Praise for *The Mask Falling*

Amazon Editors' Pick for the Best Sc

A Bustle Most Anticip

"I can only stress how intricately plotte
out this series is . . . Part political thrill., ,... ,...........,
with some dark, dystopian bite tossed on top, *The Mask Falling* is
Samantha Shannon at the top of her game." —Cultures

"Keenly imagined . . . Atmospheric and unnerving . . . Once
again, the predicaments are complicated and suspenseful, the new
and returning characters are intriguing . . . For all its superbly
choreographed action and paranormal inventiveness, this is, at
heart, a gripping tale of trust and love, valor and sacrifice, and
equality and justice." —*Booklist*

"Thrilling . . . A tantalizing, strategic setup for the next
installment, which has all the ingredients to be
a knockout." —*Kirkus Reviews*

"With each new novel Shannon continues to prove that she
is a formidable voice in the fantasy genre. Her writing style is
intimate but the gritty realism that both her worlds and characters
embody are filled with razor-sharp teeth. This book bites and
refuses to let go. Filled with an amazing range of introspection,
this quiet tension hurtles the reader through constantly evolving
problems with higher and higher stakes towards an ending that's
as explosive as it is devastating." —Nerd Daily

"Shannon expertly blends genres to create a story that is at once
a political thriller, a dystopian epic, and a paranormal adventure.
This bold series installment will leave fans eager
for more." —*Publishers Weekly*

Praise for The Bone Season Series

New York Times Bestseller

USA Today Bestseller

Huffington Post Book of the Year

Today Book Club Pick

Goodreads Choice Award Fantasy Nominee

"[*The Bone Season*] invokes both the political tyranny
of George Orwell and the . . . mythmaking of
J. R. R. Tolkien." —*USA Today*

"A great imagination at work." —*People*

"Plenty for readers to get absorbed in . . . [With] an author clearly
driven to go deeper and deeper into a unique world, many will
surely follow her." —*The Wall Street Journal*

"Shannon is likely on the brink of
literary stardom." —*New York* magazine

"[An] intoxicating urban fantasy series . . . Fans will be calling
for more." —NPR.org

"Gripping." —*US Weekly*

"A dazzlingly brainy, witty, and bewitching tale of outrageous
courage, heroic compassion, transcendent love, and the quest for
freedom." —*Booklist* (starred review)

"Real entertainment. Shannon has continued to build on this
imagined world with intricacy, and Paige's voice comes through to
deliver a suspenseful story." —*The Washington Post*

"Epic in every sense of the word, a dystopian drama set in a future
version of London . . . [Shannon's] worldbuilding is next-level
good." —Culturess, "Why You Should Read Samantha Shannon's
The Bone Season Series"

THE MASK FALLING

The Mask
Falling

Samantha Shannon

BLOOMSBURY PUBLISHING

NEW YORK · LONDON · OXFORD · NEW DELHI · SYDNEY

BLOOMSBURY PUBLISHING
Bloomsbury Publishing Inc.
1385 Broadway, New York, NY 10018, USA

BLOOMSBURY, BLOOMSBURY PUBLISHING, and the Diana
logo are trademarks of Bloomsbury Publishing Plc

First published in 2021 in Great Britain
First published in the United States 2021
This edition published 2022

ISBN: HB: 978-1-63557-032-8; INDIE SIGNED HB: 978-1-63557-772-3;
PB: 978-1-63557-033-5; EBOOK: 978-1-63557-031-1

Library of Congress Cataloging-in-Publication Data

Names: Shannon, Samantha, 1991- author.
Title: The mask falling / Samantha Shannon.
Description: London; New York: Bloomsbury Publishing, 2021. | Series: The bone season
Identifiers: LCCN 2020016554 (print) | LCCN 2020016555 (ebook) |
ISBN 9781635570328 (hardcover) | ISBN 9781635570335 (trade paperback) |
ISBN 9781635570311 (ebook) Subjects: GSAFD: Fantasy fiction.
Classification: LCC PR6119.H365 M37 2021 (print) |
LCC PR6119.H365 (ebook) | DDC 823/.92—dc23
LC record available at https://lccn.loc.gov/2020016554
LC ebook record available at https://lccn.loc.gov/2020016555

2 4 6 8 10 9 7 5 3 1

Typeset by Integra Software Services Pvt. Ltd.
Printed and bound in the U.S.A.

To find out more about our authors and books visit www.bloomsbury.com
and sign up for our newsletters.

Bloomsbury books may be purchased for business or promotional use.
For information on bulk purchases please contact Macmillan Corporate and Premium
Sales Department at specialmarkets@macmillan.com.

For Ann Preedy
(1938–2019)

The middle of the series—its heart—is for you.

Qui regarde au fond de Paris a le vertige. Rien de plus fantasque, rien de plus tragique, rien de plus superbe.

Anyone who looks into the depths of Paris is seized with vertigo. Nothing is more fantastical. Nothing is more tragic. Nothing is more sublime.

—Victor Hugo

Contents

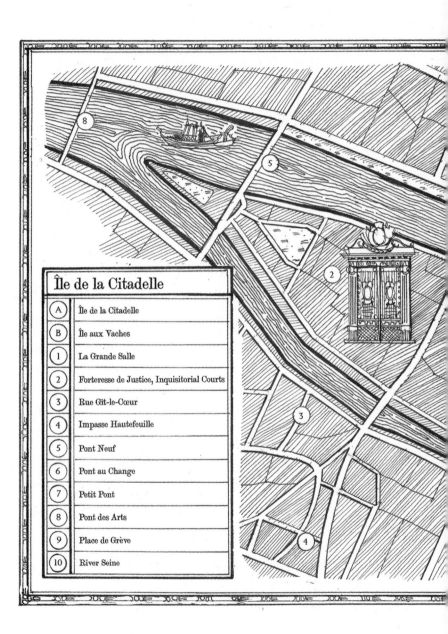

Île de la Citadelle

(A)	Île de la Citadelle
(B)	Île aux Vaches
(1)	La Grande Salle
(2)	Forteresse de Justice, Inquisitorial Courts
(3)	Rue Gît-le-Cœur
(4)	Impasse Hautefeuille
(5)	Pont Neuf
(6)	Pont au Change
(7)	Petit Pont
(8)	Pont des Arts
(9)	Place de Grève
(10)	River Seine

Île de la
Citadelle

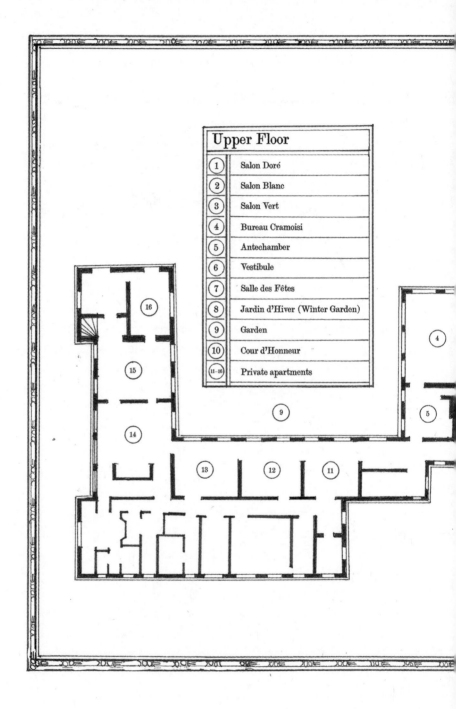

Upper Floor

①	Salon Doré
②	Salon Blanc
③	Salon Vert
④	Bureau Cramoisi
⑤	Antechamber
⑥	Vestibule
⑦	Salle des Fêtes
⑧	Jardin d'Hiver (Winter Garden)
⑨	Garden
⑩	Cour d'Honneur
⑪–⑯	Private apartments

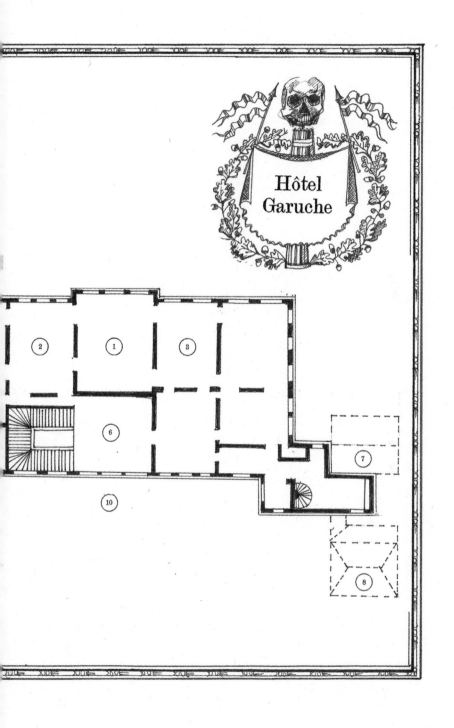

Hôtel
Garuche

Prelude

Dawn had set its match to a clear sky when our cargo ship sailed out of Dover. Now, rain thundered from sullen clouds and the gray sea raged itself to spume against the Port of Calais.

At least, that was what I imagined was happening outside, from the jolting and the noise. All I could see was the corrugated steel of a shipping container and the bruised daylight that leaked between its panels.

I was curled up on a plywood floor that smelled of brine and rust. Warden had stayed at my side for the journey, trying to warm me as I listed in and out of sleep. Even though I was wrapped in his coat, my hands were still like ice in my gloves, and I shook in the sodden chill of the ship. Beneath my oilskin, I was sticky with blood. Whatever painkiller had padded my bones was starting to wear off.

Years I had dreamed of leaving England, but never as contraband. Damaged contraband.

As we waited for the ship to dock, I remembered another journey I had made to an unknown land. Back then, it had been my father who kept watch over me as a plane carried us across the Irish Sea, away from our war-torn home.

My memories of that night still glinted. Splinters of glass, buried deep, sharp enough to catch me when I least expected it.

I had been sound asleep. Before dawn, my father had lifted me from bed, carried me downstairs, and buckled me into his car. My grandmother must have heard him, or sensed it—she had always said she could feel my fear, like a hook lodged in her chest—because she had come running from the farmhouse, a fleece thrown over her pyjamas, shouting at him to stop. I had beaten on the window, pleaded with him to let me out, to no avail.

He had let her tuck me into bed and read to me, as always, neither of us knowing it would be for the last time. After weeks of silent planning, he was defecting to the Republic of Scion. And I was going with him.

Under cover of darkness, he had driven through rebel-held territory to Shannon Airport. The car was pitted with bullets by the time he parked it. The rebels had already marked his vehicle, suspecting Scion might have turned him.

My father had come prepared, with a suitcase and a coat for each of us. Other people sleepwalked through customs with blood on their faces and little more than the clothes on their backs. Later, I had come to understand that all of the passengers on Flight 16— Shannon to London Docklands Airport—were collaborators. They had sold their friends and our secrets to Scion, and the laochra scátha, the rebel militias, had named them traitors to the nation. Marked for death, they had seen no choice but to flee to the country they had been serving.

There were others, too: Scion diplomats, sent to negotiate a surrender, returning home in defeat. Then there were people like my father, enlisted by the enemy, who, for whatever reason, had chosen to answer the summons from London. Aside from a grizzling baby, I was the only child.

Soon enough, the plane had touched down on the other side of the Irish Sea, and we, the uprooted, formed a column at the border—all of us waiting, in hollow-eyed silence, to throw ourselves on the mercy of the anchor.

Our first steps outside had been too much for my senses. Raised on green pastureland cupped by low mountains, I was dazzled and terrified by London, with its cobalt streetlamps and blinding screens and skyscrapers—bright as the sun—that knifed toward the godless blue. It had seemed grotesque in its immensity, stretched out of all rational proportion, this place I was supposed to call home. My father had bought a black coffee from Brekkabox and brazened out the citadel, unaware that London would be the death of him.

London, monstrous and marvelous and magnificent, too wild for even tyranny to tame. It had eaten me whole, and in its gut, I had grown a skin hard enough to cocoon me. I never imagined that I would burst out of that skin as Black Moth, leader of the revolution. Never predicted that I would find a new family in the Seven Seals. Never guessed that I would be the one to tear the mask off London when I found out who and what controlled it.

No, we were blind to our fates that day. Just as I was now, approaching the Scion Republic of France. I had no idea what would befall me in this new theatre of war. What names and faces I would wear. Who I might become.

If I had, I might have turned back.

****

The dockworker who had met us in Dover appeared at the door to our container, face creased beneath the peak of his cap.

"They're searching all ships that arrive from England." His breath clouded. "We have to leave."

When I lifted my head, pain bolted down my nape. My eyes felt tightly screwed into my skull.

The dockworker watched, impenetrable. His hair and eyes were gray as slate. No distinctive features. Through a dense headache, I wondered how many fugitives he had abetted, and how far this network stretched.

"Paige," Warden said. "Can you stand?"

My nod ripped out the bones of the world. All at once, nothing had structure. The dockworker shed features and edges until he was a frameless smear. Everything spread, like paint in water. Colors leaked across boundaries. I unfolded my legs, keeping hold of the dossier Scarlett Burnish had pressed into my arms only a couple of hours ago. It contained my new identity.

As I tried to get up, something deep inside me cracked. Pain thumped through my bones and bruises. With a sharp intake of breath, I stopped, my face glazed with cold sweat.

Warden knelt in front of me. As soon as I shook my head, he gathered me to his chest and stood. I clasped my arms around his neck as he followed the dockworker out of the container.

Our escape registered in fits and starts. Warden sheltered me from the rain and brutal cold. From the nest of his coat, I caught my first glimpse of the Port of Calais. Though it had to be mid-morning, the sky was dark enough that everything was still illuminated. Floodlights cast shadows onto walls of shipping containers. Ferries and freighters waited to depart, their gangways sheened with ice, and a transmission screen shone a message through the downpour:

YOU ARE NOW ENTERING THE REPUBLIC OF SCION FRANCE
VOUS ENTREZ MAINTENANT EN RÉPUBLIQUE FRANÇAISE DE SCION

The dockworker splashed ahead and ushered us into a mail van. "Keep quiet," he said, and closed the doors.

Darkness enfolded me, as it had in the cell I had barely escaped. The never-ending void, broken only by the light above the waterboard, the fire of Rephaite eyes.

Warden shifted a few of the sacks and boxes in the van. As I crawled into the space he had cleared, I caught the stale reek of the sweat beneath my oilskin and the thick grease in my hair.

"He could hand us over," I rasped.

Warden covered me with his coat. "I have no intention of letting Scion take you again."

The engine rumbled to life. Icy perspiration trickled down my face.

"I want to sleep." I breathed the words. "I just want to sleep."

He settled in beside me, and his hands closed around mine. My wool-clad fingers seemed brittle in his grasp.

"Sleep," he said. "I will keep watch."

****

The poltergeist in Senshield had left a web of fine cracks on my dreamscape. As I dozed fitfully beside Warden, shunted by the motion of the van, memories rippled through the flowers in my mind, which were steeped in murky water.

I saw my grandparents, hauled into the shadow of the anchor. I saw their farmhouse, its briar roses, the hand-carved sign above its door that showed a honeybee in flight.

I saw my father, murdered by a golden blade.

****

Somehow the dockworker drove out of a guarded port with the two most wanted fugitives in the Republic of Scion. After an eternity, the van stopped, and Warden scooped me back into his arms. I was starting to hurt again. Pain seethed like the red heat under the earth, waiting to burst forth.

The dockworker had parked on a quiet street. He shepherded us through a door, into a small hallway.

"This is your safe house," he said tersely. "You will hear from someone in the network soon. Do not go outside."

The door clicked shut behind him.

Only my labored breathing disturbed the silence. A staircase led up to the next floor. Warden was still for a time, his hand at the back of my head.

In the colony, he had found ways to help and protect me. He had wielded a degree of power, even if it had been a façade. Now he was a fugitive. A god in exile. He had no means of stopping my pain.

Upstairs, he set me down on a four-seater couch, mindful of my injuries. Its cushions were so wide and deep I sank right into them. I stared at the parlor: the plasterwork ceiling, the cream walls and herringbone floors. A table stood by a wall-length window, promising long breakfasts in the amber glow of morning. All was clean and comforting.

"The fireplace is false," I said.

Warden glanced at it. "Yes."

"But how are you—" A wild laugh was bubbling up. "How are you going to cope?"

"Cope," he repeated.

"You need a fire. To stare into, pensively. Did you know," I said to him, "that you do that a lot?"

He tilted his head, which set off a fit of silent mirth. My ribs ached. When I lifted my hands from the couch, blood lingered in their wake. Warden turned to close the nearest set of shutters.

"Is there anything you need before you rest?" he asked.

"I need to—to shower."

The stutter. The hitch in my breath. Whatever it was, something made him look back at me.

"Perhaps a bath would be more sensible," he said, after a silence.

Somehow he knew. A bath would feel less like the waterboard than being drenched from above.

"Yes," I said.

He left. I listened to the swash and gurgle of the taps, the liquid oozing through the pipes.

You sound thirsty. My hands scrunched into fists. *Perhaps the Underqueen would care for a drink.*

"Paige."

I looked up. Into Rephaite eyes, demonic and soulless. Suhail Chertan, come to drown me on dry land again.

My muscles seized up. I was chained to the waterboard again, smothered by sodden cloth. Before I knew what was happening, I had scrambled away from those terrible eyes and smacked into the floor, and then my skeleton was made of glass. The impact splintered me. I reached for a breath that refused to be drawn, groped for a knife that was no longer there.

A familiar aura called me back. When my vision had throbbed itself clear, Warden crouched beside me. Not close enough to touch. Just enough for me to sense him. To remember him.

"Warden. I'm sorry." My voice shook. "I thought—"

I wished I could find the words to explain.

"We are likely to be in this apartment together for some time." Warden held out a gloved hand. "Perhaps we should begin by agreeing that there need be no apologies between us."

It took a moment to muster the courage. When I placed my fingers into his grasp, he got me to my feet and helped me hobble to the bathroom.

"Warden," I said quietly. "No matter what you hear, don't come in. Not unless I call you."

After a moment, he nodded. I closed the door behind me.

A row of lavender-scented candles lit the bathroom. Once more I was unsettled by the cleanliness, the space. Stone floor tiles, warm underfoot. Fluffy white towels and a starched nightshirt. With my back to the mirror, I removed the jacket and sweater, the trousers, the bloodstained shift I had worn in my cell. The sweater pulled at the sneer of stitches on my upper arm.

When I turned to face my reflection, I knew why Warden had chosen to light the room with candles. Even the faintest illumination was too much. South of the chin, not an inch of my body had been spared.

Little by little, I absorbed my reflection. As I counted my injuries, I relived each one. Hands around my throat. An armored fist striking my stomach. Hobnailed boots against my ribs. Anything to make me talk. All of it in a blinding white room—white walls, white floor. Surgically clean, at least at the start. Nowhere to hide from the laughter and questions.

Blood streaked me where shards of glass from Senshield had torn my skin. I traced a cut above my eye, a shock of red against my pallor. My chin pinched. I had seen myself in bad shape before, but this was different. The work of people who had viewed my body as an instrument of torture.

It had taken months to scrape back the strength I had lost in the colony. Now I would have to start again. I would have to live as a house of cards, so fragile that a breath could knock it flat.

The bath was sinister in its stillness. When I touched its surface, my arms bristled with gooseflesh again, and my shoulders ached where I had pulled against my chains.

I needed to get the blood off. If I didn't nip this fear in the bud, I might never be able to stand water again. Taking a deep breath, I submerged one foot, then the other.

As I lowered myself into the bath, my arms shook and my wounds stung. When I was up to my waist, I exhaled. I was warm. I had almost forgotten how good that felt—to be warm all the way to my fingertips. They had left me soaked after each session on the waterboard, with the cold skin of a corpse.

My shivering worsened. Before I could stop it, a heaving sob racked my whole frame. I had tried so hard to be strong. I had said nothing under torture. I had not broken. Now, at last, I folded in the wake of all that time in darkness, stripped of my name and pride again.

Warden honored my wishes. He never came in. When I had wept until I was hoarse, I leaned against the side of the bath and held myself with both arms, fingers pressed into my bruises.

The water had almost cooled by the time I forced myself to sit up. Slowly, I cupped the bathwater in my hands. I brought it to my face. It covered the tip of my nose. Then my lips.

It was too far. In an instant, every muscle in my body turned to iron. Darkness ruptured before my eyes, and I was hauled back to my cell, down to the basement. Frantic, I groped for the edge of the bath. *Filth*, Suhail hissed from my memory. *Drink*. Black waves reared over my head. *No one is coming for you*. I crashed onto the floor, slick as a fish, and threw up into the toilet.

There was nothing solid in my stomach. Each retch mangled icy sweat from my pores. By the time I was done, I felt as if I had been ripped inside out.

"Paige?"

"I'm fine, Warden." Tears scalded my face. "I'm fine."

When I could move, I spat out the last of the bile and climbed straight back into the bath, insides writhing in protest. I needed to do this. I needed to wash my imprisonment off me.

Perhaps the Underqueen would care for a drink. To celebrate her short-lived reign.

"I can't." My throat had a thick lining. "Warden, I can't breathe—"

Drink.

For a terrible instant, I thought I would pass out and slide under the surface, never to emerge. Then Warden was there, holding my elbows.

"Breathe in," he said. My hands went to his shoulders. "Paige, look at me." I tried, through a dark haze. "Breathe in. Slowly."

Easier said than done. I managed to inhale, but it did little to wring out the soaked cloth of my lungs.

"Good," he said. "This will pass." I had to blink several times before I believed he was really there. "Breathe out."

His voice guided me back to myself. My fingers dug into his shoulders. When the surge of terror had receded, Warden drew back, his shirt wet from my touch, and saw the extent of my injuries.

His gaze darted to mine, asking permission. I gave a small nod. He took in every cut and bruise on my upper body, lingering for no longer than necessary, ending on my ravaged wrists.

"Who did this?"

The pitch of his voice was so low, it was little more than a vibration. "Vigiles," I said. "Sometimes for information. Sometimes for the fun of it. Suhail was the one who . . . poured."

Banked heat flickered in his eyes.

"You must be angry with me," I said. "For giving myself up to Scion. For not telling anyone I had a plan."

His attention dropped to my hands, which rested on his wrists. Half of my fingernails were black.

"I resented you. For eluding us all," he said. "For knowing exactly what she does to those who defy her, yet still gambling with your life, all for a strategy with little chance of success."

"I don't regret it." I whispered the confession. "It was the only way to destroy Senshield, and it had to be then."

"To those of us who care for you, your life would not have been an acceptable exchange for that victory. Every night, I wished you had not thought it was. That you had not done it." With the barest touch, Warden lifted my chin. "I also expected nothing less of you."

I managed a short-lived smile.

With him beside me, I was calmer. All I wanted now was to be out of the water and into a bed. Warden moved to sit on the floor, while I reached for a cake of soap.

"Jaxon was in the Archon. He told me things." The bathwater rusted around me. "He said it was the spirit of the Ripper that scarred you twenty years ago."

Warden was silent for a long time.

"We were hung in chains to await our punishment, to learn whether we would be sequestered—executed—for our crimes," he said. "That was not our fate. The Sargas do not destroy their fellow Rephaim lightly."

"Nashira destroyed Alsafi."

The skirr of her blade. The thump of his head. I had barely known Alsafi, yet he had sacrificed himself to buy me a chance to escape.

"That, I imagine, was a rare instance of passion. His betrayal must have incensed her," Warden said. "No, the scars were a far more imaginative solution to our disloyalty, marking us forever as traitors."

"Did you ever stop seeing the room where it happened?" I dragged a cloth up my arm. "Did you ever stop thinking you were still trapped there?"

Another silence.

"Some rooms," he said at last, "are hard to leave."

At least he was honest.

"I'm going to try to wash my hair," I said. "I think I'm all right now."

"Very well."

He left me to it. With what little strength I had left, I dumped shampoo on my head and scrubbed my scalp until it stung, forcing myself to keep scouring and rinsing until all the blood and grime was gone. Only then did I let the water drain and slither out of the bath.

For a long while, I sat on the floor, shattered. It had taken so *much* to do something that had once been effortless. Fatigue rushed over me. Almost drunk with it, I levered myself up on straw legs, hair dripping. A bead of blood welled between the stitches on my arm.

Only once, in the three weeks I had been detained, had I been allowed to clean my teeth. The bristles on the brush turned pink. When I had used about a pint of mouthwash, I towel-dried my hair and drew on the nightshirt, pulling the buttons through the wrong holes.

I was dead on my feet by the time I emerged. Warden led me into a darkened room with a high ceiling, where a double bed waited by a window, heaped with blankets and pillows.

"You ought to sleep." He let go of me. "You will feel your injuries soon."

The space between us was taut with the knowledge of what was to come. Not just the war beyond the window—a war that would not wait for me to heal—but the one my body was about to wage against me.

"I will bring you a heat pad," Warden said. I pressed my ribs. "Do you need anything else?"

"No." I looked up at him, so tired I could hardly focus. "Warden . . . I know Terebell must have only let you come with me because none of the other Ranthen wanted the job. And I know it must be embarrassing to be demoted to minding a human." Speaking was starting to hurt. "It might take me a while to recover. I don't know if I ever will."

"It is no demotion. No dishonor," he said. "And you will not rush your recovery on my account."

The gentleness in his voice almost broke me. Too exhausted for restraint, I turned back to him and nestled against his chest. Just for a minute, I wanted to be held. I wanted to convince myself that he was really with me, and not a drug-induced illusion. His arms came around me.

"Forgive me, little dreamer." His voice resonated through us both. "For letting them take you."

I closed my eyes. "I gave you no choice."

His hand was a reassuring weight between my shoulders. I listened to his steady heartbeat, and mine slowed.

At length, I sat on the bed. Droplets seeped past my collar. Before I could swallow my pride and ask, Warden left the room and returned with a comb and a blow-dryer.

"You don't have to," I murmured.

"I am aware." Warden sat at my side. "Lean on me."

I did. Heat gusted through my hair. I sat between his arms, heavy-eyed and leaden, until he switched off the blow-dryer and guided me to the pillows.

"Sleep this way if you can." He used them to prop me up. "It will make breathing easier."

I was too drowsy to so much as nod. My hair feathered warmly against my cheek.

For a long time, I waited for the trap to spring. It was too much to hope, or to believe, that I could be warm and clean and safe. The part of my brain where fear dwelled was telling me, even now, that this room was a figment of a desperate imagination—that I was alone and condemned, and the executioner was on his way.

No one came. Outside, Paris was awake, and birdsong fluttered through the window.

Before the pain could reach me, I was gone.

PART I

To Pay Thee Free

Oh yes, I've got some gold for thee,
Some money for to pay thee free;
I'll save thy body from the cold clay ground,
And thy neck from the gallows-tree.

—Child Ballad 95,
"The Maid Freed from the Gallows"

1

Beyond the Sea

A blade flashed, kindled bright by moonshine. Death lathed thin and sleek. I thrashed against my chains, retching as if I had been washed up by the tide. Someone was stabbing me.

The basement with its blind gray walls. The light, so bright it scored circles on my vision. And the water—I was choking on it. Suhail Chertan loomed from the shadows and stretched a gloved hand toward the lever.

Instinct led me to the lamp. My bedroom in Paris snapped into relief. As quickly as the fear had hit, I remembered that the shackles were only sheets, that the blade and the white-knuckled hand that grasped it were both mine, and that I was fighting my own memory.

Cold sweat dripped from my hair. Each breath strained through leagues of bruising. The alarm clock glowed—12:23 A.M.—and I was gripping the knife I kept under my pillow.

Some nights it was the waterboard, or the bleach-white room where the Vigiles had beaten me. Some nights it was the Dublin

Incursion. I would have taken insomnia over this: sleeping too deeply and for too long, only to wake with no tether to reality, half-trapped in the past.

The door to my room opened. "Paige."

I wiped my brow with my cuff.

"I'm all right," I said. "I just thought—" Wisps of my hair clung to my temples. "Was I screaming?"

"No. You were speaking."

In the Archon, I had not asked for mercy. In my sleep, I often did.

"Since you are awake, I wonder if you would care to join me in the parlor," Warden said. "Unless you wish to rest."

"No, it's fine. I won't be sleeping again." I coughed. "Give me a minute."

"I will need ten. Wear a coat."

This was mysterious even for him. Curiosity kindled, I untangled myself from the sheets.

The safe house was on Rue Gît-le-Cœur, in the ancient heart of Paris, a skip and a jump from the River Seine. Two weeks had passed since our arrival. In that time, I had seen no evidence of neighbors. Past whatever legal shadows were in place, I suspected all the nearest buildings belonged to Scarlett Burnish, or the organization that secretly employed her.

The Domino Program. The network of spies that supported Burnish and had ordered her to get me out of the Westminster Archon. As yet, I had no idea what they wanted from me—only that they had risked a valuable agent to save me from the executioner.

Once I was warmly dressed, I went to the parlor. A sweet scent hung in the air, the record player crooned, and a note waited on the table.

The locked door.

I raised an eyebrow.

One door in the parlor had been locked when we arrived. Now it was ajar. I padded up the wooden stairs beyond, to a deserted attic, and climbed a ladder into the night.

Warden gave me a hand through the hatch. We stood side by side on the roof of the safe house, beneath the stars.

"Well, look at that," I breathed. "Who knew we had a view like this?"

The snow-covered quay trimmed the river with lace. Beyond it were the louring rooftops of the Île de la Citadelle, home of the Inquisitorial Courts and the Guild of Vigilance.

"I suppose Domino did not mean for us to access the roof," Warden said, "but when I found the key, I thought we might use it to celebrate."

"Celebrate what?"

He nodded to something behind me. I turned.

On a flat section of the roof, overlooking the Seine, a rug had been rolled out. Candles flickered in jars around dishes of food, which surrounded a small and ornately decorated cake.

It was past midnight. My twentieth birthday. After everything, it had slipped my mind.

"I know this is a modest celebration." Warden spoke to the chimney. "After all you have endured, you deserve—"

"Warden." I gave his wrist a brief squeeze. "It's perfect."

That made him look back at me. No smile. Unlike humans, Rephaim rarely signaled their thoughts or emotions through facial expressions, but his features softened a little—at least, I liked to think they did. I liked to think I was learning to read him.

"Many happy returns of the day, then, Paige," he said.

"Thank you."

We sat on the rug, Warden with his back against the chimney. I swung my legs over the edge of the roof and basked in sweet, unbottled air. He knew I had been restless indoors. Here, I could lie under the stars without risk.

He had somehow assembled a picnic for me. A cheese board accompanied by sliced bread and butter. A bowl of crisp salad, tiny potatoes and hard-boiled eggs nestled among its leaves. Pears and red apples and oranges. Pastries so delicate they looked as if they would vanish if I picked them up. There was even a dish of sugar-roasted chestnuts—my favorite.

"Where did you get all this?" I went straight for a chestnut. "Don't tell me you made it from scratch."

"I am not so impressive. Albéric delivered it at my request."

Albéric was the contact who provided our supplies. Even though all our requests had been fulfilled—Warden had illegal wine, I had coffee—I had never seen our mysterious benefactor come or go.

"Cake was, apparently, not available," Warden continued. "I acquired this one elsewhere."

A smile pulled at the corners of my mouth. "Are you saying you *stole* me a birthday cake?"

"A tribute to your vocation, Underqueen."

My smile widened.

We listened to Paris. Citadels were never silent. *Blue tone*, Nadine called it—that low and ceaseless roar, like one long exhalation, the rush of lifeblood through vein-like streets. Sirens and traffic and an undersong of voices from the transmission screens, which spoke all the way through the night. I took a bite from a wheel-shaped pastry filled with praline cream.

"A drink?"

Warden was holding a silver jug. "What is it?" I asked.

"Le chocolat chaud." His voice deepened when he spoke French. "Do you care for chocolate?"

"I do," I confirmed.

He poured some into a gold-rimmed demitasse and passed it to me. It was thick and sweet as molasses. I sipped it between bites of food.

For our first week here, I had barely eaten. Now I was ravenous. Once I had sampled everything, I made a start on the cake, which was swathed in coffee-flavored icing. It had been a long time since I tasted something so good, something meant to give pleasure.

"What would happen if you had a bit of this?" I asked Warden as I cut a second wedge.

"I would rather not say while you are eating."

"Now I'm really curious."

He waited until I had finished my next mouthful before he said, "I would vomit."

A surprised laugh burst out of me. "You're joking."

"I think we can agree that humor is not my forte."

"Don't be so hard on yourself. You have a firm handle on *unintentional* humor." A gust of wind blew my hair into my eyes. "So you'd throw up if you tried to eat. But you can drink."

"Nothing thicker than broth. I cannot digest solid food."

"Do you not have a stomach?"

"I do not know which organs I possess in your terms. Rephaim have never consented to physical examination by humans. Nashira prefers to keep our anatomy a well-guarded secret."

"Right. Otherwise we might be able to design weapons that can harm you."

"Precisely."

I had so much to learn about the Rephaim. Now I had Warden to myself, I meant to caulk the gaps in my knowledge.

"Well," I said, "I'm sorry you'll never know the joy of cake. But more for me, I suppose."

"Indeed."

I polished off the rest of my slice. Comfortably full, I lay back on the rug to stargaze, watching my breath rise like steam from a kettle.

It felt like eons since my nineteenth birthday. A year ago, Nick had baked me a strawberry cake and served it for breakfast, and Jaxon had afforded me nineteen minutes off to eat it ("What could be a better gift than a day of hard work for your mime-lord, darling?"). Later, Nick had given me an exquisite chatelaine he had wrangled at the black market and a stack of records for my collection, and we had gone out with Eliza for a slap-up supper.

We had been happy then, in the corner of the world we had scratched out for ourselves. I had been able to close my eyes to the real Scion and pick a living from the bones it tossed me.

Warden lay on the rug beside me and folded his arms under his head. It was such a relaxed, human posture, I had to look again.

"Thank you for this," I said to him. "And for everything you've done since we arrived. I know I haven't been much company."

"You are not here to entertain me."

One had to wonder what he really thought about birthdays. To an immortal, it must seem masochistic, to celebrate each step of my journey to the grave. Still, it was sweet of him to play along.

A row of three stars flickered right above the safe house. "Rephaim are named after stars. Their old names, I mean," I murmured. "Why is that?"

"Most humans cannot speak our true names. Since your kind have long associated stars with the divine, Nashira decreed that we would use their names here."

"Did you all choose your own?"

"After consulting the æther," Warden said. "On the subject of my name, I never did invite you to call me by it."

"Arcturus?"

"Yes. Warden is a title—a title that was stripped from me, at that," he said. "We have known each other for almost a year. If you wish, you are welcome to call me Arcturus."

He had a point. I should have stopped calling him Warden months ago, but to me, it had become a name. Or perhaps I had used it to draw a line between us—a tissue of formality that kept me from growing too close to him. Whatever the reason, it was long past time.

"I'd like that," I said. "Arcturus."

Another siren in the distance. Somewhere in the night, Nashira Sargas was considering her next move.

I had always had a healthy fear of her power and her reach. I had always known that, in the end, she was the one we would have to defeat to win this war. Yet before my imprisonment, Nashira had never kept me up at night. There had always been a reassuring sense of distance.

No longer. I had seen the fire in her eyes when I escaped her clutches for the second time. After everything I had done to defy her, I had also refused to break. I had refused to be silent. I had refused to die. She would never give up her pursuit.

A tiny sound drew me back to the present. Warden—Arcturus (it would take a while to get used to that)—had placed a small object beside me.

"A gift."

It was an oblong parcel, neatly wrapped in newspaper. "Arcturus—" I sat up. "You didn't have to get me anything."

"I was under the impression that a gift was traditional on the anniversary of a womb birth."

"Womb birth. Great."

The parcel was heavier than I had expected. I opened it with care to reveal an ornate box. A moth gleamed on its oval lid, fashioned from smoked glass, perched on a bell-shaped oat blossom. I remembered telling him once that it was my favorite. In the language of flowers, it meant *the witching soul of music*.

I turned a gold key on the side of the box. The lid opened, and a figurine of a bird—a ring ouzel, black with a pale breast—emerged from inside. It beat its tiny mechanical wings and whistled like a living thing.

"Arcturus," I said softly. The artistry of it was exquisite. "Where on earth did you get this?"

"Originally, it was one of my snuffboxes. Now it is a boîte à oiseau chanteur."

A songbird box. "It's beautiful." I looked at him. "Wait, you made it by hand?"

"A modest conversion."

Even the underside of the lid was stunning, painted to resemble a poppy field. He moved to sit beside me and turned the key the other way. The bird stopped moving, and instead, the box played music. As I listened, I had a muted recollection of my grandfather restoring a harp in his workshop, singing in his pebbly voice. An air about a long-lost soulmate.

A hollow ache stretched out within me. It started in the chambers of my heart, in a place that reached eternally for Ireland. I imagined Arcturus working on the music box while the Ranthen watched over his shoulder, wondering why he was squandering time on a trifle.

He had made me a memory I could hold. I leaned up and placed a soft kiss on his cheek.

"Thank you."

"Hm." He lifted his wine in a toast. "To you, Paige. And the next twenty years."

"Sláinte." I touched my cup to his glass. "May they be significantly less horrific than the first."

We drank. I rested my head against his shoulder, and we watched the stars until dawn painted the horizon.

****

The days of waiting for contact from Domino wore on. So did the long crawl of my recovery. After two weeks, my bruises had gained more earthen tones, but I was still weak as a haystalk.

My mind was just as slow to mend. Time refused to blunt the edges of the memories. I could no longer sleep through the night. Sometimes I relived my father's death, saw the open bottle of his body. Sometimes I would get so cold that my fingernails turned gray. More than once, Arcturus checked on me in the night and found me next to the radiator, enveloped in a blanket.

It was the dark that got to me the most. I had never been able to sleep well with a light on—yet without one, I couldn't convince myself that I had ever left the pitch-black cell. I had meant to die there, and a part of me had.

The sedative, at least, was out of my system. Now it was a rattling cough that kept me up at night. That and a sharp pain in my chest, on the right side, when I took too deep a breath.

At first, I had watched the news every night—to make sure Scarlett Burnish was still alive, to keep one eye on London—but it made me itch to get back to the streets. Never more so than when the news offered glimpses of Georges Benoît Ménard, the Grand Inquisitor of France.

He was said to be a fanatic, his bloodthirst unrivaled among the leaders of Scion. Certainly he sent hundreds of people to the guillotine each year. His spouse, Luce Ménard Frère, had come to London as his representative in December. Other than that, I knew very little about him.

Arcturus did his best to distract me. He taught me chess, which I enjoyed even though he always won. I could still wipe the floor with him at cards, having spent years in and out of the gambling houses of Soho. I taught him the finer points of cheating as well as fair play.

"There is little honor in duplicity," he pointed out one night.

"None," I agreed, "but if everyone is duplicitous, honor is a disadvantage." I threw down another card. "And whoever said there's honor among thieves was talking absolute shite."

In the colony, he had been named my keeper. In London, I had been his queen and his commander. Now we were just two fugitives, each with no power over the other. At last, we were on level ground.

I liked spending time with him. It had taken me months to fully admit it to myself, but it brought a smile to my face to see him each morning. I had worried we might run out of things to say within a few days, yet we never did. Sometimes we stayed up talking all night.

He was intelligent and perceptive in conversation, solicitous, a good listener, with a bone-dry wit that I was never wholly sure was intentional. I told him things I had never told anyone—about my childhood in Ireland, on my grandparents' dairy farm, and about my time with the Seven Seals. We talked about music I had saved from piles of salvage at the black market, about books he had discovered in the colony. He told me stories Scion had erased.

He described the Netherworld, so I could almost sketch a map in my head. He conjured its buildings in exquisite detail—colossal, carved from iridescent stone, cities that shone like shattered glass— and described the river, the Grieving, with its bed of pearl-like pebbles.

"Your river was called the Grieving?" I raised an eyebrow. "The Netherworld sounds like a riot."

"It is a poor translation."

We shared an interest in languages as well as music. One evening, he asked me if I might consider teaching him my mother tongue.

"You realize almost nobody speaks Gaeilge these days," I said. We were playing chess, and I was waiting for him to make his next move. "Not in public, anyway."

"All the more reason to learn it."

We were into our endgame. There were more black pieces on the board than white, which definitely meant I was winning.

"Scion made a concerted effort to destroy all evidence of the Irish language after the Molly Riots," I said. "You won't find many books, and you're not likely to be able to talk to anyone but me."

"I enjoy our conversations very much." Arcturus moved one of his pawns. "And I would like to be fluent in another human language."

"How many do you already have?"

"Six," he said. "English, French, Swedish, Greek, Romanian, and Scion Sign Language."

"Only six?" I slid my black queen across the board. "You've been here two centuries, lazybones. I already have half as many as you and I haven't had unlimited decades to learn."

"Clearly yours is the superior intellect, Paige—"

"Well, I didn't want to say—"

"—but you still cannot best me at chess." He set down his white bishop. "Checkmate."

I stared at the board. "You . . . infuriating bastard."

"You only had eyes for the king and queen. Remember not to overlook the other pieces."

With a sigh, I sat back. "Well played. Again." I shook his hand. "Fine. I'll teach you Gaeilge if you teach me Gloss. Deal?"

"Humans cannot learn Gloss. It is the language of spirits."

"Polyglots can speak it."

"They do not learn it. They are born with it."

"Try me," I pressed. "Say a word in Gloss and I'll copy you."

He humored me and made a soft, chime-like sound, which I had a stab at mimicking.

"Wrong," he said.

"How?"

"You are not Gloss-articulate. Even if you were to perfectly imitate the sound I made, you would only be speaking with your vocal cords, not your spirit."

I tried not to look crestfallen. Gloss was beautiful, and I would have liked to call him by his real name.

Still, the thought of holding a real conversation in *my* mother tongue was tempting. My grandmother had been born on an island where Gaeilge had once been spoken daily, and had passed it onto me—a bright jewel, a shared joy, that I had kept buried for years.

Scion had outlawed all the Celtic languages during the Molly Riots. They would die out soon; now families were too afraid to teach them to their children even in secret. I liked the idea of a Rephaite knowing mine. Through him, it would be immortal.

"All right," I said. "I'll teach you. But fair warning—nothing in Irish sounds like it looks."

"I enjoy a challenge."

"Good." I took a pen and paper from the table and scribbled the longest word that came to mind, *grianghrafadóireacht*. "Your best conjecture, then. How would you pronounce this?"

Arcturus considered it, then served himself a large glass of wine.

"This may take some time," he said.

****

We found a collection of films and took to watching them together in the evenings. I looked forward to that time, when we would sit on the couch and I would eat my supper. Often I would fall asleep there. In the morning, over breakfast, he would tell me how the film had ended.

One such evening, not long after my birthday, found us sitting in the parlor as usual. Arcturus was immersed in the film. After weeks of stress and separation, it was strange to be resting at his side. The set of his jaw was softer, his hand at ease on the arm of the couch.

A month ago, I might have moved closer. He might have drawn me to his chest and pressed his lips to my hair.

Sometimes I wished we could talk about how it had been. Not that there was much to say. I had ended our trysts because as Underqueen, I could put nothing and no one above the revolution—and because if they had found out, the Ranthen would never have tolerated it.

And yet I was Underqueen now only in name. And there were no Ranthen here to see us.

As if he had sensed the thought, Arcturus glanced at me. I looked away a second too late.

"Are you all right?"

"Fine." I put my plate aside. "I just can't believe you're here sometimes. That we both are."

"Hm. We have come a long way since you last contemplated killing me."

"We have."

Out of habit, I traced the silver marks on my palm. When I had banished the spirit that powered Senshield, it had joined the scars there, forming the word *kin*. I had no idea what it was supposed to mean, or how I had banished the spirit without knowing its name.

Women with damson lips and penciled eyebrows glided across the screen. There was just enough light to remind me that I was no longer chained underground. Curled up next to Arcturus, I slipped into a drowse. I was warm. I was clean. I was safe, if not entirely free.

I jolted awake when a spirit glided through the window, frosting the panes. A psychopomp. I held still as it approached Arcturus.

"What did it say?" I asked when it had gone.

"That Hildred Vance's replacement has been summoned," he said. "Vindemiatrix Sargas, the blood-heir, is on her way to London. She will assist Scion with Operation Albion."

"Vance isn't dead?"

"No. Hospitalized."

Alsafi should have finished her off. I might have known she would cling to life with every finger.

"Operation Albion." I rubbed my eyes. "That sounds familiar."

"It is the formal name for the eradication of resistance in the homeland. This includes the complete dismantling of the Mime Order."

A military operation *within* Scion. I sat up a little. "You think this . . . Vindemiatrix Sargas is going to help with that?"

"Her principal duty for the last two centuries has been to monitor the free world. She likely intends to put some of her skills to use to find and infiltrate the Mime Order."

"I assume the Ranthen have warned Glym and Eliza."

"Yes."

The Mime Order was still very young. Its divisions had made it fragile from the beginning, then Senshield had paralyzed it for weeks. Now this. A coordinated effort to destroy it.

The capital was still under martial law, thronged with ruthless soldiers. Eliza and Glym, who were ruling in my stead, would have to work around the clock to keep this operation from snuffing the flame of revolt.

"What are the Ranthen doing at the moment?" I asked.

"We cannot entrust too much information to psychopomps, since they can be intercepted," Arcturus said, "but before I left, Terebell told me that her current aims were to reconstruct Alsafi's network of human contacts, and to continue making Rephaite allies."

"Good."

The film ended. Arcturus gave a half nod of approval—I took that as a seven out of ten—before he rose.

"I must take aura," he said. "I will not be long."

It was a risk for either of us to go outside, but he had no choice. "Be careful."

He stopped beside me on his way out, to cover me with a second blanket and tuck it around my shoulders. As the door closed behind him, my thoughts returned to the threat in London.

I had faced an army, but never had to contend with spies. Ognena Maria had once told me it was thanks to espionage that Scion had crushed the rebel militia in Bulgaria. Leaks had opened in its ranks, one by one, until it sank without a trace. That could happen again.

I was still Underqueen. Even though I was over the sea, I had a duty to protect my syndicate.

My body was still reclaiming lost sleep. Close to midnight, the sound of the door woke me. I traipsed downstairs, collected the supplies, and restocked the fridge and cupboards.

Under a warm loaf of bread, I found an envelope. Inside was the map of the citadel I had requested from Albéric. Once I had looked it over, I folded it and tucked it into my pocket.

There was no reason Scion should know I was in Paris. To avoid damaging faith in the regime, it was possible they hadn't even told the Vigiles I had escaped the executioner.

I knew how to avoid detection. I had done that before, under worse circumstances. I could go outside. It would be a risk, but the news from home—that the revolution was once again in danger—had galvanized me. I could not just sit and wait for Domino.

I had arrived in London as a frightened child. I had left as the ruler of its underworld. If there was one thing I knew how to do, it was twine myself into the sinews of a citadel. I needed to acquaint myself with Paris, find its voyants, and help the Mime Order.

Not long after our arrival, I had glimpsed some hair dye in the bathroom cabinet. I dug it out, scrubbed it through my curls, and set a timer. As always, it took a while to negotiate the shower, and I shook as I rinsed out the dye and watched it drain away, red as old blood. When I blow-dried my hair, it sprang back richly copper, each curl shiny as a coin. And I almost looked—

—like my father.

My father.

Saliva washed into my mouth. I hunched over the sink, gripping its edges so tightly it hurt.

He was gone. He was dead. I saw the block again—the swing of the gold-plated sword, the blood that had dripped from its blade. I met my own eyes, the eyes of a daughter who had abandoned her father to his doom. Who had defied Scion, knowing he might pay the price, and had not lifted a finger to protect him.

I would make it right the only way I knew how.

And I would start tonight.

2

Paris

When Arcturus returned, he looked stronger, as he always did after a feed. He found me sitting at the table with a coffee. I had pinched my cheeks and dabbed concealer over my dark circles.

"Hi," I said.

"Paige."

He made no comment on my hair. Just took off his coat and hung it up.

"Albéric came," I said. "We have more wine." I cleared my throat. "Can I talk to you?"

"Of course. No need for a formal request."

"Says he who talks like he just rolled up in a horse-drawn carriage with Queen Victoria."

"Touché."

He left his gloves on the mantelpiece and sat. I slid a glass of wine toward him. Red wine was all he ever drank, even at the crack of dawn. I had tempted him with coffee and tea in vain.

"I'll cut to the chase," I said. "I've decided to go out." When he was silent as a church, I clasped my hands on the table. "Nothing strenuous, I promise. I just want to find out where the syndicate is based. If we play our cards right, the voyants of Paris could be valuable allies to the Mime Order, and we need allies now. It's time to escalate the revolution."

"And you believe your fatigue no longer presents an issue."

"I'm fine."

"The darkness under your eyes serves as compelling evidence of that. As does the full bowl of coffee."

I cocked my head. "Did you just master sarcasm?"

"Paige."

"It's a *cup* of coffee. With . . . no handle." I rubbed the bridge of my nose. "All right. It's a bowl, and I'm knackered, but I can handle a couple of hours on the streets. Half a morning."

"I need not remind you that behind the curtain, you remain the most wanted individual in the Republic of Scion."

"Most of the Republic of Scion thinks I was shot dead in Edinburgh. I doubt more than a handful of officials know the truth."

"I cannot stop you from leaving, Paige. Your choices are your own."

"I'm asking for your blessing. And your help." He remained impassive. "Look, any day, Scion could shatter the Mime Order," I pressed on. "All our work and sacrifice from last year will have been for nothing. I won't hide away when there are things I can do to protect it."

"You deactivated Senshield."

"I can do more."

He studied my face.

"It was not easy for any of us to watch you surrender yourself to Scion." His voice was low. "The others believed the bullet had killed you. I knew otherwise. I sensed your fear."

That silenced me for a moment. "Why didn't you use the golden cord?"

"I did. Every day."

Not once had I felt him in the darkness. My thoughts had been trained on survival, but I had listened for his voice, or some hint of his presence. It would have helped me to hold on.

"You have not always acted prudently in your desire to move the revolution forward," he said quietly. "In London, you fell into a trap that resulted in deaths." I looked away. "I do not remind you of this to be cruel, Paige. Only to point out that it was your hunger for action that blinded you to the peril that night. That, and your exhaustion. If you push yourself too hard now, if you are impatient, you will put both yourself and others at risk."

"Terebell was pressuring me to score a victory at any cost," I reminded him. "I shouldn't have let her turn the screw. Those deaths are on me, but I've learned from them. I won't put anyone else in danger."

"Except yourself."

"I know I can survive out there. I plan to find the syndicate, and I'd stand a much better chance if I have your help."

"Domino ordered us to wait for contact."

"They won't know," I said. "I'd like us to work together. Isn't that what we've always done best?"

He deliberated for some time. If he called my bluff, I would have to accept defeat for the time being. It would be madness to strike out on my own while I was this physically weak.

"I gave you my word that I would stay with you," he said at last. I looked up. "As you say, we have accomplished a great deal together. Let us see what comes of this." He picked up the wine. "How shall we find the syndicate?"

My face broke into a smile.

"Well," I said, standing, "how the tables have turned. Time for me to be *your* mentor."

I turned down the lights and opened the shutters. Streetlamps shone along the quay, their lilac glow rippling on the Seine.

"First, you need to learn to see the underworld," I told him. Arcturus came to stand beside me. "Think of it as a chain. You look for the people at one end, and they'll lead you all the way up to the other." I nodded to the street. "Tell me what you see."

"Denizens."

"Look harder. Look for outliers." I pointed out a boy in a peaked cap. "What's he doing?"

"Waiting for a guardian, perhaps." When the child blended into the crowd, Arcturus narrowed his eyes. "No. A thief."

"Good. His mark is the dark-haired woman in the pencil skirt, third in line at the coffee stand." I watched her. "Not paying attention to her handbag."

The bag was dusty pink silk, tempting as a cake in a window. The pickpocket snuck up to the owner, who was deep in conversation with the man beside her. With a deft cut, the boy liberated the bag from its strap and melted back into the crowd, leaving his mark none the wiser.

"There." I had to grin at his nerve. "He'll be taking that to the kidsman in charge of his gang. Follow him, and we'd get to the next link in the chain and bribe our way up." I closed the shutters and sat on the sill. "That's one way."

"And the other?"

"We go straight to the top. That might be our only option, since neither of us has two pennies to rub together for bribes."

"Do we not?"

"You've got a big pile of money lying around somewhere, have you?"

Arcturus rose and disappeared into his room. When he returned, he placed a brick-sized wad of banknotes on the table.

"You . . . do indeed have a big pile of money lying around somewhere," I observed.

"The Ranthen would never have sent me abroad without my fair share of our assets."

Slowly, I leafed through the crisp notes. "Arcturus," I breathed. "What is this, ten grand?"

"Twelve. It is yours to use as you think best."

"You're giving me twelve *thousand* pounds. Just like that." I looked between him and the notes. "Have I ever mentioned how deeply I treasure our friendship?"

"Hm. Call it another birthday gift." He sat. "Perhaps we should begin our search in the Court of Miracles."

I knew of it. Jaxon had spoken often and fondly of the slums where the outcasts of Paris met.

"All right." I laid the money down with appropriate reverence. "Where?"

"The largest of the slum districts is north of the river. Or was," he said, "when I last visited Paris."

"And we can just walk in." I was skeptical. "There's no watchword, no need for someone to vouch for us?"

"I have never tried to enter it myself."

"Right." I tapped my fingers on the table. "How long to get there on foot?"

"Perhaps half an hour."

"All right. We'll go in the morning, to avoid the night Vigiles. And we'll be careful," I added. "I promise."

"I still do not like this idea, Paige. I wish to make that known."

"Noted." I shot him a winning smile. "But I think we'll make a decent syndie of you yet, Arcturus Mesarthim."

****

The sky was cloudless in the morning. Sunlight striped the floors with gold.

Exhilaration crushed my hurts. I danced along to the record player. I wolfed some porridge with apple butter, then prepared for the Court of Miracles.

I was heading into a citadel I had dreamed of seeing since I was a child. Anticipation thrummed in every limb. For the first time in weeks, I was a live wire, raring to run.

The wardrobe was a room of its own. Domino agents must have stayed here in the past and needed a range of disguises. I chose a white blouse and a charcoal sweater, which I tucked into high-waisted trousers, and button boots with low heels. Smoked lenses hid some of my face. A peaked cap would hide a little more. I straightened my hair, scalding my neck and one hand in the process—I debated asking Arcturus to do the back for me—before I swung a green coat onto my shoulders and a scarf around my neck. I took the knife from under my pillow, wrapped it, and slipped it into my pocket.

On my way downstairs, I glanced at a mirror. My sleek auburn hair was off-putting.

Arcturus was in the hall, dressed from head to toe in black, as usual. His new overcoat suited him.

"Good morning." He was pulling on his gloves. "I trust you slept well."

"I did." I turned on the spot. "Est-ce-que j'ai l'air suffisamment française?"

"Très française, petite rêveuse."

His pronunciation was impeccable. "You've a cut of the money?" I asked.

"Yes."

"Watch out for pickpockets." I belted my coat and drew on my own gloves. "We shouldn't walk together. You go first. If the Vigiles get wind of us, we call it off, lose them, and meet here later."

"Very well." Arcturus took me in. "Are you certain you are ready for this?"

"Absolutely."

In truth, my palms were slick. Before my capture, I had always been confident that if a Vigile spied me, I could climb and fight my way out of danger.

As soon as I opened the door, a breeze whipped my hair across my eyes. Arcturus strode out first. I checked no one was looking before I pulled on my cap and went after him.

My boots crunched into an ankle-deep snowbank. Once the door was locked, I walked up the four steps to the street and stepped out of the shadow of the safe house.

Paris roared its welcome.

The noise and light were overwhelming. At eight in the morning, cars and people thronged the Quai des Grands Augustins. A vintage moto rattled past, close enough for me to smell its exhaust. I blinked and looked east, to the twin bell towers of the Grande Salle de Paris. A place of worship in the monarch days, it was now used for some of the most significant events and ceremonies in France. I had to stop myself from staring at it. Beyond it lay two more natural islands of Paris—the Île aux Vaches, where many wealthy officials lived, and the Île Louviers, home to some of the most famous Parisian markets and arcades.

Arcturus had crossed the road. I followed at a distance, craning my neck to take in the sky. London was a vertical citadel, all 'scrapers and high-rise apartments, but Paris seemed far wider.

I looked down, to the stern gray waters of the Seine and the streets I had pored over in travel guides. Tearooms and boutiques and tiny chocolate shops. Florists with windows framed by winter-flowering blossom. Branches of the Bank of Scion France, white doors embellished with gold leaf, façades whittled from marble. Printers sold broadsides and mysteries beside children with red brooches on their lapels, marking them as official vendors of the *Daily Descendant*. Stalls with candy-striped awnings stood cheek by jowl, boasting penny toys, artwork, souvenirs (I resisted the compulsion to spend three pounds on a miniature Eiffel Tower), and all manner of curiosities. I spotted a snow globe with London inside it and felt a pang of longing.

Even though English was the official language of the empire, taught in schools before any other, France had clawed back some of its own—many of the establishments had French names, and the chapbooks were all printed in French. There was no trace of a Brekkabox from here to the horizon, but there would be one somewhere. No citadel could get away with not having a Brekkabox.

Paris was her own creature. She had her own underworld, lurking like crude oil beneath her surface. Somewhere very close to here, the River Bièvre slunk past a district of tanneries and shambles, licking up blood and dye as it went. Thieves conspired in slums. And perhaps—just perhaps—there were whispers of insurrection.

Arcturus turned his head a little. I spotted the camera and obscured my face with one hand.

A transmission screen was mounted on the first bridge we passed. I slowed to watch the cycle of photographs. My face was no longer among them, but the other fugitives were still there. Nick Nygård. Ivy. Julian Amesbury.

I clenched my fist in my pocket. More than five months since I had last seen Julian, and I still had no idea if he was dead or alive. After the faces, a series of messages appeared.

WE MUST SAVE SPAIN FROM ITSELF
NOUS DEVONS SAUVER L'ESPAGNE D'ELLE-MÊME

SUPPORT THE IBERIAN EFFORT
SOUTENEZ L'EFFORT IBÉRIQUE

The white-hot flash and smoke of tankfire. Bloody hoofprints. Limbs entangled on the bridge. Bodies flung into the river. I walked on, faster, ears ringing, but the memories screamed after me.

The Iberian Effort, as it was known to the average denizen—or Operation Madrigal, as it was called behind the curtain. Scion had revealed it to the public on the twelfth of January. How much of Scion's progress was propaganda, I had no idea, but its aim was to annex Spain and Portugal. If the operation succeeded, Scion would control eleven countries.

Arcturus waited by a streetlamp. We fell into step on our way down to the riverfront, where there were no cameras and not many people.

"What is it?" he said.

I glanced at him. He was looking straight ahead.

"Paris." I cast my gaze over the river. "It's magnificent. So much of Scion is. Isn't that sick?"

"It is a beautiful mask, but all masks fall. In the end."

"Not fast enough." I thrust my hands into my pockets. "Spain and Portugal will be under the anchor soon. Not one month ago, they had emissaries in London, like they had a chance of stopping this."

"They may be able to resist ScionIDE, as Ireland did."

"Ireland was defeated on the day of the Dublin Incursion, when an army marched in and murdered hundreds of unarmed people," I said, my tone clipped. "Scion does its worst in the early days. It goes straight for the soul. Everything after that is just . . . death throes."

We walked beneath a bridge, past skeletal trees and moored barges, painted red and white and gold. Frost glittered on every surface.

"We may not be able to stop this invasion," Arcturus said, "but we can keep building our own army. We can cooperate with Domino. We can make a difference."

I tried to believe it. I had to believe it. When we reached the steps to a footbridge, Arcturus pulled ahead again.

A breeze dredged a heavy green smell from the Seine. Halfway across the bridge, I stopped and rested my elbows on the railing, giving him a chance to put some distance between us. Sunlight sparkled on the water. Despite the danger, I allowed myself to imagine that I was an ordinary woman, taking in the sights of a new country. It took my mind off war and blood.

The illusion shattered when I spotted two Vigiles at the other end of the bridge. I joined a long column of sightseers, who were gossiping in Swedish. Neither of the Vigiles spared us a glance. As soon as we were past them, I deserted the group and kept walking. Day Vigiles might be amaurotic, unable to see or sense auras, but it was best for them not to get a close look at my face. Smoked lenses and a coat of dye would only do so much.

The Swedish tour group bustled in the opposite direction. While vacationers still came from elsewhere in Scion, I realized it had been months since I had last seen any free-world tourists.

Outsiders had once been allowed to visit the Republic of Scion under strict conditions. It was how Zeke and Nadine had first come to London, on a tour for students. Zeke had later told me their phones and recording devices had been confiscated at the airport, and they were told not to leave their hotel without a Scion-approved guide, presumably to stop them seeing any evidence of executions. Of course, they had found ways to break that rule.

That was when Scion had cared about foreign relations. Now it seemed Nashira was starting to cut ties.

I followed Arcturus up one street for what felt like an eternity. Stabbing pain echoed my breaths. By the time we met beneath a red plaque reading RUE DES FORGES, my brow was clammy.

"The Court of Miracles." Arcturus nodded to a crumbling brick archway. The smells of sizzling grease and woodsmoke oozed through it. "It would appear it still exists."

Too winded to do anything but nod, I leaned against the wall and pressed a hand flat to my chest.

"We can turn back," Arcturus said.

"No." Taking the deepest breath I could manage, I straightened. "Time to make some friends. Or enemies, knowing my luck."

No one stopped us from passing through the archway. The street beyond was unpaved, wet with snowmelt. From the first step, there was evidence of hardship—shedding paint, broken windows, families sleeping rough.

The Court of Miracles was not the cauldron of decadence Jaxon had promised. The reality was quieter. Rubbish was strewn across Rue des Forges, where the vagabonds of Paris talked and dozed and cooked beneath tarpaulins. None of them were dressed for snow. One group was split between two mattresses, sharing a few bags of chips. Over the largest of several pit fires, a muddy stew bubbled in a pot.

I knew from the map that the shantytown hooked around a block of flophouses. As I followed the path, I remembered what Jaxon had told me about the people who had lived here in the past, the malingreux. They had crafted the appearance of disease in the hope of earning more generous alms from the public, but once they returned to the slums, their rashes and sores evaporated. That was how these pockets of deprivation had first earned their name.

There was only one miracle I could see here now, and that was voyants and amaurotics sharing one cramped street in peace, with the rotties clearly aware of the unnaturals in their midst. They spoke in a mix of French and English, switching seamlessly and often.

Two women danced while a whisperer played an air on a fiddle. In the middle of one cluster of people, a hydromancer stirred a pail of murky water, watched with interest by several amaurotics. Everyone seemed to be getting on like wick and flame.

"This isn't the syndicate," I muttered to Arcturus. "Not enough voyants."

Still, it was worth taking a look around this place. Nobody protested as we picked our way through the slum. We had no valuables on show. A few people eyed Arcturus, intrigued by his appearance or his aura.

Definitely not the syndicate. Outsiders would have been challenged by now.

The sound of a lullaby caught my attention. It came from one of the few voyants here—a seer, hunched and shivering. A shew stone glinted in her lap. Her cheeks were windburned, her hands almost swallowed by heathered arm-warmers, and she sang to a newborn in the crook of her arm:

"J'ai fait un rêve horrible, mon cher,
Lorsque je fus dans l'ancien jardin de mon père.
Je rêvais qu'il y eut une ancre sur la tour,
Et que des tyrans envahirent notre cour."

I stepped close enough to draw her attention. She took one look at Arcturus and screamed. Shock jerked my hand to my knife, though I just stopped myself drawing it. The seer scrambled into her shelter, the baby and the stone clasped to her chest.

"It's him, it's him!" She stabbed a finger at Arcturus. A tiny cry split the air. "L'Homme au Masque de Fer. Il est venu m'enlever—"

"Ta gueule," a woman barked at her. "Enough of your raving, Katell. And shut your brat up, before I drown it."

There were muttered agreements before everyone returned to what they had been doing, but glances kept darting back to us, some hooded with suspicion. We needed to be gone before they got too interested.

I crouched in front of the seer. She peeked at me from behind a tuft of black curls, showing a bruise on her cheekbone, stark against her light brown skin.

Katell was a Breton name. Even though the people of Brittany had never mounted any major rebellions against Scion, all Celtic regions had been tarred with the same brush as Ireland. With that name, this woman had probably never been able to secure full-time work.

"I'm not going to hurt you, Katell," I said. "Neither is my friend. I think you might have mistaken him for someone else."

Her face was careworn, gnawed by hunger, but I thought she was about my age. She stared up at Arcturus, who seemed to sense that getting any closer would spook her.

"Yes," she finally said. "This man is taller, I think."

"L'Homme au Masque de Fer," I said. "That's who you thought he was. Who is that, Katell?" When she retreated farther into her lean-to, I lowered my voice a little more. "Maybe we can help each

39

other. I need information. If you can provide it, there's coin in it for you."

Katell shushed her grizzling baby and glanced over her shoulder. Her collarbone jutted.

"Not here," she said, so only we could hear. "I will meet you in Rue de Ponceau. You know it?"

Arcturus gave me a subtle nod. "Yes," I said.

As I stood, I made a point of pursing my lips, as if I'd tried and failed to wring something from Katell. Arcturus led me straight out of the slum.

"Interesting development," I said.

"Indeed. Do you intend to investigate?"

"Naturally."

A short walk brought us to Rue de Ponceau. It was a foul-smelling alley, starved of sunlight and paved with cobblestones. Katell soon came, her baby asleep and tucked into a sling.

"Hello, Katell," I said.

She gave Arcturus a wary look. "What is it you want to know?" she asked me.

"A few things," I said, "but first, tell me about this . . . Man in the Iron Mask. You piqued our curiosity."

It was starting to snow again. Katell wrapped some of her shawl around her baby.

"He took my spouse, Paul Caron," she said. "I saw the mask he wore—made of metal, with bars over the eyes. Others have seen the same figure. I have heard whispers of his name."

"For how long?"

"I don't know. A few weeks."

"And he took Paul?"

"He and his followers. I ran after them, but they hit me with something, and when I woke, they had disappeared. No one believes me." Katell stepped forward then and clasped my hand. "Madelle, do you work for Le Chevalier des Deniers? Have you come to help me find Paul?"

"No. I'm sorry." I gently broke her grip. "Is Le Chevalier des Deniers your . . . boss?"

Disappointment stiffened her face.

"Yes. The patron of this district," she said, her voice flat. "Le Chevalier des Deniers rules the Court of Miracles. We give him our earnings. In return, he keeps us fed and safe. Or so he claims."

Katell was describing a mime-lord, or something akin to one. She was our first link in the chain.

"I suppose he reports to someone else," I said.

"The grands ducs." Katell stepped back. "You must be new to the district. To the citadel, perhaps."

"I'd like to introduce myself to the grands ducs. Any idea where I might find them?"

A frown pinched her brow. "No one sees our leaders without invitation. If I wished to see them, I would ask Le Chevalier des Deniers, and he would—he might—petition for me."

"They'll want to see me."

"Madelle, they will never receive you unless you petition. Save yourself a wasted journey."

"A name or a place. That's all I need."

Fresh hope jumped into her eyes. I had dredged my words with false impatience. Impatience pointed to desperation, and desperation pointed to need. This woman knew those refrains.

"Our leaders hold court in les carrières," she said under her breath. "For a price, I can give you a name. An old friend who knows the way inside." She held out a hand. "Two hundred."

I almost let her fleece me, just to throw her a bone. "No name in Paris is worth that much coin, as you well know," I said. Her cracked lips pressed together. "Since I'm feeling generous today, I'll forgive you for trying to rip me off. Fifty."

"I cannot risk my life for fifty. If anyone finds out I have shared information about the carrières with a stranger, I will leave my child an orphan." Her hand trembled. "Ninety."

"Seventy, Katell, or I walk. I'm sure someone else around here could use the money."

I kept my nerve until hers failed. When she gave a stiff nod, Arcturus took the right amount from his coat. Katell snatched the notes from him and stuffed them into her skirt pocket. She beckoned me close and whispered into my ear: "Montparnasse. Find Mélusine."

"Where in Montparnasse?"

"She could be anywhere in that district."

"Do you have unregistered cabs in Paris, the sort that will take voyants without questions?"

"Anormales, or anormaux," Katell corrected. "That is what we call ourselves here." She took a step back. "The cabs have blue paint over the wheels. Look for them beside any triumphal monument. The nearest is the Porte Nord." Another step. "Please, ask no more of me."

I nodded and turned to leave. A few paces later, I realized Arcturus wasn't with me and looked back just in time to see him give Katell an extra few notes. She took them as if they would bite her.

"She cannot have given birth more than a week ago," Arcturus said to me, once he caught up.

Tenderness surged in me. "I know. I wanted to give her more, too," I said, "but we have to be careful how much of that cash we spend. With Alsafi gone, I presume we're going to have a lean period."

"Most likely. Unless Burnish can help us, Terebell fears the line of communication with our financiers could be lost." Arcturus fastened the top of his coat. "You are right to recommend frugality."

I wished Scion had more room for compassion. I wished I didn't feel the need to curb it in him.

"So. This Man in the Iron Mask." I pushed my hands into my pockets as we pressed on. "Think it's a Rephaite?"

"A Rephaite would not abduct a human. My kind would leave such work to underlings."

A disquieting thought occurred.

"The Rag and Bone Man vanished after the scrimmage," I said. "No one saw or heard of him again after that night, even though I put a substantial bounty on his head. He has an unusual aura, like you. If *he* was the attacker, that could be why Katell mistook you for him."

"You believe he may have fled here."

"Maybe. If he did, I'll wager he's up to his old tricks. Selling voyants to Scion again."

"There is no reason to fear that the gray market has resurfaced. Caron may simply have been arrested."

"True. I suppose he could also have had a run-in with debt collectors. Or vigilantes. All kinds of ways to disappear in Scion." I spoke with more conviction than I felt. Something felt off. "For now, let's just find the syndicate. Remind me what *carrières* means?"

"Quarries. Katell was referring to the system of abandoned mines and ossuaries that lies beneath the skin of Paris, which covers at least two hundred miles. Scion has never been able to map it."

"Sounds like the perfect hideout. And Mélusine could be our key to it. Our next link."

"She will still be in the citadel tomorrow, Paige. It can wait."

"I'm not tired."

A barefaced lie. We both knew it. I also knew that if I didn't push myself, I would never get my strength back.

"It will be safer if we separate for the journey," Arcturus said. He stopped and handed me a roll of notes. "For your cab. I will meet you at an establishment in Montparnasse—La Mère des Douleurs. Ask the waitron for a café sombre."

"Café sombre." I raised an eyebrow. "Is the goal to sound as much like a tourist as possible?"

"Indeed. An ostensible mistake that will not attract unwelcome attention."

"You really are the prince of mystery, you know that?"

"Yes."

I tamped down a bout of nerves as I tucked the cash away. I couldn't be afraid of striking out alone. If I let that sort of dread set in, it would mean the torture had broken something I might never fix.

"A gloomy coffee at the Mother of Sorrows." As I turned away, I threw him a smile. "You really know how to show a girl a good time, Arcturus."

I was sure the corner of his mouth flinched.

3

Gloomy Coffee

It was a short walk to the Porte Nord. Two pickpockets trailed me for a while, but when I turned and gave them a level stare, they melted away.

Carven faces gaped down at me from the triumphal arch, which honored the French soldiers who had fallen at the Battle of the Iron Gates during the Balkan Incursion. Idling across the street was a car with dabs of azure paint above its wheels. I climbed in, gave the address, and we were off. The cabbie smoked like damp kindling and paid me little mind.

Dull pain throbbed in my temple. Twice I snapped out of a drowse. The car rattled back over the river and into the south of the citadel, where it braked outside the shell of a church. I paid the cabbie and waded through a snowbank, toward a coffeehouse on the corner.

La Mère des Douleurs didn't look as if it hid any secrets. The awnings over its outdoor tables were heavy with snow, its façade peacock blue, and bay windows flanked its door, each square pane laced with frost. The menu promised hot spiced mecks and Lyonnaise-style cuisine.

Inside, I scraped mud and snow from my boots. Customers lounged on wicker chairs, eating and talking. I checked my lenses were still in place as a waitron approached me.

"Bonjour," she said.

"Bonjour." Hoping I wasn't about to make a fool of myself, I went for it: "Je voudrais un café sombre, s'il vous plaît."

She didn't miss a beat: "Très bon choix, Madelle."

I followed her to the back of the building, past tables and framed photographs, and she took a key from her apron. She led me through a concealed door and down a winding flight of steps.

We descended into a tunnel, which resonated with chamber music and the beehive hum of a hundred conversations. It seemed many Parisians had a taste for gloomy coffee.

The waitron escorted me past a statue of a veiled woman, who seemed to be holding her own heart. Candles glimmered at her feet. An amaurotic was on his knees before her, hands clasped, head bowed. Dim impressions came to me: fragrant smoke, voices raised to a vaulted ceiling. Tendrils of a memory.

The coffeehouse was a warren of cozy spaces, lit by tapers and cluttered with tables. A peppery fug of tobacco and regal hung in the air. The vast majority of these patrons were voyant. I was getting closer.

In the largest chamber, where a quartet of whisperers played baroque violins, several alcoves served as private booths, cut off from the rest of the coffeehouse by red velvet curtains. I took the last vacant one and slipped into an upholstered seat. The waitron set down a glass of hot blood mecks and a basket of bread before she closed the curtains. I removed my gloves and read the menu, which boasted such delicacies as cassoulet au cimetière and tarte ténébreuse.

My eyelids were heavy. Now that I had stopped moving, all my aches had crept back in. I kept my coat on and burrowed into it.

Arcturus soon joined me in my alcove. The curtains fell together in his wake, muffling the clamor again.

"This place is so . . . you." I took a slice of bread. "How on earth do you know your way into a secret coffeehouse?"

"You sound surprised," Arcturus said. "I have been a revolutionary for a very long time."

"Oh, yes. Such a rebel, with your organ-playing and gramophones and good manners."

"Are you mocking me, Paige Mahoney?"

"Fondly." I smiled into my glass. "Seriously, how did you find this place?"

"After France pledged to Scion, this crypt was used first for clandestine religious services. Later, artists and musicians discovered it, too," he said. "Nine years ago, Nashira sent Alsafi to find a seditious painter, and his investigation led him here. He told me about it."

"Did he turn the painter over?"

"Yes, though he did not betray the crypt. Alsafi did only what he believed was necessary to keep his place beside the blood-sovereign."

Alsafi had made ruthless choices. He had sacrificed others to maintain his cover, but given his own life to save mine.

I pushed the memory aside. "Why are we here?"

"Two reasons," Arcturus said. "The first: since this is a crypt, it may connect to the carrières, or serve as a meeting place for those who know their way in. Perhaps you can find a link to Mélusine."

"The thought had occurred." I stole a glance between the curtains. "And the second?"

"To give you an opportunity to rest."

That made me look back at him sharply. "I've rested for three weeks," I said. "We need to start looking for Mélusine now if we're going to make it back to the safe house by dusk."

"Half an hour to eat and warm yourself." He held my gaze. "Tell me you do not feel drained. Tell me this day has not taken its toll on you, and we will leave."

I drew in a breath to lie to him. As if to mock me, pain sliced into my chest, so deep I had to set my jaw against it.

"I hate this," I said. "This weakness." My exhalation made the candle flicker. "I used to be able to run all night. Fight off thugs twice my size. Now this." I wrapped my hands around my glass. "Our mutual friend might not have killed me, but she's left me essentially useless."

"You believe all those she has tortured are rendered useless, then."

That made me look up.

"Sorry." I reached across to touch his wrist. "I didn't mean that. Of course you're not."

"Tell yourself the same." The candle made shadows feather over his face. "There are always other ways to fight."

Perhaps it was the low pitch of his voice. Perhaps it was the warmth of him beneath my fingertips, a reminder of when his arms had drawn me close. Perhaps it was the red drapes that concealed us.

His eyes darkened, and I was sure we were recalling the same night. I let go of his wrist.

"All right," I conceded. "I'll eat one of these morbid-sounding meals. And then we're going to find Mélusine. Agreed?"

"Agreed."

While I drank my hot mecks, I thought of how I had instinctively reached for him. Only two weeks ago, I had been racked by fear that I would never share that casual intimacy with another person again. While Suhail Chertan tortured me, he had told me over and over that I was repulsive. Then the Vigiles had taken their turn to beat and waterboard me.

For over a week after the escape, I had shied away from Arcturus, afraid that Suhail had been right—afraid of any touch at all, because for too long, every touch had caused me pain. The fact that I could reach for him now, without thinking, was a small victory.

A different waitron came to take my order. "Your French is excellent," Arcturus said, once we were on our own again. "You speak as if you were born to it."

"Thanks. I started learning it in Ireland, but I was lucky to have a very good teacher in London, too," I said. "She thought my speaking Irish was an asset. I was conversationally fluent in French by the time I left school, and I've worked on it ever since."

After a pause, he said, "Did something happen to her?"

He was getting better at reading my expressions. I looked down.

"After we left Ireland," I said, "I begged my father to keep speaking Gaeilge with me at home so I wouldn't lose it. He refused. I'd hold long conversations with myself in secret, but I was only eight when we left Ireland. There were words I didn't know. Madelle

Alard somehow got hold of a dictionary so I could keep teaching myself." The candle flickered. "She was hanged for sedition about two years ago. I suppose she helped one too many outcasts."

"I am sorry."

I nodded, trying not to remember the day I had walked past the Lychgate and seen her.

The waitron came back with a silver tray. She placed my food in front of me—served in a burial urn, no less—and shut the drapes behind her.

"They're committed to their theme down here." A casserole of sausage, white beans and mutton was baked into the urn. I dug in. "Enough about me. Tell me how you get around citadels so fast without anyone seeing you."

"I am surprised that interests you," Arcturus said. "You have been able to evade Scion for months."

"Tell me anyway." I blew lightly on my forkful. "Now that I've got the chance, I'm going to ask you everything I can."

"Rephaim are not wholly corporeal," he said, as I ate. "Our sarx allows us to circumvent some laws of the human world. Cameras see little more than a shadow when I pass."

"I knew there was something."

"I do not wish to seem opaque to you, Paige. You may ask me whatever questions you wish."

"Will you answer?"

"When I can." Once I had eaten some more, he spoke again. "How do you mean to find Mélusine?"

"I know the underworld."

"Paris is not London."

"No," I agreed. "Which is interesting, because Scion tries hard to regulate its citadels. The blue streetlamps, the cohorts, the white cabs and buses." I scraped up some more of the casserole. "I suppose you can never tell a city what shape to take. Still, Scion has done us a favor by attempting to standardize the unstandardizable. The underworlds will have similarities, because they were created as safe places in citadels designed to give us no safe place. They're the gaps between the bones. Similar bones, similar gaps—which means I should be able to navigate them."

48

Arcturus looked at me, long enough that it made me more aware than usual of the way I was sitting, the fall of my hair, the space between us. Not for the first time, I wished I could hear his thoughts.

"I am glad to be with you in this particular citadel," he told me. "No matter its shape."

"Likewise."

"And I think you are enjoying being my mentor."

"I would never be so petty."

"Liar."

"Fine. It does give me a little satisfaction."

"I daresay you have earned it."

I polished off the sauce with some more bread. As I did, I kept one eye on the customers through the sliver between the curtains.

For a while, nothing caught my attention. Then a medium passed a group of soothsayers, and I watched a note scrunch from one hand to another. The medium crossed the chamber and was gone. Not long after, having skimmed the note and finished his cup of saloop, the soothsayer picked up his coat and left in the same direction.

"I may have just found that link." I shifted out of my seat. "Meet me at the church. Twenty minutes."

****

In the short time I had been underground, clouds had stonewashed the sky. Snowflakes wafted around me as I shadowed the soothsayer, keeping him just in sight. When he waded through a snowdrift and into a backstreet, I followed my hunch and went after him.

The street was a dead end. I hung back in a doorway while the soothsayer waited under a lantern. Before long, a girl appeared and handed him a package from her satchel. He gave her an envelope in exchange. I retreated farther into the doorway so he could leave without seeing me.

That parcel would either contain numa or ethereal drugs. Either way, the girl had a supplier. This was the next link in the chain.

She tucked the money into her coat. At my end of the alley, she stopped, like a hare catching a scent. Before I could so much as tense, she sprinted between two cars, leapt up to catch the top of a barrier, and vaulted over it.

Using my gift to keep track of the girl through the walls, I ran straight for a parallel street. She had taken a path that wound through the courtyards of the nearest buildings. I pulled ahead of her, into a crowded section of the district, and hid behind a tree.

The girl reappeared outside a cookshop and peered across the street. Once she had judged it safe, she set off again. I tailed her at a distance through a pair of rusted gates. Even before I saw the silver lettering above them—LE CIMETIÈRE DU SUD—I knew what the place was.

The cemetery was a citadel unto itself. Tens of thousands of graves spilled across this part of Montparnasse, all of them from the centuries before the anchor descended on France. Scion mandated cremation or composting after death, to save on space and ensure its denizens were never tempted to speak to the dead. Grief and remembrance were permitted to a point, but believing that your loved ones might still linger was unnatural behaviour.

It was easy to stay out of sight among the headstones. I followed the girl to where a woman leaned against a mausoleum, pocket watch in hand. The girl presented her with a bundle of money, a phone, two fat purses.

As soon as I stepped into view, the girl was off like a shot. Her kidsman spun to face me, one hand on the hilt of the dirk at her side.

"Busybodies," she said, "are bad for commerce. Fortunately, there is room for all manner of bodies in this ground." She rested her boot on a ledger stone. "Why did you follow my courier?"

"No need for threats. I'm looking for a local," I said. "Goes by the name of Mélusine."

"Never heard of her." Her knife rasped from its sheath. "Now, piss off, busybody. Before I slice the nose you stuck into my business."

"I serve the grands ducs." I stood as still as the graves. "Help me track Mélusine down, and perhaps I'll put in a good report for you. Refuse, and I'll be delighted to piss off . . . but so will all the merchants who would otherwise have bought those stolen goods of yours."

Her expression changed.

"What are you?" she said. From her tone, my bluff was working. "A bounty hunter?"

I just raised my eyebrows.

Kidsmen were seldom risk-takers. They had gutterlings to do their dirty work. After trying to stare me out for a few moments, the woman let go of her knife and beckoned me closer.

It turned out that Mélusine was the leader of a small gang of hydromancers. Once I knew that, the search went smoothly. One roll of notes to an augur in a public garden, one whisper on the right corner and in the right ear, and I had a list of places Mélusine was known to frequent. The local open-air bath struck me as her most likely haunt at this time of day. Hydromancers were always drawn to water, especially large bodies of it. Just my luck.

The bath was an ancient-looking building, all columns and stone lintels. I walked into the foyer, wondering how the hell I was going to get beyond it, only to glimpse the receptionist on the phone with his back to me. Quick as a whim, I slipped under the turnstile and through a pair of sliding glass doors.

As soon as the gloom enfolded me, I smelled water. Pressing down my nausea, I pulled off my boots and socks, the floor clammy underfoot. I tried not to breathe too hard, or think about anything but my task.

There were no voyants in the bath itself—just a throng of amaurotics, all naked as the day they were born. But sitting alone in a steam room, I found a slender woman with an aura, combing her waist-length hair. A ring bridged her nostrils, and her brown skin was varnished with sweat.

"Mélusine?"

A flash of dark eyes through the gloom. She sprang up, like a fish leaping clear of a river, and I found myself pinned to the tiles, a crooked knife at my throat. I caught her wrist.

"I'm from the London syndicate," I said under my breath. "Help me, and I can make it worth your while."

Mélusine searched my face.

"Katell sent you," she said at last, her tone resigned. "Didn't she?"

****

Sunlight glittered on the snow again by the time we emerged from the bathhouse. I savored the crisp air, willing the steam out of me. Beneath my coat, I was uncomfortably damp.

Mélusine walked at my side. Gaiters covered her heavy-duty boots, she wore a puffer jacket, and her hair was scraped into a ponytail. Now we were outside, I could see it was mossy green.

"How is the syndicate structured in Paris?" I asked her.

She glanced at me before she answered.

"We call it Le Nouveau Régime," she said. "There are three grands ducs—Le Latronpuche, La Reine des Thunes, and Le Vieux Orphelin, who each control two of the six cohorts. Within those cohorts, there are local officers, the patrones, who oversee the districts. They are all named after tarot cards."

"Is there an overall leader?"

A snort escaped her. "Not officially, but Le Latronpuche thinks himself king." Her lips pressed together. "If you wish to see Le Vieux Orphelin, you will be disappointed. He has been missing since New Year. No one knows what has become of him."

Another missing voyant. Now I was suspicious. "And what do the other two grands ducs say about this?"

"They are trying to find him. Or so they say."

"You think otherwise?"

"If I did, I would not tell you so." She looked straight ahead. "Thoughts like that are dangerous."

Arcturus was waiting for us in the derelict church. He stood in a pool of sunlight where the roof had caved in.

"Mélusine," I said, "this is my . . . associate."

She had to crane her neck to look Arcturus in the face. Her eyebrows crept up, and I knew she was trying in vain to read his aura.

After the scrimmage, I had asked Eliza, who was sighted, what she saw when she looked at Arcturus. She had described his aura as resembling a dark cloud that spat occasional glints, like embers. *All their auras look unstable*, she had told me. *Like sparking wires.*

Mélusine finished her examination with a shrug. "Is it just the two of you?" she asked.

"Yes," I said.

"It is forbidden to show anyone the way through the carrières without express permission from the patrones. I was caught once before."

She showed me her tongue, solidly black. I remembered now. In Paris, revealing the secrets of the syndicate earned you a spoonful of l'encre ardente, a poison that discolored the mouth and caused a week of excruciating cramps. It could take months for the stain to fade.

"Should it happen again," she went on, "I will be banished. And I cannot let that happen."

"I wouldn't be asking you to do this if it wasn't urgent."

Mélusine looked hard at my face, as if she could remove my lenses through sheer willpower.

"You say you are from the Mime Order," she said. "Tell me, did you work for the Underqueen?"

"You could say I still do."

At this, she chewed her lip. Uneasy allies were rarely reliable, but she was our best shot at getting to the syndicate.

"Katell is an old friend," she said at last, "and I know she has been desperate for coin since Paul was taken. For her sake, I will guide you to the grands ducs. You are clearly not Vigiles."

"How do you know?"

"Because no Vigile would seek to enter the carrières. They're not stupid." A thin smile. "I do have a condition."

"Name it."

"My fellow anormales patrol the tunnels for outsiders. Once we are down there, you must keep your distance from me," she said, "and if we do run into a patrol, you must say you were following me."

"We'll be convincing," I said.

"Good." Her neck was tattooed with green scales. "You are confident the grands ducs will receive you?"

"Trust me."

"I wish I could. Most likely they will abandon you both in the dark and leave you to die of thirst. And I'm afraid I won't be able to help you if they do."

"Understood."

Mélusine hitched up her backpack. "Follow me. Not too close," she said, and strode back into the snow. I waited a few moments before I went after her.

She walked down the boulevard. Arcturus and I followed at a reasonable distance until she stopped near a bus shelter and beckoned us.

"Here is our door." She tapped her foot on a manhole. "I have the equipment to pull it up," she said to Arcturus, "but you look as if you might be quite strong."

Arcturus picked up the cast-iron cover as if it were made of cardboard. Mélusine shot him an impressed look and slithered into the manhole. I tucked my lenses into my pocket and checked no one was watching before I went after her.

My boot found a rung. I climbed down the ladder, darkness coagulating around me. Above, Arcturus slid the cover back into place. My knuckles strained as I clung there, sightless and unmoving.

"Paige?"

When I could speak, I said, "I'm all right."

I forced my legs to keep going, one rung after the next. Mélusine waited in a circle of light at the bottom.

"Welcome to the carrières." She wore a headlamp. "Home of Le Nouveau Régime."

The blackness formed a wall before us. "Do the Vigiles not know about the manholes?" I asked her.

"Oh, they know—but as I said, they don't come down here now. You'll see why."

Arcturus stepped off the ladder. I set my back against the wall, hands on my hips. There were hundreds of thousands of spirits around us, pressing so hard on my aura that cold sweat prickled on my brow.

"First-timers always find it hard," Mélusine said. "You will get used to it."

"How many spirits are here?"

"Several hundred thousand, at least. Hard to count. Be grateful there are not more," she added. "The remains of about six million people lie in the carrières." She pulled a second headlamp from one of her pockets. "Many of the dead remain with their bones. We do not banish them. In return, they let us share their domain."

"I don't see any bones," I said.

"You will." She tossed me the headlamp. "At points, the ceiling is very low," she warned Arcturus. "Mind your head. And remember, keep your distance."

She set off down the passage. I turned to Arcturus, whose eyes lit the absolute darkness.

"Paige."

The silence was so thick around us that it ate the echo of his voice.

"I'm not letting this trail go cold." I switched on the lamp. "In the syndicate, you take what opportunities you can."

"It is too much for one day."

Faced with the abyss, I had never been more tempted by the thought of retreat. I was already shivering in my boots and woolen coat, which were about as waterproof as paper.

"No," I said. "If we go back now, we'll never find her again."

Mélusine was already far ahead of us, almost out of sight. Before I could change my mind, I walked on. A long beat passed before I heard footsteps in my wake. He had promised me we would stay together.

We moved in single file, Arcturus behind me. I let Mélusine disappear around each corner before I followed.

I had seen my share of the subterranean, but this was something else. A labyrinth beneath the earth. Moisture dewed like tears above our heads. Here and there, graffiti streaked the walls.

I could see why Mélusine was confident in the security of this place. Any Vigile would piss themselves at the prospect of trying to navigate down here. Perhaps some of them had wandered themselves to death in these passageways, searching in vain for the heart of the syndicate, or perhaps they had been put off by the sheer volume of spirits. They were like sandpaper on my sixth sense. Too many of them in too little space.

Arcturus had explained to me once that it was an excess of restless spirits, unable to move on after death, that had caused the Mothallath—the former leaders of the Rephaim—to cross over to the human realm, to chase our unquiet dead to the Netherworld. One of their visits had gone terribly wrong, and the veils between the worlds had thinned. That was what had started the civil war that had led to the destruction of the Mothallath.

Here in the carrières, I could feel how threadbare the veils had become. The reverberation in the æther was overwhelming.

I flinched to a stop when my boot knocked something across the rubble. The beam of my headlamp revealed part of a jawbone. The herald of what lay ahead, in the next tunnel.

Bones packed tight as bricks. Human skulls, buffed to a high shine—some as perfect as they must have been in life, others missing jaws or sporting holes. Candles sat in some of their eyeholes, weeping tallow. Crowning these eldritch walls were yet more shards of skeleton. Orphaned ribs and shoulder girdles, littered like a morbid game of pick-up-sticks.

Arcturus beheld it with no expression. I wondered again what he was thinking. One day, every human he had ever met, and had yet to meet, would look like this. I would look like this. The lips he had kissed would rot away. Yet he would remain. Untouched and unchanging.

There were murals on some of the walls, as beautiful as any in a gallery. Mélusine led us through a cleft and down a flight of steps. I was about to follow her when I froze. Several dreamscapes were closing in fast.

"Wait," I hissed after Mélusine. "There are people coming."

She was too far away to hear. Moments later, the thunder of footfalls filled the tunnels.

Somewhere ahead, Mélusine shouted. Boots pounded up the steps she had taken, and then they were on us, a swarm of masked voyants. I made out grinning skulls, fingerless gloves and dirty nails, the gleam of carabiners—then one of them slammed me to the floor, pinned my arm, and twisted the knife from my grasp.

"What do we have here?" A knee dug into the small of my back. "Intruders in the dark."

Several pairs of hands took hold of Arcturus and shoved him against the wall. He made no attempt to resist.

"Regardez ça les gars," someone called. "Ce mec est un colosse."

Laughter abounded. The weight on my body wore my breath thin, made my fists clench and my chest heave as I tried to writhe away. I couldn't be trapped again, I couldn't . . .

"Hey, hey, bouge pas." A hand fisted in my hair and jerked my head up, and a rusty switchblade flashed in front of my face. "Parle, maintenant. Who the fuck are you people?"

Arcturus watched with hot eyes. I gave him the barest shake of my head.

"Mélusine," a polyglot barked. "Letting outsiders into the carrières again, are you, nymph?"

A scuffle on the stairs, and Mélusine was hauled back into view. They threw her down beside me, and she, too, was pinned with a knee.

"What are you talking about, Trouvère?" she said thickly. Her lip bled. "What outsiders?"

"This pair of rats were lurking in the dark." A flashlight blinded me, then shone toward Arcturus. "How much coin did they pay for you to let them in, and was it worth your life?"

"We followed her," I cut in. "It's not her fault."

The nearest mask tipped. Mélusine wiped her mouth on her sleeve.

"Dear lady, thank you for your honesty." Warm breath prickled at my ear. "Unfortunately, you and your handsome friend will both have to die for it. No one enters la ville souterraine without invitation. You understand. We must defend our domain from the Vigiles."

"I demand to see the grands ducs."

More uproarious laughter. "And who are you to make such demands?" A hoarse chuckle to my left. "Another lowlife mendiante who thinks she can drag herself up from the Cour—"

"I am Paige Mahoney," I said. "Black Moth. Underqueen of the Scion Citadel of London."

My voice was a guillotine blade, ending all sound. The one with the knife gripped my hair a little tighter.

"Paige Mahoney is dead. Slain in Edinburgh," a medium said coldly. "You insult her memory."

"Wait."

The polyglot grasped my chin and raised it, so the lamplight reached my face. Pale eyes assessed me from inside his skull mask.

"Her face is familiar," he conceded. "A red aura, yet it does not belong to an oracle. They say the Underqueen was another kind of jumper. And that she walked with the gods of the æther."

"Lies to shift penny dreadfuls," came a sharp reply from the medium, even as a few of the masks turned toward Arcturus. "If there are gods in the æther, they abandoned us a long time ago."

"No. He is one of *them*," someone else muttered. "Look at his eyes. Did you not read the pamphlet?"

The Rephaite Revelation. I had organized its publication to warn the syndicate about the Rephaim, and the Spiritus Club had distributed it all over London. It seemed it had made its way here, too.

"Whispers from over the sea mean nothing," the medium insisted. "And this could be a trap."

"That is for Le Latronpuche to decide," the polyglot said. I jerked my chin free. "Come, then, my new friends. Walk with us. And do try to keep up, or we will not be friends for very long."

****

They escorted us farther into the labyrinth, past free-standing towers of bone that looked like altars to some nameless divinity of death. Though I tried to remember the turns we took, I soon lost track. Arcturus would remember the way.

Water trickled beneath our boots. It set me on edge, but I could stand it so long as it was away from my face.

At some point, rubble and shards of ceramic overtook the bones. One passage was so cramped that we humans had to duckwalk through the knee-deep water, while Arcturus was almost on all fours. I clenched my stomach to keep myself from heaving. When we emerged in a small chamber, I stopped. One of the voyants was up to his waist in a milky pool.

He took a deep breath and went under. One by one, the others followed. Mélusine stepped in last, hair drifting like seaweed on the surface.

"Thank you," she said. "For covering for me." She tucked the slack tresses back into her ponytail. "This is the final test. Le Couloir des Noyés. I trust you can hold your breath for a while."

I couldn't take my eyes off the water as it closed over her head. The light from her headlamp dwindled to nothing.

"Paige."

There was soaking cloth over my face, rancid water in my mouth. Worming down my throat, swelling my abdomen, rusting my lungs. I was alone and suffocating. A living corpse.

"I can do it," I said, more to myself than to Arcturus. I took off my coat and knotted the sleeves around my waist.

Cold swashed up my body as I lowered myself into the flooded basin. I shuddered at the feel of the water, the dank smell of it. It had almost reached my chin before my heels scraped the bottom. With an uncontrollable shudder, I turned back and gripped the edge of the pool. Chalk smoked around me.

Arcturus sank into a crouch. "Look at me," he said. I did. "This is not the waterboard. You are not trapped. I will be with you all the way."

"It's all over m-me."

"You are not going to drown, Paige Mahoney. You are a dream-walker," he told me, "and you know how to go without breath." I clung to the side like a limpet. "Would you like me to go first?"

"No. Don't leave." I closed my eyes. "I n-need you to come straight after me. Promise."

"You have my word."

He joined me in the water and held my elbows, keeping my shoulders above the surface. The stretto of my breathing filled the tunnel.

If I waited any longer, our guides would think we had lost our nerve. It was now or never.

"Okay," I whispered.

Arcturus let go. I counted down from three, took a breath that stoked fire in my chest, and kicked off the side of the pool.

A bubble stoppered my throat at once. My headlamp kept work-ing, but the water was almost opaque. Chest bucking, I scrabbled for purchase, using the crags of the tunnel as handholds.

Something knocked against my cheekbone. Shock made me inhale. My nose burned, my eyes stung, and then I was back in the dark of the basement, arms chained above my head, stomach bloated with foul water, and there was no light and no escape and no one was coming—

A hand plunged through the whiteness and took hold of my arm. Next thing I knew, I was back on solid ground, my vision furred with black.

"Bravo," the polyglot said.

Behind me, Arcturus broke the surface. The voyants traded glances as I tried to get my cough under control, and as Arcturus lifted himself from the pool. He knew not to help me stand.

My fingers curled into a fist. I was shaking violently, my heart pounding. If I could survive the swim, I could get back on my feet. I braced my hands on my thighs and rose.

There was no more water after that. Soon we were dripping our way through dry tunnels. My clothes were soaked and smudged with chalk, and blood seeped from a graze on my cheek.

At last, we entered a long cavern, warm and dimly lit. A gauze of sand covered its floor. Numa were tucked into every nook and alcove, stashed beside all manner of personal effects: toothbrushes and combs, board games, ornaments. Voyants cooked over stoves and conversed in low voices. Some were enveloped in sleeping bags. Perhaps this was the only place they could rest, far below the surface, in a place where Scion remained blind.

Art mediums worked together to paint a mural across one wall, all with the blank expressions of the possessed. Their brushes trailed surreal patterns. People bathed and floated on their backs in another flooded passage. Beside a column, a cartomancer studied a tarot deck with the eye not concealed beneath a patch. He suddenly looked up at me, took me in, and crooked a finger. The urge to go to him was terrible.

When Liss Rymore had performed a reading for me in the colony, the final card had been lost. Part of me wanted to know the end of my story—except there was no time, and we were too conspicuous. Stares and whispers followed us across the cavern. Over and over, I heard the same word: *Réphaïte*.

Our escorts stopped beside a beaded curtain. "They followed me down here," Mélusine said to the others. "They are my responsibility. I will introduce them to the grands ducs."

None of them protested. When they were out of earshot, Mélusine turned back to me. "So." She folded her muscular arms. "Are you really the Underqueen?"

"In the flesh," I said.

"We thought you were dead." A weighted pause. "I will . . . announce you to the grands ducs."

"Just say that someone's here to see them, if you would. I'd prefer to introduce myself."

"As you decree, Underqueen."

With that, she went through.

Water sloshed in my boots. My nose ran. I wrung out my hair, which was already curling again, and draped my sodden coat around my shoulders like a cape.

When it came to amicable relations with other syndicate leaders, my track record was spotty. In Edinburgh, I had forged a good alliance with the Spaewife—it helped that Liss had been her niece—but the Scuttling Queen had not welcomed me in Manchester. The grands ducs might not open their arms to a fellow clairvoyant ruler.

"Tell me I look regal," I said to Arcturus. "This isn't the grand entrance I imagined."

In answer, he cupped one side of my face and brushed his thumb across my damp cheekbone, smoothing back the wisp of hair that had been stuck there.

"Thank you," I said.

He let go. "You are trembling."

"I'm all right."

With a last, scrutinizing look at my face, he turned his attention to the curtain. When I followed his line of sight, I realized. What I had thought were beads were, in fact, teeth. Hundreds of human teeth. Before I could think better of this audience, Mélusine returned.

"They are not pleased," she said, "but you may enter. They are bored today." She held back the curtain. "Tread carefully, Underqueen, or your blood will be their entertainment."

4

An Empty Throne

A cavern loomed before us, far larger than the first. Its ceiling had been smoothed into a dome and decorated with breathtaking skill. The chandelier illuminated the twenty-two scenes of the Major Arcana, the trumps of the tarot.

The painting was an illusion, designed to make the ceiling appear higher than it was. A sky beneath the earth. Among the clouds I saw the Hermit with his lantern, and the Wheel of Fortune, and Justice with her sword and scales. There was the Devil—its staring eyes followed me—and there were the Lovers, torn to opposite sides of the assembly, reaching for each other.

The Devil and the Lovers. Those had been the third and fourth cards in my reading. In Edinburgh, the Spaewife had warned me of their meaning: *Follow the path of the Lovers. Stay close to the person you think the card might represent, and make sure you've identified that person correctly. If you stray from whoever it is, I suspect you'll be vulnerable to the Devil.*

Jaxon had often waxed lyrical on clairvoyant life and history in France. There was some debate about whether the ring of fortune-tellers involved in the seventeenth-century Affair of the Poisons should be considered the first French syndicate, or whether that honor should be given to a secret society founded later by a cartomancer named Louise Gilbert. In 1782, she had attracted the interest of a lady-in-waiting at the French court, who had invited her to read for the Queen of France. Seeing bloodshed in the cards, Gilbert had not been able to keep the dread from her face, and the Gray Queen, in turn, had started to fear her.

Having earned the disfavor of the Queen, Gilbert had made a swift return to Paris. By the time the French Revolution began, she had befriended a younger cartomancer, Marie-Anne Lenormand, whom she took under her wing. Together, they had resolved to take advantage of the chaos and make themselves indispensable to key figures of the Revolution—after all, never was a clairvoyant more useful than when the future was both dangerous and uncertain. The pair had founded a secret circle of influential voyants, which had evolved into the present Nouveau Régime. That must be why this ceiling venerated the art of cartomancy.

Three thrones of raw crystal stood before us, raised on a dais enshelled by stacks of polished bones and skulls. Behind these thrones loomed a statue representing Jeanne of Arc, a medieval oracle. She was clad in armor, had chin-length hair, and raised a sword and shield in defiance. The shield was emblazoned with a message.

JE TROUVERAI
LE CHEMIN LIBRE

A paunchy binder, who I guessed was in his seventies, was draped across the throne beneath her sword. Rouge smeared his pasty cheeks. Despite his posture, he was stately, crowned with an abundant gray wig that belonged in the courts of the monarch days. Plump feet hung over the right arm of the chair, clad in a pair of steel-buckled shoes.

Beside him, a younger cryomancer picked at a bowl of sweets. Thin as a flute and with dark circles to rival mine, she had umber skin and black hair that rippled to her collarbones. Her gown was a wash of pale blue satin and lace. She wore a diamond brooch, shaped like two interwoven ribbons, and matching diamond bows in her ears, each of which supported a teardrop-shaped pearl. More pearls hung around her neck.

The third seat was empty. That must belong to the missing grand duc.

"Who dares stand uninvited before the rulers of Paris?" the binder drawled. "Who disturbs the lords of misrule?" He peered down at us. "Oh, Nostredame deliver us, a pair of panhandlers. Begone, or I shall have you both thrown into the ossuary. Drip your destitution all over someone else."

I schooled my face into a smile. With a smart flourish, I bowed to them.

"Grands ducs de Paris," I said, "merci de nous avoir reçus."

"A courteous vagrant." The cryomancer rolled a dark, sugar-dusted sweet between her fingers. "La Cour des Miracles earns its name again."

The binder guffawed.

"We are not from the Court of Miracles." I stood tall, hands tucked into my pockets, boots a shoulder width apart. "I would have appeared before you in something more befitting of your court, but I'm afraid I left all my finery in England. Along with my crown."

They both did a double take so abrupt it was almost comical.

"Crown," the rouged binder spluttered. "Crown! Who *are* you, rogue?"

"Paige Mahoney, Underqueen of the Scion Citadel of London. I'm here to forge an alliance between our two syndicates." I cast a cool gaze over the scene. "If you're not too busy, of course."

The cryomancer dropped her sweet. Beside her, the binder swung his legs from the arm of his chair.

"Paige Mahoney. What a notion," he scoffed. "Raise your head and let us see you, imposter."

I did, so the candlelight could reach my face. He stuck a peevish lip out.

"You look nothing like Paige Mahoney. Nothing," he said, and all of a sudden his accent was not quite French. "The Underqueen is in the æther." He peered at me again. "And yet, I do believe I hear a charming Irish lilt. And I do see a red aura. Red as a rosy-fingered dawn."

"Forgive me," I said, "but are you from London?"

"Gracious, no, but I did live there for fifteen years. How the accent clings," he sighed. "I only meant for it to be a holiday. Alas, it is so very easy to find oneself *anchored* in London."

"May I ask why you left?"

"Oh, you would have abandoned ship if you'd had to wither away under that utter *bore* of an Underlord, Jed Bickford. Getting himself skewered in the kidney was the first noteworthy thing he did." He rubbed the corner of his eye. "My half brother stayed behind. Didion."

"Didion." My lips twitched into a smile. Surely not. "Your brother is Didion Waite?"

"Half brother," he stressed. Improbable though it was, I could see a resemblance. "He always was a vexation. And a ghastly poet. Dire." He squinted at me. "If you truly are Black Moth, you will understand that we really must have some proof of your identity, Madelle."

"What proof can I offer?"

"The Underqueen was said to have been a dreamwalker. A marcherêve. Your aura, while unusual, could be that of an oracle." He clapped. "Come. Possess one of us! We would relish a display of your talents. To feel the power of a dreamwalker must be a most exciting sensation."

I kept my smile nailed in place.

"Such displays are only suitable for my enemies," I said. "I'd hate to leave either of you with permanent damage."

The cryomancer lifted a fine-boned hand to her lips, showing off yet more diamonds, this time confined to a ring on her finger.

"Perhaps I can offer you some other evidence of who I am," I said. Turning my face, I indicated the scar on my jaw. "A mime-queen gave me this at the scrimmage, when—"

"Common knowledge," the binder interrupted. "That scar could be self-inflicted. Part of a grand deception." He leaned forward a little. "But the Underqueen is said to have another scar. On the back of her shoulder, always concealed. The mark of a Scion brand."

First he had wanted me to make a spectacle of my gift, as if it were a parlor trick. Now he wanted me to take off three layers of clothing and show him my bare skin.

At this point, the cryomancer stood with a rustle of silks. The light sparked off her brooch and earrings as she descended from the dais, making her glitter like moonlight on ice.

"We cannot expect a fellow ruler to compromise her dignity, mon frère. If this is the Underqueen, it does not set a good precedent," she said. A beauty mark perched to the left of her mouth. "Must you always be such a disciplinarian?"

"I'm afraid I must insist, ma chère sœur." The binder tapped the arms of his throne. "The mark."

The cryomancer pouted.

Silence descended in the chamber. Slowly, I reached for the top button of my coat, maintaining eye contact with the binder. In a minute, I would be half-dressed, exposing my scar—my scars—to two strangers. They would see how bruised and brittle I still was. That was all they would ever see.

"Allow me to serve as your evidence," Arcturus said.

My fingers stilled as he came to stand beside me. "And who is this . . . individual?" the binder said delicately.

"My bodyguard." I had already slotted my hands back into my pockets. "Just a precaution, you understand."

"Of course. He has a mesmerizing aura," the binder remarked, a glint in his eye. "Perhaps your bodyguard would care to explain why he serves as confirmation of your identity."

I looked up at Arcturus, realizing.

"Because he's a Rephaite," I said. "I assume you know of them, and my alliance with them. Your voyants certainly do."

They both stared, mouths ajar. Arcturus stared right back at them with those inhuman eyes.

"Yes," the binder admitted. "We had heard. But I never imagined—"

He looked Arcturus up and down again, searching for evidence of a trick, finding none. I could empathize. I had never imagined, either.

"Very well." The binder regarded me as if for the first time. "I bid you welcome to the Scion Citadel of Paris, Underqueen. I am Le Latronpuche, and this is my sister-in-chaos, La Reine des Thunes."

"Enchantée," La Reine des Thunes said. "You are most welcome on our streets, Votre Majestée."

Arcturus stepped back. "Thank you, Vos Altesses," I said, hoping it was an acceptable way to address them. With a nod to the empty throne, I added, "I understood that there were three grands ducs."

"Oh, Le Vieux Orphelin seldom joins us down here." Le Latronpuche settled deeper into his seat, while La Reine des Thunes returned to hers. "He and his perdues prefer the pleasures of the surface."

Deep within me, instinct drummed. "I see," I said. "When was the last time you saw him?"

"Oh, two or three days ago, or thereabouts. Time is so difficult to reckon here among the bones."

"Strange. I heard he went missing around New Year."

La Reine des Thunes stroked the pearls around her neck and shot a look toward Le Latronpuche, who intertwined his fingers on his stomach and looked down his nose at me.

"You have been talking to our anormaux," he said.

"A few."

"You have made yourself very much at home here, then, Underqueen. And now you come to our court with questions. I hope you will forgive us for asking one or two in return." Intelligence crouched in his fishy eyes. "For instance, I should very much like to know how you survived a bullet to the abdomen. Many of our subjects witnessed the broadcast."

"It was a rubber bullet," I said, "likely coated in a fast-acting anaesthetic that induced a coma. Scion wanted to interrogate me before my execution."

"Dreadful business. How did you escape?"

"I had some help."

"Yes, you do seem to inspire loyalty. Not initially, perhaps—betraying your own mime-lord, tut tut, I'm surprised no one carved your throat for that—but now we hear tell of a very popular young queen. A queen who sacrificed herself for the dream of revolution."

"And now you come to us." La Reine des Thunes spoke quietly. "Why?"

Something was off here. Every instinct told me so. Still, I had come this far.

"The Mime Order faces a serious assault by Scion, codenamed Operation Albion," I said. "Scion has reclassified my syndicate as a terrorist organization, acknowledging the threat we pose."

"As well it should." Le Latronpuche muffled a yawn. "We hear it is because of the Mime Order—because of you—that Senshield will never threaten Paris. We hear that you are on your way to refining your thieves and murderers and bully-rooks into a formidable army."

"It could be more formidable. With your support, we might stand a chance of achieving our purpose."

"And what is your purpose, Underqueen?"

"To overthrow Scion."

At this, Le Latronpuche offered the sort of smile one might use to indulge a petulant child.

"Underqueen," La Reine des Thunes said, "it is a noble purpose, but Scion has endured for more than two centuries. In the words of the Gray Queen, your ambition is . . . un beau rêve. Voilà tout."

"Voyants don't dream. And in the Mime Order, we strive for more than petty treason. We act," I said. "In less than a year, we've shut down a penal colony where voyants were being brutalized and indoctrinated. We've deactivated Senshield and stopped the Grand Commander. We have no intention of slowing down. We can defeat our enemy, but only if we have enough soldiers to call upon in the war we mean to bring to Scion. And only if we have enough allies."

"Ah. That is what you want," La Reine des Thunes said. "For us to open our carrières to anyone who flees from London."

"I'm offering you a partnership. We are two age-old underworlds. You would be our esteemed allies. Join us."

"And how does Paris benefit?" Le Latronpuche inquired. "What do *we* gain, Underqueen?"

"Freedom, in the fullness of time. For now, I think there are a number of ways we can help one another," I said. "Perhaps you'd like to share in the proceeds of our black market, the most lucrative in Europe. Or perhaps you could use soldiers." I raised my eyebrows.

"I hear your Grand Inquisitor is a little more assiduous than ours. That Ménard is true anachorète. He sings in the language of the guillotine, the blood lottery. Perhaps it's time for you to sing back."

"Oh, the Butcher of Strasbourg is no threat to us." Le Latronpuche waved an idle hand, as if he were swatting a slow-moving fly. "His blundering Vigiles will never find us here. They have tried, many times. And their friends have tried to find their bodies. And *their* friends have tried to find *their* bodies, and so on. Meanwhile, *we* are never found."

"But what if someone else finds you?" I asked. "A voyant. One of your own."

"Of whom do you speak?"

"Before I became Underqueen, I discovered the existence of a trafficking ring in London," I said. "Mime-lords and mime-queens were selling their own voyants to the Rephaim." La Reine des Thunes stiffened. I pretended not to notice. "I have reason to believe this so-called *gray market* has moved here, to Paris. It's run by a voyant called the Rag and Bone Man, who fled London when his involvement was expo—"

"Madelle," Le Latronpuche cut in, "I'm afraid you are telling us what we already know."

"I beg your pardon?"

"I grant it." His blue eyes were fixed on me. "You see, we are familiar with the Rag and Bone Man—or the Man in the Iron Mask, as he calls himself now. He came to see us when he arrived here in November. And we came to an arrangement."

I turned numb.

"An arrangement," I repeated.

"Yes. He offered us a deal, which we accepted."

Without a word, Arcturus came to stand just behind me. I fought to maintain my composure.

"What sort of deal?" I asked, knowing the answer.

"A simple one. Any clairvoyants among us who breach the peace, our new friend can . . . remove. And he pays handsomely."

I swallowed the first two words I wanted to spit at them.

"You hold with the trafficking of voyants?" I said. "And you accept money from Scion?"

"We accept money from the Man in the Iron Mask. We really care nothing as to its source," Le Latronpuche said. "He assured us that the voyants receive a home. And a purpose." He inspected his nails. "Understand that we only alert him to those who richly deserve to be swept from our streets. Murderers. Sadists. Vicious traitors to our syndicate. We take the coin to protect worthier voyants while Inquisitor Ménard does his level best to eradicate us all."

"You don't consider *this* treachery, then," I said coldly. "Collusion with the anchor."

"With a fellow clairvoyant. In exchange for much-needed funds." He was shameless. "Can you offer us more favorable terms?"

Alsafi was gone, and with him, our financial security. Even if I had been able to match whatever Jaxon was paying, I would not have given tuppence to this pair of traffickers.

"You should know that I have personal experience of the gray market," I said. "I was sold on it by the late Underlord, Haymarket Hector. Not because I was violent. Not because I betrayed the syndicate. He did it to settle a score with my mime-lord. And because he was greedy."

"So we heard," La Reine des Thunes said. "Hector abused the market. We will not make the same mistake."

"We are very sorry, of course, that you suffered," Le Latronpuche added. "But be assured, *we* are careful in our selection. Careful and objective." He grasped the arms of his throne. "To many of our clairvoyants, you are a hero. A martyr of the revolution. If you find that you can accept our arrangement with the Man in the Iron Mask, we might find ourselves in a position to offer the hand of friendship to the Mime Order. We will not fight alongside you— there is no desire for war here—but we could give sanctuary to you and yours."

I longed with every twine and sinew of my being to tell them where to shove their friendship.

"We have miles of empty carrières," La Reine des Thunes said. "With coin from the gray market, we could make them habitable, Underqueen."

I thought of Glym and Eliza, ruling London in my stead. Even with Senshield deactivated, Scion would smoke the Mime Order out eventually. When the spies undermined it and the soldiers descended in force—and they soon would—how long could it last?

"And if I don't respect your arrangement?" I said, as calmly as I could. "If I decide to interfere with the gray market?"

"That would be a pity. Close as our two countries are," Le Latronpuche said softly, "you are still very far from home."

The threat hung like vapor in the stale air. Le Latronpuche shot me a last, dead-eyed smile.

"We hope you enjoy your stay in our citadel, Underqueen. And that you will respect the peace we have worked so hard to maintain," he said. "Do return to see us soon. Until then, farewell."

Behind him loomed Jeanne of Arc, unseeing. I turned my back on the grands ducs and left.

****

Le Trouvère led us out of the carrières, taking a different path from the one Mélusine had used. I had hoped to strike an alliance today. Instead, I had found another corrupt underworld. The grands ducs had all the voyants in Paris under their control, on the streets and far beneath. They could hinder me at every turn.

My muscles scorched with the effort of walking. Just when I thought the nightmare would never end, we half crawled up a final passage and emerged into the fading daylight.

We were under a bridge that crossed what could only be the Petite Ceinture, the derelict railway south of the river. Dead weeds jostled for space between its sleepers. The entrance to the carrières was the narrowest of openings in the ground, impossible to stumble upon by chance.

"Thank you, Underqueen, for gracing our Empire of Death." With a flourish, Le Trouvère handed back my knife. "Should you wish to return, you need only come to this door. Someone will find you."

He favored me with a bow and marched away. I waited for him to get well out of earshot before I let my fury rip into a rust-bitten fire bin, which crashed onto its side. The kick burned up the last of my strength, and I slid to the ground, my back against the nearest wall.

Snow formed curtains on either side of the bridge. Arcturus came to sit beside me.

"After everything we did to get the gray market out of London, the Rag and Bone Man just flees the country and starts again under a new name. And now he has another syndicate to feed on." I closed my eyes. "Jaxon arranged this. His bony fingers are all over this mess."

"You think he is involved in this branch of the gray market," Arcturus inferred. "Despite the fact that he now serves the Sargas."

"I don't just think it. I know it."

"He wrung money from Nashira for years, forcing her to pay exorbitantly for clairvoyants of interest, all while concealing himself in the underworld. She would never support its return."

"Oh, I don't think for a moment that she knows about this Parisian branch. In fact," I said, "I'll wager that as soon as Jaxon found out Sheol II would be in France, he planted seeds here, so he'd have a new base of operations if anything happened to the first market. He might even have met Le Latronpuche in London years ago and identified him as a potential marketeer."

Arcturus seemed to digest this.

"He had to shut the first one down. Not just because we exposed it, but because he couldn't be too closely involved when he lived right under Nashira's nose," I went on. "But when I last saw him, he told me he was being sent to France—away from her—to oversee Sheol II. It must be ready to receive prisoners. And Jaxon must be ready to profit from their misery again."

"It would still be a grave risk now he works for Scion. Jaxon does not strike me as a brave man."

"That's because what he did to you wasn't brave. He stabbed you in the back and ran," I said, "but trust me, he can find his spine when he wants something. And he always wants coin."

"On the subject of coin," Arcturus said, "there is a missing link in your theory."

"Go on."

"The Rag and Bone Man is paying for voyants, possibly with money from Jaxon. This time, however, they cannot sell their victims onto Nashira. How, then, do they profit from this enterprise?"

He had a point.

"Either I'm wrong," I said, "or someone else is involved. And I don't think I'm wrong." A headache was building. "I'd say Benoît Ménard, but I don't see why he'd cough up any amount of money for voyants. He captures enough of us without help from the gray market."

The wind threw a flurry of snow in our direction. I crammed my icy hands into my pockets.

"This missing duc. Le Vieux Orphelin," I forced out. Even my jaw shook with cold. "I'd bet my last penny he found out about their deal and threatened to expose it."

"So they sold him to the Rag and Bone Man," Arcturus finished. "To silence him."

"Exactly."

He glanced toward the hidden entrance to the carrières.

"This knowledge puts us in considerable danger," he said. "I imagine Le Latronpuche and La Reine des Thunes considered killing us, but some of their voyants had seen us arrive. And needed to see us leave. I suspect you are too popular to murder in plain sight."

He nodded to the opposite wall, which was smothered in graffiti. In the morass of tags and caricatures, spray-painted messages shone out in yellow, each with a black moth behind it.

LONG LIVE THE BLACK MOTH

AVENGE THE UNDERQUEEN

IL EST TEMPS DE VOLER CE QUI NOUS APPARTIENT

Le Latronpuche had said that some of the Parisian voyants considered me a hero. Here was evidence.

"We need to find out who wrote those," I said.

"Another time." Arcturus stood. "Night Vigiles will be on duty soon."

The sky was the deep blue of a bruise. When he offered a hand, I grasped it and let him pull me up. "Better find a cab, then," I said. "Do you know where the nearest arch is?"

"Yes."

Sloping walls flanked the railway. Our boots ate into deep snow. Now we were out of the darkness, I was conscious of my bruises, old and new.

Under the fatigue, my sixth sense trembled, and I looked up to see a silhouette at the top of the wall to our right. When a second figure appeared, my stomach turned. Arcturus had clocked them, too.

"Shit," I muttered. "The grands ducs have either told these clowns to kill us, or to knock us out so they can sell us on the market."

"Your advice, Underqueen?"

"Keep moving."

A service ladder took us up to Rue des Plantes, where the wind scourged my cheeks and the tips of my ears. I had never wanted to be inside more. When we reached the end of the street, we stepped up the pace. So did our pursuers.

As soon as the illuminated arch came into view, we crossed the road and strode toward it. Two painted cabs loitered nearby.

"Go." Arcturus pressed some money into my hand. "I will distract them."

"Wait." I kept hold of his wrist. "The cabbies might report to the grands ducs. I see a better option."

On the other side of the arch, a man in a suit had just climbed out of an expensive-looking car. I watched him shove the key into his pocket. He was almost shouting into a phone, too absorbed in his argument to notice his surroundings.

This had to be the easiest mark in the citadel. With my lenses in place, I marched toward him and braced myself.

We collided hard enough to set off my bruises like a row of mines. "Pardonnez-moi," I wheezed. "C'était un accident."

My hand was already out of his pocket. He batted me away, oblivious to the loss of his key. I waited until he had rounded a corner before I unlocked his car. Arcturus went to the passenger side.

"So," he said, "we are choosing larceny."

"Always so surprised when his criminal friend commits crimes." I opened the door. "Relax. Scion has far more nefarious things to do than go after a couple of small-time car thieves."

I climbed inside and fit the key into the ignition, lighting up the dashboard. Arcturus sat in the other seat.

"Bonsoir, Laurent," a cool voice intoned. "Gloire à l'ancre. J'espère que vous avez passé une journée productive au travail."

"Oh, perfect. Just what I've always wanted." I reached for my seat belt. "Propaganda on wheels."

I locked the doors, put my foot down, and swerved off the pavement. Arcturus gripped the armrest.

"Not a car fan?" I asked as I checked the rearview camera. The anormales were starting to run.

"I do not enjoy vehicles." He fastened his seat belt. "In general."

"Noted."

My hands were clammy on the wheel. Nick had taught me to drive, but I had only attempted it a handful of times, and had never got my license. I preferred the rooftops. Still, I held my nerve as I drove away from our pursuers. They kept running after the car.

"We need to avoid main roads and cameras. Guide me." I took a sharp corner a little too fast. "I'll try not to kill us."

Arcturus seemed to welcome the distraction. He directed me down a long street to put distance between us and the anormales, who soon gave up. After that, it was a winding course through the backstreets to avoid surveillance. We abandoned the car a good distance from the safe house and walked the rest of the way.

"Do you not have vehicles in the Netherworld?" I asked him as we strode through the snow.

"Not of that sort."

I was grateful to see the safe house. Even with gloves, my hands were so cold that it took me a few tries to get the door open. Once inside, I sank onto the hallway stairs, threw my coat over the banister, and unbuttoned my boots.

"There you go," I said, between shallow breaths. "Your first step up from cake theft."

Arcturus secured the latch. "And what is the next step?"

"Well, if you can stretch yourself to robbing banks, that would solve a few problems." As I pulled off my boots, the æther resonated, raising the fine hairs on my arms. "Someone else is here."

75

We looked at one another through the gloom. "No sign of forced entry," Arcturus said. "Domino."

Of course they had turned up on the same day we decided to leave the safe house. Of course.

"I'll speak to them." I got back up. My legs trembled under my weight. "You keep out of sight."

I went upstairs with one hand curled around the handle of my knife, too weary for fear. When I entered the parlor, where a single lamp glowed, I thought at first that my sixth sense had been wrong. There was no one there. Then my nape prickled, and I turned to see a woman step from the shadows to my right, as silent as if she had never touched the floor.

"Hello, Flora," she said coolly. "I trust you have had a pleasant evening."

5

Domino

The stranger was tall and amaurotic, sharp in a tailored coat and trousers. Dark hair gusted around her face. Equally dark eyes took me in, from my knotted curls to the filthy knees of my trousers.

"Fine, thanks," I said, and cleared my throat. "Just went for a quick—"

"We can dispense with the pleasantries." She sounded Parisian. "You were instructed to remain in this safe house until your briefing, but you took it upon yourself to leave. Why?"

Except for the crow's feet around her eyes, her brown skin was impeccably smooth. Cosmetic enameling. At a push, I would have guessed she was in her late thirties or early forties.

"You'll have to explain how it's any of your business," I said.

"Because your life is in my hands." She stripped off her gloves. "Isaure Ducos. Domino Program."

"Paige."

"Flora. Your name is Flora Blake, and you are now a member of sub-network Mannequin."

Isaure Ducos walked to the nearest window. She was a striking woman, yet her every move was so precise, so silent, that she must have been able to pass unnoticed in any room. I imagined that she had never so much as knocked a glass over without intent.

"Now we are acquainted, Flora, I will ask you again," she said. "Where have you been?"

"To the river."

"From your appearance, I can only assume you swam in it."

"I needed some air. I've been indoors for weeks."

"Because you are the most wanted fugitive in the Republic of Scion. If you were in such dire need of air, you might have considered inhaling." No smile. "Leaving the safe house without consulting the network was reckless and foolish. Reckless fools are dangerous in this line of work. Ignore a direct order again, and you will be deemed a rogue agent."

"What happens then?"

"Guess." Ducos snapped the shutters closed. "Where is your associate?"

"Still at the river."

"Naturally," she said under her breath. "Since he is not an agent, I have no choice but to overlook it."

"What is he, if not an agent?"

"He is your auxiliary. A support role. Usually, auxiliaries are trusted contacts, or agents drawn from elsewhere in the network. Then again . . . nothing about your employment is usual, Flora." She looked me up and down. "How is your recovery progressing?"

"As well as can be expected."

"Our medical officer will examine you in due course. Until then, you should rest as much as possible."

She sat in the armchair and set a briefcase on the coffee table. The lamplight touched on sharply etched cheekbones and heavy brows.

"I'm here to explain your initial assignment. I remind you—since you seem to have cloth in your ears—that you are not to begin active duty until February, after your period of convalescence," she said. "Clear?"

Her tone rankled, but there was no point in arguing with this woman. And I wanted to hear what she had to say.

"Clear," I said.

"First, you should know the raison d'être of the Domino Program," Ducos said. "We are a network of intelligence agents, mostly from the free world, working within the Republic of Scion."

As I took a seat, I caught sight of myself in the mirror. My cheeks and nose were pink. "How long has this network existed?"

"Domino was founded after the end of the Balkan Incursion—Scion's first use of military force, which claimed five nations in less than two years. Our primary objective is espionage, but we are now authorized to destabilize the republic from within, and to lay the groundwork for future conflict."

"Are there plans in place for total war with Scion, then?"

"We share information on a need-to-know basis."

"So I can't ask how big the network is."

"All I can say is that we work in pièces, or sub-networks, of two to twelve individuals."

"And my sub-network is Mannequin," I said.

"Yes. Mannequin currently has six agents, including the two of us." She opened her briefcase. "I'm told you have the required skill-set for the job and are at least conversationally fluent in French. Je suppose que vous l'avez appris à l'école. Vous n'avez jamais été en France auparavant."

"Non, mais je parle couramment. C'est ma troisième langue," I said. "Interrogez-moi si vous voulez."

Ducos fired a few questions at me, each faster and more complex than the last. I answered with ease.

"You speak very well," she concluded. "A pleasant surprise. As you know, English is compulsory in all territories of the Republic of Scion, but some of our contacts prefer to use French. We must adapt to all situations." She reached into her briefcase and passed me a tube. Inside was what looked like bunched-up cling film. "This is called a dissimulator, a technology unknown to Scion. You will be unrecognizable while you wear it."

Scarlett Burnish had worn one when she helped me escape. "Seems more like magic than technology."

"Welcome to the new decade." Next was a dropper bottle, full of inky fluid. "This will darken your eyes for an hour. One drop in each eye."

Two more containers appeared from the briefcase. One held a pistol with a built-in suppressor, the other a fountain pen. Unscrewing the barrel revealed a three-inch blade.

"To be used in a crisis," Ducos said. "I take it you don't need a lesson in how to use a gun."

"I won't lie," I said. "I've never been a crack shot. I'd be marginally better with a revolver."

Ducos eyed me with fresh interest. "I can request one," she said. "I understand you were a gang-affiliated criminal in London. I assume you used a revolver to further your . . . activities."

"Just to take out the odd kneecap, you know. Nothing fancy."

I kept a straight face. Without comment, Ducos removed two identical vials from her briefcase.

"This is a stimulant." The first one she passed me contained a circular white tablet. "And this is a suicide pill."

After a moment, I accepted the second vial. The capsule inside resembled a tiny bullet.

"Please commit the difference between those pills to memory," Ducos said. "Should Scion capture you again, bite down hard on the silver pill to break its coating, then swallow. Painless brain death occurs within a minute."

"Thank you."

With a nod, Ducos shut the briefcase and dug into her coat pocket.

"Europe stands on the verge of war. The continent is a tinderbox, hungry for a spark." She took out a steel case and removed a slim white cigarette. "The Domino Program is financed by sixteen free-world nations with concerns about the Republic of Scion. We have gathered enough intelligence to know that Scion aims to keep expanding its empire."

"You don't need any special intelligence to know that. Frank Weaver declares it in his motto."

"The ongoing invasion of the Iberian Peninsula," Ducos said, as if I hadn't spoken, "has naturally raised concerns among our financiers that they could be next on the list of targets."

I remembered the scale of military preparation I had witnessed at the depot in Edinburgh. Just a taste of the force Scion could wield against other countries.

"At this stage, further invasions seem inevitable." Ducos fit the cigarette between her lips and lit it. "At the present time, they would likely succeed. Our imperative is to slow Scion down. To give these countries precious time to prepare, and to fortify their borders. It may give them a chance."

A younger, more naïve Paige died in that moment. The girl who had believed the free world held the key to defeating Scion. The girl who hoped those countries had only ever been biding their time.

"An asset of extraordinary value was put at risk to save your life. It is time for you to prove that risk was justified." Ducos blew smoke out of the corner of her mouth, away from me. "Georges Benoît Ménard, the Grand Inquisitor of France, has been avoiding contact with the government in England. Domino would like to know why."

I nodded slowly. "He never came at New Year. Didn't show up for Novembertide, either."

"Despite the fact that England gave his imminent visits a great deal of publicity. Frank Weaver clearly wants to meet with him, and to display the strength of their relationship," she said. "The question is: why is Ménard not accepting these overtures? Why avoid a fellow Scion leader?"

My mind had been so full of the revolution, I had never really questioned those absences.

"You are able to inhabit other bodies." Ducos examined me through a haze of smoke. "A unique ability, as I understand it. There are no others like you."

"Not to my knowledge."

"Then let us hope you are up to the task." She never took her gaze off me. "You will infiltrate L'Hôtel Garuche—the official residence of the Grand Inquisitor of France—and extract the information we require by possessing his spouse and chief representative, Luce Ménard Frère. You will use her influence to find out what England has done to rankle him."

Luce Ménard Frère. The woman who had smiled at the prospect of my death, told me she was glad their children would grow up in a world without me in it.

"That's out of the question," I said. "For one, I can't perform long possessions. Not without life support."

"I am aware." Ducos tapped her cigarette over the hitherto-unused ashtray. "A ventilator will be delivered to a safe house near L'Hôtel Garuche."

"For another, Frère will clearly become suspicious if she keeps losing hours of memory."

"Over time, perhaps, but not if you are quick. I'm told you're resourceful. Frère may also be reluctant to report any symptoms that smell of unnaturalness."

"Ménard would hardly put his own spouse on the guillotine, would he?"

"Don't underestimate his commitment to Scion." Ducos handed me a dossier. "This is everything we know about Frère, as well as the staff of, and regular visitors to, L'Hôtel Garuche."

"And you just want to know the reason Ménard won't see Weaver." I leafed through the dossier. "Why?"

"Because if there is tension between them, we can use it to sow discord within Scion. And when the time is right, we can fan the flames of that discord. To weaken internal unity."

"And when do you want this done?"

"Ideally, in the first week of February. The sooner we have this information, the sooner we can act on it."

Ever since I had discovered the truth behind Scion, the underworld had been my arena. I had fought to effect change from below. This was a grander stage—the world stage.

"This period of peace—if we can call it peace—is fragile. One misstep on your part could push us into all-out war," Ducos said. "We set fires in the Domino Program, but only fires we can control. Interfere in any unauthorized manner, and there will be severe repercussions. You are *only* to extract information pertaining to Benoît Ménard and Frank Weaver. You are not to use our support, money, or equipment for any other purpose."

"I get a salary, then."

"Not for your first assignment." She eyed my clothes. "I don't believe you went to the river today. You're covered in chalk. I suspect you found a way into the carrières."

I elected not to answer.

"I suspect that a woman like you—a woman used to giving, not following, orders—has found her own ends to pursue in the citadel," Ducos said. "Cease and desist, Flora Blake. Domino has given you sanctuary. Domino pays for this apartment, your food, your medicine. On top of that, you owe us a life debt. This assignment is how you pay it." She crushed her cigarette into the ashtray. "Enjoy your last few days of convalescence. I'll be in touch."

With that, she picked up her briefcase and left without a backward glance.

The front door closed. I tilted into the cushions and curled up, catlike, on my side. My temples ached. Arcturus walked into the parlor and took the seat Ducos had vacated.

"And now to sleep for a thousand years." I tucked a folded arm under my head. "Did you hear all that?"

"Yes."

"So Domino thinks Ménard and Weaver are at odds. And they want to know why," I said. "I don't suppose Alsafi told you anything useful on that front?"

He considered.

"As I told you in the colony, Benoît Ménard was invited to the Bicentenary. The guest of honor," he said. "During the event, he was to sign the Great Territorial Act—that is, the agreement that Sheol II would be founded in France."

"Remind me why he didn't show?"

"According to his representatives, he could not travel due to illness. Nashira was both displeased and unconvinced by his excuse. In October, she apparently lost patience and sent a Rephaite emissary to Paris for his signature and seal. The emissary disappeared without a trace."

Interesting. "But Ménard did eventually sign?"

"Yes, in December. Luce Ménard Frère brought the signed document to England on his behalf—Alsafi confirmed this before he severed contact. Clearly Ménard could delay no longer."

"Then we already know the source of the tension. The Great Territorial Act," I said. "Ménard didn't want Sheol II in his country. What we don't know, and what Domino *needs* to know, is why."

Without the distraction of movement, I could feel every step I had taken. A deep, relentless ache. All I wanted was to sleep, but first I needed to wash the chalk off. The thought kept me on the couch.

"Working with Domino could allow us to escalate the revolution," Arcturus said. "Are you willing, Paige?"

"Right now, I don't have much choice. This assignment is how I pay off my life debt, and it seems like we only have this hideout for as long as I keep working for them." I shifted my weight off a bruise. "And there could be all manner of useful secrets in the Hôtel Garuche."

He said nothing, but the golden cord stirred.

"What is it?" I asked. He glanced away. "Go on. If you have something on your mind."

Some time passed before he spoke.

"I wonder if you were entirely frank with me about how far you intended to go today," he said. "If you always meant to follow each lead to its end, even in the face of jeopardy."

Tiredness blurred my thoughts. It took me a moment to absorb what he was saying. "You think I misled you?"

"I prefer to prepare for all potential outcomes." He avoided the question. "To guard you to the best of my ability, I would know the conceivable extent of your plans in future."

"I told you what I planned to do this morning."

"Yes. You also stated that you would not do anything strenuous," he said. "Perhaps you feared I would not support you if I knew how far you meant to go."

"I had every intention of taking it slow," I said coolly. "Then I adapted. You know I strike while the iron is hot."

"Yes, Paige," came his quiet reply. "I am well aware."

"You might not like it, but it got rid of Senshield." As I spoke, I braced my ribs with one hand. "Maybe the Ranthen don't know how to adapt. Maybe that's why you need help from humans to make any actual progress."

"Perhaps so," Arcturus said. "In fact, I believe we complement one another in that regard. My rigor, your inclination to play for high stakes—these make for a well-balanced alliance."

84

"Fine. We're on the same page. So what's your problem?" When he fell silent again, I rubbed my raw eyes. "Arcturus, I'd really like to get some rest. Are you steering for a point?"

"Rest. We can speak tomorrow."

"No." My headache was thickening. "Just . . . say your piece."

"As you wish." Arcturus looked me in the face. "We were ill-prepared in the carrières. It was dangerous and unfamiliar territory that placed us both at the mercy of strangers."

"And if we hadn't taken the chance to go down there, we'd have no idea about the gray market being in Paris. That ignorance could have put us in danger further down the line."

"The grands ducs could have trapped and assassinated you. Even I might not have been able to protect you from all of their followers."

I huffed an incredulous laugh. "I'll thank you to remember that you've put me in danger yourself in the past. More than once," I said, "when it served *your* purposes, blood-consort." His eyes flared. "Yes, you heard me."

It was too far. As we stared ice at one another, I was distantly aware that I should quit while I was ahead, but I had said it now, and I couldn't unsay it.

"You chose to risk my life," I heard myself say, "when you chose me as the human face of your rebellion. If you hadn't made that choice, I wouldn't have been tortured into a shell. And my father would still be alive." Each breath scissored into my chest. "You helped set me on this path. Don't you ever tell me how to walk it."

Arcturus looked away, jaw set like cement. I forced myself up and made for the bathroom.

"I'm going to bed." My voice cracked. "Find someone else to lecture."

✳✳✳✳

By the time I reached the bathroom, I was aware of my own skeleton—its joints, its marrow—in a way I had never been in my life before now. I shut the door a little too hard and came face-to-face with my reflection. Against the chalk that covered me, my dark circles seemed even darker.

He was *maddening* sometimes. Immovable, sanctimonious carving, too set in his ways to bend in the wind. No wonder his side had lost the civil war, if he needed advance notice every time we fine-tuned our approach.

Even as I had the thought, I knew it was unfair. I pressed my temples and willed the headache down.

Turning the taps hurt my fingers. Peeling off my sweater hurt my back. I ran a shallow bath, just deep enough to cover my hips.

It took an age to climb into it. I gripped the edges and told myself over and over that I was in control, that no one was going to shove my head under. I wiped the dirt away with a cloth, then carefully soaked my hair and worked apple-scented shampoo through it. At last, when the water ran clear, I pressed my forehead to the lip of the bath and tried to govern my breathing.

He had said I had *stated* my intentions not to do anything strenuous. In fact, I had promised him.

I got out and pulled on a nightshirt. Combed my hair, too drained to do any more than towel-dry it. I carried my clothes to the washing machine, bundled them inside, and ate a plate of leftovers from the fridge.

Arcturus had retired for the night. Aching from head to toe, I brushed my teeth and retreated to my own room. The heating had been off all day, yet when I crawled into my bed, I found it warm. He had still left me a heat pad.

Shame cooled the last embers of frustration. Feeling worse than I had in a couple of weeks, I turned down the lamp, towed the duvet and blankets over me, and pressed the heat pad to my chest.

Though I was physically and mentally spent, sleep refused to come. Each breath raised brutal pain. My skin was so sensitive it almost hurt. I was hot and cold. On top of that, remorse lay heavy in my stomach.

Blood-consort.

Calling him that had been inexcusable. That was the title he had endured against his will for two centuries while he was trapped in a betrothal to Nashira, mocked and judged by his fellow Rephaim. I had known how it would make him feel. Tiredness was no excuse.

By half past ten, my cough was back with a vengeance. At wits' end, I stumbled to the bathroom in search of relief. A spoonful of cough syrup cushioned my chest and finally let me sleep.

It never lasted. Not for long. At some point, my hand strayed above my head, finding its old position on the waterboard, and I jerked awake, nightshirt plastered to my skin.

I stared at the ceiling for a long time. When it was clear I would never get back to sleep, I took a long cardigan from the bedpost, drew it on, and crossed the parlor to knock on his door.

"Come in."

I took a moment to collect myself before I entered.

Except for the position of the bed, his room was almost identical to mine. Arcturus lay on his side, a book open on the sheets in front of him. A lamp penciled shadows across the high ceiling.

He looked up. I had seen him bare-chested before, but this was the first time I had really noticed that he had no navel. His sarx —the warm gold of brass—was taut and seamless over slabs of muscle, limned by the dim light from the lamp.

"Paige," he said, his tone questioning.

I realized I was staring like a gamal at him.

"Sorry," I said, face warm. "You just don't have—" I indicated my own abdomen. "But you wouldn't, I suppose."

Rephaim were not born. He had never been tethered to a womb, nor grown inside someone else. When he had first emerged, alone, he had looked exactly as he did now.

"You are curious about other differences." Arcturus closed his book. "There are none. Externally, at least."

"But Rephaim don't reproduce," I said, thinking aloud. "So you probably don't have a—"

I stopped dead, willing the floor to disappear, the ceiling to collapse and bury me. Arcturus looked at me, expressionless.

"I presume you did not come to discuss the particulars of my anatomy, Paige," he said.

"I did not." I picked up the shreds of my composure and started again: "I came to apologize for earlier. I shouldn't have lashed out at you like that, or called you what I did. I'm sorry."

He closed the book and turned over, so his back was against the pillows. "You spoke true," he said. "By asking you to lead the rebellion, I did bring all of this on you."

"I didn't mean any of that. It's not your fault I was tortured. Or that Vance killed my father," I said. "I ate the head off you because I was overtired. You didn't do anything wrong."

When I came to sit on the bed, he returned his book to the stack on the bedside table, and I wrapped myself a little more tightly in my cardigan. His room was colder than mine.

"You were right. I was trying to prove something to myself by going down there," I said, "but I pulled you into danger with me, knowing you wouldn't leave me alone. That wasn't fair." I looked him in the eye. "I didn't lie to you about what I aimed to do today. Having said that, I know I'm a chancer. I shouldn't have made a promise I knew I might not keep."

His answer was hushed: "I did not intend to imply that you deceived me out of malice."

"I know what you meant."

He studied my face. I raked my fingers through my frizz-addled curls.

"I know I'm quick to snap at you sometimes. If it helps, I've done it to most of my friends," I said. "Eliza always said my name was perfect for me. A page looks soft, but it has sharp edges."

"Hm. And paper cuts never sting for long."

"Why are you excusing it?" I asked quietly. "I'm not Nashira. You don't have to absorb whatever I throw at you."

"Because I have felt the same anger you aimed at me," he said. "When you were tortured, every facet of who you are came under assault. For a long time, you may feel even the smallest criticism as an extension of that attack. Instinct will tell you to defend yourself."

His words rang with truth. The moment he had tried to express a concern, something inside me had bared its teeth. A shadow of the thing I had become when I was tortured.

"And because I confess to a fear of losing you. Stronger now than it was before," he continued, softer. "I cannot be certain that it did not spur my desire for you to turn back today."

He had tried to stop me giving myself up to Scion. In answer, I had pointed a gun at him.

"That fear—my fear—is not your cage," he said. "I will never ask you to mold yourself to it."

I held his gaze. "I don't want us to argue," I said. "Do you forgive me?"

"If you will forgive me. For my fear."

"I do."

Quiet fell between us. I knew I should leave now. Toss and turn in my own bed until I wore myself out.

"I can't sleep." It was out before I could stop it. "Would you mind if I stayed here tonight?" I cleared my throat. "I keep thinking I'm still chained up in that basement. Alone."

His eyes were embers. After a long moment, he shifted to the left side of the bed.

"By all means," he said.

"Sure?"

"Quite sure."

Before I could second-guess myself, I went to the other side. Arcturus retrieved his book. Once I had found a position that let me breathe, he reached for the light.

"Oh, don't turn it off on my account," I said.

"I have my own reading lamps." He indicated his face. "Unless you would sooner not be in darkness."

"It's fine. I should try to get used to it again."

With a *click*, the room turned black. My throat pulled tight. "What are you reading?" I asked, to distract myself.

"Poetry." Arcturus turned a page. "Do you like to read, Paige?"

"I've flicked through my share of penny dreadfuls, and my grandparents both used to tell me stories," I said, "but I've never had the patience to sit and read for hours. I'd like to."

"I am of the considered opinion that for every person, there exists a book that will sing to them. I trust that you will find yours."

I smiled. "I'll keep an eye out."

In the past, I had found him unnerving in the dark. Seeing him now did give me a chill, but not an unpleasant one.

For a while, the only sound was turning pages. It reminded me that I was no longer alone. Just as I was on the cusp of sleep, Arcturus said, "In the colony, I told you that the golden cord may have formed because we had saved each other's lives several times."

"I remember." His words took a while to take root in my sleep-thickened thoughts. "You weren't sure, though."

"No. It was simply all I knew of the cord. An obscure myth of a bond between two spirits, forged by mutual loyalty. I have never found another Rephaite who confessed to having one."

"Mm. It's strange," I murmured into the pillow. "Just us."

"Yes." A long stillness. "Paige, there is something I have concealed from you."

My eyes fluttered open again. "Okay." When he was silent, I said, "I'm listening."

"Forgive me. I took an oath of silence."

"Arcturus, as your friend, I think it's my duty to inform you that you're not a twelfth-century monk."

"It is not only monks who honor such oaths."

"If you say so." I was so deeply burrowed into the duvet in that I had to squirm a bit to face him. My blood ran like honey. "If you can't tell me the secret, why tell me it exists?"

"You will work it out yourself. You are perceptive, and you have all the pieces. Sooner or later, you will fit them together," Arcturus said. "When you do, I want you to know that I did not wish to keep it. That it is the last truth I will hide from you."

At length, I said, "All right."

There was nothing else to be done. Still, it was rare for him to be in a confessional mood. I folded the pillow in half and returned my head to it, so I was propped up a little. Sleep could wait.

"You didn't trust me with your secrets in the colony for a long time," I said. "When did that change?"

"The night you saw Nashira strike me in the tower. Later, you followed me to the chapel. It showed that you cared for me in some measure. If you cared, you could not mean to betray me."

He had been forced to greet her on his knees. It had taken me too long to see that he was also her prisoner.

"Did she often hurt you?" I asked softly.

"When she judged me in need of instruction." He was impassive. "Our betrothal was a private war. Nashira believed that, sooner or later, she would cleanse me of my traitorous ideals. That I would come to see what her loyalists saw, and desire her. For two centuries, she sought to break my resolve. Perhaps it is the nature of a binder to believe all spirits can be claimed."

Likely. Jaxon certainly thought he could own anyone, living or dead.

Had I been more awake, I might not have asked what I did next. Drowsiness had softened my inhibitions.

"Terebell used to be your mate," I said. "She isn't now." The cord tensed. "Sorry. I'm prying."

"I sifted through your memories more than once. You have a right to ask for mine."

I sat up a little more. My body gathered the black threads of sleep, like a bird collecting pieces for its nest, but I wanted to hear this.

"I have taken several mates," Arcturus said, "but I had no great desire for a long-term companion until I met Terebell."

I had glimpsed his memory of their first meeting. Terebell, dressed in sleek garments, dark hair pouring down her back.

"We were still together when the Waning of the Veils began," he continued. The civil war. "Throughout the chaos, Terebell was always at my side. We fought hard for the Mothallath. When they were defeated, Nashira chose me as blood-consort."

"Did you know Nashira before that?"

"Yes. Her opinions were very different from mine, but I respected her for expressing them." His voice darkened. "Sundering a Rephaite from their mate would have been unthinkable under the Mothallath. Nashira made it clear she had no interest in old customs."

"But why you?"

"She knew the public surrender of the Mesarthim, who had been most faithful to the Mothallath, would cement her new position. So she took their leader as her war trophy," he said. "She promised to eradicate my family, as she had the Mothallath, if I refused. When she sent me the head of one of my cousins, I knew what I would have to do."

"But Terebell is nothing if not proud. When Nashira summoned me to plight my troth to her in public, Terebell challenged her to single combat." A brief silence. "Nashira had honed formidable skills during the war. She came very close to destroying Terebell."

Terebell carried herself as if she expected a fight. Her body was a battle cry.

"I stepped in. I swore to Nashira that I would bind myself to her without question or contest, that I would be her servant in all things, and that I would pledge the Mesarthim to her cause in perpetuity, if she spared Terebell," Arcturus said. "She agreed to these terms."

As he spoke, his attention drifted to his hands. When I searched his face, he gave me a small nod, granting permission.

It was hard to see by the light of his eyes alone, but I could feel. Carefully, I turned his hand over, brushing my thumb across the heart line of his palm, his broad knuckles. The scars coursed just below them and snaked round to the undersides of his fingers.

"How did you get these?" I asked.

"I stopped her blade. Our weapons are made of a Netherworld element named opaline. It is the only substance that can hew through Rephaite bone."

Her sword had almost severed his fingers. I wondered if it was the same one she had used to behead Alsafi.

"Terebell has never forgiven me," Arcturus said. "She believed we should both have given our lives in defiance."

I realized I was still holding his hand and let go. He gave me an indecipherable look before he clasped them on his chest again.

"You told me once that the flame never goes out," I said.

"Even the strongest flame can be starved. I will always care for Terebell, and she for me. She has my affection and my allegiance," he said. "But I will never again be her mate."

A feeling thickened in my stomach. Not jealousy, but a touch of yearning—for the intimacy they shared, or had once shared. Terebell must know everything there was to know about him.

"I'm sorry," I said.

"Hm."

There was a hush between us. I had no idea how to comfort a Rephaite, or if he even wanted it.

"I want you to train me again," I said. "In possession. I'll need practice if I'm to possess Frère."

"Of course." He turned onto his side, so we faced each other. "Goodnight, Paige."

"Night."

I settled into the pillow. At first I was too aware of each tiny movement, worried I might disturb him if I fidgeted too much. Before long, exhaustion towed me down.

Sleep closed me in a tighter vise than it had in a long time. When I stirred in the night, roused by a dog barking in the street, I found that I had moved close enough for my hair to brush his elbow. The glow of a streetlamp had stolen into the room, revealing him to me.

The night we met, I had thought he was the most beautiful and terrible thing I had ever laid eyes on. There was nothing terrible before me now. Sleep had stripped him of his Rephaite armor. He was in the same position, features soft and unburdened, one hand on the sheets between us.

In silence, I turned my hand so it lay palm up, and the shadows of my fingers fell across his knuckles. Then I drifted back to sleep.

6

March of a Marionette

I woke in a cocoon of covers. When I opened my eyes to the faint light of morning, it took me a moment to remember why the windows were in the wrong place.

The other side of the bed was cold. I started to sit up, then stopped. Under the languor and the general aches, I was distinctly tender. After almost a year of absence, my period was back.

A sigh escaped me. Now I understood the headache. Roused by the thought of coffee, I checked the sheets, rubbed my eyes, and edged off the bed. A glance at the mirror confirmed that my hair was in rag order—in fact, I looked and felt as if I had rolled backward down a hill.

Once I was done in the bathroom, I crossed the sun-drenched parlor to the kitchen, where Arcturus was steeping coffee. He had cracked open a window, letting in the sounds of rush hour.

"Good morning," he said.

"Hi." My voice came out hoarse. "I didn't keep you up all night with my cough, did I?"

"I am not lightly woken." Steam rose from the coffee press. "Did you sleep well?"

"I did. I hope you didn't mind me sharing."

"Not at all."

A stillness followed. When I reached past him for the jar of painkillers, his aura raised gooseflesh.

"So," I said, "still up for training?"

"If you feel strong enough." He prepared the coffee as if he had all the time in the world. I supposed he did. "We will start gently, with dislocation."

"Gently." As I sat at the table, a cramp tightened my stomach. "That would be nice."

"Are you unwell, Paige?"

"Fine. My uterus is just confirming that it will not be growing a baby this month. With good reason," I said, "since a tiny, defenseless human is not *really* what I need while I'm on the run from the agents of tyranny."

"You are menstruating."

"I am menstruating," I confirmed gravely.

"I see." His eyes darkened. "Is it very painful?"

I considered.

"I've never had to describe it before," I said, musing. "I suppose it's like having all my lower organs crammed right down to my pelvis, then soaked in boiling water, so they're sore and swollen. It's a heavy, aching . . . downward-ness. But then it also feels like I've been kicked in the back. And the stomach. And the legs. Oh, and I've got a splitting headache."

Arcturus had stopped plunging the coffee.

"And you feel able to train," he said, after a long pause. "While experiencing those sensations."

I rubbed the corner of my eye. "I'm grand."

He watched me for several moments, then returned to the coffee. I was sure he was being gentler with it.

"Once we have practiced dislocation for a day or two," he said, while he poured, "you can attempt to possess me."

A daunting prospect. I had walked in his dreamscape, but never controlled him. The one time I had possessed a Rephaite—Nashira—it had been for a matter of seconds, and it had ripped the stuffing out of me.

"Possessing Rephaim is difficult." I kneaded the small of my back. "From what I remember."

"That is why that skill will prove useful. If you master it, you should find possessing humans easy in comparison."

He presented me with the coffee. I resisted the urge to rest the warm mug on my abdomen.

We sat in companionable silence. Arcturus folded the shutters back. The sky was tender pink, and the sun cast a hazy, dreaming light over the citadel.

"Paris is more volatile than London," he remarked. "These streets have already coursed with the blood of revolution. Something will happen here soon. Something that will push us over the brink."

"You sound like Ducos." I blew on the coffee. "She said Europe was on the verge of war."

"Which is why you must be careful when you possess Frère."

I glanced at him. "I really don't know what you're afraid I'll do in there."

"You might be in a position to kill the Grand Inquisitor of France. As we have established," Arcturus said, "you seldom ignore an opportunity." I sipped my coffee without comment. "There will be many temptations, but I advise you to maintain your focus. We agreed to follow orders from Domino."

"I was a mollisher for years. I can follow orders. That doesn't mean I shouldn't try to further *our* ends," I pointed out. "There could be hundreds of official secrets in that place."

"If you seek them out at the cost of your mission, you risk jeopardizing our relationship with Domino. An alliance with them could be invaluable to the Mime Order."

"As if they'd ever work with us. They're the real deal," I said. "A state-funded intelligence network. You really think they'd stoop to rubbing shoulders with undisciplined criminals?"

"The Mime Order could be far more than that. It has the potential to wage guerrilla warfare against Scion. If you can forge a strong relationship with Ducos and prove your reliability, she may be able to persuade her employers to funnel some of their funds toward your army."

I tried to picture it. Our motley legion, supported by countries with vast resources. No longer terrorists or thugs, but a credible threat to Scion.

"Maybe," I said.

"I understand your instinct to exploit every opportunity you see. Such an instinct is well-placed in war," Arcturus said. "I only ask you once more, as your friend, to exercise caution."

I watched him as I drank my coffee.

The truth was that there *was* something I wanted from inside the Hôtel Garuche. Something I needed.

I could tell Arcturus now. Except it would only trouble him, and I had put him through more than enough worry of late. Besides, I was certain I could get what I wanted without anyone having to know.

"I'll bear it in mind," was all I said.

****

We spent the next few days in the cellar, which doubled as a training room, complete with weights and a pull-up bar. Arcturus started us off with some light combat to ease me back into drills.

It took great effort to meet his mock punches. I was graceless, my reactions slow. What had once been a dance of equals—my agility, his strength—was now painfully one-sided. He could outflank me so quickly I might as well have just sat on the floor.

Dislocating was no easier. My gift had been suppressed while I was imprisoned, and now it shied away from me. It took several excruciating tries before I could peel my spirit from its seat in my dreamscape. I couldn't imagine being able to take a flying leap from my body the way I had before.

Arcturus did his best. Sometimes he would make me laugh with some archaic turn of phrase, and I could relax enough into the fight that it flowed. That only lasted for so long.

It wasn't just my inelegance that frustrated me. It was the sharp pain that shadowed each breath. It was never having *enough* breath. It was how often I had to call time for a rest. On top of that, Arcturus seemed reluctant to push me. When I started to cough during one session, he steered me back upstairs and set me up on the couch with a heat pad for the evening.

He cared too much. If he wouldn't push my limits, I would have to push them myself. In the small hours of that same night, I wrapped my hands and stole back to the cellar. If I rebuilt the strength in my body, my gift might return, too.

A rack of weights stood in the corner. I made for the ones I had been able to handle before the scrimmage, hefted them into my hands, and lifted. My arms shook, but the tug in my muscles meant progress. I relished it.

That was when my wrist folded. I had thought the sprain was healing. With a hiss, I dropped both weights, and they fell with a terrific clangor to the floor. Racked with coughs, I folded onto the mat and hunched over my hand.

Silence filled the room to its corners. I drew my knees to my chest and rested my brow against them.

"Paige."

Arcturus had appeared in the doorway. My face was hot as a stove, beaded with sweat.

"What is it?" he asked.

When I just shook my head, he came to sit beside me. I braced my wrist and flexed my fingers.

"They broke me," I said. "In that fucking basement." The taste of salt filled my mouth. "I don't know how to get back to being who I was before."

"You never can. That person is dead. So is the person you were yesterday," Arcturus said. "Death is not an ending. It is only a change of seasons. Passage from one state to another. Your new form is fragile, but in time, it will grow strong. Be patient with yourself."

I managed a weary smile. "Patience isn't always easy for those of us who won't live forever."

"I would like you to live for as long as possible, Paige Mahoney." Arcturus rose. "When Ducos returns, you should ask to see the medical officer."

With a reluctant nod, I took his proffered hand and stood. I felt like a fool for wanting to cry.

We went back upstairs together and sat in the parlor, where Arcturus opened a bottle of red wine.

"I'll have one," I said.

"As you wish." He took another glass from the cabinet. "I did not know you cared for wine."

"I can't hold it to save my life," I said ruefully, "but I'll survive a splash." I arched an eyebrow. "Can you . . . get hammered?"

Arcturus cast me a look. "Hammered?"

"Drunk. Battered. Ar meisce. In a state of alcohol-induced intoxication."

"Not to my knowledge."

"Pity." I put my feet up on the couch. "I'd have proposed a drinking game."

"How does one make a game of drinking?"

"Well, Nadine and I once watched the news and had a shot of absinthe every time someone said *unnatural*. We were absolutely locked." I pulled the throw down over my legs. "I always meant to ask you."

"Yes?"

"When you first trained with me, were you just running on instinct?"

Arcturus filled the first glass.

"In part," he said. "It is easier now, since I can sense your spirit through the cord." He poured again. "However, I based my initial approach on a dreamwalker I knew before you."

I stilled. 'What?'

"Did you never wonder how Nashira was so well-informed about dreamwalking?" He slotted the cork back into the bottle. "You are the second of your kind to slip between her fingers."

This was unexpected. Even Jaxon, self-professed authority on clairvoyance, had never found living proof of other dreamwalkers. I had come to accept that my gift was a one-off.

Yet it did make perfect sense for there to have been someone else. Nashira had been consumed by her desire to dreamwalk long before I arrived in the colony. That obsession had to have grown from a seed.

"Emma Orson," Arcturus said, seeing my face. "She was captured after the third Bone Season and brought straight to the colony." He held out a glass. "In secret, we Ranthen contrived her escape. It was too dangerous to have such a powerful clairvoyant near Nashira."

Gaze fixed on him, I took the glass. "You learned about dreamwalking through her."

"Enough. Terebell and I were only able to speak to her twice. She did not call herself a dreamwalker, of course."

Because Jaxon had coined the term. "What happened to her?" I pressed. "After you let her escape."

"I have one theory."

I waited. Arcturus sank onto the couch and rested his glass of wine on its arm.

"When she discovered that Emma had escaped," he said, "Nashira sent a red-jacket to find her. Not long after, several women were brutally murdered in Whitechapel."

My back prickled. "The Ripper."

A stiff nod. "The final woman was identified as Marie Kelly. I discovered later that she had been known on the streets by several other names—one of which was Fair Emma."

"You think Marie *was* Emma."

"Or it was a case of mistaken identity. Either way, to my knowledge, Emma was never seen again."

I had seen photographs of that crime scene. Tinkers sold copies on the black market.

"Nashira must have been fuming." I tried to blot the picture from my mind. "I always wondered how she got the Ripper. Your theory would solve it. He returned to Sheol I, only for her to kill him and bind his spirit—either to punish him for not finding Emma, or for her murder."

"Yes," Arcturus said. "As you know, Nashira turned the bloodshed to her advantage. She had been waiting for the right chance to bring down the monarchy. As soon as Prince Edward was crowned, she sprang her trap, and he was forever known as the Bloody King."

She had framed him for the murders, painting him as the bringer of unnaturalness, so Scion could rise in his place. If Arcturus was right, it had started with a dreamwalker.

"You are the only dreamwalker I have met since," he said.

"No wonder." I drained my glass. "Nashira is never going to stop hunting me, is she?"

"No."

At least he didn't sugarcoat the truth. I would return the favor.

"Arcturus, I need you to push me harder in training." I sought his gaze. "We agreed to always do whatever was necessary. Not to let anything get in the way."

As I spoke, I remembered that night in the dark, when I had crushed whatever had been flowering between us. I had done it so we would never put each other above the revolution.

I can't afford to feel the way I do when I'm with you.

Silence fell between us, thick and deep. Arcturus drank before he said, "As you wish."

"Okay." I got up. "If you don't mind, I want us to only speak in French for a while. I imagine that's what Frère uses in private."

"A sound idea," Arcturus said. "Bonne nuit, petite rêveuse."

"Bonne nuit."

****

As February loomed, Arcturus met me in the training room each day, and he helped me draw my spirit out. It was hard work. I responded best to danger, and there was none in the apartment. In the end, I was forced to use my imagination to ignite my gift.

I pictured the waterboard. I pictured my friends gunned down by faceless soldiers. I pictured the massacre I had witnessed as a child. At last, with supreme effort, I dislocated and concentrated the ensuing pressure on Arcturus. My nose bled, but it was a start.

When I wasn't in the training room, I was memorizing everything there was to know about Frère from the documents Ducos had given me.

Luce Isabella Frère had been born in the Scion Citadel of Toulouse, the eldest of the three daughters of the Minister of the Exchequer. After her parents had separated, she and the middle sister had moved with their mother to Marseille.

Since childhood, Frère had fostered ambitions of becoming Grand Raconteur, and she had earned a first-class degree in Scion History with that end in mind. At twenty-three, she had met the future Grand Inquisitor of France at a dinner party in Grenoble. They were engaged in 2049, the same year he became Minister for Justice, and had married five months later. Now they were two sides of a coin, rarely seen apart, and had three children—Onésime, Mylène, and Jean-Michel—with a fourth on the way. Frère had formally announced her pregnancy on the fourteenth of December, when she was three months along.

The dossier on Frère included a video file of her public appearances. I watched for any habits, took note of her bearing, listened to her feathery laugh. Frère crossed her legs at the ankles when she sat and only smiled with the left side of her mouth. When pregnant, she often placed a hand on her stomach. Years in the capital had eroded her southern accent, but occasional words lured it out. I took note of those words.

Like her spouse, Frère was ardent in her hatred of clairvoyants. When England had unveiled NiteKind—a form of painless execution for voyants—she had been its fiercest opponent, arguing that brutality was essential to keep unnaturals in line. NiteKind had never made it to France. She had also represented Ménard at many of the so-called blood lotteries, where prisoners in the Grande Bastille were selected at random for execution.

The main guillotine stood in the Place de Grève. I found one recording of a triple execution, where Frère could be seen in the witness stands, a newborn Jean-Michel in her arms, while the voyants waited to die. The corner of her mouth lifted when one lost control of his bowels.

All this served as a reminder that Frère was the enemy, a disciple of the anchor who craved the extinction of clairvoyants. I would still treat her body with as much respect as I could afford it, and not abuse my power any more than necessary. She had her morals. I had mine.

There was one more thing to consider. To guard against my ability to infiltrate its buildings, Scion had taught some of its personnel to recognize the signs of possession. I had learned that the hard way in Manchester. There was no telling who in the Hôtel Garuche—if anyone—had been informed I was still alive. Who might be able to catch me out. This possession had to be flawless.

****

Early one morning, Arcturus found me chewing oatmeal in the kitchen, eyes puffy. My soul-destroying cough had kept me up all night again. It seemed as if it was getting worse, not better.

"Possess me," he said, in French. It was all we spoke now.

I finished my mouthful of oatmeal. "It's half past five."

"We do not have long until February. You have regained your ability to dislocate your spirit. Now you need to dreamwalk."

He had kept his promise to push me. I abandoned my half-eaten meal and followed him.

In the cellar, we faced one another on the flagstones.

"To kill with your spirit, you must be fast and firm, as you know," Arcturus said. "For a silent possession, however, you should glide into the dreamscape. The gentler you are, the smaller the chance that your host will bleed."

"It's hard to breach the dreamscape without some force. If I'm too slow, Frère will notice the pressure."

"Then be quick. Quick, but light-handed. In any case, Frère is amaurotic. She will have few defenses."

His own defenses were lowering. "Maybe we can skip all this," I said, thinking aloud. "You and I combined our gifts to steal a memory from Vance. Could we do that to Frère?"

"Not without alerting her."

"She might not realize what was happening."

"And if she does?" he said, even-toned. "If Vance warned anyone of what we can do?"

He had a point. In this case, possession might carry less risk. I weighed up whether to take it slow, or to be ruthless.

"Brace yourself," I said.

I cast off all restraints and jumped.

It was agony. Red-hot agony. A moment later, I was too far away to feel it. I slipped into his dreamscape and walked past the red drapes that hung there, my fingers luminous against them. They lit an otherwise dark place. In his mind, I glowed like a candle.

103

Arcturus waited for me in the centre of his dreamscape. Seeing me approach, he stepped aside so I could take control. I was careful not to make contact with him as we switched places.

Possessing him was far harder than taking hold of a human. I fought to find purchase, to fill him—but little by little, my host accepted me, and the training room shivered into relief.

Arcturus was sighted. Three ghosts appeared as glowing threads in front of him. I had a moment to marvel before my senses were blown open, and I almost crashed to my knees. His knees.

I had never experienced the æther like this. Not only could I see its inhabitants, but I could feel it in a way I had never imagined was possible. He carried it within him, in his very blood. In my own dreamscape, I was a bubble in black water—aware of the æther, in touch with it, yet shielded from it, too. Though I was voyant, I was human, and flesh muffled the æther. Sarx conducted it.

The initial shock began to fade. When I willed his fingers to move, they rewarded me by flinching.

Very good.

"Wait, how are you talk—?" I started when his voice rolled out. "Oh, wow. I forgot I was going to sound like you."

I am sorry if my voice disappoints you.

"It's a beautiful voice. I'm just feeling the pressure to use fancy vocabulary," I said. "At least you sound less of a Sasanach now." My accent lilted up his words. "Seriously, though, you should be out of action. Why can I hear you?"

Another side effect of the golden cord, no doubt.

"Great. A body with a back seat driver."

If you would prefer silence . . .

"No, no. It's your body. Bloody hell, your voice is deep," I ground out. "It's almost *tiring* to have a voice this deep." I squared his shoulders. "I thought I was sensitive to the æther, but this is something else. It's as if you exist on both planes."

Not restfully. To be a creature of the in-between is to not belong on either side.

As he said it, I felt the strain in his aura. I had the distinct impression that what I was feeling—the swallowing vastness of existence—still paled in comparison to what I would have felt if his aura had worked the way it once had, before the Rephaim had needed to feed on clairvoyants. Where mine linked me smoothly to the æther, something hindered his.

"It's like hunger," I said. "In your aura."

A mercy for you. If my aura was at its full strength, I imagine this experience would have shattered your sanity by now.

I didn't doubt him. Humans were not supposed to comprehend immortality.

My body stood nearby, surrounded by scarlet radiance. He had taught me how to keep it breathing even while I possessed someone else, but it took concentration. On the mission, at least, I would have a ventilator, allowing me to leave altogether and focus on Frère.

"I've always thought of it as feeding when you use clairvoyant auras. Like you're parasites. But that's not quite right," I said, thinking aloud. "You're not consuming anything, are you?"

Go on.

"Our auras are like solder. They seal the rift between yours and the æther. You're not feeding. You're . . . bridging."

It exhausts the clairvoyant if they try to fight it. In that sense, we do drain you. I looked down at his scar-riven hands. *Walk to the mirror.*

Easier said than done. He was so much larger than me, his limbs so much longer. I moved like an automaton. Even without trying, I knew how easy it would be to break anything I touched—his body coursed with tremendous strength. I almost envied him, moving through the world with bones too solid to be broken and a frame too robust to be thrown to the ground.

I almost envied him. Not quite. Though Rephaim were intrinsically strong, a single red flower could strip their might away. Then there was the pain in his back. It gnawed at him, deep and constant, as if someone had beaten him with a mace.

You feel them.

Jaxon was responsible. It was his betrayal of the Ranthen that had led to this punishment.

Do not pity me, little dreamer, Arcturus said. *I have lived with those scars for twenty years.*

"I don't pity you, but I am sorry."

Your sympathy is noted.

I finally reached the mirror. Just comfortable enough to be fascinated, I leaned close to see how my presence affected his face. All that gave me away was the stillness of his eyes. Usually they were living flames—their light would brighten and flicker and dim in ways I could occasionally interpret. Now that light was flat.

"I'm tempted to indulge in some real vulgarity, just so I can hear you swear," I mused.

I trust that you are above such low humor.

"You think too much of me."

Never. For your first task, Arcturus said, *raise my hand. And try not to make it look as if a string is pulling it.*

7

Rootless

For the last few days of the month, he taught me how to move him as I moved myself. Possessing him was always a challenge—it was hard to keep my foothold in his dreamscape—but I kept at it. If I could do this, Frère would be easier to grasp.

While I controlled her, she would effectively be unconscious. I needed a cover story to explain her memory loss, and I found it when I went through her medical history again. Frère had low blood pressure, which had caused fainting spells during two of her pregnancies. If I was careful, she would think she had blacked out for the time I possessed her.

This would only work once—twice, perhaps, at most. After that, she would know something was amiss.

Once I was confident that I could handle the jump into Frère, I gave us both a break from my possessions. Rephaim usually only needed rest once every four days, or thereabouts. Since I had started using Arcturus as my host, he took to his bed almost as often as I did. Sometimes I joined him. One night, when I woke disoriented yet again, I found his door ajar, and him asleep on one side of the bed, leaving room for me on the other.

By day, I turned my attention to other tasks. I studied a floor map of the Hôtel Garuche. I watched endless recordings, rehearsed speaking and acting like Frère. And I absorbed everything I could find on the Scionet about my target.

Georges Benoît Ménard. Born in the burning summer of 2019, he had spent his childhood in Strasbourg, a port city on the Rhine. In a rare personal interview, Ménard recalled seeing free-world children beyond the electric fence that separated it from Germany.

There was a French-speaking Swiss family who lived on the other side. They had several children, and every few days, those children grew bored and strayed to the border to mock us as we walked along the riverside path on our way home from school. Sometimes they would bring unnatural paraphernalia and throw it over the fence.

In Germany and Switzerland, there are clocks mounted with wooden birds that pipe the same notes every hour. They are called pendules à coucou, and coucous is what these children called us— mad and mechanical, unable to do anything but sing our anthem, which we often did when they approached. They were blind to the truth: that it was they who were automatons, their clockwork wound by unnatural hands.

Pendules à coucou. That gave me pause. Only a few weeks ago, Nick had seen a vision of a waterboard and a cuckoo clock.

I had to get this possession right.

Disgusted by the influence of the free world on Strasbourg—its architecture, its cuisine, its river that had the absolute gall to run from the mountains of Switzerland—Ménard had moved to Paris to study law. Not long after receiving his degree, he had secured his first job as a judicial clerk at the Inquisitorial Courts.

Ménard was a man on the rise. He had been a fixture in the Forteresse de Justice, praised for his intelligence and his meticulous approach to every task. It seemed odd, then, that at twenty-six he had suddenly departed for the Scion Citadel of Lyon, where he had served as "expert counsel" to the Ministry of the Interior. With a vague title and no further record of his movements at that time, I was certain he had been involved in the hidden cruelties of Scion. Interrogator, perhaps.

In 2049, he had returned to Paris as Minister for Justice. Within four years, his devotion to Scion was repaid in full when, upon the death of Jacquemine Lang, he became the youngest ever Grand Inquisitor of France at thirty-four. One of his first acts had been to almost wholly remodel the city of Strasbourg, and to increase the voltage of the electric fence on the border. Now that fence was lethal.

His official photograph showed a clean-shaven man with a high forehead and dark walnut hair, neatened with pomade. A crescent-shaped birthmark curved under one cheekbone. Small brown eyes stared out from beneath solid brows. His popularity seemed to be rooted in his impeccable manners, good looks, and a hard-line approach to unnaturalness.

He was forty now and had been Grand Inquisitor for almost seven years. In that time, he had given only a handful of interviews. I watched them all. They revealed a cool and self-possessed demeanor that gave me a chill. He would consider for a long time before he answered a question, knowing the journalist would wait on tenterhooks for as long as it took for him to speak. He was all mild courtesy. He never gesticulated, and his smiles were lukewarm at best.

Frank Weaver behaved like the dummy he was. You could almost see the hinge on his jaw. Ménard was entrancing. Without ever raising his voice, he commanded attention.

I asked Arcturus to test my knowledge. When I could answer each question off the cuff, I devoted myself to refining my French, seeking obscure and technical words that had eluded me before.

Sometimes the sheer audacity of the mission daunted me. All I knew of Frère was her public veneer. I was going to be dealing with people who lived with her, who knew her intimately. Then there was the security unit of eighty elite Vigiles, some of them former soldiers, who protected the Inquisitorial family and must know exactly how their employers behaved.

I had so little time to obtain the two pieces of information I needed. One of them—the source of the tension between Ménard and Weaver—I would pass to Domino. The other I would share only with Arcturus.

Everyone had a key. No matter how complex the lock, Benoît Ménard was no exception.

****

I sensed Isaure Ducos again on the last night of January, while I was perusing a thick French dictionary in bed, having spent the day with a fever, coughing myself to distraction. Arcturus had brewed me a mug of hot lemon water and honey to help. I finished it as I joined him in the parlor.

"Ducos is coming." I sank into a heap beside him. "You may as well stay. She'll want to meet you sooner or later."

"Very well," he said. "How is your fever?"

"Better, I think."

He handed me a thermometer. I stuck it into my ear and held it there until it let out a tiny *beep* and turned red.

"It's come down a bit. One hundred degrees." I passed it back to him. "I'll be fine by tomorrow."

"I know you are finding it difficult to drink, but you must. You are likely dehydrated."

"I drink all the time."

"Yes. Coffee." He took my mug. "I will brew you some more lemon water."

"All right." I nudged him with my foot. "You big hen, you."

"Cluck," he said, straight-faced.

My smile faded when I noticed the news. ScionEye was providing regular and enthusiastic updates on the invasion of Portugal. According to the report, the battle for Lisbon had now begun.

A map appeared on the screen. Lisbon sprawled beside a vast estuary of the River Tagus. Graham Harling, the Grand Admiral of Scion England, had sent a fleet of warships to blockade it. Meanwhile, soldiers marched on the capital from two sides and air strikes hammered the heavily populated cities of Coimbra and

Porto. Weaver vowed the bombardment would stop the moment the President of Portugal, Daniela Gonçalves, issued her formal and unconditional surrender. Portugal needed the anchor. It must accept the inevitable.

At twenty-nine, Gonçalves was a young leader. ScionEye described her as inexperienced and weak. So far, she seemed to be holding her nerve.

"I urge President Gonçalves to accept the inevitable," Weaver said from the screen. "You are infested with unnaturalness. Only Scion can cleanse it. Lay down your arms and embrace the anchor, and it will embrace you in return. Your people will be treated with dignity. Continue to fight, and we will treat you as we would a house tainted with plague. Only ashes will remain."

He meant it. If Portugal fought to the end and still lost to the anchor, it would suffer the way Ireland and parts of the Balkans had. Its people would forever be marked as troublemakers, stained by their defiance. Still, I willed them to fight on. I willed Gonçalves not to bend.

"Can we trust any of this?" I said, when Arcturus returned. "They wouldn't share their actual tactics with the public, would they?"

"No. Scion will report whatever it thinks will ensure continued support for the invasion."

"Then for all we know, Portugal might be winning."

"It might."

He didn't believe it. I didn't, either, but it made me feel better to consider the possibility.

Ducos stepped into the room a few minutes later, hair pin-curled, the collar of her dark gray coat turned up.

"Good evening, Flora." She appraised Arcturus. "And you must be the auxiliary."

Arcturus inclined his head. "Good evening."

Though her face resisted scrutiny, I could see her trying to make sense of him without letting on that she was doing it.

"I am pleased to see that neither of you has risked another late-night jaunt to the river." She folded her arms. "I came to confirm that you are ready for your assignment, Flora. Command awaits your report. You would ideally make your first attempt at a possession tomorrow."

So soon. "I can do it," I said, "but I suspect I'll be caught quickly."

"You don't need long. Find out what is between Ménard and Weaver, then get out."

"Fine, but I'd like to see your medical officer first. I haven't been able to shake off this cough."

"Cordier is due to join us tomorrow, but she may not have time to examine you before the possession." Ducos paused. "Do you feel well enough to proceed?"

I thought about telling the truth, which was that I barely felt well enough to get up in the morning. "Does Cordier know anything about how my gift works?" was what I said. "Does she know how to monitor me?"

"She knows as much as I do, but an experienced assistant would be useful," Ducos said. "I rather hoped your auxiliary might feel able to step in."

"I am able," Arcturus said.

"Good. I feel warmly toward people who make themselves useful. Especially when Domino is providing those people with free accommodation." Ducos handed me a key with an address tag and a code attached. "Our intelligence indicates that Frère begins her day around seven. I will meet you at this address at six. Any problems, call the number on the back of the tag."

With that, she turned on her heel and was gone in a waft of rose-scented perfume.

"Did she just call you a freeloader?" I said to Arcturus, one eyebrow raised.

"I believe that was the insinuation."

"Must have been covering her nerves." My drink had gone cold. "She had no idea what to make of you. Interesting, since Burnish must have told her supervisors the truth behind Scion."

"Burnish may not have been able to safely communicate the specifics. Even if she did, I do not imagine her supervisors have shared the information with agents in the field, like Ducos."

"Right. Need-to-know basis." I set the mug aside. "I'd better get an early night."

"You have not eaten."

"It's fine. I'm not hungry."

"You have had little appetite for several days." He watched me rise. "Your condition is not improving. Ducos will postpone the assignment if you ask her."

"There's no time to postpone," I said, thinking of all I wanted to accomplish inside. When he narrowed his eyes, I wiped my expression clean. "We're on the brink of war, remember?"

"Yes." After a moment, he returned his attention to the evening news. "Sleep well, Paige."

"I'll try."

In the bathroom, I locked the door, then hacked something thick and yellowish into the sink. With a shudder, I rinsed the stuff away. It was just a cough. It would go in the end.

By the time I got to bed, Arcturus had tucked a heat pad under the duvet. For once, it did nothing to drive out my chill. I lay sleepless, nerves in knots, exhausted past the point of no return.

Tomorrow I would enter another Scion building. The news was not conducive to a restful night. Every time I thought I might drift off, memories of my torture crested.

By half past eleven, I was desperate. I needed sleep. If I was tired in the morning, I would never be able to dreamwalk. After half an hour, still wide awake, I hauled myself back out of bed.

Jaxon had always slept like a stiff after his nightcap. I could take one leaf out of his book. I took a glass from the cabinet and opened a decanter of what looked like red wine.

I took tiny sips at first. Just enough to sedate me. But the wine was rich and sweet, and suddenly I had drained the whole glass, and I was warm all the way through. As I poured out more, I remembered long nights with the gang. Their laughter and companionship. The family I had found in London.

I was a ghost untethered from its haunt. Having Arcturus with me had stifled the homesickness, but now I was alone, it burst its banks. I missed Maria. I missed Eliza. Most of all, I missed

Nick, my best friend, my rock, who had also been snatched away to work for Domino. A splintered part of me, buried deep and leaking shame, even missed Jaxon Hall.

And then I missed Ireland. It had been twelve years. Twelve years since I had last seen my grandparents. I drank until I could see the bottom, then flooded the glass with red-black comfort again.

"Paige."

I raised my spinning head. Arcturus was in the doorway, hair tousled from the pillow.

"Hello, you." My words slid out a little too fast. "Can't sleep?"

"No."

"Me neither." I held up the glass. "Thought this might help."

"It might also dull your gift." Arcturus picked up the decanter. Only a small amount of wine was left. "This is a fortified wine."

"Good. I need fortification." With a heavy-eyed smile, I patted the couch. "Keep me company?"

"If you refrain from finishing that glass."

I placed it dutifully on the coffee table. Arcturus sat beside me.

"I might ask why you would risk drinking so much," he said.

"Why do you?" I asked slackly.

"To quell pain. Perhaps you are trying to do the same."

"Think you're onto something there." I slumped deeper into the couch. "I was thinking about the fact that I don't have a home any more. Wondering if I'll ever have one again."

Arcturus looked toward the window. "I wonder the same."

His home was in decay, and mine lay in the shadow of the anchor. Scion had made wanderers of us.

"Humans cannot remember their own births. An oneiromancer forgets nothing," he said. "I emerged into a forest, under eternal dusk. Amaranth made wreaths around the trees."

The light from the streetlamp washed him in blue. He was all clouded edges and strange beauty. Carved in a human shape—yet this close, I could see the fine details that set him apart.

"Except for the birds, there was a silence I have never found on this side of the veil," he said. "A stream flowed through the forest. After passing through the domain of the Mesarthim, it reunited with the Grieving and poured into the Fall."

"Fall?"

"The door to the æther from our realm. When spirits were ready to accept their deaths—to go to the last light—we would lead them to this chasm, and they would cast themselves over."

"Sometimes I wonder what comes after it," I said, sobering up a little. His intention, perhaps. "If there's a final resting place."

"The Mothallath claimed to know. They told us they were sent from it by higher beings—the Anakim, the creators of the æther—and compelled us to worship them. Some Rephaim resented being told they were inferior. Nashira was the most outspoken of these dissidents."

"You believed it."

"I kept the faith of my sovereigns."

"And now?"

"I have seen too much for blind devotion. If higher beings do exist, I wonder that they did not intervene to stop the war. To avert the foundation of Scion. To prevent all of this."

When he spoke about the war, he sounded as ageless as he was. It was too easy to forget.

"I saw your home in your memory," I said. "It was beautiful."

The barest nod answered me.

"It is a cruel thing," he said, "to find oneself rootless."

Fields walled by sweet yellow furze that lured the bees in spring. Hills where castles were enthroned beneath a wide-flung sky. A windfall of golden apples in our orchard. Frost on the kissing gate. The mountains—white in winter, green elsewhen. Green as far as the horizon. I sometimes thought I must have misremembered Ireland—that it could never have sung with such beauty—but still I yearned for it.

"I would like to have seen your home," Arcturus said.

"I would have liked that, too."

It still existed in my memory. I could show him. He could reach into the annals of time and resurrect the place I remembered. I wished I had the courage to let him take me back.

"If the Netherworld is never restored," I said, "could you ever think of this world as home?"

It took Arcturus a very long time to answer.

"Yes," he said. "For a time, at least."

Silence thickened between us. The parlor swayed like a pendulum.

"Why are we connected?" I could barely hear myself. "The æther pulled us together for a reason. Why us, and why now?"

"Would that I knew."

The ache started low in my stomach. It fought against the restraints I had put on it. Before I knew it, I had reached out and gently turned his face toward me, and his gaze was on mine.

"Do you mind it?" I asked softly. "Being linked to me?"

The silence rang with something I recognized.

"No." His voice was a shadow. "It roots me again. You remind me what it is to have a home."

A laugh escaped me. "Dreamwalkers are rootless. Scion wants me dead because I have no anchor." I traced his stone-cut features. "If you make me your home, you'll wander forever."

"I am not known for my wise choices, Paige Mahoney."

His sarx was warm under my fingertips. I could feel the strong bone of his jaw, its solidity, so at odds with his nature as a being of the in-between. He felt human. Present. Real.

For once, I didn't want to be reserved with him. I wanted to solve the puzzle of his features. I wanted to glide into his dreamscape again and slow dance with his most intimate self. I wanted to embrace his dream-form, and to know it—know him—like no one else ever could. His gaze was a world I had yet to discover, an open door to the infinite.

And I understood what else I wanted. I wanted him to take me in his arms. I wanted to kiss him, as I had before.

I wanted him to want me.

The realization warmed my blood. My touch drifted from his face to his nape, and I drew him close.

"Paige."

A firm hand stilled mine. His touch woke me up enough to focus on his ever-burning eyes. "No one can see us now," I whispered. My other hand rested on his chest. "I want you."

"You have had too much to drink. This is not you."

"It is me." I nuzzled his neck. "Just without a mask."

"No. This *is* the mask. To hide your fear," he said, softer. He was so warm. "Trust has no room for façades. I would look on your true face, little dreamer. And know that you had looked on mine."

I had to make him understand that this was real, that words spoken behind a mask were no less genuine. I had to tell him about my fourth card, the Lovers, the warning, *stay close*. But I was so drowsy, so heavy, and the words were too slippery to figure into sentences.

"Paige." Arcturus cupped my lolling head. "Can you stand?"

The room was a carousel. When I sank against him, he gathered me into his arms and rose.

"You have a lovely jaw," I murmured into his shirt. "Did anyone ever tell you that?"

"Goodnight, Paige."

He carried me to my own room, set me down on my side, and tucked my good hand under my cheek. I felt him cover me with the duvet before the pillows swallowed me whole.

****

I woke in a series of painful stirrings. My skull was an overfull glass, too heavy and precarious to lift.

Shards of memory. My fingers on his jaw. His voice and mine, the words muddled. No clarity. All I remembered in excruciating detail was how much I had wanted him to hold me. He must have felt that want through the cord. Thick and sweet as summer honey.

I should never have touched that wine. I had risked the assignment. Nothing mattered more than what I was supposed to do today.

It was almost half past four. Bleary-eyed, I switched on the lamp and dressed in the clothes I had laid out early the previous evening, trying not to move my head too much. Every time I breathed in, a blade cut into the back of my shoulder. My skin had a grayish tinge, like newspaper.

Once my hair was straightened and I had darkened my eyes with the dropper, I found the dissimulator and stole into the parlor. Arcturus was nowhere to be seen, but the decanter was just where

I had left it. I emptied its contents into the sink and forced myself to drink a full glass of water.

By the time Arcturus emerged, the water had restored me a little too well. I could remember loose threads of our conversation. The position I had woken up in, with my head supported in a way that would have stopped me choking if I threw up in my sleep. I really was a class act.

"I did not expect you to be awake," he said.

"I'm just as surprised." I brushed my hair back. "I'm sorry about last night. Like I said, I'm not good with wine." Before he could get a word in, I went on: "I was just thinking, there's no need for you to come with me today. You should look for more of the graffiti we found, establish who in the citadel supports me. We should try to secure allies within the syndicate."

After a long silence, he spoke. "Your body should be monitored by someone with experience of your gift. This assignment will strain your limits."

"I'm sure the medic will manage."

He seemed to digest this statement. I could see him contemplating whether or not to press the issue, questioning the fact that I was pushing him away when I most needed him.

Had I been brave, I would have told him the truth. That I needed space to nurse my pride.

"When you find the graffiti, mark the locations on our map," I said. "We'll see if there's a pattern."

Without looking at him, I did up my bootlaces and tied back the smooth hair that felt nothing like mine. "I will do as you ask," Arcturus said, "but when you return, we should speak."

"There's nothing to talk about," I said curtly, pulling on my jacket. "I was drunk."

Silence reverberated across the room. Arcturus watched me collect the key from the table.

"Paige."

Slowly, I faced him.

"I know you are still uncertain of your gift, but you are a dream-walker. This is what you were born to do. I am proud of how far you have come," he said. "Call if you need me. I will be at your side."

Heat stoppered my throat. To my embarrassment, my eyes filled, and I had to look away.

"Thank you." I fastened my jacket. "Watch yourself out there. We know the Rag and Bone Man is hunting, and he's captured you before."

"I have no intention of being a prisoner again. Neither would I see you suffer that fate," he said. "Please, Paige, do not take any unnecessary risks."

"I'll do my best."

Our gazes locked. Before I could do something really stupid, I all but fled the room, grabbing my bag as I went.

In my haste, I almost forgot to disguise myself. Just before I left, I stopped by the mirror in the hallway, took out the dissimulator, and stretched it over my face. It warmed to the consistency of oil and gradually constricted. I squeezed my eyes shut, resisting the urge to pull it off, as it remolded my features. When the pressure eased, my nose was pinched, my mouth wider, my cheeks peppered with freckles. I was Flora Elizabeth Blake, a student from the University of Scion London, here to research her dissertation. Only if I looked closely could I see the tiny crinkles in my skin.

It was remarkable. Impossible. Like short-term surgery. Shame I wasn't in the frame of mind to marvel.

Outside, it was pouring with rain. The dissimulator made my face feel badly sunburnt. I trudged through the dark, freezing and dismal, until I saw an illuminated entrance to the Métro. I bought a return ticket and waited on the platform, trying to iron out my breathing. At this rate, I would be lucky if I made it to Rue de Surène without throwing up.

When the train arrived, it was almost deserted. I took a seat at the back and burrowed deep into my jacket. Now I had a twenty-minute journey and only my thoughts to occupy it.

Eliza could spend a night with a stranger. She could share herself and walk away, all in the time it took the sun to set and rise again.

Nick could fall for kind eyes or a smile, not knowing what lay behind them. For him, love was a dive into deep waters. He trusted himself not to hit any rocks.

I had to see the depths before I jumped. I only seemed to want someone—to truly want them—when I cared for them too much to run. I wanted in ways that would always have consequences.

The first time I kissed Arcturus Mesarthim, I had known that there would be a price.

I hadn't truly wanted him that night. Not beyond that minute in his arms and the comfort it had offered me. Faced with death, I had felt alone. He had been there and willing. That was all. Then he had come back into my life, and little by little, I had started to notice.

That I looked forward to seeing him. That he made me smile without ever smiling himself. That he challenged me. That I always wanted to hear his voice. And that even though he was a mystery, and there were shadows in him I might never disperse, I somehow knew him.

The train arrived at the right stop. I tottered back outside, into the blistering cold, feeling as if my head was stuffed with steel wool. At least the pressure on my face had eased.

A bakery glowed across the street, tempting in the predawn gloom. In my haste to leave, I had forgotten to eat breakfast. I stepped into the toasty warmth and ordered a large coffee and a chausson aux pommes. With this face, I was no longer a wanted criminal. I could do anything.

Rue de Surène was a short walk from the station. No cameras watched over it. I threw my half-finished pastry away before I found the right door and tapped the code into a pad beside it. The hallway beyond had a checkered floor. I trudged up to the third floor.

It was a postcard apartment, made up of a bathroom and a parlor with a tiny kitchenette. Beside the compact bed was the ventilator Ducos had promised. I tugged off my boots and flopped onto the couch, where I peeled off the dissimulator and pinched some feeling back into my face.

The apartment was cold and quiet. I finished my coffee. My thoughts returned to Arcturus, like birds to their branches.

I had been the one to end it. I had cut him away before I could fall for him, not realizing I had already fallen. Not realizing it was already too late.

It was also too late to try again. Even if there were no suspicious Ranthen eyes here—even if he still wanted me back, which he might not—we were better off as allies. Anything else was too complicated.

So I had told myself, to no avail. Still I wanted to know him in every way possible, down to the last secret and sinew. Our unexpected bond had paved the way for an attraction I could no longer deny. No matter how long it took, I had to crush it.

Despite the strong coffee, I dozed off, huddled into the corner of the couch, feeling as if I might shrivel into nonexistence. I woke to a familiar voice and an unfamiliar name.

"Flora." A firm shake. "Paige. Did you sleep here?"

Ducos was leaning over me, hair pulled into a severe bun. She wore no makeup today. "No." I licked my bone-dry lips. "Just got here early."

"What about your auxiliary?"

"He's not well."

I expected some kind of reprimand, but all Ducos did was flick the heating on. "I suppose he was always doomed to catch your illness, with the two of you cooped up in there. Fortunately for you," she said, "our medical officer will be here soon. She got back just in time."

She helped me sit up. My temples pounded.

"You've been drinking," she observed.

"Of course not."

"I have been in Scion for a long time, but I know a hangover when I see one." She raised a dour smile. "Something has to fill the hollow this life carves in us. For some agents, that something is drink. For some, it is sex. For me, it is smoking. An extension of a transgression I have already committed."

"What transgression?"

"Hurling myself into destruction." She held my shoulder. "You have been through a great deal, Flora. This once, I will turn a blind eye to your conduct, on the condition that this never happens again. Do I make myself clear?"

My nod was tiny. She pressed another coffee into my hands.

"Drink."

I took an obedient sip.

"While you wake up," Ducos said, "you can listen." She sat on the end of the bed. "Unfortunately, the ventilator was damaged in transit and now requires manual replenishment every three hours. You'll need to return to your body while that happens. Not ideal for creating a convincing façade."

"I'll make it work," I said.

"If anyone notices your infiltration, or if you believe your physical location has been compromised, return here at once and leave the building. Steph—our courier—is keeping watch nearby. They will guide you to safety."

"What if Scion reaches me before they do?"

"In the unlikely event that you are detained, we will not be able to assist you. Our last attempt to rescue an agent almost exposed us." She looked me in the eye. "Do you have your kill pill?"

I nodded. The capsule of fast-acting poison was tucked into my jacket.

Ducos reached into her briefcase and unrolled a floor plan I recognized. "I wanted to draw your attention to one room in particular. The Salon Doré." She pointed to the main building. "This is where Ménard is likely to store important and sensitive documents. His private study."

I kept my face blank. Even if it contained nothing of use to Domino, I needed to get inside that room. It might well hide the second piece of information I wanted.

The location of Sheol II.

"We know for a fact that Ménard has a safe in the Salon Doré," Ducos said, "and that the safe contains a number of letters that he considers too sensitive for the Scionet. Now, he will certainly be in meetings in that room all day, and for most of the evening—but watch for any opportunity to enter it. I presume a seasoned criminal like yourself can crack a safe."

"Depends on the safe," I said. "What if I find other information that could be useful to you?"

"Your assignment is to collect information pertaining to the relationship between Weaver and Ménard. Do not risk your cover for anything else."

After a moment, I nodded. "Excuse me."

Eating had been a bad idea. I locked myself into the bathroom and sighed at the unholy mess in the mirror. Bloodshot eyes, clammy face. Quietly, I heaved over the sink. All I brought up was another clot of yellow.

"Great," I said under my breath.

Something was wrong in my body. I could feel it. I was afraid to find out what it was. If Ducos thought I was too ill, she might take me off this assignment, and I needed to do it.

I set my jaw and washed the sink out. Though it made me flinch, I dabbed my face with icy water. That and the caffeine took the edge off the hangover. I was ready. At least, that was what I told myself.

There were voices on the other side of the door. When I emerged, I saw the newcomer, a woman who was probably in her early thirties. She wore a pencil dress with short flared sleeves, which flattered her hourglass figure. White skin struck a high contrast with the deep plum velvet of the dress and the raven hair that gleamed to her chin.

"—should she be doing this, if that's the case?" she was saying. "Surely there's no need to rush this job."

"There is every need, as yesterday should have taught you. Given the situation—" Ducos stopped talking at once when she noticed me. "Flora, this is our medical officer, Eléonore Cordier."

The woman regarded me with sparkling corvine eyes. Her lips were painted the same plum as her dress.

"Flora," she said with a smile. "Welcome to Mannequin." Her handshake was delicate, and her accent, as far as I could tell, was French. "I hear you've given Scion more trouble than the rest of this organization put together. And that you've had a persistent cough. I'd do a checkup now, but we're out of time. Madelle Guillotine is about to wake up."

"We would not be out of time if you had been *on* time," Ducos muttered.

"Would you sooner I had not been careful?" When Ducos pursed her lips, Cordier sighed and turned back to me. "Flora, are you absolutely sure you feel up to this?" she asked, serious. "From the little I know about what you can do, this will put a lot of strain on your body."

"I'll cope," I said. "I want to do my part."

Ducos gave a satisfied nod.

"All right." Cordier steered me toward the bed. "Make yourself comfortable, then, and we'll get you hooked up."

I lay on my back. Cordier tucked a couple of pillows under my head while Ducos switched on the ventilator. Now I wished Arcturus had come with me. It was unnerving to leave my body vulnerable with two people I barely knew.

"We're almost ready to go." Cordier reached into her bag. "Just need to give you the sedative."

"What?" I sat back up. "Why?"

"For the ventilator." Cordier showed me a narrow tube. "I need to sedate you to insert this."

Danica had custom-made my old ventilator for a dreamwalker. All it had required was a face mask. "If you sedate me, I won't be able to dreamwalk." When Cordier looked blank, I said, "Project my spirit."

She exchanged a troubled glance with Ducos. They were amaurotics, with little idea how my gift worked. "Sorry, Flora. This is all new to us," Cordier admitted. "Any ideas?"

"I can go into my dreamscape. I'll be less aware of my body."

Cordier brightened. "I have no idea what *dreamscape* means, but that sounds like a fabulous solution." She took a spray can from her bag. "Let me give you this, at least, to numb your throat. It won't make you drowsy."

"Fine." I tried to relax. "When we're ready to go, pinch me hard. I'll feel it."

"I'll do that." She gave the can a shake. "Open wide for me."

I did, and she blasted something foul-tasting into the back of my mouth. It trickled down my throat.

"Watch the clock," Ducos told me. "Remember, you have three hours. Bon courage."

With a nod, I withdrew into my dreamscape. Red flowers opened their petals around me. I was distantly conscious of a strangeness, a discomfort, before the pinch came. I jumped into the æther.

The Hôtel Garuche was close, and I had met Luce Ménard Frère before. Her dreamscape was a beacon. When I took hold of her, it was quick, but gentle. Like catching a mouse by the end of its tail.

****

The first thing I felt was silk against my cheek. My eyelids fluttered as my borrowed senses woke. In the deep blue light of morning, I could see that I was lying on my side in a canopy bed.

Slowly, I lifted one hand to find soft, delicate fingers and manicured nails. I knew I was in the right host when I saw the spousal ring—a ruby flanked by diamonds, mounted on a band of pure gold.

Frère had offered no resistance. She had never been taught to see or react to intruders in her mind. Unlike Hildred Vance, the last Scion official I had walked in, her dreamscape had not been surgically clean, though it was colorless, like every amaurotic mind. It resembled the affluent Place des Vosges, where she and Ménard had first lived together.

A floral scent crept up on me as I settled into my host. I savored it. It had been so long since I had been able to take a deep breath without a stab of chest pain. Still lethargic, I looked around the room, at the lavish crimson furnishings, the dark and polished floor, the vase of fresh white roses. Embroidered gold anchors bordered the sheets.

I checked for a nosebleed and found nothing. Time to go. Filled with resolve, I propped Frère up on her elbows—and remembered she was nineteen weeks pregnant. Her abdomen bulged.

I didn't think I'd ever even met anyone pregnant. No one purposely had children in the syndicate. Kids cost hard-earned money. Still, I had prepared for this. I could handle a little passenger.

When I was confident that I could stand, I did. Even though I was still connected to my own body through the silver cord, and Arcturus through the golden one, I was virtually cut off from the æther in this amaurotic host. Her flesh numbed me to half the world.

A chandelier glistened above me. This must be the east wing, which housed the private apartments of the Inquisitorial family. Frère and her personal stylist discussed outfits in the evenings, and the stylist would set one or two aside for the next day. I opened the right armoire and found a floor-length dress with a high collar and a low neckline, made of blood-red chiffon.

A golden clock ticked on the mantelpiece. Almost quarter to seven. Above it was a mirror with a giltwood frame. I approached it and scrutinized my host, trying to perfect her expression and keep her dark eyes attentive. Her nose sloped up a little at the end, and her hair fell in waves. Like Ducos, she had the kind of perfect skin, almost poreless in its clarity, that could only be achieved through high-priced cosmetic polishing.

A flicker low down in my stomach. When I gave the bump a tentative nudge, it nudged back.

"Shh." I gave it the lightest pat. "I'll give Maman back soon, I promise. Don't tell anyone."

Another kick.

There was a little time left to compose myself. I walked to the nearest window and looked down at the private terrace. I fluttered my fingers, rolled my shoulders, cracked my neck. Arcturus had been right. After possessing a Rephaite, this was effortless.

At the stroke of seven, a smart *rat-a-tat* came at the door. I wet my lips before I spoke.

"Entrez."

The door opened to admit a pale woman in delicate wire-rimmed spectacles. Her oxblood hair was sliced into a bob. This was Alexandra Kotzia, the personal secretary. Her father was a close friend of the Inquisitorial family—I suspected collaboration with Scion before the invasion of Greece—and at twenty-four, she had moved from the Scion Citadel of Patras to join their household staff. She had since married Charlotte-Marie Deschamps, a popular journalist.

If I could remember all that in a heartbeat, I could remember everything else I needed in this place.

"Luce." Kotzia held a white data pad, to match her bleach-white teeth. "Good morning."

"Aleka," I said, using her nickname.

"I'm sorry to leap on you right away, but Auclair called on urgent business last night." She spoke in rapid French. "I scheduled a meeting at half past seven, before your breakfast with the Société Française pour la Préservation Culturelle at eight. I did try to reschedule it, since you have more pressing engagements, but they really are insistent. It's about the state of the public gardens."

Well, at least *somebody* was thinking about the state of the public gardens.

"After that, you have lunch with Madelle Vérany, a meeting with the Minister for Industry at three, a phone call with the Chief of Vigilance at half past five, your obstetrician will visit at six, and then you have some time to spend with the children." Kotzia glanced up. "And the Grand Inquisitor has asked if you would like to join him for supper at nine."

"Yes," I said. "Of course." I tried to tug up the pitch of my voice. "Where is the meeting with—"

The Minister of Internal Security. Surname: Auclair. Arcturus in the parlor, testing me. *First name?*

"— Gabrielle?"

"Your office, as always."

"Of course." I kneaded my forehead. She seemed oblivious, but there was no harm in guarding against future suspicion. "I have a migraine. Would you fetch me something for it, Aleka?"

"Luce," she said, all concern. "Please, go back to bed and rest. Let me speak to Minister Auclair and postpone the meeting."

"Is she already here?"

Kotzia looked apologetic. "Yes."

This was a spanner in the works. Canceling would be the easiest option, but it would be out of character. I doubted anything kept Frère from her work.

"No need to postpone." After a pause, I said, "But I wonder if you could move our meeting to the Bureau Cramoisi so I can stay close to the apartments."

"Yes, of course."

I gave her a tiny nod, as if even the smallest movement hurt. As she clicked out on white kitten heels, I remembered the floor plan. The Bureau Cramoisi was very close to the Salon Doré. Two rooms away.

Frère needed a shower before she met anyone important. Mingled with sweat, I could have sworn I smelled two distinct fragrances on her skin. Ménard must have spent the night with her and risen early. In interviews, he claimed to work long past midnight and start again at five.

The bathroom was all dark marble and gold leaf. I stapled my gaze to the ceiling while I undressed, and while I showered behind a glass screen. Jets bathed my host in cool water and covered her in scented foam. Frère might never have been waterboarded, but my fear snowed her with gooseflesh.

Her loyal assistant had once been a free-worlder. I had learned all I knew of the Balkan Incursion from Maria, who had been a resistance fighter in Bulgaria. She had never gone into detail about what had happened in Greece, the first country to ever face invasion by Scion, but clearly some its denizens had escaped the taint of rebellion. Kotzia had only been three or four during the occupation—she must have little memory, if any, of a world before the anchor.

New jets rinsed my host clean and blew her dry. I stepped out of the shower. It was lucky I was accustomed to pain: Frère was riddled with it. Her thighs cramped. Her back was sore. She was breathless, almost as much as I was in my own body. Pregnancy was clearly no picnic. I enveloped her in a towel, brushed her perfect teeth—her gums hurt and bled—and took her back to the bedroom, where I found the silver watch she always wore. Next, I put on the red dress, feeling like the Queen of France. For a Scion official, Frère dressed remarkably like a monarch.

An elderly attendant soon arrived with sweet Greek coffee and some tablets. I took all of them. While I fed my host sips of the coffee, I combed her thick hair until it shone.

Two key opportunities had already presented themselves. First, a chance to size up the Salon Doré. Second, the dinner with Ménard, which I needed to prioritize.

The logistics would be very delicate. I would have to put Frère back to bed under the pretext of her migraine. Since she had been asleep when I possessed her, she would have the impression of waking up for the first time—except she would have lost about an hour. I would have to hope that nobody asked her about her discussion with Auclair, since she would have no memory of it.

I almost left the room before I remembered how much Frère liked to adorn herself. I added pearl earrings and a dab of lipstick. Finally, I spritzed her with the first perfume I saw.

Dealing with Kotzia had been relatively easy. Meeting one-on-one with a minister was my next test.

The east wing was connected to the main building by an antechamber. As I crossed it, a portrait of Irène Tourneur, the celebrated First Inquisitor of France, seemed to judge me from on high.

I was now a mere two walls away from the study that might hold everything I needed.

On a marble-topped desk, a lamp gave off a tawny glow. Gabrielle Auclair, Minister of Internal Security, was waiting in a wing chair, her dark curls scraped into a ponytail. Seeing me, she tucked her phone into her suit jacket and stood. Freckles sprinkled her brown face.

"Luce."

"Gabrielle." I kissed her on both cheeks. "Have you been offered something to drink?"

I hoped Frère was usually this gracious. She had spoken cordially enough with Scarlett Burnish.

"Yes," Auclair said. "Coffee is on the way." She smiled at my stomach. "How are you both?"

"The little one is very well." I touched my temple. "I wish I could say the same, but I've woken with quite the migraine."

"Oh, Luce—you mustn't worry. I had one or two with Nora." Auclair squeezed my elbow. "Why don't I come back later?"

"I have a full schedule today." I went to the chair on the other side of the desk. "And I understand this is urgent."

Auclair returned to her seat. Sweat pricked my scalp as I clasped my dainty new hands in front of me.

"Luce," Auclair said, "you told me to keep careful watch for the fugitive, Paige Mahoney."

So Auclair knew my execution had been staged. It made sense. If anyone needed to know the secret of my survival, it was the Minister of Internal Security.

"Mahoney." I dredged my own name with scorn. "And?"

"I ordered my teams to take note of anyone who seems to be avoiding the cameras. There are no small number, but none matched Mahoney." Auclair pushed her data pad across the desk. "Until this was captured near the Pont des Arts. Ten days ago."

Shit.

The data pad showed an image of me on the morning I had ventured out with Arcturus. It had been taken at a distance, and my face, obscured by my hair and lenses, was tilted away from the camera.

"Ten days," I finally said. "Why was this not brought to my attention earlier?"

"There was no recognition alert. Accuracy decreases when the face isn't captured head-on, and as you can see, this individual has covered their facial landmarks," Auclair explained. "An operative spotted it last night by chance, while reviewing footage in relation to a reported assault. I arranged to see you at once."

The attendant entered with the coffee, and Auclair stopped. I kept hold of my composure by a thread until he left.

"All estimable biometrics tally with the data we have on Mahoney," Auclair said. "I consider this a strong potential match." She breathed out. "You saw her in the Archon. Is it her, Luce?"

I pretended to take my time studying the photograph.

"Impossible to tell," I said at last. "But nobody is safe if she has brought her violence here." I handed back the data pad. "Find this person, whoever they are. I will have two additional squadrons of night Vigiles posted to the area. Our resources are at your disposal."

"Glory to the anchor." Auclair hesitated. "Will you alert the Archon?"

I waited a moment, considering my response.

"I suppose I must," I said.

I had struck the right chord. Auclair shook her head in disgust. "Unbelievable that they let a terrorist slip between their fingers. They've created the greatest security risk in decades, and now they expect us to clean it up for them. As if we don't have enough to do." With a sigh, she slid the data pad into her handbag. "I'll call you with any developments."

She kissed my cheeks before she marched out, leaving her coffee untouched. The moment the door shut behind her, I combed through the desk drawers and an antique cabinet. There was nothing inside them but stacks of letterhead paper and some history books.

I turned to face the two sets of doors to my left, which led to the next office. Beyond *that* office lay the Salon Doré. In this amaurotic body, I couldn't sense whether or not Ménard was there.

He would be. Most of his day must be comprised of meetings. I could still get a brief look at the entrance. With all the confidence I could muster, I opened the nearest door and stepped through.

The Salon Blanc was spotlessly white, from its carpet to its ornate ceiling to the lilies perfuming the air. Against my will, I remembered the white room where I had been beaten, and my heart thumped harder.

Six people in suits sat around a table, clearly gathered for a meeting, their heads bent over a collage of paperwork. My appearance made them all look up.

"Luce. Good morning." The nearest removed his gold-rimmed spectacles. "Can we help you?"

Name: Jakob Coquelin. Position: Second Minister of the Exchequer. I could almost hear Arcturus again. *Known to Frère as—*

"Jaquot," I said, with an apologetic smile, "is the Grand Inquisitor in his study?"

As I spoke, I looked past him, to a pair of gilded white doors. One armed Vigile stood beside a fingerprint scanner.

"Indeed," came the reply. "I believe he is on the phone to Chief Tjäder. Shall I give him a message?"

"No, it's all right. I'll try again later."

I retreated back into the Bureau Cramoisi and shut the doors behind me.

That confirmed it. Getting in to the Salon Doré would be almost impossible. As Ducos had anticipated, Ménard would be ensconced in there all day, dissecting reports, meeting his advisors and ministers, making calls. His soldiers were helping to drive the invasion of the Iberian Peninsula, and he would be in constant contact with his commanders there.

No, my energy was best spent on the meal in the evening. All I had to do now was tuck Frère back into bed.

"Luce?" Kotzia popped her head in. "The representatives from the Société Française pour la Préservation Culturelle are ready for you downstairs."

"My migraine is worse," I said. "A little more sleep will help, I think. Can you entertain the representatives for a while?"

"Of course." She came straight to my side. "We'll serve coffee. I'll return to wake you in half an hour. Is that all right?"

"Yes. Thank you, Aleka."

Kotzia took me back to the bedroom and drew the curtains. Once she was gone, I removed the earrings, wiped off the lipstick, changed into a nightgown like the one I had woken up in—the original had been whisked away—and roughed up my hair. I returned the red dress to where I had found it.

Once I left her, Frère would stir at once, with a genuine headache and no memory of what had just happened. Kotzia would take her down to the coffee morning, which she already knew about. Hopefully Kotzia would be in too much of a hurry to mention anything that had just occurred.

One last touch. I opened the back of the golden clock and set the time to half past six. When Kotzia returned to wake her, Frère would think it was seven, exactly when her day should begin. An attendant would correct the clock during the day. It would be as if I had never been here.

When my host was tucked back into bed, I released her spirit and returned to the æther. From here, everything rested on Frère.

8

Into the Fire

A room with pale blue walls. A hairline crack in the ceiling above me. Something was clamped onto my left forefinger, hard enough that I felt my pulse there. Eléonore Cordier patted my cheek.

"Flora?" she said. I managed to nod. "Welcome back. Can you tell me where you are?"

"Rue de Surène." My tongue felt like rubber. "Scion Citadel of Paris."

"And the month?"

"February."

"Perfect." Cordier shone a small flashlight into my eyes, then snapped her fingers in front of them. I blinked. "Your reflexes are working. So far, so good. Did anyone suspect?"

"Not that I could tell."

"Great." She took the clamp off my finger. "Ducos might actually crack a smile when she hears."

"Where is Ducos?"

"I put her on lunch duty. Espionage is hungry work." When I tried to sit up, Cordier stopped me with a slight laugh. "Cool your heels, Lazarus. You just rose from the dead."

"I've done it before." My thoughts ran thick. "Who the hell is Lazarus?"

"Long story." She powered down the ventilator. "You know, Flora, I've heard all kinds of interesting rumors about what clairvoyants can do, but seeing is believing. You could be anyone. Go anywhere. If I were you, I'd be all over the world, inhabiting the rich and famous."

"It's not as easy as it sounds. And I take no joy in treating people like puppets. Even people like Frère."

"Of course." She glanced at my face and smiled. "Just kidding."

"Oh. Sorry." I rubbed the bridge of my nose. "The half pint of coffee clearly wasn't enough."

"I'm surprised you're awake at all, after what you just went through. My nerves were down to nothing." Cordier unclipped a small case and took out some equipment. "Scion must be terribly afraid of this ability of yours. Are there many anormales who can do the same?"

That word felt different when an amaurotic said it. Then again, I supposed she might not know the right one. "I'm the only dreamwalker," I said, too tired to explain. "As far as I know."

"That must get lonely."

"I've never known anything different. No one knows exactly what it is to be you, either, do they?"

"True." Cordier wrapped a cuff around my upper arm. "Just taking your blood pressure, if I may." She activated the monitor. "Flora, is your cough productive?"

It took me a moment to work out what she meant. "A little."

"All right." The cuff began to constrict. "And you've had this cough for how long?"

"Couple of weeks." It was only half a lie. "I'm fine to carry on."

"I'd still like to rule out anything serious," Cordier said, somehow gentle and firm at once. The cuff squeezed my arm tight. "I came straight here from my last assignment, so I don't have everything I need, but I'll give you a thorough checkup once you're finished with Frère."

A dull throb filled my arm. I stared at the wall and flexed my fingers in and out of a fist.

An intelligent creature would have ended the pain by now. It would have answered my questions. The bite of iron at my wrists, screwed tight. *A dull, filthy beast must be chained. But all it has to do is speak . . .*

"There we are." The cuff loosened with a sigh. I opened my eyes to see Cordier check the reading. "You should get some rest until Ducos gets back. Your blood pressure is a little low."

With blurred vision, I looked at the faint, matching marks on my wrists. "I need some air."

Cordier looked up in surprise. "What?"

I was already off the bed, my only thought to get outside. Then red-hot pain stabbed into my temple, and I caught the back of the couch, too dizzy to take another step. Cordier carted me straight back to bed before I could protest. She was stronger than she looked.

"I am ordering you to rest now, Flora." Then, softer: "I'll give you something for the pain."

A quick prick in my arm followed. It dulled the headache enough to let me slip into a fitful doze. Now and again, I stirred and glimpsed a silhouette by the window, but by the time I woke for good, Cordier was gone.

Rain freckled the apartment windows. I cautiously sat up. While the last of my headache dwindled, I wrote down everything I had heard in the mansion. Everything that might be of use.

Most of it pertained to the invasion. Frère was meeting with the Minister for Industry, who was in charge of ordnance, and lunching with Françoise Vérany, spouse to the Grand Commander of France. Ménard was—as expected—wholly focused on the invasion.

Ducos turned up at noon, looking as tired as I felt. She had brought a meal in a cardboard box.

"Where's Cordier?" she asked.

"No idea."

A muscle started in her cheek. "Eat." She set the box down in front of me. "Tell me about this morning."

"I couldn't get into the study. Too many people." I paused, then decided to use what Arcturus had told me. "I met with the Minister of Internal Security. She referred to a document from Weaver that

Ménard was reluctant to sign. He eventually did, and Frère took it with her to England for New Year, but I got the impression he was still opposed to it."

"Do you know what the document was?"

"Not yet, but Frère is eating with Ménard tonight. I thought that would be the best time to get to the root of it."

Ducos breathed out through her nose. "That sounds . . . a promising avenue of inquiry. Is anyone suspicious?"

"Not as far as I can tell," I said. "But they do suspect I'm in Paris."

"How?"

I told her about my image being captured. Her lips thinned until they were almost nonexistent.

"Now, perhaps, you understand the importance of the dissimulator," she said. "Fortunate that they didn't identify you categorically."

She motioned for me to eat. I opened the box to find a salad of diced tomato, cucumber, onion, and bell pepper, all covered with crumbled white cheese, accompanied by a slice of fresh bread. "Ducos," I said, once I had eaten some of it, "do you know anything about me?"

She sat in the nearest chair. "I know everything I need to know about you, Flora."

"Not Flora. Me."

Her stance changed.

"You were born in Ireland," she said eventually. "You exhibit a rare form of extrasensory perception. You were the commander of an insurgent militia in London. You sabotaged Senshield. And now you seem determined to sabotage my sanity by asking needless questions."

"I still am the commander of that insurgent militia."

"No. You are an intelligence officer. There is no time or place for divided loyalties behind enemy lines."

"What if they didn't need to be divided?"

She flung me an exasperated look. "What?"

"What if your organization could work alongside mine?" I kept my voice low and steady. "Domino wants to set fires across Scion. My people can do that. Would your superiors consider funding a militia?"

"I'm not at liberty to say." Ducos regarded me. "We have not known each other for very long, Flora. Carry out your assignment. Demonstrate that you can follow orders to the letter. Then, perhaps, we can discuss this in more detail." Her gaze was unyielding. "Eat. Rest."

Perhaps it was because I was exhausted; perhaps I was finally learning diplomacy. Either way, I decided to leave it.

My appetite had been waning for days. Once I had eaten as much of the salad as I could, I lay on the couch. Ducos took a thin file from her briefcase and settled down to study it.

While I waited for sleep to claim me, I reached for the golden cord. A muted vibration rewarded my effort. In all our training, we had never mastered the art of mental conversation.

I could feel him on the other side. He was fine. Holding that knowledge close, I slept.

****

At half past eight, I looked through brown eyes once more. I saw a white marble floor, a painted ceiling lit by chandeliers, and a girl with sable locks and a small, upturned nose. Her black silk frock had puffed sleeves and a lace collar. This was Mylène. Middle child in the Inquisitorial family.

My fingers moved. I blinked discs of light away. Frère was sitting with her back against a wall, barefoot and wearing flounced cherry silk. Matching shoes were tucked into the corner.

This vast chamber was the Salle des Fêtes, where Frère and Ménard hosted dances and dinners. Their children had turned this corner into a playroom. Jean-Michel, who was only four, leaned into my side. His hair was the brown of dark chocolate, falling in curls around his face. Alexandra Kotzia sat in a chair in the corner, bent over some paperwork.

Mylène was absorbed in her data pad. "Onésime, t'es trop doué. C'est pas juste," she said crossly. "Laisse moi gagner pour changer."

"Si je te laisse gagner, c'est pas gagner pour de vrai. Papa ne sera pas d'accord."

"Tu m'embêtes."

It took a moment for my hearing to adjust, and for their voices to sound less than a mile away. This time, I had seized control of Frère while she was wide awake.

"Maman." Jean-Michel rested his head against my stomach. "When will the baby come?"

He spoke in English. "Soon," I said, mirroring him.

Jean-Michel looked up at me, brow crumpled in thought. "If your head still hurts when she comes out, will she have a headache, too?"

I had to smile at that. "No, mon trésor. I don't think so."

Frère had been left with enough of a headache for me to keep up that charade, then. Good.

"Maman will be all right soon, Jean-Mi," said another voice. "Papa will make her feel better."

An older boy was leaning against another pillar, one eye on his data pad, dressed as if for a formal dinner. Onésime. He took more after their father than his siblings. I had known I would have to deceive the children, but it felt wrong to involve them more than necessary.

"Of course he will." I gave Jean-Michel a brief pat on the head. He yawned. "Speaking of Papa, I think it's time I got ready for supper. And time that Jean-Mi was asleep."

Kotzia was up faster than a jack-in-the-box. "Come, then, children," she said. "You can have milk and cookies before bed."

"Cookies!" Mylène sprang up, fist clenched in triumph. "Yes!"

"Calme toi, petite sotte," muttered Onésime, with a flick of his forefinger. "And . . . you lose."

Mylène stared back at her data pad and stuck her lip out. "Cheat."

As Kotzia picked up the drowsy Jean-Michel, I glimpsed the toy in his hand. A doll with its head twisted off.

"The Grand Inquisitor will see you in the Salon Vert," Kotzia told me in French as we proceeded upstairs. "He may be a little late. He is on a call with Chief Tjäder."

"Very well."

Birgitta Tjäder commanded Scion's invasion force. What was the Butcher of Strasbourg whispering to the Magpie?

Focus, Paige.

After Kotzia had handed the children to another member of staff, she returned to do my hair, securing it with a ruby-studded comb. She passed me an ivory shirt with an overlay of bobbin lace, then helped me into a crimson evening gown, unbuttoned to the waist to show off the lacework of the shirt, with sleeves that cut off at the elbow.

"Will you need anything else?" Kotzia said, once I was ready.

"No, thank you, Aleka. Give my regards to Charlotte-Marie."

She looked mildly surprised. "I will. Thank you." A proud smile. "She has a front-page piece tomorrow, about our moral obligation to the people of Portugal. It's very good."

"I look forward to it. Every word furthers the cause."

Her smile widened. When she was gone, I gave myself a final appraisal in the mirror. I looked the part.

All I had to do now was convince a tyrant.

The Salon Vert, true to its name, had mint-green walls and curtains. A table set for two was covered by cloth of a deeper green, and a fire roared in the hearth, its light reflected by gold adornments on the walls. So far, there was no sign of Ménard. I took a seat.

"Madelle." An attendant looked into the room. "Good evening. Something to drink?"

"Rose mecks, please, Émilien," I said. It was what Luce was usually seen drinking at engagements.

"Of course."

I waited, hands clammy, every muscle tense. The attendant brought my drink and a basket of bread. The clock ticked.

At ten past nine, Georges Benoît Ménard, Grand Inquisitor of the Republic of Scion France, emerged from his study. As usual, he wore a black suit and a red tie. Nothing too flashy.

His face creased into a smile when he saw me. How strange that someone feared for his cruelty could almost look kind.

"Luce."

I was about to say his name, but stopped in favor of a warm smile of my own. Ménard used his middle name officially, but I had no idea what Frère called him in private.

Ménard walked around the table. As he embraced me, I stole a glance toward the Salon Doré. He had left the door just slightly ajar. A moment later, I was looking at his face, and he touched his mouth to mine. To hers.

His lips were smooth and soft. His skin smelled of soap, his breath of lemon. He smelled clean.

"You are beautiful. As always." Ménard placed one hand on my stomach. A plain gold spousal ring shone on one finger. "Is all well with the little fish?"

He spoke French, like all his staff. I was starting to wonder if it was a small act of defiance against England.

"Kicking away," I said, locking my hand over his. "Impatient to meet us."

His brow darkened. "You never told me she had started kicking."

"I felt the first one this morning," I said smoothly. Hard as it was to hold his penetrating gaze, I kept going. "I came to tell you earlier, but Jaquot said you were on the phone."

Ménard smiled back at me. "I think this one will be Inquisitor. If Mylène doesn't get there first." He placed a kiss on my temple. "Onésime joined me for breakfast this morning. He still seems very worried."

A memory. The Archon. Frère had said that her elder son always thought a new baby would take her away from him.

"Of course he is." I let out a light, Frère-esque laugh. "Yet he was the first to love Mylène and Jean-Michel."

"I reminded him of that. But perhaps you should talk to him again, too."

"Of course."

He took off his dinner jacket and folded up the sleeves of his crisp shirt before he sat. His olive skin looked golden in the fire-light. There were shadows under his eyes that aged him by ten years.

"It will have to be a quick supper. I'm expecting another call. And you must be tired," he said. "Aleka said you had a migraine earlier. The pressure of this charade is affecting you."

Charade. The blood froze in my stolen veins.

"I wish I could deny it," I said carefully. "But when the anchor calls—"

"—we all must answer." Ménard reached across the table to hold my fingers. "Well said, as always. But this is not your burden, Luce. Perhaps you should see the consultant tomorrow."

I kept an iron grip on my composure. By *this*, he was referring to something I had yet to understand.

"Your burdens are mine. And there's no need," I said. "Migraines are common in pregnancy."

"You never complained of them with the other children."

"Well. Each time is bound to be different." I willed my hand to remain dry. "Gabrielle was telling me that she had them with Nora."

"Auclair." Ménard nodded. "How is she?"

"She brought disturbing news." I looked deep into his eyes. "She believes Paige Mahoney may be here, in Paris."

"Mahoney." His hand tightened, just a little, around mine. "How sure is she?"

"The suspect's face was obscured, but the biometrics matched."

His nostrils flared a little. I hoped that if he had any suspicions, this would allay them. A fugitive would surely conceal her own detection, not inform him of it.

"I stationed additional Vigiles in the area," I went on. "In case she is correct."

After a moment, Ménard released my fingers. "Good."

Two attendants arrived then with the meal. For Ménard, a whole buttered crab on ice and a glass of pressed lemon, unsweetened. For me, a bowl of stew I thought was bouillabaisse—a dish from Marseille—and a well-done beef steak, served with mushrooms and laced with dark sauce.

Of course it had to be beef, one of the few things I avoided eating. My stomach braced itself.

"I will call Gabrielle for an update tomorrow." I picked up my cutlery. "Is there anything more you need her to do in preparation?"

As Minister of Internal Security, Auclair would know all about the agreement to establish Sheol II here.

"Preparation." Ménard was focused on prying the crab open. "For what?"

"For the—" The shell cracked. "Saison d'Os."

Shit.

I had just made a grave misstep. *Bone Season* came from a corruption of the French *bonne*. I had drilled what I presumed was the

141

official Scion translation—La Bonne Saison—into my skull, only to botch it.

Incredibly, Ménard didn't even look up.

"No. Auclair has everything in hand." He snapped a claw off. "Be assured, the site is well-protected."

A bead of perspiration rolled down my nape. I had to cover my error. I creased my brow, put down my fork, and circled my temple with one finger, as if the pain was rising.

"Luce." Ménard lowered the knife. "Should I call someone?"

"No need." I met his gaze head-on. "Benoît, the colony in England was sordid. A breeding ground for sedition and disease."

Straight away, another possible slip-up. I had used his middle name. He regarded me mildly.

"We must keep a closer watch on Sheol II than Weaver did on its predecessor," I pressed on. "If there is another rebellion and the prisoners escape into our citadels, there will be chaos in France. Just as there has been chaos in England."

His attention was back on his crab. "I have no interest in how the Rephaim choose to maintain the rotting places they inhabit."

He said that word, *Réphaïm*, as if it were a poison. That was puzzling. And interesting. I should stop.

I couldn't.

"They are in our country," I said. "On our doorstep."

"As I said, the site is well protected. We are not fools or marionettes, like Weaver. There will be no repeats of what happened on his watch." Ménard picked white flakes of meat from the crab. "The Suzerain will have to purge her own house if there is another uprising."

He peeled the finger-like lungs from the crab and placed them on a dish. I was about to retrieve my fork when I thought better of it. The steak would turn my stomach, which I might not be able to hide. As for the bouillabaisse, the smell of it was making my mouth water, and not in a good way. I could imagine the slime on those fillets, the cottony wetness of the eel.

"Luce." Ménard had been spooning the mustard from the crab, but stopped. "Are you not hungry?"

I forced a weary smile. "I must admit the migraine has left me feeling a little delicate."

"Ah, mon cœur."

I slid the plate of steak aside, out of eyeshot. Ménard watched it move across the tablecloth, then started to eat again.

"Benoît," I said, after a brief silence, "we should visit Sheol II ourselves. Just once, to show our support."

At this, he raised his dark gaze to mine once more. *Tell me, you bastard. Tell me where it is.*

"I do not think that would be a good idea." He dabbed his mouth with linen. "Let us not speak of this tonight. You know how I detest the subject."

I clenched my fist under the table.

"Of course," I said. "What did Chief Tjäder have to say?"

Ménard considered me for a beat too long.

"She and I are in agreement," he said. "It will take time to arrange the counterstrike, given the . . . situation in Sweden. But we have her loyalty."

I sensed this subject was very important, but I had absolutely no idea what he was talking about. Perhaps this was exactly what Domino wanted Nick to discover. He and I could be working to complete the same picture.

Two attendants returned to clear away the plates while a third set down a cheeseboard and cut a blue-veined wedge for Ménard. I shook my head when she offered it to me.

"So," Ménard said, when we were alone once more, "what are we going to call our little fish?"

I raised my glass to my lips again to buy myself some time. In spite of myself, my hand gave the slightest tremor.

Surely they would have discussed baby names by now. Luce was almost five months into her pregnancy. Then again, running a tyrannical republic must be at least moderately time-consuming.

Ménard kept looking at me, his face now utterly expressionless. A wrong answer would shatter the façade, which would stop me returning. Even I had a line when it came to taking risks. With a tiny sound of discomfort, I let my head fall and pressed my knuckles to my brow.

"Luce." Ménard stood. "Come. You should lie down."

"Sorry." I affected a strained laugh. "I've been looking forward to seeing you all day, and now this."

"You are exhausted." He slid an arm around my waist as I got up. "Aleka will rearrange your schedule so you can rest in the morning."

"There's no need, Benoît, really."

"I know. When the anchor calls, we all must answer," he said gently. "But it can wait for half a day."

Next thing I knew, he was guiding me away from the table. Away from his study. He escorted me through the deserted Bureau Cramoisi, past the stern portrait, through the private apartments, to the bedroom. I stood very still as he eased the clasp from my hair, so it tumbled around my shoulders.

"I wish I could stay." His lips brushed my neck. It took every grain of my self-control to not stiffen. "There is much to be done, but all of it will come to fruition, Luce. Soon."

"Let me help." I touched my fingertips to his nape. "At the least, I can keep you company."

"Another time. Tonight, you must rest." He kissed me once on the lips before he moved away. "Sleep well."

I forced a smile. As soon as the door closed behind him, I wiped my mouth on my sleeve, tasting lemons.

I had learned enough to fill in some of the gaps in what I already knew from Arcturus. But I had needed more. Not just for Ducos, but for myself.

I needed the exact location of Sheol II. No matter how great the danger, I would have to return. I carefully laid Frère on the floor on her side, and arranged her hair as if she had fallen.

As I left her body, an idea occurred.

****

I woke feeling cold and heavy. A silhouette appeared above me.

"Flora," a voice said. "Can you hear me?"

I nodded. The tube was already gone, like before, leaving my throat sore.

The agent standing over me was amaurotic, tall and lean, about the same age as Cordier. They wore a navy sweater tucked into trousers, the sleeves rolled up to show toned brown forearms, and their dark curls were pulled into a ponytail that clouded at the base of their neck.

"Stéphane," I said hoarsely. "I presume."

"The courier. Hello." A ring glinted in their nose. "I see Ducos put you straight to work."

"She did." I rubbed my throat. "Thanks for keeping an eye on me."

"Yes. Very weird to be watching your body while you are . . . out and about." Stéphane raised a thin eyebrow. Like the other agents, they sounded French. "Hungry?"

Now that I thought of it, I was. I accepted a shard of almond brittle.

"So," I said, "what does being a courier involve?"

"I take intelligence and equipment from the sub-networks of Paris to other agents across France."

"That sounds dangerous."

"The most dangerous job in Domino. When I am not doing that, I sometimes cover for Albéric, who is spread thin, and Cordier, who does as she pleases. And Ducos thinks *she* is the overworked parent of Mannequin." Stéphane checked their watch. "She asked if you got what we need. If not, you can stay here tonight and make a second attempt in the morning."

I swallowed. The brittle was hard on my throat. "I'd like to stay," I said. "I have some promising information, but I think I could get more."

"Super." Stéphane pulled on their jacket. "If you want more food, there is a very good Greek place next door." They slapped some banknotes onto the counter. "Welcome to Mannequin."

I had barely managed a thank you before they were gone, leaving me alone in the apartment.

Now I had the whole night to myself. And a plan. What I intended was a risk, but I had my doubts that the façade with Frère would hold up for another day. Ménard was far too sharp.

No, I would do what I needed to do tonight, prove to Domino I was a safe bet, and carry on working for my own ends. Before anyone else woke, I would possess Frère one more time and get into the Salon Doré. I would crack the safe and steal its contents, anything that might hint at where Sheol II was.

I would have to do it without a ventilator. For that, I would need to be quick—and much closer to my host. With my dissimulator in place, I locked the apartment and stepped into the evening chill.

An enticing scent drifted from the Greek cookshop next door. I bought a slice of spinach pie and two hot flatbreads to go. While I ate, I walked south.

The Hôtel Garuche loomed sinister in the blue light of the streetlamps. I sensed Frère inside. Even though it was past sundown, day Vigiles stood guard, armed to the hilt. Ménard must not want to employ clairvoyant Vigiles on his own doorstep, even if he saw the use in stationing them elsewhere.

Unsurprisingly, there were no derelict buildings near the mansion, nowhere to use as a hideout. It would have to be the rooftops. I took note of how the nearest buildings connected, spied a service ladder that would allow me to get up high without the Vigiles seeing me.

The golden cord gave a soft ring. Arcturus, wondering if I was on my way back.

Tomorrow.

He would only tell me not to go. I needed to do this now, before my window of opportunity closed.

I would not leave another colony standing.

****

With my approach sketched out, I returned to the safe house and slept until the alarm went off. Moments later, I was heading back toward Luce Ménard Frère.

I used a drainpipe to climb one of the buildings I had scouted. The service ladder took me higher. For the first time since my arrival in Paris, I could see the spire of the Eiffel Tower, shining as if with moonlight. Nick and I had planned to climb it together one day.

I could marvel later. Once I was off the chimney, I picked my way along the mansard roof until the Hôtel Garuche was back in sight, then used my belt to fasten my ankle to a flue. I didn't want to slide to my death while I was only semi-present.

Do not think of it as splitting yourself, Arcturus had told me once, *but leaving a shadow behind.*

The last thing I saw through my own eyes was the stars above Paris, half covered by cloud.

****

Unbroken darkness. The scent of fresh linen. I took a few slow breaths and reached blindly to my left. Smooth fabric slithered under my fingers. Frère had closed the curtains around her bed.

It had worked. I was distantly aware of my own body, the chill of the metal roof beneath it. If I could get the hang of this, I could take or leave my life support.

My hand slid across the disheveled sheets, searching for any trace of another body. Nothing. Frère was alone. Either the couple slept in separate beds, or Ménard was still working.

Frère was slow and heavy with sleep. I drew back one of the curtains and craned her out of bed.

I felt my way to the lamp. There was a tiered box of accessories on her dresser. I opened it and selected two hairpins. With tweezers from the bathroom, I bent one of them and straightened the other. A lever and a pick. As if to tell me off, a little flutter came from my passenger.

The bedroom door opened without a creak. Every breath, every tiny rustle of nightdress, seemed painfully loud. The carpet hushed my footsteps as I padded into the Salon Blanc, where the only light was the glow from the hearth.

I glanced over my shoulder before I tried the door to the Salon Doré. It was locked. Ménard had retired for the night.

Good.

The lock was a dead bolt, to blend in with the old-fashioned grandeur of the mansion. I slid the hairpin in, the way Eliza had shown me when I first joined the gang. I edged the pick in above my lever and used it to hook the closest pins. Once I had a feel for them, I worked on the first one until it gave way.

Sweat pearled on my brow as I coaxed the next pin, and the next. At last, the lock admitted defeat. Now for the electronic defense. Heart in my throat, I turned to the scanner beside the door and pressed one finger to it. With a tiny *beep* and a click, the door opened.

I was in.

Darkness hung thick in the Salon Doré. I retreated a few steps, took a candle from the mantelpiece, and lit it on the embers of the fire. Beneath my heartbeat, there was another patter. Rain against the windows.

My own body would be soaked to the bone before long. I needed to get this done and get out.

I stepped into the study and closed the door. Gold leaf reflected the candlelight. A chandelier, dripping with crystal, adorned the white ceiling. And there was the desk, near the north wall. As I made toward it, I glimpsed my host in the mirror. Frère looked as if she was sleepwalking. When I reached the desk, I turned the lamp on low and blew out the candle.

In this amaurotic body, I almost missed the threat. Elsewhere in the mansion—two rooms away—a creak sounded.

For a displaced spirit clinging to the mind of a pregnant woman in a nightdress, I moved fast. I switched the lamp off, rushed back into the Salon Blanc, and gently shut the door to the Salon Doré. I had barely turned around before a man appeared on the threshold.

Not Ménard. A little taller. And as his features came into relief, I remembered them.

Remembered him.

Light brown skin and asymmetric eyes, one hazel and one dark. His hair had grown out a little since I had seen him last, forming small russet curls. A face from the past.

David.

From the Bone Season. The red-jacket who had known too much. The oracle who had spoken in riddles.

His gaze was intent. I was so stunned to see him at all, let alone here, that I half-forgot I was in Frère. I watched him slide the bolt across. How had he escaped the colony? Why the hell was he here?

"Madelle Frère?"

He came to stand right in front of me. Close enough for me to count the freckles on his nose.

"Luce," he said, softer, "what is it?"

I was too shocked by his appearance to speak. Before I could form another clear thought, my face was cupped between his palms, and a moment later, his mouth was on mine.

The shock hurtled me back to myself. My own eyes snapped open—rain, darkness, bitter cold—before I looked through hers again, at the bolted door, the gilded walls. I felt as if I was in freefall. Heart thudding, a high-pitched note in my ears, sweat on my palms.

Muscular arms wrapped around me. Strong hands roved over my hips, my back, up to my waist, gathering me against a hard chest. A tongue roamed in my mouth, tasting of mint. A white wind of panic blasted through my mind. What the ever-loving *fuck* was happening?

Raw instinct jolted me out of my freeze. I wrenched free, took aim, and socked David right in the face.

Frère had a weak arm, but her spousal ring caught David on the cheekbone. He managed to strangle his own shout of pain. I plastered myself to the wall as he reeled back, staring at me like I had lost my mind.

"Merde—!" He covered his bloody cheek, eyes watering. "When did you learn to punch like that?"

"How dare you put your foul hands on me?" I made a grab for the sharp letter opener on the desk. "I will send you to the guillotine for this, anormal. When I tell the Inquisitor—"

"Paige?"

We stared at each other through the gloom of the study. "How did you know?" I whispered in English.

"It's my job to know. I sensed a voyant lurking near the mansion, but I never imagined she was already inside." He nodded east. "Your body is that way, isn't it?"

I turned cold to the marrow. "You're an oracle. You can sense the æther to that extent?"

His smile was grim. "You're close," he said. "Very close. Roof of the Swedish Embassy?"

"Is anyone coming?"

"Not yet." He looked at the blood on his fingers. "There were four hundred people you could have used to spy on him, and you chose her. The person he would raze citadels to protect. You have a death wish, dreamwalker?"

He had sounded English when I met him in the colony. Now he sounded distinctly French.

"I don't need to wish for death," I said. "Sooner or later, it always comes back for another go." I kept a tight hold on the letter opener. "What the hell are you doing here, David?"

"Catching you red-handed, apparently."

"You work for Ménard now?"

"I always did."

I didn't wait for more. Instead, I started to dislocate from Frère.

"Wait," David hissed, and I stopped halfway into the æther. "Let me give you a gift. For old times' sake. The gift of choice."

"Shove it, red-jacket."

"You came here for a reason. You're looking for something, and presumably, you haven't found it. Unless you do as I say, you never will." His gaze seared into mine. "Ménard suspects."

"How can you possibly know that?"

"He asked me to check Frère for . . . la tache de l'anormalité. He's called a doctor for her," David said under his breath. "You won't get away with it again. But there is another way."

"You can pretend you never saw me." My arm was too weak to break his grip. "Let me get what I need."

"From his study?" He nodded to the doors. "Anything important will be in the safe."

"You think I can't crack a safe?"

"Not this one."

Elsewhere in the mansion, I sensed another person moving. Apparently he did, too, because he glanced over his shoulder and pulled me close enough to smell the mint on his breath again.

"Listen," he whispered. "I need to prove my worth to survive in here. So I'll help you. But first, I need you to do something for me. Let me tell them where you are. Let them detain you."

"I didn't come up the Seine on a soap bubble, you shit." I shoved him away. "That's not a deal. It's an execution warrant."

"Ménard won't kill you. You're too valuable. You'll be imprisoned, like I am—but in a perfect position to spy. And I'll help you. If that's what you want." He drew away. "Allow yourself to be captured."

"And then what—you'll *help* me onto the guillotine?"

"I'll help you get out of here. You know about me and Frère. It's in my interest to keep my word."

I searched his face for deceit.

"If you leave now, you'll never know what's going on in here," David went on, "and believe me, you want to know. It will change everything you think about Ménard. About the Rephaim. If you don't want to stay after that, I swear I'll help you leave. If I break my word, send me and Luce to the guillotine. She deserves it. Maybe I do, too." Those striking eyes held mine. "Choose."

"I don't trust you," I said. "I couldn't prove your affair to Ménard. There's no evidence."

His gaze flickered. A moment passed before he swallowed.

"Yes," he said, "there is."

Slowly, he looked down, and I followed his line of sight. To the bump. The words died on my lips.

"Time to choose, Paige. I'm going to raise the alarm." He wrapped an arm around me. Around her. "If you want to run, this is your head start."

I didn't need a second invitation.

My silver cord hurled me back into my own body. On the rooftop, in the downpour, I scrambled to release my leg from the flue. I was soaked to the skin, my nose streaming, shivering so hard my teeth rattled. Coughs wrenched my insides as I wrestled with the belt.

If you leave now, you'll never know what's going on in here. My fingers were clumsy with cold. *And believe me, you want to know.*

The Trojan horse. I could almost hear Hildred Vance, the flat-toned voice that had betrayed a shadow of approval. *An ancient stratagem. You presented yourself like a gift to your enemy, and your enemy took you into their house.*

The belt came undone. I yanked my ankle free and ran. My boots slewed on wet metal, almost throwing me over the edge.

You have a death wish, dreamwalker?

Chest heaving, ribs aflame, I lunged for the chimney and caught it with one hand. Stayed to catch my breath, to draw my panic-stricken thoughts into some semblance of order.

The deal David offered was madness, suicide. Only a reckless fool would try to trick the anchor twice . . .

Arcturus would never forgive me for risking my life again. And yet wasn't this the way of war?

Wasn't this a chance to get everything we needed?

I was torn between the streets and the mansion. If I ran now, there was no way back in. No guarantee I would ever find the location of Sheol II, or the truth about Ménard and the Rephaim. Domino would discover what I had done and cut me off. There would be no money, no support. I peeled off the dissimulator and shoved it between two bricks in the chimney.

Reckless fools are dangerous in this line of work, Ducos had told me.

Dangerous.

And necessary.

****

When the squadron of Vigiles reached the roof, they found me sprawled by the chimney—as if I had slipped and twisted my ankle. They were not gentle. I put up a convincing fight as they handcuffed me and hauled me up to face their commandant.

Armored hands. Steel-capped boots. Like those that had battered my body in the Archon.

"Your Majesty." A red visor burned in the dark. "Welcome to Paris."

His baton snapped out. The last thing I felt, after the shattering blow, was a shock wave from the golden cord.

PART II

Turn the Anchor

You will soon hear of me with my funny little games.

—Jack the Ripper

9

The Butcher of Strasbourg

FEBRUARY 2, 2060

I woke on my side, wearing a loose nightshirt that smelled of dust and pepper. A throb above my temple kept time with my heart. Sunlight gleamed onto my face through a tall window.

The room was in a state of neglect, its grandeur long since faded. There was a free-standing wardrobe, a coffee table, and the daybed I was lying on. A heavy mantle covered me to the waist. I found the lump on my head, fingers barely surfacing from the cuffs of too-long sleeves.

"Arcturus?"

A figure moved to my left. It took human shape, and a warm hand touched my upper arm.

"Paige. Are you all right?"

Every breath hurt. The light made a smear of him, but now I remembered his voice.

"David," I croaked.

"Sorry to disappoint, but yes." A cut flecked his nose where I had punched him, and he sported two black eyes. "I take it this means you've accepted my deal."

Little by little, I remembered where I was, and why. What I had done.

"How long have I been out?" I said.

"All night and half the day. They kept you under for a while, to make sure you didn't, er, act up." His brow pinched. "You were coughing a lot."

"Even dangerous fugitives get colds." I pushed my weight onto my elbow. "What time is it?"

"Almost one." When I let out a small groan, he got up. "Let me shut the curtains. You must have the mother of all headaches."

The Vigile had hit me like he had wanted to take a good look at my brain. While David went to the windows, I thought as fast as one could after being clobbered with a steel baton.

Someone from Mannequin would have long since returned to the apartment and found it empty. They would have gone straight to Rue Gît-le-Cœur, only to find Arcturus alone. The thought of him sealed my throat. He had sensed my pain and dread before I fell unconscious. He knew I was in danger again.

Just not that I had chosen it.

David returned to his seat. "So," I said, "is this my cell?"

"Mine is on the other side of the attic. We're kept out of sight of the officials." He blew out a breath. "You're lucky. Luce wanted you hung by your wrists."

"Yes, what a constant gift it is to be me." Gingerly, I touched my temple. "You didn't tell me your Vigiles would knock me senseless."

"They didn't want to take chances with a preternatural fugitive. And they're not *my* Vigiles."

"But they listen to your tip-offs."

"For reasons I will explain." His voice softened. "I promise you're safe, Paige."

"Right, of course. No safer place."

Whatever sedative they had given me had worn off. I could use my gift. The knowledge gave me the confidence to look him in the eye.

"Go on, then," I said. "Explain."

"Let me get you a hot drink before I start. You were soaked when they brought you in."

"I'm fine."

A lie. I had a deep-rooted chill.

David reached for a teapot. "This doesn't have anything nasty in it. They might drug you later, though, before you see Ménard," he said. "Something to cut you off from the æther."

"What kind of drug can do that?"

"You don't want to know. But don't worry," he said. "Its effects aren't permanent."

He poured some black tea. I took it, if only to warm my hands. My stomach gave a rumble I hoped he couldn't hear.

"I have a lot to explain," he said. "I know I must have seemed a little shifty in the colony."

"Yep."

With a thin smile, he poured a cup of his own. His arms were freckled and corded with muscle.

"David Fitton was my alias. My real name is Cadoc Fitzours," he said, "but call me Cade."

"Cadoc." To rhyme with *haddock*. "Welsh?"

"Think so. I'm not," he said. "I'm from Brittany. Little place called Île-d'Arz." He cleared his throat. "Éire go brách."

"Breizh da viken." It was the only Breton I knew. "Are you fluent?"

Cade grimaced. "Rusty, at best. I stopped learning it when my family died." He glanced at me. "House fire. I was the only survivor."

"I'm sorry."

"Long time ago." A muscle flinched in his cheek. "I was on the streets for a while before I got a job at the Port of Lorient. Eventually, one of the other dockworkers guessed what I was and reported me. The Vigiles raided my flophouse, and I was sent to the Bastille."

It was among the most notorious prisons in the Republic of Scion. A stone-built fortress without a single window.

"I was in there for almost three years before I won the blood lottery. The night before I was meant to die, the guards hauled me to a car. It brought me here." He blew on his tea. "Ménard was visiting his mother in Athens. That meant it was Luce who greeted me."

Ménard's mother had moved to Greece not long after Mylène was born. He flew to see her several times a year, leaving Frère to run the country.

"Love at first sight?" I said.

Cade snorted into his teacup. "Not quite." He drank. "Luce explained that the Grand Inquisitor needed an exceptionally rare voyant to work for him as a spy. If I took the job, I'd be pardoned for my unnaturalness."

"And you were so enchanted by this offer that you . . . took a flying leap into bed with her?"

He cocked an eyebrow. "You want some fangs with that venom, Paige?"

"Trust me, I wouldn't usually care who you or anyone else is riding. But Madelle Guillotine herself?" I sipped my tea. "That's a very special kind of masochism."

"I have my reasons."

"Did you have your *reasons* for propositioning me in the colony?"

Cade had the decency to look contrite. "You remember that." He rubbed his face with one hand. "Look, I know you won't believe me, but I didn't actually want to sleep with you."

"Could have fooled me."

"It was an act, Paige. When I saw you, I did feel drawn to you. You were a fellow jumper, and I wanted to help you survive, so I gave you some of the information I had been collecting for Ménard." Cade breathed out. "And then you threatened to tell the Rephaim what I knew. And I thought you might mean it. That they'd find out why I was in the colony."

He ran the same hand over his reddish curls. With pursed lips, I waited for him to finish.

"I covered my tracks by acting like it had all been a ruse to get you into bed," he said, sounding tired. "Fucking stupid, I know, but I panicked. Better you thought I was a lowlife than a spy." A mirthless huff. "And then I felt shit for doing it, so I tried to help you again."

I wasn't sure whether or not to believe him.

"I'm sorry. You know what it was like in that place. Made you paranoid." Cade looked at me. "I knew your rebels had spiked the drinks, that last night. I never betrayed you. We're on the same side."

It was true that he had at least kept his mouth shut. Sedating the red-jackets had gone to plan.

"Fine." I set the tea down on the table. "Carry on. Before all this, what exactly did Frère propose?"

Cade settled back in his chair, one ankle resting on one knee.

"Ménard had received a summons to the Bicentenary," he said, "to sign the Great Territorial Act. A formal agreement between the Republic of Scion France and the Suzerain that the former would host a penal colony for unnaturals. Now, most Scion staff with first-level security clearance are aware that there's a power above Weaver, but they have no idea who—or what—it is. Ménard needed someone to find out."

"You're saying Scion is spying on itself?" Ducos was going to love this. "In the colony, you said there was still a grain of sense left in the Archon. You meant the Hôtel Garuche."

"I could hardly just come out and tell you I was spying for the French," Cade said, amused. "But, yes. Frère issued me with a false identity and sent me to London to get myself arrested. As a rare voyant, I was sent to Sheol I. The whole time I was there, I was observing on Ménard's behalf."

"He wanted to know what he was agreeing to host in his country," I said. "Before he signed up to it."

"Exactly. I was his canary in a coal mine."

The pieces of the jigsaw were at last forming a picture. "How did you escape the colony?"

"Do you remember Aloys Mynatt?" Cade said. The former Grand Raconteur of France, who had retired in November. "He was there to extract me. He got me onto the next train out."

"And that's when Frère became pregnant," I said. A tiny nod. "I don't know why you're still working here. She's due in June. If the baby is yours, shouldn't you run while you still can?"

"When you've spoken to Ménard, you'll see why I want to help him for as long as possible. You might even want to do the same."

"You think I'd work with a tyrant?"

"Sometimes you need to shake hands with the enemy. You trusted the Warden, didn't you?"

I wanted to point out that my alliance with Arcturus had been forged when I realized he was a fellow prisoner, and that Arcturus had never betrayed any desire to behead hordes of innocent people with a weighted blade. Cade cracked his neck and stood.

"Ménard expects you at nine, after the staff and officials have gone. I put in a good word for you," he said. "Cooperate and you won't be restrained."

"Words to inspire an alliance of equals. You should write the propaganda."

"Just friendly advice, Underqueen." He had the cheek to wink. "You can keep the shirt."

He rapped his knuckles on the door and was let out. I heard the distinct *click* as the guards locked it behind him.

Already I had useful intelligence for Ducos. Tonight would bring more. High risk for high gain. Still, no matter how many secrets I unlocked during my stay, they would be no use to anyone unless I got out of this place alive.

I got up from the daybed. When I parted the dusty curtains, I found myself looking at a significant fall to a lower rooftop. Even if I somehow got down there without breaking my legs, I would be shot before I could reach the ground. Ménard had put snipers on the gate.

You have risen from the ashes before, Arcturus had told me. *The only way to survive is to believe you always will.*

The memory of those words tempered my nerves. I had survived this once—I could do it again. I would hear what Ménard had to say.

****

For the rest of the day, I observed the Vigiles who patrolled in the front courtyard of the mansion. There was no clock in the room, so I used the sun to estimate the time. I also took note of my position. My room was in the west wing. Ménard had placed me as far away from his living quarters as possible.

I could sense hundreds of people working downstairs. Staff and guards and officials. Close to sunset, a Vigile delivered me a cup of water and some clothes. A simple white blouse, gray trousers, a black sweater. Slip-on shoes with liners—flimsy things, not snug enough to run or climb in.

There was a sink in my cell, beside a door that led to a cramped toilet. The tap dripped. Beside it sat a hard-bristled toothbrush, toothpaste, and a bar of soap. Better than my last prison, though I suspected Ménard wanted me clean for my guards' sake, not mine. Cast-iron radiators taunted me from the walls, icy to the touch.

I tried the golden cord. Arcturus needed to know that I was alive. Even as I willed myself to be calm, to hold the cord with both hands, everything conspired to distract me. My cough. My hollow stomach. The ever-growing shadows, which made me feel surrounded. Try as I might, there was a wall between us. In the end, I gave up. I would try again later.

At dusk, Alexandra Kotzia entered the room and looked me over, her face tight with dislike.

"Hello again, Aleka," I said.

Her nostrils flared. "Drink this." She handed me a glass, full of something gray and pungent. "Tout de suite."

Despite the hour, two day Vigiles flanked her, pistols aimed at my kneecaps. I steeled myself and drank the stuff in one go. It slid down my throat like cold grease, tasting of must and rot, like water tainted with peat.

What came next was worse. As Kotzia snatched back the glass, the æther turned woolen around me. It wasn't absent—it never was —but it seemed farther away, harder to reach. An intense feeling of dread and hollowness gripped my insides.

"What was that?" I managed to say. "What the hell is it?"

"Security." Kotzia sniffed. "Try anything, and you will be shot."

The foul taste rocked my stomach. For a dangerous moment, I thought I would throw up all over her pristine white heels. Whatever she had given me, it was obstructing my gift. I could only sense the nearest dreamscapes.

Six armed Vigiles waited for me by the door, including the commandant who had knocked me unconscious. They marched me to the floor below, to the doors of the Salon Vert, where I had eaten with Ménard. Kotzia knocked on the door, and a voice called from within.

Inside, it was dimly lit. Ménard sat beside Frère, with Cade on the other side of the table.

Frère was first to lock onto me. Her chin jutted. She took her spouse by the hand.

"Thank you, Aleka." Ménard spared me a level glance. "Vigiles, kindly wait outside."

"Are you certain, Grand Inquisitor?" the commandant asked.

"She has been neutered."

I stayed where I was as my escort retreated. When Cade patted the chair beside him, I sat mechanically. Frère looked as if she would throttle me with her necklace if I came within reach.

"I brought you here, anormale, to explain your situation. So there is no confusion as to why you are in my home, and not on the guillotine." Ménard addressed me in crisp English. "After what you did to my spouse and our child, that is certainly where you belong."

I elected not to answer.

"When I heard that Luce had complained of a migraine, I was concerned," Ménard said. "Migraines, seizures, blackouts—more often than not, such things are the heralds of unnatural influence." The very excuse I had used to cover my tracks had tipped him off. "Coupled with reports from England that the fugitive Paige Mahoney could infiltrate even the most secure buildings, and that she had escaped Inquisitorial custody, my suspicions grew."

He drew his cup and saucer toward him, slow as you please. No one else moved.

"The meal we shared included a test," he said. "You were clever to report your own detection. At first, I was sure it was Luce— that she had simply been unwell. I was at ease. Only one aspect struck me as curious. I had expressly requested that bouillabaisse was served, since Luce does not care for it, and expected her to send it away at once."

"As I would have." Frère dealt me a mocking smile. "I suppose you researched me for your deception. You imagined that because I lived in Marseille, I must like bouillabaisse, hm?"

Beaten by a bowl of fish stew. What a spy.

"You did not remark upon it. Still," Ménard said to me, "you never tasted it, either. Instead, you left it untouched. It was . . . a plausible reaction, if not the one I anticipated. Until the end of the meal, I must confess, I was convinced. You did well."

I spoke for the first time. "What gave me away?"

"When you avoided discussing baby names." He clasped his hands, so I could see his gold spousal ring. "Luce and I have already decided what to call our fourth child."

"Of course. The happy family," I said. "So happy, so devoid of paranoia, that you decided to set a test for your own spouse . . . because she told her secretary she had a migraine." I raised my eyebrows at Frère. "Is this a marriage or a noose?"

"I would be happy to demonstrate the difference," Frère said, deadly soft.

"Are you proposing, Luce?"

Frère half-rose. Ménard tightened his grip on her hand, and they seemed to have a silent conversation. Finally, she sank back into her seat, one hand on the firm swell of her stomach, her gaze roaring hatred. Under the table, Cade gave my wrist a warning squeeze. I pulled my arm out of his reach.

He was right. Sitting across a table from this pair of murderers was harder than I had expected, but I had to watch my tongue. Frère would be only too pleased to have it torn out.

"Later," Ménard continued, "Fitzours summoned me to the Salon Vert, where he had found Luce wandering in the dark. When he told me he had sensed unnatural influence on her, it confirmed what I had already supposed. A criminal had stolen her body. Violated our family home."

I dared not look at Cade.

"You are here, in our country," Ménard said, "because Frank Weaver failed to execute you. I imagine he would like you back so he can remedy that mistake—urgently, if he is to placate his Rephaite masters." His tone was almost clement. "You are a shrewd woman. You will have already grasped that this situation makes you a valuable bartering tool."

"You're no friend of Weaver," I said. "A fool and a marionette, I think you called him. Why would you want to barter with him?"

"To rid us of the true unnaturals." He moved the silver dish of sugar. "The Rephaim."

I waited for some evidence of a joke. The Grand Inquisitor of France did not smile.

Ménard melted a cube of sugar into his coffee and stirred. The room waited for him to speak again.

"When Fitzours brought me news of those creatures, those *things*," he said, "I was sickened to the core of my being. After all we have done to uphold this empire, to curb the threat of unnaturalness—" His lips peeled back for a flash as he spoke. "It is a betrayal of Scion."

"The Rephaim *created* Scion." I shook my head. "How could their existence possibly betray it?"

"The Rephaim compel us to hunt and imprison your kind, yet they, too, are unnatural. Unnatural parasites." He set down his spoon with a delicate *clink*. "The system they created is perfect. Necessary. They, however, are not. The hypocrisy, the deceit—the natural order revolts against it."

"On that note, you have an unnatural working for you. Living in your attic." I tilted my head toward Cade. "Would you not call *that* hypocrisy?"

"It serves a higher purpose."

"The higher purpose of saving Scion from its own makers?" My mouth twitched. "I knew you must be soulless, but not delusional. Scion would be meaningless without the Rephaim."

"Not meaningless. Liberated," Ménard corrected. "Free to use its power to benefit humanity, unshackled from its Rephaite masters—and from sycophants like Weaver, who obey them."

"Or to collapse."

Not that I would mind. If Scion buckled under the weight of its own contradictions, it would save me a lot of time and effort. No, in poking holes through his logic, I had no intention of putting him off this line of thought. I just needed to understand how he had drawn it.

"Believe what you will," Ménard said, his attention fixed on me. "I mean to rid us of this infestation. To purge every last Rephaite. To clean unnaturalness in all its forms from the face of the earth. And to make a human-controlled Scion the one and only power in this world."

He made blood and destruction sound practical, reasonable. It unnerved me in a way few people ever had.

"Weaver made a mistake when he announced that you had been killed in Edinburgh. If your survival were to be exposed, it would end him, and someone else could take his place. Someone who knows the truth of the Suzerain, who sees her for exactly what she is. I am that someone. I mean to forge a new and purified Scion, unsullied by *any* unnaturalness." He raised one of his temperate smiles. "You were interested in Sheol II. I may have been forced to host it, but make no mistake—I will use it not to glorify the Rephaim, but to bring them to their knees."

And there it was, in a nutshell. The secret Ducos needed, that Domino could use to sow discord between England and France.

Georges Benoît Ménard was plotting a coup. He wanted to seize control of England, the head of the anchor, so that he could get rid of Nashira Sargas and rule the empire himself.

And he wanted to use me to do it. To oust Frank Weaver by turning public opinion against him, or to blackmail him into quietly stepping down.

"Right," I finally said. "Very impressive. You are mighty and righteous indeed." Frère looked at me as if I were a fly that refused to be swatted. "Cade here said you had a proposal I might find interesting. Do enlighten me."

At length, Ménard took a sip of his coffee.

"Fitzours will have told you that I offered him an extended stay of execution in exchange for his services," he said. "You have connections to well-placed Rephaim who despise the Suzerain. You front a terrorist organization dedicated to her downfall. Cooperate with us. Help us carry out our goal of destroying the Rephaite scourge, and I will not hand you back to them. I will provide you with immunity from execution."

"And then what?" I said. "You let me open a bookshop in a pretty Provençal village, live out the rest of my life in peace?"

"I can make you someone else." His gaze drilled into mine. "So long as you are out of my sight."

He sounded like Jaxon, offering me an illusion of freedom at the cost of my integrity. This tie-wearing murderer wanted me to loan him the Mime Order—my army of rebels, thieves, and misfits, which I had nearly given my life to protect—as if it were open to the highest bidder.

"You will have realized that I don't seek the destruction of all Rephaim," I said. "Only the Suzerain and those who follow her. I will not convince my Rephaite connections to work with anyone who means them harm. As for the Mime Order . . . you can't seriously think I would ever compel my soldiers to serve the Butcher of Strasbourg's cause."

"Our cause is the same until we defeat this common enemy."

"What if we do?"

"Well." He gave his coffee another stir. "We will cross that bridge, as they say, when we come to it."

"And we know what will be on the other side. You'll want to erase all evidence that you ever colluded with unnaturals. The guillotines will work around the clock," I said. "Between you and the Suzerain, I don't know who I'd rather have. The Rephaim, at least, need some voyants alive to feed on. They're also our principal line of defense against the Emim."

For some reason, that made Ménard smile.

"Yes. The monsters from across the veil." He sipped his coffee. "On that count, at least, you need not trouble yourself."

The way he said it made my nape prickle. I had no idea what he was driving at.

"I will give you time to consider my proposal," Ménard said. "Work in my service. Lend me your allies, Rephaite and human. Commit to a new Scion. Or die in whatever way Luce desires."

From the look in her eyes, Frère would have me torn apart.

"I'll consider it," I said.

"Very good." Ménard glanced toward Cade. "Fitzours, take our visitor back to her room. You may stay with her for half an hour. Perhaps you can join your voice to our cause."

Cade dipped his head. "Yes, Grand Inquisitor."

When he stood, I half expected him to bow. I pushed myself from my chair and followed him toward the door.

"One more thing," Ménard said, calm. I stopped. "Frank Weaver did not seize his chance to be rid of you. I hear that was because the

Suzerain wanted something from you first. Be aware, anormale, that I am not so generous. I will give her nothing she desires."

A slow-moving cold licked up my back and across my shoulders. The disquiet of a hunted thing.

"If you choose not to see things my way, you become a liability. Nothing more or less. I will have no incentive whatsoever to keep you alive. Pollute my spouse, or my children, or any of my staff, and I will send you to the highest cell of the Grande Bastille. They have a machine there, la mâchoire. I will ensure it tastes some pieces of you before you lose your head."

Silence followed. I was dismissed. Cade took me by the elbow, giving me the jolt I needed to walk on.

When he returned to France, Cade must have told his employers that Nashira Sargas wanted my gift, and had kept me alive for months so I could die in the right way, at the right time. Ménard had no need for that kind of restraint. He would only spare me if I proved myself useful, and there was no end to the ways he might hurt me if I refused his bargain.

I had once entertained the fantasy that destroying Nashira would be all it took to topple Scion. Now I realized that her creation had become a monster all of its own. Hatred of clairvoyants had washed across nine countries in two centuries, with countless more set to fall. Nashira might have forged the anchor, but humans had latched onto it willingly.

I learned that humans have a mechanism inside them, she had told me, the last time we came face-to-face. *A mechanism called* hatred, *which can be activated with the lightest pull of a string.*

An empire founded on human hatred. That was what she had called Scion. If Ménard got his wish—if that were possible—she would learn the hard way that human hatred was too strong to be constrained.

Cade walked me back to the attic. When we reached my room, the Vigiles locked us in together.

"So," I said, "that's why you still work for him. You think he can take Nashira down."

"Yes." Cade faced me, purpose in every crease of his face. "Imagine it. A new Grand Inquisitor of England *and* France who hates the Rephs. Think of the colossal money and power he would be able to turn against them."

"He's lost his mind. So have you," I said. "The money and power comes from the Rephaim. They *are* Scion."

"No. It's the other way around, Paige. It's *our* money. Our power. Rephaim can't hold bank accounts, can they?" he said, with feeling. "Legally, they don't exist. They have to operate through us. What if we revoked our support? If the Rephaim aren't lording it in our buildings, wearing clothes we made for them, feeding on *our* auras—what are they, really?"

Something in his words rang true. Without high walls to hide behind, without the comforts Scion afforded them, the Rephaim were scavengers. Powerful scavengers, yes. Difficult to take down —but scavengers, nonetheless. Scavengers could be picked off. Starved out.

"Ménard is not the only one who feels this way," Cade went on. "He's already found a firm ally in Birgitta Tjäder. She's as much of a fanatic as him, and she has Inquisitor Lindberg of Sweden under her thumb."

Tjäder had been at the Bicentenary, too. I remembered how unsettled and tense she had looked.

"We can turn their own anti-unnatural message against them, Paige," Cade said in a low, urgent tone. "Don't you see?"

"You heard him, Cade. He wants us all dead. A human-run Scion would still be Scion."

"Humans are easier to overthrow. This is only the first step."

Without answering, I paced to the window.

I thought of a world in which Nashira was no longer revered. It was tempting. Yet it would go against every principle I had to work with a Grand Inquisitor.

The Mime Order needed to expand its horizons, but I had other irons in the fire. If I got out of here alive, I might be able to strike an alliance with Ducos. I might also have the Parisian syndicate, if I could crush the corruption and find the people who supported my cause.

"Sorry," I said at last. "I will not ask my soldiers to work with Ménard. I will not put him in touch with my allies—Rephaite or human—and I will not be staying here to discuss the matter any further. It's a pipe dream." In the dim reflection, I saw his brow furrow. "What?"

"I hoped you would give it some more thought," Cade admitted. "I thought you, of all people, would see the gray."

"Meaning?"

"You worked with the scarred ones."

"Don't insult my judgment, Cade. The scarred ones aren't perfect, I grant you, but they've worked for decades to help us. Ménard has worked for decades to kill us." I nodded to the door. "Go on. You're wasting your breath here. And I'm sure the love of your life is waiting."

"Do you think I don't know what she is, Paige?" He spoke too softly for the Vigiles outside to hear, but with passion enough to draw my gaze. "Why do you think I let it go so far?"

"I have no idea."

"I thought if she fell in love with me, she might start seeing us as people. Might find it harder to watch us die." His voice was flat, hollow. "I've made mistakes. I also want to do the right thing for voyants. I believe you do as well."

"Don't underestimate what I'd do to defeat Scion."

"I always thought you'd do anything."

"Look, this is war. There are always going to be different factions," I said. "I see your perspective. I just don't agree with it. I'm sorry, but I can't work with you on this."

Cade considered my face, lifting his hands to the back of his head. At last, he heaved a sigh.

"I don't want you to leave," he confessed. "I could use some voyant company in here, and I think you could have furthered the cause—but I do understand. Having said that, I would appreciate it if you'd at least give it a day or two. Pretend you're considering. It would help me keep my head."

"Fine," I said, "but I'll need a bit more freedom. There was a reason I came here, and it wasn't to sit in an attic."

"I'll try," Cade said. "And you keep my secret." He stood and offered a hand. "Deal?"

I shook it. "Deal."

"Good." He smiled, the corners of his eyes crinkling. "Thank you. For listening, at least."

"Cade," I said. He stopped halfway to the door. "Thanks for the shirt."

"Keep it. Luce wanted you to freeze," he said, with the facial equivalent of a shrug, "but I guess I can screw her in more ways than one."

One knock on the door, and he was gone. The silence of the attic wound like rope around me.

I had the information Ducos needed. Now for the task I had set for myself. Whatever plans Ménard had for Sheol II, I needed to know where it was, or where it would be. I needed to take control.

The foul drink had worn off, and the æther embraced me like an old friend. I went to the window and pressed my brow to the glass. Outside, the stars were scattershot on a black canvas.

I'm alive. I willed him to hear me across the divide. *In the Hôtel Garuche. Give me two days—then be ready to help me get out of here, Arcturus, or the next string I get caught in will be around my neck.*

10

Revelation

It was a long night. Snow fanned across the courtyard, a fine layer of frost silvered the windows, and the dripping tap in my cell picked at the edges of my sanity. Beneath the mantle, I muffled my vicious coughs on a cushion. It eased the pain a little if I lay on my right side.

To distract myself, I sought Ménard in the æther. Logically, I knew he couldn't feel me unless I touched his dreamscape, but even using my gift covertly now felt too much like playing with fire.

Drip, drip.

He was in his study with Frère. They stayed there for a long while, then retired together to the private apartments, leaving only a handful of dreamscapes on the move. The mansion had a skeleton staff at night, including the armed Vigiles who stood outside my door.

Cade was in his room. I still wasn't sure what to make of him, just as I had never been sure in the colony. His commitment to Ménard was a riddle. So was his liaison with Frère.

Drip, drip.

I wondered about Frère. Cade had a clear motive for the affair, if a naïve one, but all Frère seemed to have gained was a pregnancy that might spell her undoing. No matter how much he adored and relied on her, Ménard could not allow an unnatural progenitor to remain at his side. She would lose her opulent lifestyle, her children, and in the end, her life. All for a fling.

Frère was devoted to Scion. Now I considered what else she might be. Bored of the many constraints of naturalness, even as she preached them. Hungry, after a lifetime of comfort, for a taste of real danger. Cade was good-looking, and he had a certain assurance about him that she must have found attractive. Attractive enough, apparently, to risk her head.

Drip, drip.

Every muscle in my body was spring-loaded. I stared at the wall, my head full of voices.

Drip, drip.

That fucking tap. I fantasized that I could tear it off the sink, smash it to bits, burn the whole mansion to the ground so that good-for-nothing tap could never drip again. I thought of shoving the mantle into the sink, knowing I would be too cold without it. Finally, I clamped the cushion over my ear. With the sound muffled, I started to slide into a doze.

Paige.

I bolted upright, every fine hair on end. A whisper in my mind —my name, clear as a stricken bell.

Arcturus?

Silence answered on both planes, but he was closer than before. He was coming. Solaced by the thought, I clapped the cushion back over my ear and slept.

****

A Vigile slammed a tray on the coffee table, jerking me awake. Before I could fully remember where I was, he was gone, and the door was locked.

I remembered soon enough. Sore all over, I sat up, the mantle around my shoulders, and examined the meal. One heel of stale bread, scabbed with mold, and a small glass of milk. I nibbled around the mold, but left the drink. I knew spoiled milk when I smelled it.

The Hôtel Garuche was beginning to wake. When dreamscapes started to trickle in, and Frère stirred in her room, I knew it must be almost six. Cade was already up and pacing.

Fear warred with my resolve. I could defy Ménard. Steal another body. Search the Salon Doré. Grow a spine. How many times had I stared death in the face before, and how many times had I cheated it?

If I failed to find Sheol II, I was condemning the voyants there to enslavement and death. I needed to be brave for them. Yet every time I started to dislocate, I saw myself trapped in another dark room.

Cade had promised to get me out of this cell. I would wait and see if he came through.

The sun ascended. I brushed my teeth. Another Vigile threw down my lunch, which consisted of an apple bruised with rot and a slab of white meat I decided not to touch. Thirst scraped my throat dry. I could have killed for a coffee.

My hunger was so distracting, I failed to notice the subtle changes in the æther. Suddenly the door unlocked and creaked open, and a dark-haired child appeared.

"Oh." Mylène blinked as if I had startled her. "You're a person."

There was no way Frère or Ménard would have allowed their daughter to visit me in my cell. When I probed the æther, I realized the Vigiles had left their posts.

"Last I checked." I offered a smile. "I don't think you're supposed to be here."

"I know. I sneak up sometimes, even though I'm not allowed." Mylène spoke in fluting English. "I heard Maman say there was a bad thing in the attic, but there's just you. Are *you* the aboma . . . abunash . . . aba . . . " She blew out a frustrated breath. 'I don't remember how to say it."

"Abomination," I said, pronouncing it the French way. "Is that it?" She gasped. "Yes!"

"Do you know what that word means?" I spoke gently. "It's not a very nice thing to call someone."

Mylène scuffed her buckled shoe along the floor. "Maman says." There was dust all over her red frock. "I like your hair," she ventured. "It's not like monster hair."

"How do you know about monsters?" I asked her. My grandfather had thrilled me with tales of headless riders and children transformed into swans when I was little, but they told far duller stories here.

"It's a secret," Mylène informed me.

"I should think so." I sat back. "Go on, then. What kind of hair do monsters have?"

"Green?"

In spite of myself, I smiled again, and Mylène smiled back. Against the odds, an amaurotic child had found a way to dream of green-haired monsters in Scion. There was some hope in that.

To my dismay, little Jean-Michel appeared behind her. He held a fleecy blanket that looked as if it had been gnawed at every corner.

"I'm Jean-Michel," he whispered. "Excuse me, but who are you?"

"Jean-Mi," Mylène hissed, "we're not supposed to tell strangers our names."

Jean-Michel just chewed his blanket and gazed at me with huge calf eyes. I got off the daybed and crouched in front of them.

"Hello, Jean-Michel," I said. "I'm Paige. It's very nice of you to let me stay in your house."

"Your voice is funny," Jean-Michel said.

"Well, my accent is different from yours. I come from a country called Ireland."

His eyes somehow grew even larger. "Isn't that a bad place?"

"Maman says it's bad," Mylène said, before I could get a word in. "I don't think we're supposed to talk to you. I just wanted to see what an abomination was. Onésime says we should always do exactly what Maman tells us."

"Is Onésime your big brother?" I asked.

"Yes. He went back to school today. He's ten this year. I'm Mylène Édith," she said. "I'm seven and a half. And Jean-Mi is four. Look, he has all his baby teeth."

Jean-Michel proved it with a big smile. Suddenly, painfully, I remembered that my grandmother would leave a silver coin under my pillow whenever I lost a tooth.

Scion had conscripted my father when I was only a little older than Mylène. He had uprooted me from Ireland, but I had clung to the memory of it. It had kept me sane, reminding me each day that there were other ways to live, a world beyond Scion. Mylène and Jean-Michel had known nothing else.

"Will you play with us?" Jean-Michel asked shyly. "We like to play hide-and-seek up here."

"Do you, now?"

He nodded. "When Maman and Papa are busy."

"This used to be where Mamie Caroline lived," Mylène said. I knew from my research that Luce had brought her late mother here to nurse her during her final illness. "Maman stopped us coming here after she died, but I found a secret way in, and Jean-Mi followed me one day. The Vigiles aren't supposed to go out all at once, but they sometimes do, so we play here until they come back."

This could be useful.

"That sounds like fun." I smiled. "You must do a lot of exploring. Can you show me the secret way?"

Mylène eyed me. "But then you could escape. And you're a monster."

"Hey, I thought we agreed I'm *not* a monster?" I crossed my eyes, and they both laughed. "It's all right if you don't want to tell me, though. I know it's your secret. I have secrets, too."

"You do?"

"Lots." When I sat down on the floor, they copied me. "You said you come here when your parents are busy. Are they busy now?"

"Yes, with the war." Mylène looked resigned. "It's so boring. And Papa is always too cross and tired to play with us."

"Cross?" I tilted my head. "About what?"

"He never *says* he's cross. I just know."

"I wish we had friends," Jean-Michel said wistfully in his tiny voice. "Onésime does."

"Onésime goes to school in Valençay," Mylène told me. I knew from the dossier that it was the most expensive boarding school in France. "We have tutors. Maman doesn't like us to go outside, except in the gardens. She says the bad anormales would kidnap us." She considered me. "But maybe you are a nice one, like Cade."

"Onésime says there are no nice anormales," Jean-Michel said, his voice muffled by his blanket.

"Cade must be, silly, because Maman and Papa have let him stay in our house."

"Oh."

"I don't know about Paige, though," Mylène added, giving me a look. She was the spitting image of Frère, but she had inherited that piercing stare from Ménard.

"Maybe I can prove I'm a good anormale." I looked between them. "We could play hide-and-seek, and I promise I won't try to escape. If I keep my promise, that proves I'm not a monster. Deal?"

Jean-Michel scrambled up, shyness forgotten. "Yes, please!"

"Are you good at it?" Mylène asked, bright eyed. "I'm the best."

These poor kids were so desperate for friends that they wanted to hang out with a prisoner in the attic. Good old Scion parenting. "I'm *very* good at it," I confirmed. "I've had a lot of practice."

"All right. We can play. But you can't be cross if I win. I always do." Mylène spoke as if this skill were a great burden. "Do you promise that, too?"

"Promise."

I followed the kids out of the room. Mylène took a set of keys from the lock and tucked it into her pocket.

It turned out that the room I had been confined in was one of several in the attic, which had clearly been a grand apartment at some point in the recent past. Dust swirled in wide bars of sunlight. Furniture had been pushed against the walls and draped with heavy-looking sheets.

I was out of my cell. Now I had to get out of the attic.

Mylène spun as she crossed the floorboards, making her frock wheel around her. "Do you live somewhere nice, Paige?"

"Very nice," I said, thinking of the safe house. "I'm staying with a friend."

"Maman says that all anormales live in squalor."

"What does *squalor* mean?" Jean-Michel piped up as he clambered over a dust-covered chest.

Mylène hesitated and looked to me. "Dirt," I said.

Both children looked solemn for a moment. "Well," Mylène said, pulling on a ringlet, "some anormales must deserve it. They do bad things and hurt people and steal and lie. Onésime said that—"

"Good morning, everyone."

I stopped. Ahead of us, Cade was leaning against the wall, arms folded. When Jean-Michel ran to him, Cade scooped him up.

"Cade!"

"Hello, you." Cade chuckled. "Showing our guest your secret hideout, are we, Mylène?"

"We are testing Paige," Mylène informed him. "If she plays hide-and-seek with us and doesn't run away, then she's a good anormale. If she's mean or tries to escape, we tell Papa and she has to have her head cut off."

His gaze darted to me. "That sounds like a fun game."

I stared him out.

"I've got to take Paige to see someone now," he said, setting Jean-Michel down and ruffling his hair. Mylène looked sulky. "Hey, you can play another time. Your maman wants you to join her in her apartments. Better get there quick, or the baby will eat all your breakfast."

Mylène sucked in a huge breath. "No!"

She grabbed Jean-Michel by the hand, and they took off, back toward my room, leaving me alone with Cade. I watched the kids until they were out of sight, none the wiser as to how they had got up here in the first place.

"I take it the game was your idea." Cade sighed. "Paige, you need to tread carefully for both our sakes. They're sweet kids, but if they get overexcited and tell Luce—"

"—I'll be sent to my death. Which will happen anyway," I said, "once Ménard realizes I'm worse than useless to him."

"Help him, then."

"We've been over this. Over my bones will the Butcher of Strasbourg have the Mime Order."

"I know," he said. "But I want to show you something that might just put the issue in a new light." He strode toward the stairs. "Come on. I'd like you to meet a friend of mine."

****

We made our way down to the next floor, where a single day Vigile guarded the door to the attic. Her hand strayed toward her baton when we approached.

"Vigile." Cade lowered his gaze. "The Grand Inquisitor granted us permission to leave."

"I am aware." She opened the door. "Keep to the agreed route."

We stepped through. Cade held a finger to his lips, then hurried me across a corridor and down another flight of stairs to the ground floor. We passed a room full of voices and dreamscapes before he swung me around a corner and stopped next to a velvet curtain.

"You're about to see the greatest secret in Scion."

"I thought the Rephaim were the greatest secret in Scion," I said.

He gave me an odd look as he pulled the crimson fabric aside. "There's more."

"Right. Anytime you want to stop being unnecessarily enigmatic, Cade, be my guest."

The curtain hid a small door, which he opened with a key. I had to duck my head to fit into the passage beyond, which led to yet another set of steps, this time made of stone. Cade pocketed the key and took a flashlight from a wall-mounted charger. I tried to ignore the sense of the walls closing in as we made our way underneath the Hôtel Garuche.

When we reached the end of the staircase, Cade tapped a code into a keypad, unlocking a foot-thick door. Once we were inside, he directed the flashlight toward the ceiling.

"This is a safe room. Protects the Inquisitorial family from invasion and disaster, including nuclear warfare," he explained. "Used to be a wine cellar, apparently, before Scion."

"The greatest secret in Scion is hidden in this cellar." I stifled a cough. "Is it a stash of wine?"

"Actually, Ménard is one of the few Scion officials who doesn't secretly drink. In fact, I doubt he's ever broken a law. Scion is in his bones, his blood. He's the embodiment of the anchor." He glanced over his shoulder at me. "That's what makes him the perfect man to fight the Rephaim. Other officials—the ones who taste forbidden pleasures and benefit from voyant knowledge—could ignore the hypocrisy of working for the Rephaim. Ménard can't."

"You're not endearing him to me."

"I'm not trying to. He's a cold-blooded bastard, but he's a cold-blooded bastard with power and money. And that's what we'll need if we're to stand a chance against the Rephaim."

He had a point. Without Alsafi and his network of embezzlers, the Mime Order would soon burn through its reserves.

"You're considering it." Seeing me shiver, Cade said, "Do you want my jacket?"

"I'm fine."

He nodded and pressed ahead, past crates and shelves, before he stopped and pointed his flashlight. I stared at what its beam revealed.

A Rephaite.

Even though he sat on the floor, I could see he would be taller than Arcturus standing—taller, in fact, than any Rephaite I had ever laid eyes on. His muscled arms were shackled to the wall above his head, each thicker than both of mine put together. Iron chains twined with familiar red blossoms crisscrossed his torso, which was gray where the flowers touched it. He looked as if he could tear me in two with his bare hands.

He was also asleep, or unconscious, his face still. Dark hair fell in waves to his waist.

"What is this?" I asked Cade under my breath. "And *who* is this?"

"Nashira sent him in October. He was meant to . . . persuade Ménard to sign the Great Territorial Act, then to stay on as a keeper in Sheol II." Cade handed me the flashlight and gave one of the chains a tug. "Morning, Kornephoros. I brought someone to meet you."

Kornephoros. That was a name that tasted of power.

The chains scraped and clinked. Slowly, I shone the flashlight at the Rephaite. His sarx was silver, warmed by the faintest undertone of copper.

"Fitzours." The voice was deep and scorched. "Here you are again."

Cade saluted. The Rephaite lifted his head, and his eyes, subdued by hunger, settled on me.

"Another red aura," he said softly. "How perfectly you match. I hope this one is for me."

"Absolutely not," Cade said. "And you treat her like food at your peril."

"Why, you *are* defensive today, Fitzours. Could this be your mate?"

"I'm not his type," I said. Cade pursed his lips.

The Rephaite looked between us. He bore a close resemblance to Terebell, with the same strong features—though his mouth, which had an amused set to it, was more generous than hers. A scar cleaved his chest from his left shoulder all the way down to his last rib on the other side. I should have sensed him as soon as I'd gotten here, but his dreamscape was little more than a watermark in the æther.

"Who are you, then, human?" he asked me. "Why does Ménard have you in his home?"

"You first," I said. "Who are *you*, Rephaite?"

"You have the privilege of standing before Kornephoros, Warden of the Sheratan."

"Never heard of him. The only Warden of the Sheratan I know is Terebellum."

"My Ranthen cousin." Kornephoros reclined into his chains. "She gave up the right to be Warden when she chose the losing side. It is my title now. Just as it always should have been."

"You sound very impressed with yourself," I remarked. "I'm looking for a reason why."

His lip curled. I had grown used to Rephaim over the past year —their stature, their auras—but, even chained to a wall, this one reminded me how brittle and mortal I was.

"Perhaps you do not need to introduce yourself," Kornephoros said. "Could it be that you are Paige Mahoney, the dreamwalker who has tempted the great Arcturus Mesarthim into flesh-treachery?"

"How disappointing," I said, "that someone of your clear importance should trouble himself with gossip."

"But you are the human in question."

"I am."

"Paige Mahoney." He regarded me with newfound interest. "I expected him to be drawn to someone taller."

"Okay, first off, I am taller than average," I said, nettled. Beside me, I heard Cade snort. "Second, the whole thing is a fabrication. Arcturus and I are allies."

Kornephoros kept looking at me, relentless.

"I thought so," he said. "The blood-sovereign is judicious in so many things, but even to discredit the Ranthen, it was unwise of her to tell what was so plainly a lie. Even the former Warden of the Mesarthim—a wanton traitor to his kind—would not stoop so low as to lie with a human."

I doubt even his standards are this low.

My wrists began to ache. All at once, the underground shelter was the basement, and I was tied like cold meat, basted with my own vomit, and a red-eyed Rephaite was whispering in my ear.

"Have I upset you?" That charred voice brought me back to the present. "If you wish to cry, do. We Rephaim cannot weep. I find it charming."

I recovered my composure. "Another Rephaite sadist," I said. "Are you friends with Thuban Sargas, by any chance?"

"Do not liken me to that craven. He spends his time pulling the wings off mayflies. I prefer prey that fights back." His eyes grew just a little hotter. "Tell me, how *is* Arcturus?"

"Far away, I imagine." I pointed the flashlight at Cade. "So this is your big secret. Does he have a gift we can use, or have you worked out how to weaponize arrogance?"

"He does have an interesting gift," Cade admitted, "but that's not why I brought you to see him." He turned back to his prisoner. "I'm afraid we're not here for a heart-to-heart, Kornephoros. I'm here to give Paige a demonstration."

The trace of a smirk left Kornephoros, turning his face to metal.

"When I leave this place, Fitzours," he said, "I will make you rue the day you helped them incarcerate me."

"Yes, I'll die with my head on backward. We've been over the details." Cade glanced at me sidelong. "Paige, you might consider taking a step back."

I raised an eyebrow and stayed exactly where I was. Cade approached a steel trolley. When he came back into my flashlight, he was holding a syringe.

"Sorry, my friend," he said to Kornephoros. "You know I hate this."

"Head on backward," was the cold reply. "I will hear your spine *crunch* between my—"

Cade struck. The needle hit Kornephoros hard in the crease of his right arm.

What happened next was swift and brutal. The light in his eyes guttered. His aura pulled inward, as if it were bound as fast as the rest of him. Mottled bruising spread from the puncture in his arm, all the way to his fingertips, and fanned across his shoulder, into his chest.

A chill sharpened the air. My flashlight shook. Kornephoros strained against his chains—so hard I heard the crack of bone—and let out an awful noise, rough stone across metal. It woke a memory I had tried to suppress.

A forest in the dead of night. Endless trees, and that buzzing, like a swarm of carrion flies. Running across a land strewn with mines, pursued by a thing that screamed for my flesh. My wrist snapping under the weight of my fall.

Emite . . .

"Stop," I barked at Cade. "I've seen enough."

He was already back with a syringe of darker fluid. Kornephoros snarled at him like an animal, teeth snapping together. Cade flinched beyond their reach and stabbed him in the abdomen.

Kornephoros went limp. His head rolled forward. I tightened my grip on the flashlight as he shuddered, his giant hands clenching into fists.

For a long time, all I heard was my own breath. Finally, Kornephoros looked at Cade. Light waxed back into his eyes, embers blown into red flame. His aura brightened to match. Cade took a few drunken steps backward, and I steadied him before he could topple over.

"You okay?"

"Yeah," he said in a strained voice. "Never feels any better when they feed." Blood seeped from his hazel eye. "You understand now."

You will work it out yourself, Arcturus had told me. *You are perceptive, and you have all the pieces. Sooner or later, you will fit them together.*

"Yes," I said softly. "I understand."

Arcturus had been right. I had seen more than enough to work it out. Yet never once had I allowed myself to fit the pieces together, because never once had I imagined that the Ranthen would have kept a secret of that magnitude from me. Especially not him.

In 1859, the English government had secretly relinquished control to the Rephaim, believing only Nashira Sargas could protect humankind from the Emim—the flesh-eating creatures of nightmare that had come from their world to ours. They had thought she was a benevolent guardian, come to save us from the monsters at our door.

She had declined to mention one very fine detail.

They all had.

"The Emim," I said. "The Emim . . . are Rephaim. Or were, at least."

I couldn't take my eyes off Kornephoros. Bone-jolting aftershocks racked his frame.

"They call it the half-urge." Cade walked back to the trolley. "As far as I can tell, Rephs are immune to all human pathogens. I've injected him with smallpox, malaria, syphilis, even plague—no dice. This is the one and only sickness they can get."

Distantly, I wondered just how many times Cade had tried to make this Rephaite ill.

"To pass on the half-urge," Cade continued, "all an Emite has to do is bite or claw a Rephaite, hard enough to break their sarx. As soon as that happens, the Rephaite starts to run out of time."

The Emim carry an infection called the half-urge, which causes madness and death if left untreated.

Arcturus had told me that in the colony, before I had learned enough about the Rephaim to question him. Terebell must have already sworn him to secrecy. I closed my eyes for a moment.

"How did you infect Kornephoros just now?" I asked.

"Injected him with pure Emite blood, which speeds up the process. Don't ask how I got it."

"Is there a cure?"

"Yeah. Aura." Cade took a tissue from his pocket and dabbed his eyes. "Unfortunately, they lose the ability to feed as soon as the half-urge is in them. Salt and human blood restore that ability long enough for them to find a voyant and start healing."

183

Sealed vials of blood in the colony, ready to be delivered to the Ranthen. Just in case.

"You learned this through experimenting on Kornephoros," I said.

"I didn't have a choice in the matter, Paige. Ménard told me to find their weaknesses, their secrets. He doesn't want to get his own hands covered in this sort of unnaturalness."

Kornephoros himself seemed unable to speak. He was heavy in his chains, chest heaving.

"The Rephaim told us they would shield us from the Emim. We swallowed it whole," I said. "What we actually did was let a bunch of potential Emim into the highest circles of power." I breathed out through my nose. "Humans. The chumps of the universe."

"Not all humans, in this case," Cade muttered. "England has believed for centuries that it has a divine right to do whatever it wants. The fact that these angelic figures chose it as their seat of power . . . I assume it only deepened that sense of superiority."

"Oh, yes," Kornephoros said throatily. "I was there. Worthless, proud, hidebound men. All too willing to exchange their true power for the delusion that gods had descended to bless them."

I could believe it.

"When I got back, I told Ménard about the Rephaim training us to fight the Emim." Cade scrunched up the tissue. "Even though he was sickened, he thought, like our ancestors, that we might need their protection. But he still didn't want them in France."

"So he avoided signing the Great Territorial Act. Nashira sent Kornephoros to intimidate him," I recounted. "Ménard imprisoned him, and together you discovered . . . this. That the Emim are former Rephaim. And that ended any doubts Ménard had about the need to overthrow them."

"He realized they were two sides of a coin. Vectors of unnaturalness."

"Has he told Tjäder?"

"If not, he will. Not that Tjäder needs further persuasion that the Rephs have to go. She saw them herself."

As I stood there, cold inside and out, a thought occurred to me.

"Cade," I said quietly, "is this also what happens if Rephaim don't take aura for long enough?"

"I wondered the same, but I haven't tested it. Kornephoros is my only lab rat. I don't want to lose him just yet." Cade cut him a glance. "I asked, but he hasn't been forthcoming."

"I can't imagine why."

Kornephoros looked between us.

"You must be clever, Paige Mahoney, for my cousin to have chosen you for an ally," he said to me. "Perhaps you are beginning to understand the dangers of your little revolution."

I looked back at him. A picture was forming, darker by the moment.

"At present, the Emite threat remains . . . in hand," he went on. "Should Inquisitor Ménard oust us from Scion, however, we will be forced to the outskirts of civilization, leaving us more vulnerable to the half-urge." He canted his head. "We Rephaim can be ruthless, but we can also be reasonable. We can be moved to mercy, or persuaded to promote human interests. Where would you find yourselves if that compassion was engulfed by mindless hunger?"

"In hell," I said. "The only way to stop it would be to seal every last one of you back in the Netherworld."

"Yes. Sadly, that is no longer possible, since the veils are now eternally torn." His gaze bored into mine. "Scion is how we coexist, dreamwalker. You ought to leave the anchor well alone."

11

Changeling

C ade had a cleaner and larger room than mine, upholstered with tawny satin. There was even a radio. A Vigile had brought us a platter of cold meats and fruit, hot saloop, and a log of white cheese. A fire crackled beside us. This, then, was how Ménard rewarded submission.

"You should eat, Paige." Cade swallowed his mouthful. "You need your strength."

The meats glistened in the ashen sunlight. I looked toward the window, my gaze distant.

I was more clearheaded now that we had left the cellar. Down there in the dark, with Kornephoros, every word had rung with doom. Up here in the attic, I was calmer. I could think.

"My first thought was that Ménard must plan to expose the Rephaite presence in our world," I said, breaking a minute-long silence. "To rally people against them. Drive them out." I shook my head. "But no. He wouldn't do that. It would mean open war, and he already has enough war to manage. There are too many risks. Too many potential outcomes."

"You're getting to know him already." Cade began to peel an orange. "For someone who detests fortune-tellers as much as he does, Ménard hates not being able to see the future. No, he'll keep the truth close to his chest and try to remove the Rephaim quietly."

I nodded once. Cade ate the orange and poured winter cordial into two cut-glass tumblers.

"He plans to keep everything the same in Scion, except for the balance of power." He slid one toward me. "He wants to spin the wheel. Turn the anchor. In his world, amaurotics will be on top and Rephaim at the bottom. Voyants still get crushed in the middle, naturally. He'll use Sheol II to keep unnaturals in their place. All unnaturals."

I grasped the arms of the chair. Trying not to sound too interested, I said, "Do you know where Sheol II is?"

"No. They wouldn't share that kind of state secret with an unnatural, even a house-trained one."

"Frère never let it slip?"

He glanced at me. "You mean pillow talk?"

"If the shoe fits. I assumed that was how you were getting all this information about Ménard."

"Luce isn't stupid, Paige. She just happens to get off on screwing an unnatural on the sly," he said. "Possibly because her spouse thinks any, er, loss of control invites the æther."

I raised an eyebrow. "Seriously?"

"I know. Ces amaurotiques." He gestured vaguely. "To answer your question, no, Luce did not disclose the location of Sheol II, and I would be on the guillotine by morning if I asked."

There was a trace of bitterness there.

"I thought he didn't want Sheol II on French soil," I said. Cade picked up a glass without comment, and I paused to think. "But now it's here, he'll use it."

"Exactly. He wants it to be a prison for all of us—Rephaim *and* voyants. That way, we can keep feeding them."

"He only needs a certain number of us to do that. I presume he'll kill the rest."

Cade lifted his glass to his lips. "He's not called the Butcher of Strasbourg for nothing."

Chills flickered up my sides.

"Sheol II would also keep the existing Emim away from other areas," Cade added. "Amaurotics can continue with their lives, untouched by the whole unnatural lot of us. That's how it will be until he figures out a way to remove the Rephs without creating more Emim."

"So that's why Ménard is footing the bill for all your . . . experimentation." I closed my ice-cold hands around my glass. "Someone must have come looking for Kornephoros."

"Of course." Cade tucked a slice of cured sausage into his mouth. "The Grand Overseer, no less."

Jaxon. It was the first I had heard of him being in Paris. I tried to keep my expression calm.

"He arrived here in November. Ménard told him Kornephoros never showed," Cade said. "I don't know whether he believed it or not. Still, he did finally persuade Ménard to sign the Great Territorial Act."

I could well believe that Jaxon had been the one to convince him. Words were his finest weapon.

"Is the Grand Overseer in Sheol II now?" I asked. "To your knowledge."

"I don't know everything. I'm just a canary," Cade said dryly. "But I would assume so."

"And you're okay with all of this." I raised my eyebrows. "After all we went through in the first colony, you think we should leave this second one alone and allow Ménard to execute his grand plan."

"Yes." His face betrayed his disquiet. "I don't like it, Paige, but war is a long game. I believe we should support Ménard until he succeeds in disempowering the Rephaim."

"And how does Ménard succeed in that, exactly?" I was skeptical. "He might have got lucky with Kornephoros, but he could never capture Nashira or Gomeisa. You've seen their power."

"I'll work out how to take it. I am going to find a way to destroy them without turning them. If that means I have to starve Kornephoros and see what happens, so be it."

As I scrutinized his face, I noticed the shadows under his eyes, darker than mine. Deep lines laced around them when his expression changed.

"I don't suppose *you* know anything about Rephaite weaknesses," he said. "Having worked so closely with them."

"Only that they're very averse to the poppy anemone, which you clearly already know."

"Yeah. I brought seeds back from the colony. Contact with those flowers constricts their auras," Cade said. "It also makes them *look* a bit like Emim—necrotic. Kornephoros sometimes calls that disfigurement *half-urge*, too, even though it's not the same condition. Just mimics the early stages of it. So . . . false half-urge."

"All those fancy words and that's where they choose to recycle."

Cade chuckled. "Rephs." He reached into his pocket and took out a single red bloom, slightly crushed. "Strange little things," he murmured. "Almost like someone put them here to warn us."

Without answering, I sipped my drink.

I did know another Rephaite weakness. I knew that a certain Netherworld substance could behead them, and I doubted they could get up again after, half-urge or not. Gut instinct warned me against telling Cade, perhaps because it felt for all the world like I was telling him how to hurt Arcturus.

Arcturus. Somewhere deep inside me, resentment simmered like a hearth of hot coals. He had warned me about his secret, but I was still frustrated with him for keeping it from me.

"I couldn't sense Kornephoros at first," I said.

"You wouldn't have. I've been experimenting with Emite blood," Cade explained. "I discovered it cuts the subject off from the æther. It also makes them much harder to detect."

"You've learned a lot." I tapped the arm of my chair. "That's what they gave me before the meeting."

"Yes. It makes it hard to use our gifts," Cade said. "The human body can't tolerate pure Emite blood very often, though. My self-experimentation involved a lot of puke." He sat back. "Ménard expects your answer tomorrow night, in the Salon Vert."

"You think any of this has changed my mind about working for him?"

"I hoped it would." Cade met my gaze. "I imagine he wants you as bait, or a bargaining tool. He knows how much Nashira wants you, and how much your survival will discredit the Rephaite-supporting Weaver. In the meantime, he'll treat you well and keep you safe."

He really thought this was an attractive offer. His face was full of resolve, his eyes bright with it. To my surprise, he reached across the table and placed a calloused hand over mine.

"Stay," he said. "We can make this work, Paige. Just wait a few more—"

Before I had a chance to cut him off, the door swept open, and he dropped my hand as if it were poisonous. Luce Ménard Frère stood in the doorway, dressed in black and white.

"Je veux lui parler seule." She sliced a glance toward Cade. "Quittez ma vue, anormal, tout de suite."

He left without a word. Frère didn't look at him. Instead, she watched me, and I watched her.

"Stand up," she said in English.

I rose. Frère crossed the room at her leisure, taking in what remained of the food. When she was near, she scaled and peeled me with her gaze. Her lips were red, her lashes brushed with lampblack. The last time I had seen her face this close, I had been looking into a mirror.

She backhanded me. I could feel that she had thrust every ounce of her loathing into the blow, but her hand was weak, inexpert. Her spousal ring still cut my cheek.

"That," she said, "is for polluting my home. For drawing breath where my mother lived."

I forced myself to look back at her, my cheek throbbing. That was when I saw what was in her other hand: a heavy-looking fire iron, ending in a blunt hook.

"And this is for fouling my body. For my child," she said softly. "For whatever your despicable violation might have done to them."

Before I could speak, she struck me hard in the knee, buckling my leg, then belted me across the ribs. And straight away, I was back in the room, the white room where Vigiles had mauled and spat on me. This time, I made no attempt to fight back. I curled straight into a ball.

It felt like years before the beating stopped. She hit old bruises and made new ones. The worst part was when the iron smashed my elbow, sending a shock all the way to my fingers and jolting heat into my eyes. All I could think was that I had to protect myself without hurting Frère. Ménard would not see that as self-defense. Neither would the Vigiles.

When the iron split my lip, anger overcame self-preservation. I flung out a hand and grabbed her weapon, and our gazes locked across it. My arm was stronger than hers. Both of us were panting. Her face was smeared with perspiration, pupils down to punctures.

"If you dare contaminate my body with your presence again, espèce de monstruosité, I will make sure yours is a hell to inhabit." When Frère jerked my chin up, her manicured nails dug into my skin. "Benoît seems to think you have value, but I know you will always work against us."

"I know something, too," I whispered. "I know your secret, Luce." Her nails pressed deeper. "Your child is unnatural. You're an unnatural progenitor, and your precious Benoît will kill you for it."

Her hand was white-knuckled on the iron. A flicker of apprehension crossed her face.

"Touch me again," I said, "and I will tell him." Blood leaked down my chin. "I will send you to the guillotine you love so much."

Little by little, her composure returned. So did her cruel smile.

"Benoît would never hurt me for falling under unnatural influence. Vigile," she called, and handed the iron to the one that came. When he was gone, she turned back to me. "Do not imagine you have any power over me, anormale. Here, you are the marionette."

She drew a silk handkerchief from her skirt and wiped my blood from her ring with it. The bite of metal filled my mouth. My threat had just rolled off her, and I couldn't fathom why.

"Your father tried to save his own skin, you know." She looked down at me. "They examined him for information on your whereabouts. Do you know what he told them?"

I reached for a reply, but the words refused to come. Even if she intended it to hurt me, she was offering me knowledge about his final hours, and I owed it to him to listen.

"He swore you had never belonged to him. That you were not his child," Frère told me. "He renounced you, calling you a changeling and all manner of superstitious babble." She tossed the handkerchief into the fire. "It might have saved him, had Vance's plan not necessitated his death. He went to the block despising you."

The handkerchief lay in the hearth. I focused on it. The intricate lacework. The blood-spotted silk. It would have fetched a few coins at the black market. Enough to fill a hollow stomach.

"His head is staked on the Lychgate. I hear Weaver had it boiled in brine to keep it fresh," Frère said. I kept my gaze firmly on the handkerchief, watching as the flames consumed it. "Because your father was a servant of the anchor, you could not love him enough to save his life. Do not tell me that, as Underqueen, you did not have the means to try."

Her wristwatch let out a small *ping* before I could answer her charge. Frère glanced at it, then shoved my head down to the floor and strode away.

****

The Vigiles threw me back into my own room and locked it. There was no fire or food. Even the mantle had been withdrawn. I washed the blood from my chin and huddled up on the daybed, preserving warmth as best I could.

My father had been tortured before they murdered him. I tried not to imagine what they might have done to draw my whereabouts from his lips.

He had called me a changeling. A fey creature. When I was still young enough for a cot, my grandmother had hung a pair of iron scissors nearby, to ward off any fairy that might carry me away and leave a síofra in my place. Years before, she had done the same for my father and aunt.

Frère was Scion-born. She couldn't know the word *changeling* unless he really had said it. He had never given much credence to the stories my grandmother honored, but with his last breath, he had used them against me. He had refused to acknowledge me as his daughter—or, apparently, as human.

He must truly have been afraid of me. All my life, he had been afraid. I hadn't imagined it.

I shook myself. People changed under torture. I had not given in on the waterboard, despite the pain and humiliation, but Suhail Chertan had been under strict instructions not to do any enduring damage. My father could have suffered anything.

Exhaustion sank its hooks into me. I would have a fresh coat of bruises by morning. Frère lacked strength, but anger and a foot-long bar of iron made for a powerful combination.

I had to get out of here. Ducos needed the information I had.

Except I still didn't have the location of Sheol II. Even after a sound beating, the thought of leaving without that knowledge was too bitter to swallow. Twice I had come close enough to taste it. Twice it had eluded me. Instead, I had unexpected knowledge, and I had no idea what to do with it.

Arcturus had wanted to tell me about the Rephaim becoming Emim. Whatever oath had stopped him, it must have been strong. *Trust has no room for façades.* A blurred memory, soaked in dark wine. *I would look on your true face, little dreamer. And know that you had looked on mine.*

His wish had come true. At last, I knew the secret he had kept for nearly a year.

My head listed to the side. I could allow myself a short rest, after everything. When I breathed in, a barb scored the right side of my chest. I had barely dozed off when an explosion slapped me awake.

At first, the total darkness was disorienting. When my thigh smarted, I remembered where I was. I must have slept for the whole afternoon and deep into the evening.

Another explosion. Fireworks. Bleary-eyed, I groped my way to the window, one hand on my aching rib cage. There was a commotion in the front courtyard. Shouts and cheers. Another firework wheeled over the mansion and fractured into splinters of red and white light. From the sound of it, they were going off all over the citadel.

In the courtyard, Vigiles pulled off their helmets and embraced one another. The night staff poured down the front steps to dance in the snow. I had never witnessed so much joy in Scion, not even at Novembertide or New Year. It was something like madness.

This could only mean one thing. Lisbon had fallen. I turned my back on the window, sick with grief for Portugal.

I remembered the Fall of Ireland so clearly. The day our leader, Eóghan Ó Cairealláin, had finally issued our formal and unconditional surrender. Throughout the Molly Riots, he had spurred us to resist the invaders, to protect our independence from what he had called a cult of hatred. Some had condemned him for his obstinacy, blamed him for the bloodshed, while others had declared him a hero.

Ó Cairealláin had met his end on the gallows that December. His replacement was the first and present Grand Inquisitor of Ireland, who had anglicized her name to April Whelan.

We were in London by then, of course. The night of the surrender, my father and I had gone into hiding. He had collected me from school early—before the official announcement—and got us chips for supper. Once we were home, he had explained that we needed to stay inside for a while. Ireland was now part of Scion. Things would get worse before they got better.

I hadn't been afraid for myself. Even though the other children tormented me at school, nothing could be worse than the bloodbath I had narrowly survived in Dublin. All I had been able to think about was my beloved grandparents, who would soon be dead, like my cousin.

At dusk, my father had spoken to the security guard and locked up the apartment. The two of us had huddled up together on the couch, one of my old toys squashed between us, and pretended to watch a film. That was the last time I could remember him holding me. Even though dread had squeezed my insides, I had felt warm and safe. He had drawn me so close I had felt him shivering. His parents were in Ireland. His sister, grief-stricken over her son. He had lost everyone but me.

The fireworks had gone on and on, each detonation reaching my bones. My father had not sent me to bed. Our apartment had been high up, the windows shut fast, but we had still heard their joy. In the end, I had fallen asleep against his chest, my cheeks salted with tears.

Fifty-seven settlers, most of them homeless, had been killed or beaten that night. A few Scots had died, too, the Sasanaigh hearing something other in their voices. Years later, the exultant screams rang in my memory. The same fevered crows of triumph that cracked the frozen air tonight.

My father had kept me home from school for a month, saying I had whooping cough. During that time, he had been gentle with me. Checked how I was feeling and brought treats home. The other children had pounced when I returned—they had tripped me in the corridors, spat on my hair, emptied offal into my bag and laughed when I got the blood on my hands—but it would have been worse in those early days of victory. And for the first time in years, I had walked those corridors armored with the certainty that I was loved.

My father had soon enclosed himself in ice once more. I wished he were still here so I could ask him why. Why he had never comforted me again, or explained anything, or tried to soothe me when I raged. Why he had never once acted like a father to me after that time—except on the night of my arrest. I wished he was here so I could hide from the world with him just one more time.

Portugal had fallen in little more than a month. For the first time, it occurred to me that ScionIDE might have swelled its ranks with Irish conscripts.

When another victorious bellow raked my spine, I switched my attention to the æther. There were no dreamscapes nearby. Or anywhere on the floor below. Eager to join the celebrations, the Vigiles had forsaken their post outside my door.

A chance to get into the Salon Doré. In an instant, I was at the door to my cell, rattling the handle. Still locked. I waited for another firework, ready to fling my weight against the door.

Footsteps. I backed off, heart pounding. A moment later, the lock clicked, and then Cade was in the room, wearing a nightshirt and shorts. Shadows circled his eyes.

"They've taken Lisbon," he said. "I thought—" He stared at my face. "Shit, Paige, what happened to you?"

"Not important. How the hell did you get in?"

He held up a ring of keys I had seen before. "Luce's old set. I know where Mylène hides it."

"Good." I was already brushing past him. "I need to get into the Salon Doré while they're all distracted. I need to crack his safe."

"You won't." Cade caught my bad wrist. I took a sharp breath, then regretted it. "Paige, just listen. You need a registered fingerprint to access the study, and even then, there's a manual lock to get past." He seemed exasperated. "Maybe if you told me what you were looking for—"

"I can't."

"You don't trust me."

"Nothing personal. I don't trust anyone." My voice was on the verge of cracking. "I'll find a way."

"If they catch you, you'll never leave this room again. Consider a deal. Earn his trust, like I did. Wait for him to drop his guard." Cade grasped my elbow. "Don't risk it. Think of the bigger picture."

The next firework made us both glow red as embers. Red as our shared order. Something about his aura had distracted me, and I couldn't put my finger on what. He let go.

"I can't stay, Cade." I motioned to my swollen cheek, my lip. "Frère will kill me for what I did to her."

A muscle in his jaw rolled out. "Yes." He turned away. "I can't help you tonight, Paige. Get some rest. Tomorrow, if you still want to escape, we'll work it out."

"Wait," I said. He stopped. "President Gonçalves. Do you know if she issued a surrender?"

"Not yet. Guess she's holed up in a bunker somewhere."

I could almost see her now. Caught like prey in some underground room. Ears pricked for heavy boots at the door. One hand on a gun, either to shoot the invaders or herself. Either that, or it was a pen she held, and she was poised to sign her name to the surrender.

Even if she signed, her life might still be forfeit. Only if they were in a forgiving mood would they allow her to stay on as Grand Inquisitor.

"I'm sorry," Cade murmured. "I know I can't ever understand, Paige, but I'm sorry."

With a gentle squeeze of my shoulder, he left me to the silence in the attic, and the bitter sound of the festivities outside. I sank back onto the daybed and stared at the ceiling.

Deep in the night, my eyes snapped open, and I breathed in, pain knifing into my chest.

I knew exactly how I was going to find Sheol II.

12

Moth in the Wall

The celebrations went on all night. Fireworks. Parades. Never-ending anthems and cheering on Rue du Faubourg. Half the citadel seemed to have gathered at the gates of the Hôtel Garuche to rejoice. The voices outside soared to fever pitch, shearing my nerves thin.

At some point, I must have drifted off. When I woke, golden light shone through the window and tinseled the dust in the air. There was a blanket tucked around my shoulders and two small pills on the table, along with a cup of tea. Cade had also left me his radio.

It was silent outside. The citadel had reveled itself to exhaustion.

At ten, it came back to life. Red hot-air balloons took flight over the citadel. An hour later, the aerobatic division of the Inquisitorial Air Force performed a display. Their smoke trails crisscrossed the blue sky. Wrapped in the blanket, I washed the painkillers down and tuned the radio to the news. I listened as the presenter announced a national holiday. Except for those in vital services, all denizens could leave work to celebrate. Frank Weaver called upon Daniela Gonçalves, who was still in hiding, to issue her unconditional surrender.

Gonçalves must be in a private hell. Her surrender would end the bombardment ("Scion is merciful, President Gonçalves, take heart"). It would also end all formal resistance.

In her fortified room, Gonçalves would be asking how she could justify her actions to whichever god or code she held dear. This choice would cement her place in history. It would decide whether she was remembered as a traitor or a martyr, a coward or a hero. The longer she postponed, the more of her people would die. Even though Scion had the capital, air strikes on other cities would not cease until the surrender.

At noon, I heard Ménard live on the radio. He stressed the crucial role of French soldiers in taking Lisbon—they had formed the bulk of the invasion force—and commended the Grand Commander of France for his swift and decisive actions on the frontline. Lavish celebrations were planned in the event of an official surrender, including a masquerade at the Grande Salle de Paris, with guests chosen by lottery from all around France.

It chilled me that the conflict had escalated this quickly, after such a short period of resistance. When they had set their sights on Ireland, they had been forced to wear it down over several years, in a long war of attrition.

Europe stands on the verge of war. The continent is a tinderbox, hungry for a spark.

The spark was inching closer to the tinder. Soon it might burn hot enough to set the world alight.

By one, there was more breaking news. The Second Inquisitorial Division would now split. Half its forces would remain in Portugal to oversee the transition to Scion, while the rest would continue the campaign. The meaning was clear. Without so much as a pause for breath, Scion was going for Spain.

I would make a final attempt to find information on Sheol II. I knew who might have the location, and suspected he would be willing to sell it. Afterward, whether or not I succeeded, I would leave by whatever means necessary and get my intelligence to Domino.

Cade arrived at two with pastries and coffee. He pulled the door shut behind him, laid the tray on the table, then beckoned me close.

"Unsurprisingly, Ménard has canceled our discussion. He has press conferences and meetings for the rest of the day, and he's made a reservation for dinner in Le Marais." Cade spoke under his breath. "Take the opportunity and go."

"How?"

"The night staff arrive at eight. Possess a Vigile. Open your door."

"Then what?"

"Turn right out of your room and keep going until you see a portrait of Jacquemine Lang," he said. "Behind it, you'll find the hidden opening the kids use to get into the attic. It leads to a sealed-off staircase, which will take you down to the Winter Garden."

I pictured the floor plan. The Winter Garden was on the ground floor, attached to the Salle des Fêtes.

"The cook I bribe, Claudine, is the last to leave at night. She'll let you into the grounds through the kitchen. Don't get there later than eight thirty, or she'll have clocked off for—"

"Come with me."

He frowned. "What?"

"Join the Mime Order. You don't have to stay here, Cade," I said. "Sooner or later, Ménard will decide that you're more of a danger than an asset, or find out about the affair. He'll kill you." I held his gaze. "There are other ways to fight."

His brows knitted tighter.

"I want to see the baby. If I can," he said, a little hoarsely. "Just once, so I remember."

I couldn't deny him that. "This is goodbye, then. For now."

His face softened. "Yes."

To my surprise, he wrapped me into a tight embrace. As our auras flashed together, I had the sudden sense of falling, like I had missed a step. It was a sensation that both comforted and disconcerted me.

Whatever it was, it faded in the time it took for me to dip into his pocket and slide out his key to the cellar. I gave Cade a brief pat on the back, and after a long moment, he let go of me. The hairs on my arms stood on end.

"Take care of yourself," Cade said. "It was good to see you again, Paige."

"And you."

He offered a final smile before he knocked on the door and was summarily let out. I walked to the window and risked a look between the curtains. Arcturus was out there somewhere.

Tonight. I tried to weave a picture in my mind of my position. *I have a way out, but be ready to run.*

The softest tremor answered me. As I rolled the stolen key between my fingers, I savored the brief sensation of his presence. It would give me the strength to take this final risk.

****

Another small meal arrived. I drank every drop in the tureen of soup, ate every last crumb of bread. If I was going to get out of here without being shot, I would need enough strength to run, and to dreamwalk. After that, I lay still, the cellar key tucked into my blouse pocket, the shape of it concealed by my sweater.

Cade had told me to make my escape around eight. Before that, I was going to visit Kornephoros Sheratan.

When dusk mantled the citadel in shadow, I rose from the daybed and knocked on the door. A day Vigile unlocked and opened it, visor lowered, so I could only see his mouth. He was clad in full body armor, as if that would help against the only weapon I could presently use on him.

"What do you want?" he said.

"Water." I tried to look faint. "Please, Vigile."

His hand curled around the baton in his utility belt. "Fine," he said. "Get back inside, anormale. Now."

I took a meek step back. He slammed the door in my face. Before long, I sensed one of the other Vigiles heading downstairs. Three to go. I slid into the æther.

When I opened my eyes, I saw the world as if through stained glass. I had possessed the Vigile—the squadron leader—who stood outside my door. Out of sight, I removed the key from the lock and slipped it into a pocket on his utility belt.

The other two Vigiles were smoking next to an open window. I checked my host for weapons. All I had at my disposal were a baton and a flux gun. The gun would be too slow—flux took a while to work on amaurotics.

I had a transceiver. So did the pair by the window. Either of them would call for backup at the first sign of trouble. Ideally, I would sneak past and escape through the secret door without having to knock them all out. I needed to save my strength for life-or-death situations.

"You two should take a break," I said. After listening to my guards through the door all day, I could mimic the way this one spoke. "I'll watch the unnatural."

"I wish we could accept." One of them blew smoke out of the window. "But I'm not in the mood for another lecture from Kotzia."

"I won't tell if you don't." I tried to sound bored. "Half an hour. You can owe me a favor."

The two Vigiles exchanged glances, then shrugged and left their posts. As soon as they were out of sight, I unlocked my cell, dropped my host behind the daybed, and snapped back into my own body. The Vigile stirred. I pulled off his helmet and hit him over the head with his baton. He let out a low groan as I stole his transceiver and flux gun.

When the first guard returned with the water, I was ready. The moment she realized her squadmates were gone and reached for her transceiver, I sprang from my body and knocked her senseless. By some miracle, the glass rolled across the floor instead of breaking.

The base of my skull ached. I guessed I could use my gift once more without shattering my strength.

I grasped the second Vigile under the arms and towed her into my cell, where I stripped her of her utility belt and jacket and slung them on. Only then did I shoot both the half-conscious Vigiles in the neck with the flux gun. The drug would keep them down until someone found them and brought the antidote. With the way clear, I locked them into my cell and turned right.

For as long as the other two Vigiles stayed away, I had a head start. They would raise the alarm as soon as they returned.

The last daylight strained across the attic floor. I half-ran past furniture draped with dust sheets, keeping low. Every creak of the floorboards made me tense. At the western end of the attic, I found the life-sized portrait of Jacquemine Lang, framed in gold, leaning against the wall.

There was a small flashlight on my new belt. I illuminated the ornate panels behind the portrait and tested them for give. When I found the loose one, I pressed on it until it gave way, allowing me to move it aside. Cold air wafted from the pitch-black opening.

A false interior wall. I hunkered down on my stomach and slid through.

The ceiling snowed thick dust into my hair. I tried not to cough as I replaced the panel and shone the flashlight into the dark. Its beam revealed a set of cramped and winding stairs.

I pulled off my shoes and slotted them into my belt. As soon as I had my bearings, I switched off the flashlight and tucked it away. Light could seep through any cracks and betray my position. There were still at least a hundred dreamscapes in and around the Hôtel Garuche.

The darkness was crushing. Utterly blind, I edged down the staircase. The steps creaked underfoot. Any official working late could hear me through the thin wall that hid this forgotten part of the mansion. All the while, I was alert to the æther. It would do no good to run into Mylène and Jean-Michel.

They weren't close. Their father was.

I lowered myself down a few more steps. When I felt a draft, I switched my flashlight on and cupped my hand around the beam. There was an uneven opening to my right, just above my head.

The staircase continued to the ground floor. I should keep going, try to get to Kornephoros before my guards returned to the attic —but Ménard was so close, and the prospect of eavesdropping on him was too much of a temptation. I had come here to spy, after all. Before I could think better of it, I wedged my head and shoulders into the opening and squirmed through. With the flash-light clamped between my teeth, I used my hands to pull myself forwards until I could feel colder air above me. I surfaced in a tight passage and killed the light again.

Icy air leaked under my collar. I was in the hollow space behind a lath-and-plaster wall. Quiet as a spider, I moved along on my stomach, breath setting like honey.

Small spaces, I could handle. Not the dark. I swallowed and pressed on, even as dust scored my throat.

A voice thrummed nearby, to my left. That was Ménard—and he was with someone who seemed to have no dreamscape. When I could go no farther, I stopped and pressed my ear to the wall.

"—four days ago, Rackham," Ménard was saying. "I am not accustomed to waiting upon the pleasure of unnaturals."

I stayed absolutely still.

"Show me the names." After a long silence, Ménard spoke again, still in English. "This is extortion. Do you think me a fool, that I would pay these prices?"

"I would think you a wise man, Inquisitor Ménard," said his guest. "Consider it a form of insurance."

All feeling drained from my face. I knew that metallic voice, distorted by a mouthpiece. I had heard it only once—just before the scrimmage—but I could never forget.

I freed my arm from where it was pinned to my side, flexed the numbness from my fingers, and ran them along the wall, looking for anything that might help me see through it. They soon caught on a break in the laths. There was a hole in the plaster beyond, letting in a needle-thin ray of light. I peered through it.

What I saw was the Salon Doré.

Ménard stood behind his desk, pristine in a white shirt and gold cufflinks. His guest was in front of it, back turned to me. Instead of the cap and cloth that had shrouded him in London, he wore a helmet-like contraption to conceal his identity. The dirty greatcoat was still in place. He stood with his gloved hands clasped behind him, steel-capped boots planted apart, the soles crusted with mud.

The Rag and Bone Man. He was here. And Ménard had just called him by a name.

Rackham. Find Rackham.

A dying Scion official had given me that name as I fled the first colony. Rackham, the mysterious figure who had worked alongside Jaxon and Hector to sell voyants to the Rephaim.

Rackham. I shaped it with my lips. *Rag and Bone Man.*

"The Grand Overseer empathizes with your situation, Inquisitor Ménard. To be doubted by the Suzerain is an undesirable state to be in," the Rag and Bone Man said. When Ménard glanced up, I flinched away from the spyhole, even though he couldn't possibly see me. "These prices are high, yes. Reflective of their value. The potential gains, for you, are enormous."

I listened, committing his every word to memory.

"Nashira Sargas wants these anormaux very much. Sponsor their journey to her," the voice went on, "and I assure you that your standing with the Rephaim will dramatically improve."

I stole another glance at the Rag and Bone Man. This was the specter who had tried to have me killed when I got too close to the truth. The man who had done the dirty work. He had escaped justice for his crimes in England—I was damned if I was leaving Paris until he was dead.

Ménard placed his hands on the desk. He was looking down at something, but I was too low to see what. The candlelight hollowed out his eyes.

"I know this name. Ignace Fall," he said. "Le Vieux Orphelin."

"Yes."

My ears pricked. The missing grand duc.

"If you truly have him, that price is worth paying." Ménard breathed in through his nose. "We became . . . acquainted when I served the anchor in Lyon. He has been a thorn in my side ever since."

"I make it my business to strip away thorns."

"How did you find him?"

"He discovered my arrangement with the other two grands ducs and was planning to expose it. They offered him to the gray market."

Arcturus had been right. Le Latronpuche and La Reine des Thunes had sold their fellow leader to silence him.

"Ignace Fall is mine. He has eluded me too many times, mocked me from the shadows," Ménard said softly. "Twelve years I have waited to see his blood on the guillotine, and I will not have that pleasure stolen from me by a scum-sucking Rephaite. I want him for myself. Arrange it, Monsieur Rackham."

"That is no longer possible, Grand Inquisitor. He has already been transported to Sheol II."

"I will pay you what you gave the grands ducs for him," Ménard said, "five times over."

There was a long silence. An itch in my throat warned me of an impending cough.

"Since your offer is so generous," the Rag and Bone Man concluded, "I will put it to the Grand Overseer. It may take a number of weeks to finalize the transaction."

"I want the cockroaches he calls lieutenants, too. His so-called perdues," Ménard almost spat. "Le Prince Creux. Renelde du Linceul. La Tarasque. All of them."

"The hunt for them has already begun. If you wish, they can all be yours. For a price."

At this point, the Rag and Bone Man stepped closer to Ménard, who stiffened. No doubt the stench off that coat was eye-watering.

"Grand Inquisitor," he said, "will you accept my offer, and sponsor these unnaturals on their journey to redemption?"

Ménard looked back down at the desk.

"To reassure the Suzerain of my allegiance, you will tell her that I give these anormaux to her as tokens of my loyalty," he finally said. "Once this transaction is complete, however, you will not extort another penny from me."

"It is not extortion we trade in. It is opportunity." The Rag and Bone Man extended a hand. "Sign beside the names, if you will. Your official signature."

With a starched expression, Ménard took a pen from his desk. I pressed my eyes shut, willing my breath to stop scuffing my throat. The air in this hollow was smoky with dust.

"Minister Auclair will arrange your payment in the morning," Ménard said. "Is there something else?"

"Paige Mahoney."

The sound of my own name made me inhale, and the spark in my throat burned hotter. My whole torso bucked with the effort of holding it in.

"Not only is she in Paris, but she is aware of my presence here," the Rag and Bone Man said. I clamped my sleeve to my lips. "For the sake of peace in the empire, she must be muzzled."

The bastard grands ducs had ratted me out. It was no surprise.

"If you find her," the Rag and Bone Man went on, "alert me at once, so I may deliver her to the Grand Overseer. He will reimburse you—generously—for your efforts."

"There has been no sign of Mahoney," Ménard said, sounding bored. "Nonetheless, we remain vigilant." He was a good liar. "Is that all?"

For a moment, there was only the sound of slow breathing, magnified by the helmet.

"I remind you," the Rag and Bone Man said, "that if you should discover Paige Mahoney's whereabouts and withhold that information from the Grand Overseer, there will be serious consequences. Those consequences may touch Madelle Frère. And your children."

At that, Ménard raised his head. His face gave me a chill. For the first time, I could see the killer under his façade.

"Threaten my family again," he said, "and I will deal out consequences of my own." His eyes were two blank spaces. "You are an abomination. An affront to nature. You stand here because I allow it. You breathe in my presence because I deem it acceptable. And I no longer do."

The two men stared at each other.

"My ledger," the Rag and Bone Man said. "If you please."

"Not yet. One of your pawns may collect it tomorrow. In the meantime, it will make for a thought-provoking read. I would be very interested to see how wealthy you have all become . . . from a trade I sincerely doubt the Suzerain ever formally sanctioned."

After a terrible silence, the Rag and Bone Man turned and walked with a heavy gait toward the door. At last, I could hold it in no longer. A tiny cough jolted my chest.

He stopped dead. So did my heart. I could feel his cloaked aura, but he should not be close enough to sense mine. He looked toward Ménard, who was still. Then he looked toward my hiding place.

A moment that lasted a lifetime. Finally, he trudged from the room. Ménard stayed where he was for a time, looking at whatever was on his desk, before he straightened his tie and left the Salon

Doré, drawing the door shut behind him. I heard the lock activate and sensed him walk away.

As soon as he was out of earshot, I moved. This was my chance. I pushed at the surface above my head. No give. Instead, I dug my fingers between the laths and pried at one until it broke. A splinter nipped my thumb. Throwing caution to the wind, I writhed into a different position and kicked at the wall, over and over, snapping the laths, crumbling the layer of plaster beyond. I scrambled through the gap, onto the red carpet of the Salon Doré, where I gave rein to the coughs that had been bursting to come out.

I rose and eyed the gaping hole I had made in the wall. This break-in needed to be worth the risk.

Cade had been right. Even in his own study, Ménard was cautious. All that lay on the desk was a sheet of letterhead paper, a gold fountain pen, and a leather-bound ledger with crinkled pages. I hefted the ledger open.

I knew immediately what this was. This was a list of everyone the gray marketeers had caught for the last two Bone Seasons, penned in a crabbed hand. People I knew and had known leapt out at me, as if their names were limned in gold.

Biwott, Joseph	*Polyglot*	*Vauxhall Arches, 12 Dec 2058*	*H. Brook*
Coombs, Felix Samuel	*Cryomancer*	*Frazier Street, 30 Aug 2057*	*A. Rackham*
Jacob, Divya	*Chiromancer*	*Camden Market, 11 Jan 2059*	*A. Rackham*
Mahoney, Paige Eva	*Dreamwalker*	*Barbican Estate, 7 Mar 2059*	*H. Grinslathe*

The gray market had provided just over a quarter of the prisoners to the Rephaim that year. As well as voyant types and the places and dates of arrest, a *sponsor*—whichever evil bastard had procured us for the market—was also recorded. Their names seemed to be signed in their own hands, with a fingerprint beside each one. As well as a record, this was insurance, meant to stop the traffickers from betraying the ring.

I already knew mine was Hector Grinslathe. When I saw how much coin my arrest had earned him, I stared at the figure until it blurred. There was my value to Scion, in cold sterling. Even though I had seen the glister of his intestines, his organs dumped on a blood-soaked floor, all I wanted, in that moment, was for Hector Grinslathe to die again.

He could never have spent so much money. I was asking myself why he would have entered the sum in the ledger at all—he had sold me behind the other marketeers' backs—when I noticed the tiny stains beside his signature, which was rickety. He had signed this just before his death.

Like a confession.

I turned to the next page, which recorded the voyants who had been abducted for the twenty-first Bone Season. There, at the top of a list of ten, were three names I knew, as well as the one Ménard had mentioned.

Arnett, Nadine Leiko	*Whisperer*	*Seven Dials,*	*J. Hall*
		30 Nov 2059	
Fall, Ignace	*Oracle*	*Les Invalides,*	*P. Waite*
		2 Jan 2060	
Sáenz, Ezekiel	*Unreadable*	*Seven Dials,*	*J. Hall*
		30 Nov 2059	
Wren, Michael	*Unreadable*	*Iron Bridge,*	*A. Rackham*
		11 Oct 2059	*G. B. Ménard*

Nadine and Zeke. They were alive. So was Michael, who had been missing for months. And there was *P. Waite*—Le Latronpuche, brother of Didion Waite. He had sold Le Vieux Orphelin.

Arcturus had wondered how the gray market could still be turning a profit. I was beginning to understand.

Jaxon Hall was *laundering* us.

You soulless reptile.

A dreamscape was heading for the study. I pressed down the strangling rage and grabbed the ledger. It was too important to leave, hard evidence of the traffickers' crimes. Holding it to my chest, I kicked the crumbled plaster into a corner, then released one of the curtains from its sash and drew it behind me as I crawled back into the false wall, covering the hole I had made.

I edged back to the staircase. At the bottom, I found myself in another passage and pulled my elbows in to stop them being skinned. When I reached the end, I felt an ill-fitting panel, pressed back into place by small hands, and moved it aside. It took a moment to see through the gloom.

A greenhouse-like ceiling let a small amount of light into the Winter Garden. I slid out of the wall, replaced the panel, and ran through an arched doorway, my gift keeping me alert to dangers. As I slipped into the next corridor, I shoved the ledger into my jacket and secured it with the utility belt.

Snow rushed against the windows. An attendant rounded the corner with a tray. I hid behind a pair of curtains until she passed, then ran out again, my sock-clad feet quiet on the carpet. I ducked under a desk to avoid a pair of Vigiles, and then, at last, I reached the cellar door and used the key I had stolen from Cade. Heart pounding, I locked the door behind me and lit my way down with the flashlight from the wall.

Kornephoros wore his chains like jewels. The flowers woven through the links constricted his aura, keeping him weak. When he saw me, his eyes ignited, still red as a sunset. Keeping well out of reach, I took a seat in front of him and set the flashlight down on the floor.

"It must be past your bedtime," Kornephoros said, satin soft. "To what do I owe this visit?"

"I'm here to make you an offer."

"I do not trade with your kind."

"Why?"

"If a Rephaite breaks a true oath, they must live with the ram-ifications for eternity. They will be known forever as a liar, a backstabber. Humans have no understanding of consequence. A broken oath is nothing to you. You die too quickly to plumb the depths of guilt."

"Other Rephaim have made deals with me."

"Other Rephaim were fools." He observed me like a hunter. "Does Fitzours know you are here?"

"No."

"So these are secret dealings." His voice was lazy. "I knew you would return. My suffering troubles you, even though you believe me to be allied with Nashira." He leaned toward me as much as his chains would allow. "I trust you, then, with the truth. I am no servant of the Suzerain. I am Ranthen."

"Ranthen." I tried to keep the skepticism from my voice. "What are you, a spy for them?"

"No. My Ranthen-kith are unaware that I survived the war," he told me. "I fought alongside them in the Waning of the Veils. Arcturus knows me well."

"He's never mentioned you."

"Likely he thinks I was destroyed. Likely it pains him," Kornephoros said. "We were . . . close."

I checked the time on the transceiver. Quarter of an hour until the accomplice in the kitchen finished her shift. Whatever I did next, I needed to do it fast.

"Paige."

The sound of my name on his lips raked my spine.

"Paige," Kornephoros said again, spinning out the syllable. "An archaic word for a messenger or servant, as I understand it. Incongruous, since you appear to resist authority. Or perhaps you were named for a leaf of paper, blank, its tale yet to be written. Which is it?"

"I wouldn't know," I said. "My mother chose my name."

He regarded me.

"Help me, Paige Mahoney. You are a friend to Arcturus Mesarthim. If he were here now, he would release me. I have lived for months in agony and darkness. I beseech you," he said in a whisper, "let me out of this prison. Let me return to my Ranthen-kith."

"I came down here to make a deal," I said. "You were meant to take a job as a keeper in Sheol II. If you tell me where it is—what name the city had before—I will release you."

Kornephoros leaned back against the wall. "That is all you want?"

"Yes."

"Then you mean to be rid of it," he surmised. "Compromise another of our fortified havens, and not only will we be more likely to become Emim, but those that already exist will no longer be drawn to a congregation of us. The colonies are a beacon. Without them, the Emim will scatter across your world. Is that what you want?"

"Some risks are worth taking." I raised my eyebrows. "Do you want to stay in here for eternity, Kornephoros?"

His eyes smoldered, and I knew I had him. This Rephaite was a fellow opportunist. I was a golden opportunity.

"A city lies to the west. It hides a hall of many reflections," he stated. "The Sun King held court there before the fall of his dynasty."

"Versailles," I breathed. "The Château de Versailles."

I should have known. I could have *guessed* the answer. There could be no more perfect seat for the Rephaim in France than the long-abandoned seat of the House of Bourbon.

That was it. I had everything I had come here to find. Kornephoros watched me stand.

"Fitzours has the key to my chains," he said, "but if you remove the flowers, I will be strong enough to break free."

"Not just yet."

Tendons rose in his neck. The chains jangled as gargantuan muscles strained against them.

"I've one more thing to ask you, Kornephoros Sheratan." I forced myself to stand perfectly still. "You see, I think there is a way a Rephaite can be destroyed altogether. You behead it with a blade made from opaline. Am I wrong?"

His eyes were like lava. "You have witnessed a sequestration."

"At the hand of the blood-sovereign herself."

His wolf-like gaze never left my face.

"You're afraid," I said, after a long moment. "You're afraid Ménard is going to realize there's a way to destroy you without any risk at all that you'll turn. That he'll have you all slaughtered."

"I fear nothing, dreamwalker. Least of all a human. But be warned, should Ménard learn the truth, and should he come into possession of opaline, he will spare no Rephaite," Kornephoros said. "Not even Arcturus."

"You keep talking about Arcturus. Maybe you did know him. Maybe you are Ranthen," I said, "or maybe when you saw me yesterday, you marked me for a tender-hearted fool. If I let you go, you might well run straight to Nashira and tell her I'm on my way to Sheol II."

"If you do *not* let me go, I will tell Fitzours what you plan, and he will report it to Ménard."

"Those two will never let you out of here. I might." I folded my arms. "If I find the colony in Versailles and live to tell the tale, I'll come back and set you free. On my oath. Do we have a deal?"

The former Warden of the Sheratan bared his white teeth. The links of the chains rang.

"Arcturus is not the only Rephaite with a long memory," he said, very softly. "If you do not come back within the sennight, I will find another way to escape this place, and I will hunt you, Paige Mahoney. I will take my club to your bones until you scream for mercy. And I promise you, fleshworm—you will find none."

****

I emerged from the attic heavy with knowledge. Finding the corridor empty, I broke into a light-footed run toward the kitchen. The secrets were scored onto my memory. Now all I had to do was carry them out of here.

Easier said than done. In my rush to escape, I forgot to listen to the æther. As I turned a corner, a baton bashed into my stomach, and I folded, the breath slammed out of me. Next thing I knew, I was flat on my front, and my arms were pinned to my sides.

It was the two Vigiles I had tricked into leaving their posts. They had brought friends with them, outnumbering me six to one. I launched myself into the æther.

All of them had been trained for this. None of them were ready for it. By the time someone roared for backup, two Vigiles had fallen to the floor beside me, empty, wall-eyed in the shock of death.

Escape was so close I could almost taste it. Hope spiked me with impossible strength. I could not be captured now, not when lives depended on the secrets I carried. I danced in the æther as I never had, flashing between adversaries like a bullet between walls, each strike weaker than the last. The sixth and final guard had made it halfway down the corridor by the time I clipped her dreamscape, knocking her unconscious just as she hit an alarm.

A bell drilled somewhere in the mansion. When I crash-landed back in my body, I doubled over. My fingers went to my nose and came away smeared with red. No time to stop. Chest tight, I drunkenly took the baton from my utility belt and ran—straight into the Vigiles storming in from outside the mansion. Guns snapped in my direction. I veered away from their flux darts and broke into a sprint.

Steel blinds snapped down to cover the windows. Boots thundered across the floor. With a knife-like pain in my shoulder and chest, I shot down another corridor and dived for the nearest flight of stairs. I needed to break their line of sight and get back into the hidden staircase.

Another dreamscape. A dark shape blurred from my left and slammed bodily into me. As if I had been charged by a horse, both me and the baton went flying. I hit the floor, too stunned and winded to move again, while my only weapon rolled far out of reach. Agony erupted behind my ribs. I clawed in panic at my throat, as if I could unseam it and let more air inside.

A giant of a Vigile dragged me up. He was as big as a Rephaite, all muscle and armor, his hands the size of plates. I could see my own fear-stricken face in his visor. As soon as I tried hitting him with my spirit, excruciating pain warned me to stop. He slung me over his shoulder.

The guards from downstairs had caught up. Transceivers crackled. The alarm faded. Too short-winded to scream, I grabbed onto anything I could as the massive Vigile hauled me through the mansion, up more stairs. We were back in the attic. So close to the false wall.

Cade was pounding on the door to his cell, calling my name. I made a last attempt to break free, to no avail. My fingers skidded off the Vigile's helmet. He booted a door open and flung me headlong into my cell. I just about landed on my feet, then stumbled and fell hard into the coffee table, which cut into my shoulder. The Vigile bore down on me and tore off the utility belt, but he missed the shape of the ledger. My shoes slapped to the floor.

A long shadow reached across the floorboards. There stood Ménard, flanked by two of his guards, their rifles trained on me.

"I see you have chosen not to cooperate." That restrained smile. "You were warned of the consequences of rebellion. A pity that perversion is innate to the anormale."

"As hypocrisy is innate to the tyrant. You're trying to court favor with Nashira." I wheezed out a laugh. "You're not some untainted savior, Ménard. You're like every other two-faced bastard in Scion. Taking from unnaturals with one hand, slitting our throats with the other."

"You misunderstand, Paige Mahoney," he said. "I have never used anormaux for personal gain. Only to see the extinction of unnaturalness. Preserving my own life happens to serve that aim, for I am the one who will stand against the Suzerain . . . though I must confess that it gives me some pleasure, to witness you collude in your own destruction." He glanced at the nearest Vigile. "Call the Minister of Internal Security. Tell her we have a prisoner who requires immediate transportation to the Bastille."

He left without a backward glance. The door was double-locked in his wake.

The Bastille. Shit. If I entered that windowless prison, no one would be able to reach me.

Goosebumps suddenly coursed over my arms. The golden cord was on fire, and I sensed him.

Arcturus.

13

Trust

He had come for me, as I had known he would. I threw myself toward the window and looked down.

No sign of him in the courtyard. Through the thickening snow, I could make out twelve snipers on the roof. Using my gift against even one of them would finish me off—I knew myself well enough to be sure that I was at my limit.

On the east side of the mansion, the first sniper went down. The next fired several times into the dark before he was flung like a doll off the edge of the roof, into the courtyard below, landing in a pile of twisted limbs. One by one, they fell to a faceless shadow. Arcturus was so gentle with me, it was easy to forget that he had once been a warrior.

At speed, I judged the bone-breaking drop to the roof below and took stock of the furniture. The wardrobe was heavy enough to barricade the door. I ran back across the room, braced my shoulder against it, and shoved.

My body trembled with exertion. The wardrobe refused to budge. In sheer desperation, I threw my full weight against it, planted my heels on the wall, pushed backward with all my might —and with a groan, the wardrobe tipped over and crashed to the floor, throwing up a thundercloud of dust. I landed hard beside it, the impact shuddering through my bruises, my chest. When I had gasped back enough air, I groped for the ledger, which had slipped from under my sweater, and crawled toward my shoes, coughing fit to burst.

Shouts of alarm from beyond the door. The handle rattled before the Vigiles started to batter it with their rifles. Breathless with pain, I shoved on my shoes and lurched back to the window.

Arcturus was much closer. His eyes flashed through the darkness. With a surge of adrenaline-fueled strength, I lifted the coffee table and smashed its legs into the window. Glass shattered. Snow came roaring into the room. The nearest sniper snapped their rifle toward me, only to fall in a hail of blood and brains. Their body crunched onto the gravel below.

The door splintered, and the beam of a flashlight glared in. Arcturus was right below the window now, snow flickering around him. He held out a hand.

A spray of bullets shredded the door. I had seconds. Panting, I scraped the glass from the frame and swung my legs over it. I might fear water, but heights—heights were easy. A Vigile smashed through the weakened door and shone a gun-mounted light into my cell—

—just in time to see me jump.

There were two people in the world I trusted to catch me if I suddenly hurled myself out of a window. Nick Nygård was one of them. Arcturus Mesarthim was the other. Frigid air howled in my ears before the collision. It would have buckled a human. Instead, Arcturus caught me as if I were light as a bottle, and then I was on my feet, barely shaken.

"Who sh-shot that sniper?" I could hardly speak for want of breath. "Mannequin?"

"Yes." His gaze flicked up. "Move."

I followed his line of sight to the window. A Vigile was there, her rifle pointed right at us. Bullets hammered into the roof.

Arcturus shielded me as we ran for one of the tall chimneys and took shelter behind it. Ice had turned the roof to a death-trap. My shoes had no grip, and the ledger was slipping. The instant the gunfire ceased, we struck out for the next chimney, then the next. I slid to a stop behind the fourth and tucked my limbs in tight. More Vigiles swarmed in the courtyard below, too low to get a shot at us.

"I expected this to be a somewhat quieter rescue," Arcturus remarked from his place beside me.

"That wouldn't be very me." Brick dust flew as bullets chipped at the chimney. "You have an exit plan?"

"The east courtyard." He held out my pistol. "Get to its roof."

"Take this." I took the gun and thrust the ledger at him in return. "It's important."

He tucked it into the inner pocket of his coat. I readied the pistol. When the Vigile stopped to reload again, I took the best aim I could in a snowstorm and opened fire, forcing her back into the attic.

Something flew toward us from inside. It hit the snow beside Arcturus, a canister with a blinking red light. Almost in the same instant I recognized it as a chemical grenade, I kicked it off the roof, into the courtyard below. With a flash and a *crack*, blue smoke hissed from the canister and scattered the Vigiles. I ran as hard as I could, aiming for the front of the Hôtel Garuche.

Ménard meant to kill me. That canister had contained the blue hand, the deadly nerve agent Scion used against dissenters. It would have paralyzed me. Fighting for breath, half-blinded by snow, I wended between three more chimneys, swerved hard to the right, and charged up a flight of steps, past a dead or unconscious sniper, over the arched entrance to the mansion. With Arcturus behind me, I descended on the other side of the archway, taking the steps two at a time, and vaulted a balustrade, landing on a steeper roof. My shoes slithered on frosted tiles.

Bullets sparked around us as more and more Vigiles took aim from the windows. Arcturus put himself between me and the gunfire. Fear stripped me to an assortment of body parts. Hands on the roof. Feet seeking purchase. Lips numb with cold. Chest fit to burst. The drop to the street from here was too long, and the nearest building was too far to reach.

A siren droned in the courtyard. A set of exterior doors flew open behind us, and more Vigiles stampeded across the roof. I squeezed off a few shots at them. A moment later, Arcturus swept me against his chest, his arm tight as a harness, and threw us over the edge.

As it turned out, Arcturus Mesarthim could jump like a spring-heeled devil. He cleared the impossible gap and grabbed a balcony across the street before he dropped to the ground. His Rephaite bones swallowed the impact, and then we were on the street and running.

"Are we really going to try and outrun the Grand Inquisitor of France?" I gasped over the sirens.

He pressed a dissimulator into my hand. "I thought you were good at running, Pale Dreamer."

I shaped the mask to my face one-handed as we pelted toward a public garden. Halfway across it, I threw off the stolen jacket. It might have a tracking device stitched into it.

Sirens keened from all directions. Keeping to the cover of the trees, we skirted the edge of the Place de la Concorde. Snow blew thick and fast. My sweater was damp, my hair dripping, my feet burning in the flimsy shoes. Even if there had been any Vigiles nearby—they must all be converging on the mansion—they would have found it hard to see us.

To our right, the Eiffel Tower reached above the trees. Scarlet light branched through its latticework. The same light filled the fountains, turning them to pools of magma, and the obelisk at the heart of the plaza. Across the citadel, other landmarks would be starting to glow red, indicating a serious threat. Ménard had issued a security alert.

Arcturus kept a firm hold of my hand, lending me his inhuman speed. Once I had been able to run like an engine. Now my chest was in agony.

"I can't," I rattled. "Have to s-stop. Arcturus—"

"Stéphane is waiting for us in the underpass."

Just a little farther. I could make it.

Arcturus led me around a sharp corner, onto a shallow incline. A car idled on an island between two lanes. Vehicles roared on either side of it. Arcturus opened one of the back doors, half-lifted me inside, and climbed in behind me. Before the door was even shut,

Stéphane drove off the island and onto the road, seamlessly joining the late-night traffic.

"Well done," they said. "Did anyone see you come down here?"

"No," Arcturus said.

"Good." Stéphane glanced at me over their shoulder. I coughed hard enough to crack a rib. "Are you all right, Flora?"

A nod was all I could manage.

Stéphane stuck to the speed limit. I peeled off my drenched sweater and leaned into Arcturus, a crushing pain in my chest. He wrapped some of his coat around me. When I could draw enough breath, I spoke. "Stéphane, I thought Mannequin didn't assist captured spies?"

"Your friend was the one assisting." Stéphane kept their gaze on the road. "Ducos agreed to provide cover fire and transport if he got you out."

"Thank you."

Dark eyes met mine in the rearview mirror. "You look bad. Do you need to see Cordier?"

"Yes."

Stéphane took the next right, across the gilded Pont de L'Inquisition, while a helicopter rumbled over the Seine. I rested on Arcturus and let my eyes drift closed. His warmth and the motion of the car lulled me into a stupor.

Stéphane stopped the car near the University of Scion Paris. "This is as far as I can safely take you," they said. Just the thought of moving drained me. "Walk from here and watch your backs. Ducos and Cordier will check on you tomorrow night. Until then, close the shutters and stay inside."

"Thank you, Stéphane," Arcturus said.

"Okay."

We got out, into a full-blown blizzard. Arcturus took an umbrella from the boot, drew me to his side, and opened it over both of us as Stéphane drove away. By the time we lurched into the safe house, I was on the brink of collapse. Without letting go of me, Arcturus secured the door behind us, and we sank onto the staircase together, my arms tight around his neck.

"I knew you would come this time," I murmured into his coat. It smelled of winter. "I knew."

"I could not reach you in the Archon." His deep voice coursed through both of us. "I will never leave you in a dark room again."

I pressed my burning cheek to him. Against the odds, I had survived another Scion stronghold. We were both in one piece. His hand came to rest between my shoulders.

We listened as the din of sirens and helicopters crisscrossed the citadel. A vehicle rushed past, red lights flashing through the window and onto us. Arcturus drew me a little closer.

"They took Portugal." I closed my eyes. "Gonçalves will surrender."

"I know."

He rested his chin on the crown of my head. I almost fell asleep on him. The escape had pushed my body and my gift to breaking point.

In the end, he carried me up the stairs. I stayed conscious for just long enough to peel off the dissimulator, remove my wet clothes, and crumple into bed. Sleep hit me like the flat of an axe.

****

It was the sound of rain that woke me. When I opened my eyes, the first thing I saw was the ledger, which lay beside me on the bed.

Gray light leaked around the shutters. I shivered, unable to so much as lift my head. My cheeks flamed. I was sick as a small hospital—yet somehow, by the skin of my teeth, I was alive.

No more sirens. Ménard wasn't the sort to waste time. He would have accepted that, for the time being, he had lost his bargaining chip.

Arcturus must have sensed me wake. When he came to me, it was with a steaming mug.

"Paige." He placed it on the nightstand. "How do you feel?"

"Terrible. But grateful to be here." I moved a clump of curls out of my eyes. "Thank you. I'd be in the Bastille by now if not for you."

"I am sure you would have found a way out of the mansion."

"I did. Then I scotched it." I tried to sit up. "Don't suppose you have a heat pad charged up."

"I had thought to leave you one, but you developed a fever during the night."

"Could have fooled me."

I mustered the strength to lift myself onto my elbows. Arcturus moved the pillows to support me, then skirted a thumb over my fresh bruises, the small cut under my eye.

"Frère," I said. "She wasn't happy."

"Evidently not." He lowered his hand. "Your fever has not broken. Are you hurt anywhere else?"

"Not badly." Sitting up made it slightly easier to talk. Or whisper, at least. "You were shielding me. Are *you* hurt?"

"Some trifling gunshot wounds. My body will expel the bullets in good time."

Only a Rephaite could be so blasé. He went into the corridor and came back with another blanket, which he wrapped around my shoulders. Drawing it closer hurt the small joints in my fingers.

"If you can speak, I would hear what happened." Arcturus sat on the edge of my bed. "How did Ménard capture you?"

This was going to be a difficult conversation. I sank back into the cushions and braced my right side.

"I let him," I said.

There was a tense silence.

"You repeated your tactic," he said. "Allowed them to take you."

"Listen. Just hear me out." I held his gaze. "Ménard was onto me. I needed to find out what he was plotting in there. I also wanted another piece of information for myself. For us."

Arcturus looked at me as if I were a stranger. I raked a hand through my hair again and let it tumble between my fingers.

"I know how insane it sounds," I said. "Like a death wish. And I know how you must feel about it—but I promise you, this was not a suicide mission. I meant to get out. Someone I knew was in there, someone who had good reason to help me. We struck a deal."

After a time, he spoke. "Who?"

"The oracle from the colony. David. His real name is Cade, and he works for Ménard."

Without answering, Arcturus moved to the chair, where he clasped his hands and waited for me to begin.

It took me a long time to fill him in. Between thick coughs, I told him about Cade—about his affair with Frère, why he had been in Sheol I, and his firm belief in the Grand Inquisitor of France. I told him why Benoît Ménard had avoided Frank Weaver for months. I told him about the coup Ménard was planning, and his vision for a pure Scion.

"He sees all of us as branches of the same evil," I said. "And he won't rest until all of us are gone." My throat burned. "I'll be honest: he scared me in a way Weaver never has."

Arcturus seemed to mull this over.

"Though I dislike how you obtained this information, it has extraordinary value. Ducos will be pleased," he said, "though you might not have lived to relate it to her. Cade was your only guarantee of an escape. He could have lied to you about the affair to lure you inside."

"Cade is clearly a . . . complicated person," I conceded, "but he had a few opportunities to sell us out in the colony. He didn't."

"Is that reason enough for you to have trusted him with your life?"

I looked away.

We sat without speaking for a while. In that silence, I imagined how I might feel if our situations were reversed—if he had given himself up to Scion, barely escaped, and then risked his life again, all on the word of a near stranger. Even the thought of it tightened my stomach.

"You must have been beside yourself," I said quietly.

He might as well have turned to stone. Not even a reassuring *hm*.

"When you give your report to Ducos," he said at length, "I strongly advise you not to tell her that you entered that building of your own volition."

"Even I'm not that reckless," I said dryly. "Ducos can deal with Ménard. We have something else to do."

I shifted so I was a little more upright and tried to reach for the mug. Arcturus got up and passed it to me.

"This can wait," he said. "If you are in pain."

"I'm fine." I took a sip of saloop. "I found out how the gray market is earning money. The missing link."

Seeing that I was determined, Arcturus returned to the chair.

"I think the grands ducs have been selling fugitives. Voyant fugitives, wanted by Scion, who would naturally look for sanctuary in the carrières," I continued. "The Rag and Bone Man sells those fugitives on to Scion officials, like a bounty hunter. Those officials can then choose to send the fugitives to Sheol II, and for a fee, Jaxon will let them take credit for their capture." I touched the ledger. "Ménard paid to take credit for Michael. His name is in here."

His expression flickered. Michael was the first human he had taken under his wing.

"There are other names of interest," I said. "Nadine and Zeke, and Ignace Fall—otherwise known as Le Vieux Orphelin. We were right. The grands ducs did sell him. Le Latronpuche did, anyway."

"How did you obtain the ledger?"

"The Rag and Bone Man—Rackham, that's his real name—had a meeting with Ménard." The mug warmed my fingers. "The ledger belongs to him. I stole it."

I told him about the secret way into the walls and everything I had overheard. About the Rephaite chained at the bottom of the Hôtel Garuche, willing to trade with me for his freedom.

"His name is Kornephoros Sheratan," I said. Arcturus looked sharply at me. "He . . . told me you were close."

"Describe him to me," he said, eyes burning.

"Dark hair down to here." I tapped my waist. "Big scar across his chest. He looked a lot like Terebell."

For some time, Arcturus was silent. When he did speak, his voice was low and cold.

"Rephaite hair is not like yours. It does not grow. To cut it, therefore, is an irrevocable act." His own brown hair was cropped to his nape. "If you ever come across a Rephaite whose hair is long, they were never Ranthen. Not openly."

"Then why did he say you were close?"

"Because long ago, and for a very short time," he said, "Kornephoros was my mate."

I almost choked on my saloop. Arcturus looked at me in puzzlement. By some miracle, I managed not to descend into yet another coughing fit.

"Kornephoros." My eyes watered. "You and . . . Kornephoros."

"You are surprised."

"He struck me as cruel and devious. I just can't imagine you ever finding that attractive."

"I had not seen his nature then. I soon did."

"What did he do?"

"He claimed to be Ranthen. We fought alongside him, and believed he shared our desire to keep the Mothallath in power. In the end, however, it was he who delivered our star-sovereigns to Nashira."

"Fine," I said. "Let him rot down there."

"You say he expects you to return in a sennight. If you do not, and he escapes, he will come looking for you."

"What the hell *is* a sennight?"

"Seven nights," he said, as if this wasn't the most unnecessary word in existence. "Kornephoros is an osteomancer. He used to read the bones of human children for Kraz Sargas. Not only that, but his touch causes excruciating pain."

I really did know how to choose them. "We needed to know where Sheol II was," I said. "I didn't have much choice."

"He did tell you the location, then."

"Versailles. It made sense to me, but I suppose he could have been lying."

"Likely. Deceit comes easily to his kind."

"You would know."

It shot out before I could stop it. Arcturus looked at me and waited.

"You said there was one last truth you would keep from me," I said, very softly. "Did it happen to concern the Emim?"

With his face cast into shadow, his eyes were living flame. "You know."

"That they used to be Rephaim?" I said. "Is that the secret you claimed you had to keep from me?"

"Yes."

Both of us fell silent for a time. "Well," I said, "now I know." I put the mug down a bit too hard. "If you want to explain, this is your chance."

His chin tilted down. Through the cord, I sensed a yielding, as if something had released in him.

"Terebell believed that if you knew, you and other like-minded humans might refuse to work alongside the Ranthen—that you, in particular, would not hear reason," he said. "Not long after I met you, she swore us to secrecy."

I could picture them assembled by candlelight, agreeing to keep me in the dark.

"I did not care for you then. As I came to know you, I also came to regret the oath, for I suspected it would cause the very mistrust Terebell had predicted. I asked her to release me from it. She refused."

"You could have told me the truth in confidence."

"And you would have seen that my promises were hollow." He looked at me. "For Ranthen, it is a matter of honor. To break my word, given freely—it would have stained me."

"Not in my eyes."

"Paige, know this: I would never swear an oath that endangered our trust again. But I did," he said, "and once made, it could not be undone. I am Ranthen. Terebell is my sovereign-elect."

"And I was your Underqueen. When we struck this alliance, I trusted you all to be honest with me," I said. "Instead, you conspired to keep your human associates uninformed, so we couldn't even ask questions."

He had the grace not to contest me.

"You broke your word once—to Nashira—because you knew it was the right thing to do," I said. "You could have done it again."

"It is of no import if the blood-sovereign calls me an oathbreaker," he said. "If my Ranthen-kith had, I would have been locked out of their affairs, and unable to advocate for your interests."

"You defied them in other ways." Suddenly I felt too drained for inhibition. "Every time you were alone with me—every time you touched me—you risked their suspicion and anger, but you still did it. For me."

Both our stances were rigid, our gazes in a deadlock. "I made no oaths on that front," Arcturus said quietly.

"You didn't need to. It's implicit."

"The taboo of flesh-treachery is Sargas doctrine," came his reply. "Even if many of the Ranthen have chosen to embrace it, I will never consider it to be unspoken law among us."

I lifted my chin.

"Even if I saw the bread crumbs," I finally said, breaking the tense silence, "maybe I didn't let myself follow them, because in spite of everything, I chose to trust you. And now we—"

Before I could finish, a razor blade seared under one breast. My vision bleached. Pain gored between my ribs, all the way through to my back, deep inside me, reaching places it never had before. As I tried to cushion my chest, Arcturus came to my side.

"Paige."

I shook my head. There was nothing he could do. I bent at the waist, holding myself, and waited for each excruciating jolt to pass. By the time the pain ebbed, my face was bathed in sweat and tears.

"I refuse to prove Terebell right," I said, once I could breathe without agony. "I need a bath. Then we're going to talk this out, put it behind us, and get on with the jobs we need to do. More lives than ours depend on it."

Arcturus watched me rise, his face as closed as I had ever seen it. I brushed past him without another word.

14

Necessary Truths

Even though the water troubled me as much as ever, I sat in the hot bath for a long time, my knees drawn up to my chin. The steam eased my breathing. I stared at the wall and thought back over the last year.

I knew how hard Arcturus had worked behind the scenes in London. It was because of him that I'd had the money to feed and house so many voyants, because of him that Terebell had kept backing me financially even after I botched the raid on the warehouse. Perhaps he really had believed that if he broke his oath, he would forfeit that power.

Harder to absorb was the fact that he had gambled with our hard-won trust. Our alliance had always been fragile, and by sitting on a secret for so long, he had risked shattering it.

I got out. When I had dried off, I wiped the steam from the mirror. My lips were always dark, but they were also smudged with gray now, like my fingertips. I had overused my gift.

My fresh bruises had ripened to plum. I dabbed the scrape on my thigh with antiseptic, pulled on a nightshirt, and attempted to untangle my curls, giving up when the comb snapped clean in half. All the while, the pain rose in my chest and made it difficult to breathe.

There would be time enough to rest. For now, I had to seal this fracture in our friendship.

Arcturus waited for me in the parlor, nursing a large glass of wine. I lowered myself on the other side of the couch.

The rain had turned to hail. By now, it was late in the afternoon, the sky like charcoal.

"As you know," Arcturus said, "Rephaim are not born. We emerged from the Netherworld."

"Yes."

"We did not all emerge together. There were waves of creation. Not long after the Netherworld began to fall into decay—the event that started our war—there was one final wave, the equivalent of a death throe. The Netherworld created not Rephaim, but Emim. Not many, to be sure, but we were ill-prepared, and already riven into two factions. Many were turned."

In the quiet that followed, I eased onto my right side. Breathing hurt a little less.

"I see now why *we* had to risk our necks," I said. "Going near them puts you at risk of the half-urge."

I had never understood why, when they were so fast and strong, the Rephaim had wanted to train humans to fight the Emim. At last, I could make sense of everything I had seen.

"Cade told me how it all works," I said. "Most of it, anyway. You have to be bitten, clawed, anything that breaks your sarx. Salt and human blood hold it off, but you have to take aura to cure it." Arcturus confirmed it with a nod. "There was one thing he hasn't been able to find out. Whether or not you can also develop the half-urge if you don't take aura."

"No."

I watched him with heavy-lidded eyes, one hand on my ribs.

"If we do not feed," Arcturus said, "we become delirious. We lose our gifts. Finally, we cease to function. The pollen of the poppy anemone both hastens this process and disfigures us."

"So you go into spirit shock," I said. "Like when a soothsayer or an augur loses their numen."

"It is comparable, except that voyants can die from spirit shock. For us, there is no such mercy."

I waited for him to continue.

"How much we can perceive in that state, I do not know," he said. "What *is* known is that we become considerably more tempting to the Emim. The only way to reanimate us, then, is with the half-urge. Usually, our fellow Rephaim choose to remove that possibility by sequestering us."

"That is, beheading you," I said. "Which can only be done with opaline, because nothing else severs Rephaite bone."

"Yes."

"And then?"

Arcturus watched the hailstones clatter on the window.

"Sequestration is not the same as mortal death," he said. "Our bodies do not rot. Our dreamscapes remain in the æther. So far as I know, there is no way to free our spirits at that point. We cannot truly die—nor, from then on, can we truly live."

Eternal imprisonment. Alsafi had condemned himself to that frozen state to save me.

"In the colony, I used the pollen of the poppy anemone on Kraz Sargas," I said. "Afterward, you told me he was dead."

"At the time, it seemed the best way to explain it. Kraz did not find a voyant in time to restore himself," he said. "Nashira would have sequestered him."

For all intents and purposes, I really had killed off one of the blood-heirs. I felt nothing.

"Well," I said, "thank you for the honesty. How nice it feels to be well-informed." I touched my burning forehead. "Ménard doesn't know about sequestration. Not that it would matter if he did, because I doubt Nashira leaves opaline lying around."

"No."

"Then he still thinks Sheol II is necessary to trap you. If we tear it down, we risk losing him as a potential ally. And of course, the Emim will spread."

"Yes. There will be consequences, as there were consequences the first time. But for the sake of all unnaturals—Rephaite and human —we cannot let Sheol II stand," Arcturus said. "Any civilization that must subjugate a part of itself to survive is not worth saving."

"I agree," I said. "You're with me, then?"

"If you will have me."

Usually our silences were peaceful. This one was still and heavy, like the air before a storm.

"I suppose I will," I finally said.

"You do not seem as angry as I expected."

"Trust me, I am. I'm just too tired to shout at you."

"I see."

My desire to bridge the rift between us strained against my pride. I was split in half by that tug-of-war.

"We've no time for it, in any case," I said shortly. "We need to establish if the colony really is in Versailles."

Arcturus looked back at me for a long moment, as if he wanted to press the subject.

"We could ask the perdues," he said. "They are the followers of Le Vieux Orphelin, the missing grand duc."

"You know about them?"

"You asked me to discover who painted the graffiti. Who supports you in Paris," Arcturus reminded me. "It was the perdues. It seems Le Vieux Orphelin is an admirer of yours."

Interesting. "What makes you think they would know about Sheol II?"

"Because all three of the grands ducs may know a way into Versailles. Do you recall the jewelery La Reine des Thunes wore during our audience?"

"It was hard not to notice," I admitted. "I'd love to meet whoever can cheat that bright a sparkler."

"I do not believe they were ersatz diamonds. In fact, if I am not mistaken, those jewels once belonged to a resident of the Château de Versailles," Arcturus said. "Marie Antoinette."

I tried not to wince. In the syndicate, it was taboo to speak the names of executed monarchs out loud.

"She was guillotined," I said. "Her jewels could have been stolen, washed up in the Parisian underworld that way. It doesn't necessarily mean the grands ducs know a way into Versailles."

"If I may present some more evidence," he said. "The chandelier was solid silver, identical to those that once hung in the Hall of Mirrors in Versailles. There were other treasures in that chamber. A harp. A guéridon, fashioned of marble and gilded wood. A porcelain jewel box."

"You think the grands ducs looted all that from the ruins?"

"It is possible. In order to do that, they would have needed a clandestine way in and out of the city. I imagine Le Vieux Orphelin was part of this operation. If so, his perdues may know more. I spoke again to Katell, who admitted that Mélusine is one of them."

Mélusine had kept her allegiance very quiet. "We need a meeting with them," I said. "Think you could arrange it, now you're an underworld expert?"

"Once you have seen Ducos and Cordier, I will try. We should both be here when they arrive."

****

We waited. Arcturus made me a bowl of buttered salmon and lentils. After days of almost nothing to eat, I should have been ravenous, but my appetite was gone again—as good as it tasted, I couldn't eat more than a mouthful. I settled for plain toast.

Arcturus switched on the evening news. The Chief of Vigilance explained away the security alert, claiming it was a system test. All was well. I ate tiny bites of toast and coughed.

Ménard must be furious. The thought that Cade might suffer his wrath made me uneasy. Even if he had failed in his attempt to soften a vicious tyrant, he seemed decent, if misguided.

After the local news, Scarlett Burnish appeared. She welcomed the new denizens of the empire to Scion, speaking over clips of well-behaved troops. Next, Weaver gave a speech aimed at Pilar Brugués Olivencia, the Prime Minister of Spain. He urged her to oppose King Esteban and surrender ("Will you fight to keep one man enthroned, or spare your people weeks of blood?"). Burnish returned to reflect on the pride and self-regard of monarchs, their lust for power. She was the perfect servant of the anchor. No crack in her façade.

I had never been able to thank her for saving me. Most likely, I never would.

King Esteban would die. A republican like Daniela Gonçalves could be molded into a Grand Inquisitor, but not a monarch. Never a monarch. Nashira Sargas would brook the reign of no sovereign but herself.

My skin burned through my nightshirt. Between deep stabs of pain, I dozed and shuddered and coughed. When the front door opened, Arcturus woke me with a small tug of the cord.

My arms were too weak to support me. He offered a hand, which I took, and lifted me into a sitting position. I tried to thank him, but the pain was too much to bear. Even swallowing hurt.

Cordier entered the parlor first and flashed a smile at Arcturus. Tonight she wore a cream silk blouse tucked into a high-waisted skirt, and pumps with tiny spotted bows.

"Hello," she said to Arcturus. "Again."

Arcturus offered a nod.

"Cordier," Ducos said in a starched tone as she stepped in, "see to Flora, if you please."

Cordier dropped the smile and came straight to my side. "Flora." She turned my face into the light. "You're burning up. And these bruises—" Delicate knuckles skirted my forehead. "How long have you had a fever?"

"Since last night," Arcturus said, when I could only rattle and wheeze.

"All right." Cordier placed a hand on my back. "Let's take a look at you, honey."

While Cordier moved her case to her lap, Ducos sat in the armchair. A long black coat was buttoned to her chin, and her stiletto boots gleamed.

"Flora," she said. "And auxiliary. Good to see you both alive after that little . . . interlude." Her dark hair fell in roller curls. "Flora, I can see you're unwell, but I need you to—"

"Isaure," Cordier broke in, "please. She can hardly breathe, let alone talk."

Ducos opened her mouth as if to protest before I dissolved into more bone-racking coughs. She pursed her lips.

"I'll need you to take off your shirt," Cordier said to me. "Let's send these two out, shall we?"

Shivering all over, I shook my head. Arcturus had seen me that undressed before, and I doubted Ducos gave a damn. I eased off my nightshirt and crossed my arms over my breasts.

It had been about twelve years since I had last had a checkup from anyone other than Nick. Cordier checked my temperature, listened to my breathing, attached my forefinger to the same device she had used before, and took a couple of blood samples. Next, she aimed a handheld scanner at my chest. It spat out a monochrome image, which Cordier studied, her expression grim.

"What is it?" Ducos asked tersely.

Cordier breathed out through her nose. "Pleural effusion," she concluded. "I'll need to rule out an empyema." Ducos looked as if she had developed a sudden headache. "Command should never have cleared her for assignment without a comprehensive medical. It's a wonder she's been able to get out of bed, let alone—"

"Pleural effusion?" I whispered. Every word now caused a jag of pain. "What is that?"

Cordier turned to me. "It's a buildup of excess fluid in the lungs," she said gently. "In your case, it's unilateral—just in the right lung. Given your symptoms and personal history, I suspect this is a complication of pneumonia, caused by foreign material being aspirated into the respiratory tract."

Arcturus had courteously averted his gaze during the examination, but now our eyes met.

"From the waterboard," I said.

"That seems likely. If you inhaled your own vomit, or water got into your lungs, it could have caused an infection," Cordier said. "Especially if the water in question was soiled. You're also dehydrated."

Her voice sounded distant. Instead, I heard my own terrified screams as the water carved its way down my throat. I tasted it again.

I had thought the memories were all that had followed me from that dark room. Yet ever since, I had been growing a souvenir inside my own body.

Cordier cupped my elbow, stirring me back to the present. "Is anything else bothering you, Paige?"

I pressed my ribs. Part of me was still in the darkness.

"Broke my wrist last year." I drew my nightshirt back on. "Gives me trouble sometimes."

Cordier waited for me to show her which arm, then rolled up my sleeve. She kneaded the fine bones of my hand and wrist before she used her scanner again. I had never relished strangers touching me, but Cordier was so composed, it was difficult to be tense in her presence. Even the way she spoke was calm, her voice as even as the surface of a pool.

"Scaphoid fracture," she concluded. "That bone tends to heal slowly. Did you fall on it?"

I nodded. "Scion knows she has an injury to that wrist," Ducos pointed out. "A cast will make her conspicuous."

Cordier shot her an exasperated look and probed my wrist again. This time it was harder not to flinch. "It needs support," she said. "This kind of fracture can lead to painful difficulties." She reached into her case. "A temporary brace will do. She can remove it on assignment."

Ducos chewed the inside of her cheek. Presumably taking her silence as permission, Cordier went to work, a crease between her razor-thin eyebrows. By the time she was finished, it looked as if I was wearing a fingerless glove. I gave my hand an experimental clench.

"There. Wear it when you can." Cordier tucked her sleek hair behind her ears again. "I know a medic in another sub-network who has dealt with waterboard survivors. He'll have what I need to treat the effusion." She rose and smoothed her skirt. "Give me a couple of hours. Until then, Flora, you need to rest. Lie on your right side to help with the pain."

I made a noncommittal sound. She gathered up her case and left the room at a brisk trot.

"Cordier is one of the best in the network," Ducos said. "I am sure she can ease your discomfort."

I was too tired to so much as nod. Even my fingers hurt, right down to the smallest joints.

"I need to know what happened in there." Her expression softened. "I'm sorry to make you talk, but—"

"It's fine. This is important."

Speaking in an agonized whisper, I gave her a lightly edited version of how I had ended up imprisoned in the Hôtel Garuche: I had wanted a closer look at the outside of the building and had left the safe house to scout the perimeter. Another clairvoyant had detected me. I had been able to dispose of my dissimulator before I was hauled inside and locked up.

"By hiding the dissimulator, you broke the link to Mannequin," Ducos mused. "Even in the face of arrest, you remained calm and protected the network." For once, she made no move to smoke. "Now, the million-pound question. Did you obtain the intelligence we require?"

"I did."

Ducos dropped her shoulders and exhaled. It was the strongest reaction I had seen from her. For the first time, I noticed the puffy shadows under her eyes, impossible to polish.

"Tell me," she said.

"What do you know about the Suzerain?"

"An unidentified entity or entities at the highest level of Scion. That's all I can disclose."

If only she knew.

"Weaver ordered Ménard to provide a residence for that entity in France. A city where rare anormales will be transported in tribute," I said. "Ménard hates the idea, and despises the Suzerain. The document I mentioned, the one Frère took to London, was the Great Territorial Act—his formal agreement to the deal. He signed under pressure, and it seems he's honored it."

Ducos was listening raptly. Her left hand lingered close to her pocket, where she kept her silver case of cigarettes, and I realized she must be refraining for my sake.

"Ménard is plotting a coup," I continued. "He plans to imprison the Suzerain and her supporters inside the city he was forced to build for them. He plans to take England from under Frank Weaver. And then he plans to destroy them both. To claim Scion for himself."

"Where is this city?"

"The best intelligence I have suggests Versailles."

I filled her in on the fine details as much as I could, only leaving out the affair between Frère and Cade—useful information, but it might put both Cade and the child in danger. I explained that Ménard had captured an emissary from the Suzerain, and that he was the one who had given me the location. Yes, I was confident he would keep quiet about it.

"You did well. Very well," Ducos said, at last. "All of this could have explosive potential."

"I did as you asked," I said. "Completed the assignment. Proved I could follow orders."

"Yes." She seemed lost in thought. "You did."

"Then perhaps we can discuss my militia in London."

Her gaze sharpened. "When I return, I will hear you out." She stood. "Well done, Flora. To have escaped Inquisitorial custody in one piece is a tremendous accomplishment by itself, but to have done it in your condition, *and* finished the assignment—I am very proud to have you in Mannequin."

I nodded, relieved both that Ducos was pleased and that I could stop talking for a while.

"Now that Portugal has submitted, it may take several days for me to receive new orders," she said. "Until I return, stay indoors."

The news curdled in my stomach. "President Gonçalves has surrendered, then."

"The fight was over. She must have accepted that no help was coming." She slid her hands into her pockets. "Cordier should return by noon tomorrow."

She turned to leave. "Ducos," I said, and she stopped. "Do you think Scion will take Spain?"

Her face was impossible to read, but something in her eyes chilled me.

"I think," she said, "that it's only a matter of time."

15

A Sedition of Clairvoyants

Our plans were on hold. Arcturus made it quietly clear that he had no intention of leaving me alone with pneumonia and a fever, and even I wasn't fool enough to think I could find the perdues myself in this state. Until Cordier came back to treat me, there was nothing to be done.

I lay in my bedroom and listened to the rattle of my breath. Each time, I imagined rotten water bubbling in my lung.

Even though I had slept after the escape, I was so tired and sore that I drifted off again. When I woke, it was sunset. I turned back onto my bad side and tried to remember how to just *rest*. My fever made it hard. I was too hot for the duvet, too cold not to have some of it over me.

After a while, a knock came at the door. Arcturus came in and placed a large glass of water on the nightstand.

"Cordier said you were dehydrated."

"Thank you," I said.

"And I found this in the bookcase." He handed me a rolled-up page. "It may interest you."

On any other evening, I would have asked him to stay and distract me, but speaking was still difficult, and there was a tension between us that had yet to be snapped. I nodded my acknowledgment instead, and he left. I unrolled the paper to find a regional map of the Scion Republic of France.

Kornephoros had said that Versailles was to the west. I traced a line from our location to a large area of woodland, where I found two words.

ZONE INTERDITE

A forbidden sector.

I had learned about Versailles in my Scion history lessons at school. Our classes had focused on the debauchery of its aristocrats, who had gossiped, gambled, banqueted, and otherwise frittered their time away while the poor starved on the streets. All of them, our teacher told us, had deserved to have their heads cut off and paraded about Paris. Good riddance.

With its proven suspicion of religion and monarchy, France had been the perfect candidate to join the fold of the Republic of Scion. The official story was that Versailles had been demolished within two years of the conversion.

Nadine and Zeke were in there. The last time I had seen them, they had chosen to leave with Jaxon after the scrimmage and support his claim to be the rightful Underlord. Now they had clearly joined me and Arcturus on the list of people Jaxon Hall had stabbed in the back.

And Michael. He had been imprisoned in the first colony for years, and now he had been thrown into another.

He had lasted over a month on his own before Scion had re-arrested him. If only we hadn't been separated in London, I might have been able to keep him safe.

I was certain Sheol II would be twice as secure as its predecessor. Trap-pits and landmines. Ethereal fences. Armed guards. Almost certainly some Emim, too, if there were enough auras to tempt them. I could only hope the perdues would know of a way to avoid its defenses.

If Arcturus was right. If they did have a route into Versailles.

He was proving instrumental in this search. I had underestimated his ability to navigate the underworld. I wanted to break the silence between us, to return to the warm familiarity we had shared here, but both of us were smarting.

Cordier was late. By the time she returned, it was dark, and I was settled in the armchair with a mug of tea. She carried a briefcase in one hand and her own bag on her shoulder.

"Sorry, Flora. That took longer than I expected." She set down her bags. "How do you feel?"

"No better or worse." I set my jaw against the pain. "Just made a pot of tea, if you want some."

"That's sweet of you, but I can't stay long." Cordier took off her shoes, which were dusted with snow, and draped her coat over the back of the couch. "I need to get all this back to Figurine."

"Figurine?"

"Another sub-network. Where's your handsome friend?" she added as she unclipped the briefcase.

I nodded to the doorway. Cordier looked over her shoulder to see that Arcturus had appeared from his room. "So he is." She brushed her silken hair behind one ear. "Hello again."

"Doctor Cordier," Arcturus said.

"Oh, please, call me Eléonore. We should all be friends in Mannequin." Her crimson lipstick was so flawless, I was sure she must have used a stencil. "I never did catch your name."

"Warden."

"Warden. How mysterious." Cordier smiled, then started to remove equipment from the case. "How did you two come to be . . . associates?"

"Long story." With difficulty, I shifted upright. "You met when I was in the Hôtel Garuche, did you?"

"Briefly," Arcturus said.

"Yes, we didn't have much time to speak. I hope we can remedy that," Cordier said lightly. "We work under such pressure in Mannequin. It's important to foster good relations."

Arcturus inclined his head to her, and her smile deepened. A strange feeling winged through my stomach as she took a bottle of antiseptic from her bag.

I had never seen anyone try to flirt with a Rephaite. He could flirt right back at her if he liked. It was no business of mine.

"I need to do one more scan," Cordier said to me, rubbing the gel between her hands. "Do you mind?"

"No."

Arcturus caught my eye, and I nodded. I wanted him to stay.

Cordier had me sit on a dining chair and remove my shirt again. After snapping on a pair of gloves, she slathered my back in something cold and rolled a scanner across it. After a while, she put it down.

"Good." She wiped the gel off my back and delved into her bag again. "I have a course of antibiotics for the pneumonia, but I can relieve some of your symptoms now by draining the effusion. It's a short procedure where I'd have to insert a needle between your ribs. You'll be a little bit uncomfortable."

"It's fine," I said. "Can't remember the last time I wasn't a little bit uncomfortable."

Cordier chuckled. "All right. Lean forward on the table for me, so I can reach your back." I folded my arms on it. "Perfect."

I decided not to look too hard at her equipment. A chill dab of antiseptic came first, then a sting and a throb as she injected the numbing agent. The edge of the table dug into my ribs. Arcturus brought me a cushion, which I slid between me and the table, before he took the seat opposite.

Cordier hummed spryly as she worked. Even though my back was numb, I grimaced when the pressure started. It was like she had pulled a plug from my back. I fought the sudden urge to cough again.

Arcturus offered a hand. I grasped it and squeezed until I was afraid I would crush his fingers. I was light-headed by the time Cordier said, "Needle out." A rustle of movement. "Let me put a dressing on the puncture."

She wrapped a bandage around my middle to hold the dressing in place, then came to sit beside me and placed two glass bottles on the table. They were full of something that looked horribly like melted butter.

"There," she said, with an air of satisfaction.

"Lovely." I had a strong stomach, but those bottles turned it. "All that was in my lung?"

"All lungs contain pleural fluid. You just had too much."

She slotted both bottles into her bag and listened to my breathing again. Whatever the outcome, she looked content, and set about packing the last of her equipment away.

"Breathing and speaking should be much easier now. Change the dressing every few days, take it easy, and please, drink." She patted the briefcase. "Medicine for the pneumonia. Everything you need is in here, including dosage instructions. Don't miss a dose."

"Thanks so much," I said.

"Just doing my job." She took a folded piece of paper from her pocket and slid it across the table to Arcturus. "My current number, if you need anything. Ducos will visit soon."

She stepped into her shoes, picked up her bag and coat, and was gone. Arcturus looked intently at my face.

"How do you feel?"

I plucked up my courage and took the deepest breath I dared. There was still a stab of discomfort in my chest, but now it was as if the knife was wrapped in several layers of cloth.

"Better." My exhalation turned into a sigh of relief. "Not perfect, but better."

"Good."

"Which means," I went on, "that I'm fine on my own for a bit. You have to find the perdues now, before someone else does." I reached for my nightshirt. "You need aura, too."

"I will go on the condition that you rest while I am gone."

I assented with a heavy nod. The numbing agent was already wearing off, and I was becoming acutely conscious of the fact that my lung had been flushed with a seven-inch needle.

In my room, I got back into bed. Arcturus brought a jug of water. "Cordier has left instructions for intravenous therapy," he said, as he filled my glass. "If you wish to start at once."

"Might as well. Can't wait to get shot of this cough."

For our first few days in the safe house, I had taken saline through a drip, unable to stomach water. Arcturus set everything up again, then sat on the edge of my bed. I watched as he gently attached my hand to the pouch of medicine.

"You know Cordier was flirting with you," I said, breaking a long silence.

"I had not noticed."

"She's . . . very beautiful."

"Doubtless." He released my hand. "I will return soon. Use the cord if you need me."

He was gone before I could wish him luck. Or admit how self-ishly relieved I was that throughout the time Eléonore Cordier had been with us, his gaze had been reserved for me.

****

The apartment was too quiet. I drank as much as I could. Even though breathing was easier, my chest still ached, and my face was so hot I thought the pillow would catch fire. In the end, I slid into a drowse—but a vivid image swam toward me. Arcturus, inter-twined with Cordier, her hair caught between his fingers. Then Kornephoros took her place in his arms, and I was chained in agony on the waterboard again, unable to move. Only to see. To watch.

I jolted from the fever dream, weltered in sweat, each cheek an open flame. Almost at once, I tumbled into a much deeper sleep, the hallucination drowned by darkness.

It was past midnight by the time I woke, sensing Arcturus. I released myself from the drip and went to meet him.

His hair and coat were damp with melted snow. "Did you find Mélusine?" I asked him.

The fever dream was scorched onto the front of my mind. I forced myself to look him in the face.

"In the coffeehouse." His eyes were pure yellow, no trace of the green tinge they had in their neutral state. "Those perdues who are not in hiding will meet us in Impasse Hautefeuille."

"When?"

"Half past two."

"Good." I turned away. "I'll get ready."

Disturbed though it was, the nap had refreshed me. I went back to my room, where I took the cannula out of my hand. Once I had staunched the bleeding, I opened the nightstand and lifted out a velvet-lined box I had seen, but never used. Greasepaint and brushes glinted inside.

Black Moth had slept for too long. Time to paint over the cracks in me and resurrect the queen.

First, I needed to make a concerted effort with my hair. Leading a rebellion hadn't left me with an abundance of free time to look after it, as I had when I was still in the gang. Back then, I had loved taking hour-long soaks in the tiny bathtub at the den, then lounging on my bed and working one buttery cream or another into my curls. Jaxon had usually banged his cane on our shared wall and told me to stop steaming up the windows with my faineance, whatever that meant.

At present, my hair was a mess of split ends and stubborn knots. I sat on the edge of the bath, wet my curls in stages, then worked conditioner through to the ends. Once they had a good coating, I teased out the tangles with a wide-toothed comb. Though the wetness on my scalp and nape unnerved me, I found myself relaxing into the routine: the scent of the conditioner, the small victory of undoing a knot. Finally, I rinsed out the suds and found a diffuser to attach to the blow-dryer. My hair sprang.

Back in my room, I took out some cosmetics and mixed a base to cover my bruises, leaving my scar from the scrimmage on show. Next, I dipped a brush in lampblack. From the first stroke, I could see my old self rising from the ashes, all the fear and damage left beneath. Once my eyes had wings, I painted my lips with a dark glaze that went on smooth as ink.

In the wardrobe, I searched for armor, wishing I had Eliza to offer her opinion, or Nick to tell me how fierce I looked. On days and nights like this, I felt their absence keenly. I pulled on a blouse and trousers before I found a black coat, severely cut, which I belted at the waist. My hair had grown just long enough to sit on its roped shoulders. I laced on a pair of boots and slid a blade-like clip into my hair. The final touch was a scarf over my nose and mouth.

Even with all this chain mail and greasepaint, I would have to work hard to convince the perdues that I was a strong ally, worthy of their respect. I could not show them the part of me that wanted to curl inward. The part of me that was forever trapped in the dark.

Arcturus was waiting by the door, gloved and booted. We left without speaking. Ducos had ordered me not to go out, but I would have to risk it. There was no more time to waste.

Impasse Hautefeuille was a dead-end alley, close to the safe house. When we arrived, the perdues—five of them—were already waiting under a lantern. It bathed them all in eerie blue. Instead of skulls, like the rest of their syndicate, they wore the most beautiful masks I had ever laid eyes on. They gave the effect of a shelf of dolls, turning as one to look at us.

"Réphaïte," one of them muttered.

I stopped in front of them and drew my shoulders back. Arcturus stood just behind me.

"I'm told you are the perdues," I said. "The followers of Le Vieux Orphelin."

"Five of the thirteen." Shadows filled the eyeholes of the nearest mask, which was decorated with painted wisteria and nettle leaves. "I am Renelde du Linceul. And I ask that you show us your face."

"Mélusine has already seen it."

"Yes." Renelde slid a gloved hand into her pocket. "We would like to confirm her claim that she met the Underqueen in Montparnasse. Since the Underqueen was killed in December, I'm sure you understand our confusion."

I reached up to untie the scarf and let it fall away. There was a long silence as they all took the measure of me—of my facial landmarks, as Gabrielle Auclair would have said. Renelde reached up and removed her mask, revealing angular eyes, deep brown skin, and low cheekbones. Long, dark braids framed her face. She was about thirty, perhaps a touch younger.

"Je ne leur fais pas confiance," muttered the sensor beside her. His half mask was fashioned into a vulpine face, complete with ears and a black nose. "Il se pourrait qu'elle soit une impostrice."

"The grands ducs thought I was an imposter, too," I said.

Renelde raised her eyebrows. "You speak French."

I nodded. The fox pressed his lips together. They were just visible in the shadow of the mask.

"Madelle," he said, "no offense intended, but you could be anyone. You must show us your gift, or—"

"You do not *want* a dreamwalker to show you her gift, Malperdy," Renelde cut in. "That"—she nodded to Arcturus—"is a Réphaïte. Which means that this woman is Paige Mahoney." She gave me a brief smile. "Welcome to Paris, Underqueen. We were hoping you might pay us a visit."

"How did you survive the bullet?" came another voice. "We all saw."

"It was a rubber bullet," I said. "You know about the Rephaim, then."

"Yes, the pamphlet was translated here." Renelde eyed Arcturus. "Instant bestseller."

Another one of the perdues stepped forward. "Underqueen." He went so far as to drop to one knee, making the bells in his three-pronged hat jingle. "An honor. I am Le Bateleur."

"Please, stand. There's no need." I held out a hand to him. "You're one of the patrones."

"Yes." He accepted my hand and stood. "I serve under Le Vieux Orphelin." His voice was like gravel. "He has heard tell of you, and of your Mime Order, from the merchants who go between here and London. He wanted to strike an alliance with she who destroyed Senshield—to help you, should you ever come to Paris."

Someone who had heard of me and whose first response had *not* been to want me dead. What a treat.

"Le Vieux Orphelin is missing," I said.

"Yes," Renelde said. "Le Prince Creux, his compagnon d'armes, now holds his authority – I think you would call him a mollisher in London." She fitted her mask back over her face. "We fear Le Vieux Orphelin is in the Bastille, along with Le Prince Creux's sister, La Tarasque. She disappeared the same night."

"I don't know about La Tarasque," I said, "but Le Vieux Orphelin is definitely not in the Bastille."

They all looked at each other. "You know what became of Le Vieux Orphelin?" Le Bateleur said softly.

"He was taken." I folded my arms. "You have an interloper in your syndicate. A trafficker of anormales with a network of hunters at his command. He goes after those he deems valuable and sells them to Scion." Mutters. "Le Latronpuche and La Reine des Thunes have been hand in glove with him since he arrived here. They confessed to it when I met them."

"The Man in the Iron Mask," another of the perdues muttered. "The shadow in the slums. Is he the interloper?"

"Yes. He called himself the Rag and Bone Man in London. He preyed on my syndicate, too," I said. "He means to find and sell all of you to the Grand Inquisitor. Ménard is out for your blood."

"Fuck Ménard," came a sharp retort.

"Hush, Malperdy," Le Bateleur said, just as sharply. "We have guests." He turned back to me. "Did you bring us here only to warn us of this danger, Underqueen, or do you have a plan?"

"Both. I believe that the other two grands ducs sold Le Vieux Orphelin, and that he was transported to a new high-security prison in Versailles. And I believe you know a way in."

There was a tense period in which they all traded looks again. Renelde planted her hands on her wide hips and took a breath.

"Le Passage des Voleurs," she said. "A tunnel in a very deep part of the carrières, which leads to a cemetery in Versailles. Some time ago, Le Vieux Orphelin and I found the entrance and ventured to the ruin at its end. Over several years, we mapped and explored every inch of Versailles, often visiting to plunder it."

I exchanged a fleeting glance with Arcturus. His instinct had been right on the money.

"Does Scion know about this secret way?" I asked.

"Not to our knowledge," Renelde said. "We call the entrance to the tunnel Apollyon—a shaft that goes far deeper than most sensible anormales would descend. Fortunately, we are not sensible." I could hear her smile. "That part of the mines is not for the faint-hearted."

"I've been called many things, but never faint-hearted." I pocketed my hands. "Do Le Latronpuche and La Reine des Thunes know where it is?"

Malperdy chuckled.

"No, Underqueen, they do not," Le Bateleur said. "Le Vieux Orphelin is a generous man, but he has never trusted Le Latronpuche." His bells tinkled. "With good reason, it seems."

"They know he *has* a way in, of course," Renelde added, "but not where it is. They allowed him to keep this secret on the understanding that he shared a third of the artifacts with them."

"Like the jewelery La Reine des Thunes wears," I conjectured.

"Yes. Worn by the Gray Queen herself. Le Vieux Orphelin gave them to his sister-in-chaos for her fortieth birthday." She sniffed. "See how she repays him."

"I'll be plain with you all," I said. "I want to break into Versailles and bring its prisoners back to Paris. Some friends of mine are among them. Would any of you be willing to guide us through the tunnel?"

Another silence.

"Underqueen," Le Bateleur said, "we would do anything to help Le Vieux Orphelin—his absence grieves us, as does the betrayal— but the journey could end in all our deaths, and that will not help him at all."

"The passage is too fragile now," Renelde explained. "It is an ancient mining tunnel, vulnerable to collapse. Le Vieux Orphelin forbade us from using it again."

"It might be his only way out of captivity alive," I said. "Ménard has learned of his imprisonment and wants him returned to Paris for execution. If we don't get him out of there, he's going straight to the guillotine."

Slowly, Renelde folded her arms.

"What lies at the end of that tunnel now is more dangerous than you can imagine," I said. "I'm willing. If you are."

Another look passed between them.

"Excuse us a moment," Le Bateleur said with a small bow, and the five of them turned their backs on us to confer. Renelde pulled out a burner phone. I hung back with Arcturus.

"Do you think they will agree?" he asked me, too low for them to hear.

"For a price." I tapped my foot. "In the syndicate, you learn to smell desperation."

"You believe we appear desperate?"

"Well, you have to be reasonably desperate to ask for help from somebody dressed as a fucking jester."

It was a while before the perdues returned to us. "Underqueen," Le Bateleur said, "we must put this to Le Prince Creux. If he agrees to your proposal, a small team of the most experienced perdues

247

will escort you to Apollyon and continue with you to Versailles. The journey will take two or three days."

Suddenly my stomach felt heavy. I remembered blood on the snow in London.

"I want to make this very clear," I said. "Anyone who comes with me—with us," I added, with a look toward Arcturus, "will be putting their lives on the line. We'll be breaking into a facility that Scion has very good reason to keep secret. There's a chance none of us will come out of it alive."

"If there is any chance that we can rescue Le Vieux Orphelin, we must," Renelde said. "You will need good fighters. Le Prince Creux will ensure you have them. I will join you."

"So will I," Malperdy said.

"But if you accept this alliance," Le Bateleur said, "we must ask one more thing of you, Underqueen."

"Join us in hunting down the Man in the Iron Mask," Malperdy clenched a freckled hand. "Make us this promise, and we will go with you to the depths of Apollyon. And beyond it."

"I will. Gladly," I said. "I imagine you'll need some time to prepare for the journey, but we don't have much."

Renelde nodded. "Meet us three days from now."

"Good. We'll see you on the ninth, then, at nightfall," I said. "Tell us where to find you."

****

As soon as we were back in the safe house, I scrubbed off all the greasepaint, changed into leggings and an oversized sweater, then slumped at the kitchen table to consult the map of the citadel.

I knew from the ledger that the Rag and Bone Man hunted close to Rue Montmartre. Not only was it near the Court of Miracles—a rich source of income for a voyant trafficker—but when I accessed the Scionet, it informed me that the first sewer in Paris had been constructed there. The original foundations might have survived. If so, there was no more perfect lair for him. He could drag his victims down through the manholes. When we returned with them, those victims would serve him the justice he had evaded in London.

Ducos would return soon with another task for me. I could stay and earn her approval, foster my relationship with Domino—or leave it behind altogether and disappear back into the underworld.

I had been able to hold my two selves in balance for a time. The insurgent and the intelligence agent. The queen and the subject. Now I felt them pull in opposite directions, straining fragile seams. Black Moth could not coexist with Flora Blake. In the end, one would consume the other.

I rolled the map up and stowed it away. Inexplicably, I found myself drawn to the parlor.

Arcturus was watching a news report, stone-faced, one hand wrapped around a tumbler of wine. Neither of us said anything, but the silence was softer. I sat beside him and followed his gaze to the news of more celebrations across Scion.

They would never show the truth. The violence and agony as soldiers marched into every settlement in Portugal. Religious houses destroyed, statues felled, whole libraries of books reduced to cinders in the biblioclasms. The unmaking of democracy.

Something pulled my attention to the æther. Arcturus noticed how still I suddenly became.

"Is it Ducos?" he asked.

"No. Someone else." I rose. "Someone we know."

****

I slung on a coat and boots and picked up an umbrella as I left. It would shield me from cameras as much the rain.

There was no reason she should be here, no reason at all—but while my gift had sometimes deceived me, it had never told me an outright lie. The dreamscape was farther away by the heartbeat. I shut the door of the safe house behind me and walked as fast as I physically could down the quay, following the Seine.

When I reached her, she was leaning against a streetlamp, a hood drawn tight around her face, a scarf over her nose and mouth. Dark eyes looked out at me from under a knitted cap.

"Paige," Ivy said. "I hoped you'd find me."

16

Loyalty

The last time I had seen Ivy Jacob, we had been in the deep-level crisis facility in London, where the syndicate had taken shelter from the soldiers of Scion. To convince the tosher king to let us hide in his underground domain, and to atone for unknowingly helping the gray market, she had joined his service and pledged herself to a life in the storm drains and sewers.

I took her straight back to the safe house and bundled her inside. She was soaked to the skin.

"Tell me no one's on your tail," I said to her as I shut the door.

"Vigiles caught a whiff of my aura a while back. Don't worry." Ivy kicked off her boots. "I lost them."

"You're a well-known fugitive. Coming here was off the cot." I locked up and drew the chain across. "Why would you risk it?"

"Glym and Eliza sent me," she said. When I turned into the light, her eyes widened. "Paige, your face."

"Minor altercation with a tyrant." I hung up my coat. "Did you plan to just wander about until I picked up on you?"

"Pretty much. Worked a treat, though, didn't it?"

It had been a very long time since I had last seen Ivy smile. She was disheveled and sticky with sweat, but that smile lit her face all the way to her eyes. With a sigh, I embraced her.

"Welcome to Paris," I said.

"Thanks."

Ivy pulled down her hood and took off her cap. Her dark hair was now long enough to cover the tips of her ears, almost as long as it had been before Thuban Sargas had shorn it all off in the colony. She was still hollow-eyed, but there was a new firmness about her—she stood tall in a way she never had in London.

"Someone got me and Ro out of the Beneath," she said. "I'm told it was on your orders."

"I wasn't about to leave you to rot down there." I motioned for her to follow me upstairs. "Didn't the toshers have something to say about you leaving, though?"

"Eliza and Wynn are thrashing it out with Styx. Some other much-hated voyant will take my place, but we all agreed it was best I left. You know, to stop anyone killing me for not serving my full sentence."

"Well, you're safe now."

Her only crime had been to not question her mime-lord. I had done no worse as a mollisher.

As I led her up to the landing, Ivy peeled off her gloves. "This place is nice," she said. "And so *warm*."

"Central heating. It's a wonder."

Arcturus was still in the parlor. The instant Ivy stepped in and saw him, she froze.

"Ivy," he said, after a pause. If her appearance had surprised him, he concealed it. "Welcome."

There was another silence before she replied. "Warden. Didn't expect to see you here." She took off her fleece-lined coat and left it on the nearest chair. "Paige, could you show me where the bathroom is?"

"Of course," I said.

I led her down the corridor. As soon as we were out of sight, Ivy grasped my shoulder.

"No one told me he was with you," she whispered. "Did the Ranthen send him to watch you, or something?"

"I needed someone with me. He volunteered," I said. "I was in a bad way after . . . the Archon."

"Right. I forgot," Ivy muttered. "Rephs *are* known for their caring sides."

She had just about stomached their presence in London, but she had never relished it, or gone near them. Each of us was fighting a private battle with our demons from the colony, and Ivy had more than most.

"Can you live with him being here?" I asked in an undertone. "This is our only hideout."

"Yeah. I don't expect you to kick him out," she said, gaze averted. "Can I use the shower?"

"Absolutely. Let me grab you a towel," I said, heading for the hot press. "Help yourself to clothes and anything you need from the bathroom. There's a spare toothbrush in the cabinet, I think."

"This place is like a hotel." Ivy took in the clean walls, the plasterwork. "Who's paying for it?"

I considered before answering: "I can't go into specifics, but it's a sympathizer. In Scion."

Ivy folded her arms at that, as if she had a chill. "No wonder it's so nice," was all she said. She took the towel and facecloth I offered. "Thanks. You've been here with Warden the whole time?"

"Ever since New Year."

"Okay. And how's that been?"

"More normal than you'd think. We play cards, watch films. He's cooked for me. Tried to cook for me, anyway," I added. Ivy rewarded me with a tiny smile. "Don't worry. I'll handle meals."

Ivy had known little more than cruelty and contempt at the hands of Rephaim. If she was going to be with us for a while, Arcturus needed to show her that some of them were capable of kindness. While she showered, I returned to the parlor.

"Perhaps I should find somewhere else to stay for the night," Arcturus said. "To set Ivy at ease."

"There's nowhere to go," I pointed out. "Just give her some space. Let her get used to you." I took a tissue from my sleeve and coughed into it. "She can sleep in my room. I'll take the couch."

"You have had enough trouble sleeping. Take my bed."

"If you're sure."

"Yes."

In my room, I changed the bed linen and laid out a nightshirt. On second thoughts, I put it back and left the drawer open, so Ivy could choose something she felt comfortable in. I knew from Wynn Jacob, who loved Ivy like a mother, that she had scars from her torture.

In the kitchen, Arcturus boiled the kettle and put a heat pad on charge while I prepared a hot meal. I had never been much of a cook—in the gang, we had usually eaten at cookshops, unless Nick graced us with something homemade—but I could cobble a plate of comfort food together. Mashed potatoes soaked in gravy, a heap of buttered peas, two oven-ready pies.

A creak sounded in the corridor. I turned to see Ivy in long sports trousers and a sleeveless top, hair towel-dried into spikes, skin flushed from the shower. She shot Arcturus a wary look.

"Better?" I asked.

She blew out a breath. "You have no idea."

"Good. Now, how do you like your tea?"

"Milk and four sugars, please," she said. Her top exposed the mottled scarring on her right arm, where the Rag and Bone Man had burned off her tattoo. "Can't believe I'm actually in *Paris*. And that I just had a hot shower. I'd forgotten what warm felt like."

I took a carton from the fridge. "I can't imagine."

"Oh, I reckon you can. The waterboard couldn't have been much cozier than the Beneath."

After a moment, I poured the milk. "You know about that, then."

"I didn't see your so-called death, but Eliza told me about it." She watched me stir the tea. "She and Glym made sure everyone knows who janxed Senshield," she went on. "The syndicate loves you now."

"Really?" I said, skeptical.

"Well, *love* might be too strong a word. The syndicate does not want to strangle you with your own intestines now."

"Oh, stop, I'm blushing."

Ivy grinned, giving me a glimpse of the gap between two of her bottom teeth. "Still can't believe you actually handed yourself over to reach Senshield." She accepted the mug of tea from me. "I don't know whether you're brave or stupid, Paige, but you get things done."

"I try my best."

"Seriously, though, are you all right?"

There was understanding behind the question. She knew what it was to be tortured.

"I'm . . . trying to be," I concluded. "I imagine you're doing the same." When she nodded, I showed her through the open doors to the parlor. "Make yourself comfortable. You must be tired."

"Yeah." She curled up in the armchair. "Sorry if I doze off. Haven't slept since I got to France."

"Get some food in you first." I sat on the couch. Arcturus stayed in the kitchen, within earshot, clearing up the chaos of saucepans and spoons I had left in my wake. "How did you get here?"

"From Dover. Glym bribed an old friend of his to get me across in her fishing boat, which dropped me in Boulogne," Ivy said. "Somebody else drove me to Paris."

She was fortunate to have survived the journey. "Why?"

"Two reasons. The first is because we need help."

"Go on."

"You might already know that Scion has started a military operation to root out the Mime Order. Operation Albion," she said. I nodded. "Even though Senshield is gone, there are more soldiers than ever, and it's getting harder to move around. Spot checks. Random searches for numa and weapons. Brutal interrogations. London is still under martial law."

A sharp reminder that Scion was at war on two fronts. One with the free world, and one with its own unnaturals. "Is the syndicate still using the deep-level shelter?" I asked. It was where they had all hidden from Senshield.

"Yeah. That's been a big help," Ivy said, "but a lot of people know about it, which makes it risky. As part of Operation Albion, Scion is handing out immunity from execution in exchange for information. They've also managed to plant a few spies in the Mime Order."

Her expression changed. My fingertips blanched on my mug. "Was there a betrayal?"

"The Ferryman. His whole cell is either dead or imprisoned, sold out for a pardon."

I closed my eyes. Reorganizing the syndicate into insulated cells had been hard work, but at least none of the captured voyants would be able to betray many others. A small comfort.

"He didn't give up the shelter, at least," Ivy said. Her mouth tightened. "Guess he had one shred of decency."

"What can I do to help?"

"We really need more allies. A new base for voyants who are in particular danger, or are most important to the cause. Eliza reckoned you might have already made contact with the Parisian syndicate, that they might be able to help us with sanctuary or supplies."

"I made contact with them as soon as I arrived." I smothered a cough. "Unfortunately, the Rag and Bone Man got his claws into them first. There aren't many here we can trust."

Her mouth clamped shut again.

"That's the other reason I came," she finally said. "To warn the Parisian syndicate about the Rag and Bone Man. We found out he'd fled here."

Ivy had been his mollisher. She had unwittingly helped him choose voyants for the gray market, only for him to turn on her and sell her to the Rephaim. It was because of him that she had spent half a year at the mercy of a monster. He had also sanctioned the murder of the woman she loved. If not for her testimony, we would never have discovered his illicit trade.

"His days are numbered," I said, "but we have something else to do before we get rid of him."

The oven beeped. I craned myself up and returned to the kitchen, where Arcturus was loading the dishwasher, and served up our meal.

While she ate, I told Ivy everything that had happened, from my infiltration of the Hôtel Garuche to the meeting with the perdues. I chose not to mention Domino, instead implying I had made those plans with Arcturus. Safer for Ivy not to know.

For the most part, Ivy listened in heavy-eyed silence and chewed every mouthful of food as if it were her last. When I got to my reunion with Cade, her brow furrowed in thought.

"I remember him," she said. "He wasn't as cruel as the other red-jackets. Never openly mocked me, anyway." She pulled a face. "Frère, though. That's poor taste on another level."

"I said as much to him."

I kept going. With every revelation, her face hardened a little more. When I stopped, she finished the dregs of her tea.

"I don't usually say this sort of thing, Paige," she murmured, "but I feel like the æther made sure I arrived tonight for a reason." She put the mug down. "I'm going with you to Sheol II."

As soon as I had seen her in the street, I had known this would happen. "It will be a very difficult journey," I said. "And we don't know who or what we're going to find at the end."

"Thuban will be there."

It was the first time Arcturus had spoken in half an hour. I turned to look at him, as did Ivy.

"How do you know?" I said.

"Thuban lacks the qualities necessary in a diplomat, a politician, or a strategist. He is only capable of cruelty. There is nowhere else for him but Sheol II." He spoke in soft tones, as if Ivy could be startled by too loud a sound. "I do not say this to frighten you, Ivy. Only to warn you."

"If he is there," Ivy shot back, "then all the better. I want to do everything to him that he did to me."

"I urge you not to confront him."

"Why?" she asked bitterly. "Because I'm a sad victim who'll never be any kind of threat to him?"

"Because you are alive, and there is no greater vengeance you could take against Thuban."

Ivy stared at him. I had seen that look in my own eyes many times, in the fog of the mirror, when I rose from the bath and the darkness was close enough to touch.

"He failed to break you. He failed to kill you," Arcturus continued. "You bested him by surviving, and for Thuban, there could be no greater humiliation than losing to a human. He believed your life was brittle and worthless, and you proved him wrong. Every breath you take now strikes a harder blow than any weapon. Die at his hands, however, and he wins."

She swallowed, her mouth a wavering line. Her collarbones surged out with each inhalation.

"He's right," I said quietly. "Thuban would make short work of either of us. Surviving is the best way to piss him off now."

"Whether or not I do anything about Thuban," she said, "I'm still coming. I want to do my bit."

"If that's what you want." After a silence, I rose. "I suppose we'd better all get some rest, then—we've a long journey ahead of us. There's a bedroom all made up for you, Ivy."

"I don't want to put you out of your bed." Ivy hesitated. "You don't sound very well."

"Pneumonia. Just had some very attractive yellow slop sucked out of my lung, in fact."

"Lung fever?" Ivy looked stricken. "Paige, that's really serious. People died from it in Jacob's Island."

"I'm all right." I showed her the dressing taped to my hand. "Taking my medicine."

"Okay." She lowered her gaze. "There is . . . one more thing."

I nodded. Ivy retrieved her coat and pulled a parcel from one of its pockets.

"I don't know how Eliza got this—I guess from the same person who helped you escape from the Archon." Not meeting my eyes, she held it out. "It's what your dad left you in his will."

A roar filled my ears.

"I'm really sorry, Paige," Ivy said. "I didn't know my real parents, but I know how I'd feel if I lost Vern or Wynn."

I took the parcel from her in silence. It was wrapped in waxy brown paper, tied with string. Ivy stepped out of the room, leaving me holding all that was left in the world of my father.

****

The parcel lay innocuous on the pillow, offering no clues. I sat on the bed with it for a long time before I took a knife I had brought from the kitchen and held it to the string, which was knotted too tightly to unravel.

I clenched my fingers around the knife, steadied the blade with my thumb, angled it. It sliced the string with a rasp like scissors through hair.

The paper was secured with a wax seal. I snapped it off and folded back the paper, little by little, revealing what my father had left me: a box, about the length of a cigar, carved from applewood. I lifted it closer to my face. It smelled dimly of clove, and something else.

It smelled like my grandmother. Like her perfume. I could never have described its notes, but I would have known it anywhere. My grandfather had given her a bottle on their anniversary each year, which she had rationed by the drop. It was the only luxury she ever allowed herself, and somehow, after so many years, its scent was preserved in the grain of the wood.

She had touched this box. I remembered her strong hands, the broad square palms, calloused by decades of work. When I was three, one of the cows had crushed the tip of her ring finger, leaving her with a stub. I could see her in the kitchen, her firm grip on the stamp, pressing a honeybee into rounds of hand-churned butter. People trusted that stamp. Our farm had been renowned for cheese washed in honey, which always sold out at the market.

I remembered her chestnut hair, always windswept. How stern and tired she had often looked. The sparkle in her eye, reserved for me and my grandfather. Every detail of her was impressed on my memory, as surely as that bee into our butter, unlocked by the whispered rumor of a scent.

The box was sealed. There were markings on the lid—straight lines scored into the wood, the pattern strong and deliberate. Moving it caused a rustle, as if a winged insect was fluttering inside. A letter. It had to be. Without a key, there was only one way to reach it. I picked up the blade again and started to work it into the seam, but my hands shook so hard I almost dropped it.

I wasn't ready. Whatever was in the box, it wouldn't change the fact that he had died a traitor, jeered by a thousand strangers. I shoved it under the wardrobe, too far away to reach.

Arcturus had moved the drip to his room for me and attached another pouch of medicine. I hooked myself up to it and laid my hand flat on the duvet. Somehow I was still as tired as if I hadn't slept at all.

It soon became clear that I wasn't going to drift off. I watched the drip, waited until the whole dose had gone in, then freed myself and retrieved my sweater from the floor.

As I pulled it over my head, the ground tilted. My breath thickened. I could smell the water, taste its foulness, feel the sodden cloth over my nose and mouth. A clammy membrane. My joints ached from the manacles, the chill. I reached out and dug my nails into the bedpost.

You are alive. You are safe. I smoothed down the sweater and flattened my hands on my stomach. *You are not alone.*

The apartment was dark. I headed to the kitchen for something to settle me—a glass of milk, a bite to eat, anything. On my way, I looked into my own room. Ivy was sound asleep, one arm wrapped around the pillow.

It was only when I passed the door to the attic that I realized what I needed. I stepped into my boots, picked up my coat, and half ran up the stairs.

By the time I reached the roof, my shoulders were heaving. I shut the hatch behind me, hunched over, muffled a choked sound on my sleeve. When the knot in my throat loosened, I turned to see Arcturus at the edge. I should have sensed his presence.

"Sorry." I blotted my face. "I didn't realize you were up here."

He was little more than a silhouette. "Are you well?"

"I just needed some air." Slowly, I stood. "Can I join you?"

There was just enough light for me to see him nod. I sat beside him. Across the river, the Île de la Citadelle glimmered like a bed of fallen stars. A thinly sliced crescent moon hung above it.

"Is Ivy asleep?"

"Out like a light," I said. I could breathe up here. "I can't stand to think of her near Thuban."

"Thuban will not touch her." He looked at me. "Would you wish to destroy Suhail?"

The question sat in my stomach. For all I wanted justice, I had never really considered what I would do if I ever saw Suhail again.

"Will he be there?" was all I said.

"Possibly. Like Thuban, he is inclined toward violence, above all. Still," he said, "Nashira may prefer to keep one of her torturers in London."

Even if he *was* there, there was nothing I could really do to him. Not without an arsenal of weapons I didn't have.

"You are troubled by what your father left to you," Arcturus said.

"A box with no key. I think there's a letter inside."

"You could force the lock."

"I'm afraid." I stared into the middle distance. "Frère said he called me a changeling when they tortured him. A false child, left by the aos sí in place of a human baby."

"Aos sí." He took care with the pronunciation. "You have yet to teach me that phrase."

"The people of the mounds. Fairies," I said. "Why would he have said that, of all things?"

"Frère may have been lying."

"She wouldn't have known that word." I propped my chin on my knee. "Whatever is in that letter, it won't change anything."

"You will not know until you look."

"No," I said. "Whatever it is, it will play on my mind. I'm about to be trapped underground for two full days, likely knee-deep in water. I can only think of surviving now."

"You will. You always do."

"Against the odds." The lights across the water shimmered. "I can't apologize for going into the Hôtel Garuche. To me, it was a risk worth taking. But I am sorry for putting you through that pain again."

Even though he was silent, I felt his gaze.

"I think we all have this . . . one small part of us, buried deep, that fears death," I murmured. "They shot that part of me in Edinburgh." I looked at him. "I'm less afraid of dying now. That doesn't mean I don't have the will to live."

"Good." His eyes burned from the dark. "I would see you there when Scion falls."

A breeze unsettled the fine curls at my temples.

"Oneiromancy is an unusual gift," Arcturus said. "*Clairvoyance*, as you know, refers to clarity. Many find that clarity in glimpsing the future. I find mine in the past. Hindsight is both my strength and my burden, for while the past yields wisdom, I am powerless to change it."

He was right about his own rarity. I had never met another oneiromancer. Perhaps he was alone in the world, like me.

"I cannot change the oath," he said. "But I want you to know that I regret jeopardizing our trust. I regret causing you pain. You have endured more than enough."

So we were having this out now. I tucked my hands into my coat to keep them warm.

"I'm going to admit something I thought I never would," I finally said. "I don't wholly blame Terebell."

Darkness obscured his features, so the flames of his eyes were all I could see.

"In the colony, I was angry. Justly so. I'd been torn away from another home, stripped of my name and freedom," I said. "We both know I was looking for reasons not to trust you. If I'd found out you could become more monstrous than I already thought you were, I wouldn't have listened to explanations. The rebellion might never have happened."

He didn't contradict me.

"I know myself. The ways I've changed, the ways I haven't. I've died a hundred deaths since then, lived a hundred little seasons," I murmured. "You've changed since we first met, too. Somehow you seem both more and less human."

"And yet," he said, "I am not human at all. This will not be the last time our values and beliefs come into conflict."

"I've never forgotten what you are," I said. "I see your true face. I can accept it."

Somewhere below, a piano struck up a mélodie. Strains of a sweet voice drifted up to us.

"The truth about the Emim doesn't change our aims," I stated. "We'll just have to be careful who we tell, and how." I shot him a look. "And you'd better not get the half-urge near me."

"In two centuries, I have never succumbed to it."

"Good."

We both listened to the music for a while. Even in the dark, he cut a solid figure, deeply etched onto the night. Nothing like his faded husk of a dream-form.

For the first time, I imagined what the war must have done to him. Long before Nashira had mutilated his body, having to drain those weaker than him to survive would have ripped his dignity to shreds.

"I know how much the Ranthen mean to you. You fought a war with them, and I would never expect you to always put me above them," I said quietly. "But you and I started this revolution, and we owe it to everyone risking their necks to lead it properly. If we're to do that—if we're to stay friends—there can't be any more secrets between us."

"No."

In the hush that followed, all I could hear was the citadel.

"You told me once that there was something that proved you were always on my side," I said, breaking it again. "Something that would betray you . . . if anyone but me could see."

"Yes." Even in this cold, his words were smokeless. "Have you worked it out yet, little dreamer?"

With a reluctant smile, I shook my head. I knew he would never tell. This was his puzzle for me, something I was meant to solve alone. I could allow him that.

"Perhaps I can prove it in another way." Arcturus held out a hand. "By your leave."

Curious, I accepted his hand. With the other, he cupped the side of my face, his thumb light against my temple.

"This must be spoken in Gloss," he told me, "but I will recite it to you first."

"If you could."

When he gently tipped his forehead onto mine, I grew still. This close, I saw every small detail of his face. The bow of his lips, cut as if with the tip of a knife. The eclipses of his eyes.

"Let the æther bear witness," he said. "I will never keep from you what you should know." I closed my eyes. "I will never conspire against you, nor betray you by word or thought or deed. I will never, by choice, abandon you to your enemies, nor forsake you in adversity."

The cord shivered. I could feel the heat of fever in my breath, caught in the space between us.

"In body and spirit, I am bound to this oath." He clasped my hand to his chest. "Seo í mo mhóid shollúinte."

I looked up in surprise. When he started again in Gloss, all of the nearest spirits gave a faint stir. Then came a chilling tremor, so subtle I could almost have imagined it, and a current between us, as if the æther—or something beyond it—had witnessed and hallowed the oath, sealed in our first languages.

We stayed in that position for a while. Slowly, I released a long-held breath.

"You learn fast."

He lowered his hand from my face. "Was it right?"

"Perfect," I said. A smile tempted my lips. "All right. As far as apologies go, that was impressive." I patted his chest. "Forgiven."

"Hm."

Another silence, not quite the same as the last. Even when he took his forehead from mine, I kept my hand over his heart. After a moment, he covered it again, his palm warm over my chilled fingers.

"You once asked me why I kissed you in the Guildhall."

He was rarely this direct. It disarmed me.

"Yes," I said.

"Part of me feared, before that night. That I was a fool for wanting to know you. For seeing you in everything, everywhere I turned," he said. "I thought it was a sentence. A haunting. Until I realized it was a gift to be haunted by you, Paige."

"That was when you realized." I looked into his eyes. "In the Guildhall."

"Yes."

The first touch of our lips behind the crimson drapes. The touch that should have been impossible. A collision of worlds, born of chaos and breaking, that had somehow been quiet as a moth taking flight.

"Perhaps I haunted you. But I'm not a ghost just yet," I said softly. "You can touch me."

My hand slid up his chest, until my fingertips brushed his collarbone. All I had to do was tilt my head up, and our lips would meet again.

I want you.

Words I had whispered when I was soft with drink. I willed myself to say them again now, with all the strength of a clear mind, but pride stopped me. Instead, I leaned into him.

Arcturus studied my face as if it were written in a long-extinct language. He traced the warm inside of my wrist, following the tendon—idle and intent, sure and soft. A touch that both explored and remembered. Our auras twined, like branches growing into one another.

A familiar dreamscape gleamed into range. I pulled away, and at once, Arcturus let go.

"Ducos," was all I said, and left him to the keeping of the moon.

****

Ducos arrived in a raincoat, hair tightly bound in a chignon. She smelled of cigarettes and roses. As I led her into the parlor, I willed Ivy not to emerge. To Ducos, she would register as a rogue element—a living reminder of my old life.

"Flora," Ducos said. "I understand Cordier carried out a pleural tap. How do you feel?"

"Sore," I admitted, "but better than I did. Drink?"

She paused to consider. "I could use a coffee. But I will make it."

In the kitchen, she set about preparing it. I leaned against the counter and waited until she handed me a cup. She took hers black and strong, with a thick cream of foam.

"Command has delivered your next instructions. First, however, I will keep my word." She pulled out one of the chairs and sat. "Tell me about your insurgent militia, and I will consider how—if—we might be of use to one another."

I gave her a brief rundown of our numbers, our finances, and our main victory against Scion—the destruction of Senshield. I told her about Glym and Eliza, who were ruling in my absence, extolling them as level-headed and decisive leaders who would be willing to liaise with other organizations that stood against Scion. Ducos listened without interrupting.

"Your numbers are impressive," she said, once I was finished, "but the Mime Order has not yet attempted to confront Scion.

It has only helped clairvoyants to elude it. So it is not, in point of fact, a militia."

"We deactivated Senshield."

"You did that. With help, perhaps."

"Fine. It's a crime syndicate," I conceded, "trying to become a militia." Ducos nodded. "My aim is to convert it into an organization capable of guerrilla warfare with Scion, at the very least. In Ireland, large rebel bands—the laochra scátha—were able to maintain the upper hand in Munster and Connacht for several years after the invasion."

Scion had mockingly called them *luckscores*, belittling their victories. County Tipperary had been one of their main bases of operation.

"The Mime Order could do that," I said, "but with the right support, it could be capable of more. Sabotage, for example."

Ducos nodded again, slower.

"Sabotage is one of our projected strategies, should the anchor declare war on any of our benefactors. Damaging railways, lines of communication, ordnance factories, and so on." She drank. "Coordinating local rebellions, too."

"We can do that." I leaned forward. "I'll be straight with you: we lost our main source of income in December, and Scion is doubling its efforts to destroy us. Without support, we could fall apart."

Ducos finished her coffee.

"Domino might well be able to work with your organization," she said. "But I wonder—will you want to return to your old life, or remain an agent?"

"Do I have a choice?" I asked. "Do they silence anyone who wants to leave the network?"

"Nothing so dramatic. Usually, if you were to be deemed unsuitable and discharged, you would have to submit to memory erasure by means of white aster. Once your memories are gone, Domino cuts all ties. No more supplies. You would lose this safe house."

White aster. Supplies of it were held mostly by Scion, though some of it had trickled into London.

"If you were a recognized *associate* of the network, however, they might make an exception," Ducos said. "I will inquire."

I nodded. It was a moment before I spoke again: "Tell me what my next assignment is."

Ducos drummed her fingers on the table.

"In your last report, you spoke of a city, built on the instructions of the English. A prison for clairvoyants on the site of Versailles," she said. "Domino would like you to infiltrate it."

I took a slow drink of coffee. "Interesting."

"Yes. Cordier was of the opinion that you should be allowed to convalesce for a month. Command disagreed. Your medicine is the very best at our disposal. My superiors are confident you will be fit for a stealth-based assignment in a few days."

"Does Domino have a way to get me to Versailles?"

"No. Demonstrate your resourcefulness and find your own way there," she said. "Once you reach the city, you are to take one action, and one only. You are to assassinate the official in charge of it."

"The official in charge of it," I echoed.

"Yes. You are to eliminate the Scion official known as the Grand Overseer."

That title sent a hook into my gut. I schooled my face. Ducos must not see my disquiet.

"Why?" I finally said.

"I beg your pardon?"

"Why do they want this particular official dead?"

"To continue to undermine the relationship between England and France. The Grand Overseer is a representative of England, a close associate of the Suzerain. His death in France—a death under suspicious circumstances—will inflame the wound between Ménard and Weaver."

"I see." I cleared my throat. "Am I to kill him with my gift?"

"Under no circumstances. What they want," Ducos said, "is for you to make the assassination look like a scheme by Benoît Ménard." She took something from her briefcase. "A small gift, since you requested it. One double-action revolver."

She held out the weapon. It gleamed in the lamplight. The revolver I had used in London had been a rusted old barking iron, which Danica had restored for me. This one was sleek as quicksilver.

"It was commissioned by the Grand Commander of France for his forces, and his alone. This one is a prototype. Anyone possessing it would be assumed to be in some degree of contact with French high command," Ducos said. "Use it to assassinate the Grand Overseer. England will have no choice but to respond to the loss of two of its representatives."

I accepted the revolver. Lighter than my old one, it was a Lévesque, designed by the same engineer as the Senshield guns. Ducos went into her coat and handed me a metal case.

"A military-grade stiletto, should you prefer to eliminate him at close quarters. Also of French design."

It appeared I had options when it came to killing. "The pistol is on the mantelpiece, if you want it for someone else."

She rose to take it, then returned to her seat. Another case emerged from her ever-giving coat.

"In here you will find a new dissimulator, adrenaline, and a micro-camera." She handed over one last case. "The adrenaline is from Cordier—to suppress your fatigue, should you need to fight. The micro-camera is very important. It can be attached to your clothing. Photograph the body as evidence that the assignment is complete. If you are at risk of capture, I expect you to dispose of all of this."

A camera. That was a rare thing in Scion. Recording devices were strictly regulated.

"I must leave Paris for a time, but I will be back no later than the fourteenth of February. This assignment should be completed by that date."

When I could speak, I did. "And you'll take word of the Mime Order to Domino?"

Ducos picked up her briefcase, shooting me a final look. "I will," she said. "Goodbye, Flora. I trust that you will make a success of this task."

The door closed behind her. Not long after, Arcturus found me sitting on the couch, staring at the wall.

"Jaxon." My voice sounded miles away. "They want me to kill Jaxon."

PART III

Eurydice

From the Greek word εὐρύς (*eurys*, "wide") + δίκη (*dikē*, "justice")

17

Apollyon

For the next two days, I should have been training. Instead, I was stuck in bed on a drip, sleeping as much as I could. I was grateful for the fever, which kept my mind soft and loose even when I was conscious. It made it easier to not think of my assignment.

Arcturus made sure I had nothing to do but rest. He brought me small meals, administered my doses, sat close by and held my hand when the fever disconcerted me. Meanwhile, he and Ivy gave each other space. Now and again, I sensed their paths cross in the kitchen or the parlor, and I would hear brief exchanges, too low for me to quite make out.

By the day of our journey, my fever was down, though I still had a cough. I rose late in the afternoon and forced myself into the shower, but the knowledge of what I had to do was oozing through my pores and my hair, bedded deep under my nails, and no amount of scrubbing would remove it.

Knowledge is dangerous, Liss had told me once. Months after her death, I finally understood.

You are to eliminate the Scion official known as the Grand Overseer.

I dressed in a thick-knit sweater and the waterproof trousers I had worn to Calais. I leaned over the sink and trimmed my hair so it fell almost to my shoulders, the way I preferred it. I pulled on a pair of socks and buckled the holster for my revolver and stiletto. The slender blade was perfect for piercing a kidney or a heart. I checked my backpack, which contained food, a canteen of water, three doses of adrenaline, the stimulant Ducos had first given me, and a box of medicine with instructions from Cordier.

For the first time, I also decided to carry the silver pill. I slipped the vial into one of my trouser pockets and zipped it shut. Domino might have given me strict orders about how to kill Jaxon, but if it came to it, I would choose my own end.

Arcturus was leafing through the *Daily Descendant* in the kitchen. I headed straight for the fridge.

"Hi," I said to him as I passed.

"Paige."

We hadn't spoken about the assignment. Each time I tried to come to terms with it, a ringing filled every crevice of my skull.

"How is your fever?" Arcturus asked as I took out a carton of milk.

"Down a bit." I brushed the backs of my fingers across my cheek. Still too warm. "I'll manage."

"We could ask the perdues to postpone the journey."

"It's fine."

I poured the milk into a pan and set it over the stove. While it heated up, I took my first dose of medicine in capsule form.

"I never did say how impressed I was," I said.

"Hm?"

"That you made the link between the perdues and Versailles. I would never have realized the significance of the silver chandelier or the jewelery. You did." I shot him a glance. "I said we'd make a decent syndie of you. Didn't take you long to prove me right."

"I credit my mentor."

I smiled.

The sun threw a copper-backed glow through the windows. I cooked a square meal for the journey. Ivy emerged with a yawn at five, wearing leggings and another sleeveless top, and spooned a couple of poached eggs from the pan I had left simmering. She wore a delicate chain around her neck.

"Paige," she said, "you're going to boil in that thing."

I frowned down at my sweater. "It was cold in the carrières."

"This is a mining tunnel, though. It could be warm. Maybe wear layers?"

"I'll do that. Help yourself." I slid a rack of buttered toast in her direction. "Ready for this?"

"Yeah. Kind of looking forward to it, actually."

"That makes one of us."

"I liked being underground," Ivy admitted. "I was terrified at first, but I came to like it. Mostly I was out with the mudlarks on the riverbank, but even when I was in the storm drains, it was sort of exciting. Scavenged a lot of interesting stuff." She pulled the chain from her neck and showed me the thin gold band on it. "This is my favorite. Sixteenth-century posy ring."

"Oh, that's gorgeous."

She handed it over. The initials *E* and *S* were scored inside, along with an inscription too faded to make out. I showed it to Arcturus, who leaned in to examine it over my shoulder.

"You find them now and again on the riverbank. They have little poems or inscriptions carved on their insides, though you can't usually read them," Ivy said. "They're love tokens."

Arcturus studied the ring. Without looking at him, I knew his expression would be the same as it was when he played the organ or listened to the record player—a soft, open curiosity, overlaid with intense focus. When I returned the posy ring to Ivy, she looped its chain back over her head.

"There were lots of things like that, from a time before Scion. I loved finding them," she said. "When I first got out, it was the world above that seemed more frightening." She tucked the ring under her top. "Not that there aren't dangers underground. And I doubt it's much fun on your own. The toshers always work in pairs, just in case."

"Just in case of what?"

"The stuff of nightmares, surface dweller," she purred. "Beware the wild swine of the sewers, glutted on the flesh of innocents—and rats just as big, runnin'" in swarms that'll strip a laggard bare as a pulled tooth."

Her grin made me smile. I had never seen her this light-hearted. "I'll watch out for those, then."

We finished our food and prepared to leave. I found a thin black shirt to go under my sweater, then pulled my oilskin over my layers, laced on a pair of steel-capped boots, and secured my wrist brace. Lastly, I clipped the tiny camera to the collar of my sweater, so it could almost pass as a button.

The world beneath the streets had transfigured Ivy. It had taken the clay of her and fired it into sturdy ceramic. I already knew it would have the reverse effect on me.

Arcturus waited by the door in his usual attire. "Shouldn't you wear something waterproof?" I asked him.

"The cold and damp do not affect me."

I sheathed my stiletto. "If you say so."

Ivy stepped into the parlor, now clad in fishing waders and her oilskin, a waterproof pack slung over her shoulder. A crowbar hung at her side. She looked quizzically at Arcturus.

"Is that what you're wearing, Warden?"

"Just had that chat with him," I said.

"You can't talk." She nodded to my boots. "You'll get sump foot in those."

"The perdues said they'd have spare equipment." I zipped my oilskin up to my chin, hefted on my backpack, and tightened the straps. "All right, then. Time to head back to hell."

There was a long and brittle silence between the three of us. After everything we had done to escape Sheol I, all the suffering that had followed, we were making our way back into the belly of the beast. I opened the door and stepped outside before I could lose my nerve.

Ivy had lived as a fugitive for months. As we made our way southwest, I never had to warn her to watch out for cameras or keep her face hidden—those instincts were etched into her. The glow of the streetlamps mixed like watercolor with the sunset, staining the snow lilac.

We were to access the tunnels through an underground parking garage. By the time we arrived at dusk, four of the perdues were already in a far corner, choosing items from a pool of supplies. None of them wore masks tonight. They looked more like hikers than criminals.

"Ah, Underqueen," Renelde called. "You made it." She shone her lamp toward Ivy. "Who is this?"

"A friend," I said. "Ivy."

Renelde eyed her with misgiving. "Le Prince Creux will not like this." She spoke in French. "We have some supplies for you. Mal guessed your size, so if the boots pinch, blame him."

I took the waterproof pair she indicated and pulled them on. A perfect fit. Malperdy gave a satisfied nod. At his behest, I gloved my hands and padded my calves with gaiters.

Ivy already had what she needed. I donned a headlamp and moved my supplies into a waterproof backpack. The faces around me were rendered strange and hollow by the light.

Le Bateleur had frothing gray hair. I guessed he was about seventy, each year scored deep into weathered skin. Malperdy—a redhead with a sharp nose, about my age—resembled a fox even without his mask. Finally, there was a moon-faced soothsayer in his forties, bald as a spoon and built like a keg. His huge arms bore reflected tattoos of a scythe.

"This is Ankou." Renelde smiled. "Don't ever try to arm wrestle him."

She flashed her headlamp twice, and Ankou looked up at her with raised eyebrows. Renelde pointed to me, swept her right hand in a nosedive, then skirted one finger across her throat, left to right. His eyebrows jumped higher.

"Can you sign?" Renelde asked me. "Ankou is deaf. He can try to read your lips at close quarters, but that has its limits."

"I can't. Warden can, though."

Arcturus stepped into the flashlight and presumably introduced himself. Ankou stared at him with a furrowed brow—I remembered all too well how surreal it was to see a Rephaite for the first time—before he slowly laid down what he was holding and answered, blunt fingers moving at speed. He had a short exchange with Arcturus, then looked back to me.

"I'm honored to meet you at last, Underqueen," Renelde translated, watching him. "We hoped you might visit us, after the stories from London. I look forward to finding out if they are true."

"All good, I trust," I said with a smile. When Renelde signed it, Ankou let out a stentorian chuckle, nodded, and mirrored the motion with one fist. "Will you thank him for coming?"

She did, and his smile widened into a toothy grin. He went back to sharpening a deadly-looking sickle.

"Where is the entrance?" I asked Renelde. She nodded to a crack at the bottom of a wall, just large enough to fit through. I crouched and shone my headlamp into the dark, revealing chunks of rubble.

Le Bateleur leaned down and grasped my shoulder. "Underqueen," he said, "I am only here to see you off and to introduce you to your guide. He is here."

I looked.

A very pale man had just walked into the parking garage. He was about the same age as Renelde, lean, and—incredibly—nearly as tall as Arcturus. His hair was bone-white, as was his scruffy beard. He wore a tight black shirt, trousers with capacious pockets, and a utility belt. A dark jacket was slung over his shoulder. Everything about him exuded authority. I was surprised he was only a mollisher.

"Underqueen," Le Bateleur said when the man had reached us, "allow me to introduce Le Prince Creux, compagnon d'armes to Le Vieux Orphelin."

"Prince," I said.

Le Prince Creux ran a cool gaze over me before he extended a hand. "Underqueen." His lashes were barbs of frost, his eyes a light blue, with the keyhole pupils of a full-sighted voyant. "Léandre will do."

"Paige will be fine, too." I touched three fingers to my brow. "Generous of you to guide us."

Expressionless, he returned the salute, then gave Arcturus a cursory look. "I assume you are the Rephaite bodyguard."

Arcturus returned his nod. "You may call me Warden."

"Warden. Fine." Léandre twitched his anvil of a chin toward Ivy. "Who is that?"

"Ivy," I said. "One of my allies from London."

"The passages are unstable," Léandre said, eyes flinty. "I had not accounted for seven people."

"She has experience of working underground."

The corners of his mouth pinched as he pulled on his jacket. I took that as a reluctant agreement.

When everyone was ready, Le Bateleur gathered us all together in front of the entrance. Léandre waited for a long beat before he spoke.

"There are certain rules to follow underground," he said. "I will not hesitate to leave you behind if you break them."

Ivy gave me a blank look. "Ivy doesn't speak French," I said to Léandre. "Could we use English?"

Léandre stared at the ceiling for a moment.

"We must hope we do not encounter anyone," he continued in English, "since the grands ducs are on the hunt for all of us. Do not stop. Do not speak to anyone. If you can, do not speak at all. A single raised voice could set off a cave-in." He was going to love my cough. "Le Passage des Voleurs is a very deep section of the carrières, beginning at the bottom of a mining shaft we call Apollyon. It will lead us to Versailles, but it is slow. A journey that would take a few hours above ground will last at least two days."

Two days without any daylight.

"If you get lost, you sit and wait for one of us to find you. If you are afraid, you sit and wait for us to return for you. And make no mistake," Léandre said, "you will be afraid. When we reach the bottom of the earth."

With that, he adjusted his backpack and disappeared so smoothly it was as if the wall had swallowed him whole. I let Renelde and Ankou go after him before I crouched myself.

"Good luck to you, Underqueen," Le Bateleur said. I slid my legs into the gap and dropped onto a mound of rubble. As soon as I had my balance, a hand caught my arm. Léandre had waited for me.

"There is one more rule," he said in an undertone. "You may be queen in London—but here, in la ville souterraine, I am king."

"Of course," I said. "Your turf."

He seemed to weigh my sincerity before he strode ahead, to the front of the line. As I followed, I double-checked the outer pocket of my backpack for the stimulant from Ducos.

In silence, we ventured into the dark. Arcturus walked close behind me, Ivy in front, with Malperdy bringing up the rear. Their presence, and the nodding beams of our headlamps, made it easy to stay in the present. I let my gift sleep so I could focus on the placement of my boots and head.

When we reached a half-flooded gallery, Renelde signaled for us to keep quiet. We picked our way between stepstones that jutted like teeth from the flood. Not a single drop touched my skin, but the smell of it—stagnant, lurking water—was enough to unsettle me. I used my sleeve to stifle my coughs.

At the end, Léandre steered us left, into a tunnel so low I had to dip my head. Arcturus must be bent double behind me.

The air was already too close for my liking. Straight ahead, Ivy moved fluently, used to these conditions. The silence was a bellows, smothering me even as it opened space for thoughts to prey.

I thought of the last time I had seen Jaxon, living in opulence while I was tortured. I thought of piercing his heart with the stiletto, of burying a bullet in that ever-ticking brain. I imagined how it would feel to watch the light in his eyes disappear for the last time.

I should want to see it. After everything he had done, I should wish him dead. I should want to be the one to kill him.

Just then, the æther fluted a warning. I overtook the others—difficult in the confined space—until I reached Léandre.

"There are people coming."

Léandre spared me a glance. "How do you know?"

"Marcherêve," I reminded him.

I could have sworn he rolled his eyes. "Mettez vos capuches. Vite," he said, signing into the flashlight for Ankou. He lifted his scarf over his mouth and raised his hood. "You keep your head down, marcherêve," he added to me. "You are too conspicuous."

I was getting the distinct impression that Léandre did not particularly like me.

The other voyants passed us at an intersection. Nods were exchanged, but none of them asked questions.

After that sole encounter, our group was alone. At times, we passed between tunnels using small holes in the walls. Ankou helped me through the first one, preventing me from falling through and cracking my skull on the floor. Once I had the knack for it, I could do it alone.

Monotony was setting in when the tunnels finally surprised me. One moment, Ivy was ahead of me; the next time I raised my headlamp, she was gone. So were all the others. Even though their dreamscapes had swerved left, all my light revealed was a dead end.

"In the corner." Malperdy spoke around the bulk of Arcturus. "See where the walls don't meet?"

My gloved hand found the opening. Like the entrance in the parking garage, it was so narrow that I felt a need to suck in my breath as I sidestepped into the tight space beyond. A beam of light shone just ahead of me. I followed, stale air congesting my throat, and imagined dust forming gray clumps in lungs.

At the end of the crevice, I emerged, weak-kneed, and found myself on an old iron staircase that corkscrewed out of sight. When I stepped onto it, it creaked under my weight, joining other metallic groans from below. I gripped the thin handrail. Steps had rusted away here and there, forcing me to pin my attention to my boots. At the bottom, I looked up, neck aching.

Ahead, the ground was no longer smooth. For an absurd moment, I thought the fragments were debris from a cave-in. Next, they whittled themselves into serried pieces of wood, stored down here for some unknown purpose. It was only when the truth was the last remaining option—an option too ghoulish to contemplate—that I started to pick out the shapes in the clutter. An ear-shaped curve that could only be part of a pelvis. Cracked knurls of knuckle and spine. The scalloped edge of a sternum. Bones on bones, brown with age, lying unnamed in the depths of the citadel.

I had never feared human remains. As a mollisher, I had stumbled upon more than one corpse. I had polished skulls to a shine at the black market. Death was part of voyant life.

Yet higher in the carrières, there had been a sense of dignity, of acknowledgment. A sense that the bones mattered. They had been touched with care, carefully arranged, illuminated by candles and torches. These were wretched, broken skeletons, dumped on top of one another and forgotten for three centuries.

All of these fragments had once been people. They had laughed and loved, wept and dreamed. Now they were rubble.

"This is why no one else has ever found Apollyon. They dare not come through the ossuary," Renelde muttered. She was just ahead, up to her ankles in bone. "Do you feel them?"

I swallowed before I spoke. "I've never felt anything like this."

Dust hung thick in the air. So did old, fermented spirits, enraged by their abandonment in this unhallowed ground. They were not at peace. When I took my first step into the cascade, bones cracked under my boot.

"Watch your step," Malperdy said, voice strained. "The spirits will try to block our way if we disturb their bones." He clung white-knuckled to the staircase. "I fucking hate this part."

The tunnel was piled with bones. I had no choice but to step on the skeletons, to climb them where they clustered together, to snap them underfoot.

We broke formation to forge our own paths through the ossuary. At one point, my heel crunched right through the dome of a skull. A weak poltergeist lunged at me like a guard dog, outrage and anguish spilling through the æther. I froze, my scarred hand clenched to my chest.

The poltergeist stopped as if I had slapped it, then cringed away. I swallowed as Arcturus moved past me.

"They will not threaten a Rephaite," he said. "Stay within reach of my aura."

When he took another step, the spirits only trembled. I released a long-held breath and followed him.

Some bones were sharp enough to cut through skin. Now I understood the need for the gaiters. When the tunnel forced us into a crawl, I was grateful for them, and for the thick gloves. My palms crunched into knuckles and teeth and crumbs of spine. My knees ground into other knees. I started to mutter under my breath, greeting every skull, trying to write each bone a story. This jaw had once chewed fresh oysters and whelks by the Seine. Those fingers had once held a hammer, a paintbrush, a quill. I soon lost count. Even though I was icy cold, I told myself this was another hallucination, a remnant of my fever. I was not wrist-deep in a human rib cage, not crossing an endless hallway of the dead.

There must have been murders down here. It was the safest place in the world to dispose of a body.

Heavy breathing sounded behind me. I turned to see Malperdy rummaging in his jacket, his torso racked by huge retches.

In London, Nadine had carried headphones and an audio player to muffle the voices of the dead. Unlike Nadine, Malperdy wasn't a whisperer—he must be either a sniffer or a gustant—but from the panic-stricken look on his face, he had mislaid whatever he used to get a handle on his gift. Seeing him cup his hands over his nose and mouth, Ankou grasped him by the shoulder and pushed a switch-blade into his hand. Malperdy fumbled it open and pressed the tip into his arm, hard enough to draw blood.

I had always found it harder to dreamwalk when I was hurt. The knife was creating a needlepoint of pain, pulling his attention away from the æther. Ankou clapped him on the back.

"Malperdy," I whispered, projecting my voice as much as I could. "Come closer to Warden."

His eyes were streaming. Seeing me beckon, Ankou all but hauled him up, and the two of them waded toward us, bones rattling around their legs. With every footstep, Malperdy heaved.

Arcturus had stopped to wait for them. As soon as they were almost as close to him as I was, Ankou sighed in relief and rubbed his eyes.

Ahead, Ivy was inching along the wall, blowing out slow breaths. Léandre climbed gracefully from the bones and through another crack in the wall. I followed them into a new chamber, where the ground simply fell away. Léandre turned to face me, his skin tinged blue by our headlamps.

"Apollyon," he said. "The entrance to Le Passage des Voleurs."

Ivy stood at its edge. I planted a boot on the ground and looked down, into a bottomless pit.

Apollyon. Roughly circular, the shaft was a plunge into dark-ness—a toothless maw that waited to gulp me deeper into Paris. As if inhaled by it, I leaned closer. Beyond the reach of our headlamps lay a vast and solid black. In that void, I could almost hear the whispers of my torturer. Water dripping. My own screams.

"So," I said, when I could speak, "how do we get to the bottom of the earth?"

"With this."

Renelde tapped her boot on the ground. For the first time, I noticed the rope that snaked past us and disappeared into the chasm.

"From here," she said, "the only way is down."

****

After a ten-minute rest and several long gulps from a hip flask, Malperdy looked a little less peaky. As the most experienced climber, it fell to him to instruct us first-timers.

He warned us of the many ways we could die if we failed to remember his instructions. He was soft, if stern, in his explanations, careful when he buckled me into my harness. When he was sure we understood what to do, he wove the rope through a rusty mechanism that allowed him to control the speed of his descent. It was linked to his harness with a screw-lock carabiner.

"Ne tombe pas," Léandre told him. "Je ne veux pas que tu salisses mes bottes au fond."

Malperdy snorted and planted his heels on a crag. He let himself down a short way, feeding the greasy rope, then stopped to allow the descender to cool, hanging over the black chasm. He dropped in fits and starts, lower and lower, until the darkness of Apollyon quenched his lamp.

The rest of us waited a long time. Ankou sat on a slab of limestone and drank from the hip flask. Sweat pebbled his scalp. He reached into his massive backpack and took out a handheld device, which he switched on and studied. It looked Scion-made.

Ivy was bright-eyed with anticipation, fearlessly pacing the edge of the pit, as if daring it to swallow her. I afforded it a wide berth.

Arcturus gave the golden cord a questioning tug. I glanced at him and nodded, arms folded to contain my shivering.

Léandre eyed his watch. When it beeped, he nodded to Renelde. She went down next, followed by Ankou, who mopped his face with cloth before he started the descent. Ivy was fourth. She reeled down in great leaps, a breathy laugh escaping her. Léandre pursed his lips.

"You next, marcherêve," he said, once his watch told him that Ivy had reached the bottom.

I attached myself to the rope the way Malperdy had showed me, my fingers numb on the carabiner. Once it was locked, Léandre came to double-check it. He gave a small grunt of satisfaction.

A tremor crossed the backs of my thighs as I swung my legs over the chasm. I had spidered my way up and down cranes, hung one-handed from bridges, scaled the spires of London. Never had there been such darkness waiting for me if I fell. I turned around, eased myself into the pit, and tested the rope. It took my weight.

My breath shallowed. I looked up once more. Arcturus gave me the smallest nod. I walked a short way down the wall, then pushed off and hung in midair, suspended over the abyss. The rope whirred as I began the descent.

The two small lights from above soon faded, and only mine remained. I fixed my gaze on the mechanism attached to my harness. Descending and braking required so much concentration that I could almost ignore the crushing blackness on all sides but the one I was facing. The walls were rugged and damp, more like a natural cave than anything shaped by human ambition.

I shouldn't be afraid. Here, at least, I had a harness. In London, I had been one wrong step from death. Nick, always so cautious, had a blind spot when it came to climbing—he was willing to take risks, to be foolish. He used his bare hands and nothing else.

Perspiration trickled down my nape. I could smell the water on the walls. The journey was endless, the harness so tight my legs turned numb. My muscles ached. Fear urged me to go faster, to drop farther, just to get it over with. I let some more rope through the descender and sank deeper into the pit.

At last, I heard the murmur of voices, glimpsed the light below. I kicked for a foothold, dislodging a few tiny rocks. Finally, I angled my way through a very cramped section—Malperdy had called it la gorge de l'abîme—and then I was on solid ground, breathless and light-headed, knees trembling. Malperdy was there at once to detach me from the rope. I unbuckled the harness and coughed.

I was standing in a cavern, where a mining lantern cast a warm light. Ivy was sharing a steaming canteen with Renelde and Ankou, her oilskin bundled in her lap.

"Le Passage des Voleurs," Malperdy said to me. He was holding the end of the rope, his eyes on the opening above. "You can take the gaiters off now, if you want." I crouched to remove them. "I would say the worst is over, but that depends on your perspective."

"I assume that was the worst of it for you."

"Yes." He shot me a glance. "I am a sniffer, if you were curious."

"Must have stunk to hell up there."

"You have no idea." The rope swayed. "Spirits smell of hot metal to me. Most of the time I don't mind it, but too much of it makes me sick. Reminds me of blood."

"Interesting." I removed the gaiters. "Sniffers can smell auras, too, can't they?"

"Some of us." He flashed me a smile. "Admit it. You want to know what you smell like."

"Only if it's not going to make me paranoid." I left the gaiters on the pile. "And if you don't have to come and sniff me."

His smile broadened to a grin, showing sharpened canines.

"You smell different from any other voyant I've met. So does your bodyguard," he said. "All anormaux smell a little like petrol—you know?" I nodded. Some older vehicles still used it. "But he smells of spirits, too."

Even I had caught the scent of metal on Arcturus, when I had slept beside him. Just a faint trace.

"Usually, there are other aromas laced through it. Most people in one order share a similar scent. You smell like an oracle. Bitter almond and honey. But there's something else." Malperdy considered, eyes narrowed. "Smoke. You smell of smoke."

"Could be worse," I said. "I was afraid you were going to say I smelled like week-old laundry." My headlamp picked out beads of water on the ceiling. "How far down are we?"

"Several hundred feet."

"Something tells me they didn't mine this far just for limestone."

"Maybe for gold. Or it could have been a siege tunnel." Without letting go of the rope, Malperdy blotted his face on his sleeve. "Or they were looking for another realm. We want that, I think. We crawl into the deepest caves, touch the bottom of the sea, try to reach the stars." He gestured upward. "We are forever looking for other worlds. Stranger ones."

"And that's what you found down here. A stranger world."

"Exactly."

We exchanged a smile.

Ivy had been right. This part of the carrières did feel a little warmer. I took off my oilskin and tied the arms around my waist, willing my pulse to slow. My skin had a dull sheen.

"What's he like?" I leaned against the wall, arms folded. "Le Vieux Orphelin."

"He is both leader and brother to us. Renelde was first to join him," Malperdy said. "They were both born in the Scion Citadel of Lyon, in a district under the control of a brutal anormal named Louvel, who took a special interest in Renelde."

Renelde smiled at whatever Ivy was saying. Her hands were restless, interpreting both ways.

"When she was sixteen, she met Le Vieux Orphelin," Malperdy continued, quieter. "He was only seventeen himself, but he sheltered her in his bookshop and promised to help her escape. In the end, she found her own way out . . . but it was around that time that Ménard was posted to Lyon. Somehow they drew his eye." He glanced at Renelde. "They fled to Paris, where Léandre and La Tarasque joined them. Then the rest of us. Ankou is the most recent arrival."

"I'm going to take a guess," I said. "You call yourselves les perdues because you were all lost before."

"In various ways. Ankou is a fugitive," Malperdy said. "There has been a bounty on his head for a few months."

"I've never seen him on the screens." I looked toward Ankou. "Why is he on the run?"

"I don't know. Le Vieux Orphelin does, but he has told the rest of us not to ask. We respect that."

"And you?"

"My uncle threw me out when I was twelve. It was kinder than sending me to the Vigiles." He flexed his calloused fingers around the rope. "I tried to steal from Renelde. I thought she would kill me. Instead, she took me to Le Vieux Orphelin." He looked at me. "I think that you and he are alike. Together, you could change the world for anormaux. Make it a safe place for us."

His faith was both touching and nerve-racking.

"I hope so," I said.

The rope trembled. I used the lull in our journey to dig out my box of medicine and swallow another capsule with as much water as I could manage. At last, a pair of boots came into view, then a head of white hair.

"Bon travail," Léandre said, and we all stood to attention. "Let's keep moving."

"Wait," I said. "Where's Warden?"

Cocking an eyebrow, Malperdy nodded to a point over my shoulder. I startled when I saw Arcturus, bold as a mobster's shirt, standing right behind me.

"How the hell did you get there?"

His eyes were a comfort in the dark. "Being a Rephaite has certain advantages."

"You're going to have to give me your full list of skills at some point."

"Allow me to preserve a little of my enigma."

I smiled at him. When I turned back to the others, Ivy was watching us from the corner.

"Welcome to Le Passage des Voleurs," Léandre said. "From here, the world only gets darker." He nodded to the lantern. "There are points where the air is thin. Stay close to each other, keep your mouths shut, and pray these tunnels hold."

****

For a long time, we moved on a steady course downward, into ever-smaller passageways. While there were fewer spirits, the darkness was unyielding. According to Renelde, we were somewhere deep under the Forêt de Meudon, one of the two ancient forests to the west of Paris.

"How did you haul the old treasures through these passages?" I asked Léandre in an undertone. He stiffened as if I had shouted. "The chandeliers—"

"We dismantled what we could," he said. "It took several trips to retrieve larger items."

His patience with me seemed to wear thinner every time I spoke. "It was a pity to break the harp, but we found someone to put it back together," Renelde said softly. I thought of my grandfather, who had loved to restore instruments. "The trade has made us a good coin on the black market. We will have money for the cause, Underqueen."

"If Le Vieux Orphelin chooses to share it," Léandre muttered. "It is *his* coin, after all."

Silence closed in on us. I had no strength or coherence to waste. Once again, my hand strayed to the stimulant, but surely Léandre would let us rest soon. We must have been on the move for well over a day.

He led us on at a relentless pace. After a while, a stream of water appeared, dark as spilled oil. From an underground spring or lake in the forest, Renelde told me, which the perdues had yet to find.

Perhaps the Underqueen would care for a drink.

Buried alive. No one to find me. My legs shook, my stomach cramped, and I started weaving like a drunk. Everywhere, the darkness. Crushing darkness.

At last, I could stand it no longer. I braced my good hand against the wall and tried to fill my hollow chest, but the air down here was thick as wet clay, drying in my throat.

"Paige." Arcturus stopped. "Malperdy, tell Léandre to wait."

"He won't like it."

"No," I said, but my voice was hoarse. "I'll carry on. I'm fine."

"You are not fine," Renelde said firmly. "Sit."

She guided me to the ground. Seeing the state of me, Malperdy cursed and went after Léandre.

There are ways to inflict pain. I shook my head as if I could dislodge the voice. Teeth clenched, I tried to get up, but my boots were as heavy as solid iron. My brow hit my knees. *No need to be frightened, Underqueen—*

"What is going on here?" Léandre had returned, splintering the hallucination. "Now is not the time to rest," he hissed, an undertow of genuine anger in his voice. I looked up at him wearily. "I told you what to expect down here, marcherêve. If you are too weak for the journey—"

"Back off, princeling," Ivy snapped at him. The words echoed. "She was waterboarded."

The fury rushed out of Léandre. He gave me an odd look.

"One break," he said, deadly soft. "If any of you raise your voices down here again, I will leave you to die."

Ivy stared him out, and he stalked away. Arcturus stepped into the space he had left, arms folded, back to playing the bodyguard. I took the hip flask Ankou offered and sniffed it.

"Where did you get alcohol?" I said. He watched my face intently as I spoke, glanced at Renelde, then held a hand up flat and passed it twice over his mouth, his lips tilted up at the corners.

"He's being coy," Renelde said, signing to him as she spoke. "Ankou likes his secrets."

Ankou shrugged. I thought of asking him why he was on the run, but if he hadn't told the other perdues, I doubted he would tell me. Renelde dabbed her forehead and looked after Léandre.

"Forgive him, Underqueen," she said. "He and Le Vieux Orphelin are . . . âmes jumelles. When they are parted, a fire consumes him." She tipped her head against the wall. "I want to save Le Vieux Orphelin, too. I have been with him since I was sixteen—but I also know we will be no use to him if we are exhausted when we arrive. Léandre is too in love to see reason."

Léandre was at the other end of this section of the tunnel now, staring a hole into the wall.

"I understand," I said.

"He is a little bitter, too," she added under her breath. "Before he went missing, all Le Vieux Orphelin talked about for days was you. His relief that London had bowed to a revolutionary leader instead of another lazy and brutal chair-warmer. How he longed to join our syndicates. Léandre is afraid he will be cast aside. That Le Vieux Orphelin will want *you* as a compagne d'armes."

"He's never met me. I might be a colossal disappointment."

"It's the idea of you, ma chère."

She went to speak to Léandre. Ivy stayed on one side of me, while Ankou sat down on the other.

"Sorry, Paige," Ivy murmured. "I didn't mean to tell Léandre about the waterboarding."

"Probably good that he knows."

With a nod, she leaned against the damp wall. I closed my eyes, shutting out my surroundings, and drank from the hip flask. The brandywine kindled a welcome heat in my chest.

My head was so heavy. If I didn't get up now, I never would. I handed the flask back to Ankou, stood and started moving again, before Léandre could haul me up by the scruff of my neck. The others got up and came after me.

A cave-in had almost engulfed the next stretch of the tunnel. Léandre got down on his stomach and squeezed himself into a tiny space at the bottom. I took a deep breath before I followed.

Broken rocks were packed tight above us. I hooked the strap of my rucksack around my ankle and crawled on my stomach after Léandre, the ground almost scraping my cheek. Sweat coated my nape. I imagined all the buildings of Paris cracking the thin shell of the pavement, falling into the hollowed-out earth, crushing this sliver of musty air. Mouth dry, I pressed on, holding onto the same thing that had kept me alive in the Westminster Archon. A single ember of resolve.

At last, I emerged in a tiny cave. To the left was another crawl space, into which Léandre had already vanished. Straight ahead was a jagged opening. When I shone my headlamp into it, the beam picked out a steep, wet incline. The rest of the Passage des Voleurs.

"Paige."

Ivy had stopped halfway into the chamber. The change in her was startling. She was sweating marbles, quivering all the way to her lips.

"Can't go on." Strands of hair stuck to her brow. "I can't."

I helped her out of the tunnel so Ankou could get through. There was no room to stand in this pocket of space. "What is it?" I said softly. "You seemed fine at Apollyon."

"Lost my bottle." Ivy looked at me with bloodshot eyes. "I thought I needed to do this. Face him, at least, so I can get him the fuck out of my head." Tears of frustration welled up. "But I'm just doing his job for him. Torturing myself. Every inch I move takes me closer to him. I'm n-not ready."

I recognized the haunted look I had seen in my own reflection.

"Okay," I said. "Do you want to stay here?"

"No. The cavern at the bottom of Apollyon." She wiped her brow. "I'll wait for you there."

Léandre soon returned to see what the holdup was about. Once he was abreast of the situation, he was good enough not to grouse about it. "My people need rest," he said shortly to Ivy, "but the way back to Apollyon is not difficult. Keep to the main path."

"I remember it."

"Good." He passed a cylindrical pack to her. "Sleeping bag. You have enough food and water?"

Ivy nodded and shouldered the pack. Before she left, she turned to me and gripped my arm.

"Burn that place to the fucking ground," she whispered. "Promise me, Paige. Don't let anyone else have to live with these memories."

Ducos had instructed me only to kill Jaxon, not to burn anything to the ground. I couldn't please both sides forever.

"I promise," I said.

Ivy gave me a quick, one-armed hug. I wished she could stay, to lend me a bit more strength than I had. Now I was the only human survivor of the colony to go into the next one.

Once everyone had emerged, Ivy slid back through the opening, hauling her supplies behind her. Léandre led the rest of us along the sandy passage to the left. I inched after him until we came to a dry space, just about high enough to sit up in, wide enough for us all to spread out. Léandre laid his jacket on the floor, and I realized he must have given Ivy his own sleeping bag.

"We will rest here," he said. Now that Ivy was gone, he switched back to French. "You have five hours."

Renelde lit a mining lamp, while I shed my gear and melted to the ground like heated wax, my head aching and stuffy, physically and mentally drained. I bundled my oilskin into the corner as a pillow.

Arcturus sat beside me while the others conferred among themselves. I dug out a can of barley soup, a sticky malt loaf wrapped in paper, and a bag of nuts and sundried berries.

"Are you holding up all right?" I said to Arcturus. "I'm surprised you haven't whacked your head."

"Fear not. My skull is strong."

I drank the soup cold from the can. It was lumpy and tasteless, but it would wad my hollow stomach.

"We should consider what will greet us in the colony," Arcturus said while I ate. "There may not be enough clairvoyants in the city for the next Bone Season to have begun. Usually, they are abducted over a decade."

"So there shouldn't be any red-jackets. Or harlies," I said. "If no one has been tested yet."

"No. For now, the human guards are likely to be well-paid Vigiles."

"Hopefully we'll have bypassed most of the main defenses. The traps and mines." I found my box of medicine and slid out a blister pack. "There were no surveillance cameras in the first colony, were there?"

"No. The risk of exposure was too great."

"Good." I cracked a capsule from the pack. "Just the enraged Rephaim to deal with, then."

Arcturus let me wash down the medicine and finish the loaf before he spoke again. "Can you feel any voyants?"

I hefted my attention to the æther. My tiredness rendered it woolly—a haze of distant spirits—but when I sensed the cluster of dreamscapes, gooseflesh sprung up on my arms.

"Yes," I said, "but no one familiar yet."

When everyone had wolfed down some food, the others joined us in our corner, forming a circle.

"We have a map of Versailles." Léandre rolled it out and brought the lamp closer. "We will surface in the Cimetière Notre-Dame, northeast of the palace." He signed as he spoke. "You say you have been to a penal colony like this before," he said to me. "What can we expect there?"

"Guards," I said. "Impossible to kill."

Malperdy nodded to Arcturus. "Like him?"

"Yes, but armed. And murderous."

Across from me, Ankou finished his mouthful and cleared his throat. "We stored some weapons in the cemetery," Renelde translated for me. "A few guns and blades, but not many."

"Stealth, then." I tapped the map with one finger. "This place is a Type A Restricted Sector, so it will be heavily defended, but we do have the element of surprise. I'm hoping most of the defenses will be on the outskirts, like they were in the first colony. By traveling underground, we should avoid those and have a clear path to the château."

"We should go to the front gates first, to assess its external fortifications," Renelde said. "The best way in is through the gardens. They are very overgrown. Good cover. We have all explored them and know the routes. We also have a floor plan of the palace."

Ankou spread it on the floor and smoothed the crinkles. I took in the names of each room in the vast palace. Seeing the section marked L'APPARTEMENT DU ROI, I noted its location.

Renelde laid out her proposed approach. We would enter the gardens to the east of the palace, cutting across the long-neglected groves to reach the building itself.

"We used to get in through a broken window here," she said, pointing it out. "Mal will climb up to it and let a rope down for the rest of us. Once inside, we should split into two groups to search for the prisoners. It will take us too long to cover the place otherwise. How many prisoners do you think there will be, Paige?"

"There could be up to forty," I said, "not including amaurotics and unreadables."

Renelde looked to Léandre, whose face remained stony.

"It goes without saying that getting the prisoners out will be difficult. Most of them will be weak and injured. As I said, we need to do this quietly."

Chewing her lip, Renelde nodded.

"I have an exit strategy," she said. "There is a reservoir under the main parterre, and tunnels for the pipes that once carried water to the fountains. I know a way down to those tunnels from the north wing. We never had the chance to explore them, but they most likely come up here." She indicated a street marked RUE DES RÉSERVOIRS. "We found a hatch on this street. I suspect it can be opened from below."

If the reservoirs were disused, they would most likely have dried out. The thought calmed me a little.

"Fine," I said. "The reservoir."

Renelde showed us where the entrance to it was hidden, behind a near-invisible door in the north wing.

"Moving prisoners in the north wing should be easy. Shorter distance to cover. We can escort them quietly, in very small groups," she said. "For the south wing . . . I think we will need a distraction."

At this point, Ankou took over. Among the weapons he had stashed in the cemetery, there was a Scion-made flare gun. Someone would fire it over the gardens when the north wing was clear of prisoners. The flare would both draw the guards and signal to the group in the south wing to get moving. Having the best knowledge of the gardens, Renelde volunteered.

We decided who should go in which group. Since I was most sensitive to the æther, best-placed to sneak prisoners past the guards, I chose the more dangerous south wing. As it turned out, the device Ankou carried was a motion sensor—military technology, which could detect movement, even through walls, at up to thirty feet. He would use it to escort prisoners through the north wing. With a radar on each team, we had a decent chance of getting everyone out alive. Or so I told myself.

Once we had run through the plan one more time, they retreated to their sleeping bags. There was no need for them to know about my other mission. I lay down alongside Arcturus.

"Are you ready for this?"

My voice was the softest of whispers.

"To return to hell," Arcturus said. "Yes. It is time." He was on his side, facing me. "Are *you* ready for this?"

"I don't know." I gazed at the ceiling. "I'm afraid of walking into a trap. Kornephoros could have set us up. Any of us could die, and at this point, I have no idea if it would be my fault."

"We have more evidence than rumor this time." When I said nothing, he continued. "It is your nature to act, even in the face of uncertainty. I know that I have warned you against your impulsiveness, but it has served you well before."

"I suppose Rephaim consider every risk and possibility before they dive in headfirst."

"Immortals have the luxury of time. Our councils often seemed interminable," he said, a little dryly. I managed a smile. "Can you complete your assignment from Domino?"

The question hung over us. I remembered Jaxon in his boudoir, smoking a cigar. Imparting wisdom.

A squandered opportunity is death to the thief. Should he feel even an ounce of pity for his victim, he will go hungry that night. He had stared out of the window. *Morals, O my lovely, are for the lucky ones.*

Without knowing it, Jaxon had given me his blessing to kill him that day. The assignment was an opportunity I could not squander.

"I have killed before," I said. "More than once."

"In self-defense," Arcturus reminded me. "This would be an execution. And someone you know very well."

"I don't know Jaxon. I never knew him."

As I spoke, memories gleamed. Shattered pieces of the past. All the good times I had shared with Jaxon, before I learned the truth. His rich chuckle. The spark I had longed to ignite in his eyes. Our first meeting, when he had revealed to me that I was clairvoyant, and all the things about myself that had once frightened me were rendered new and marvelous.

He had taught me to love what set me apart. If not for him, I might still fear myself.

Then came the ugly memories. When he had threatened me for trying to leave his service. All the times he had thwarted and belittled me. His betrayal after the scrimmage. The revelation of exactly who he was, and what he had done. He was a dangerous trickster who served no one but himself, capable of grave violence and utterly cold-blooded scheming.

"I don't want to fail this assignment. Not when Ducos is starting to listen." I pillowed my head on my arm. "I'll find him."

"If it comes to a choice between helping the prisoners and completing the assignment—"

"I'll choose the former. This has always been about Sheol II." My voice was little more than breath. "If that scuppers any alliance with Domino, I'll have to make my peace with it."

Arcturus reached into his coat and withdrew a familiar pendant on a chain. The protective relic he had given me, the one I had thrown back to him just before I was captured.

"Some protection against Jaxon." He offered it to me. "It may also ground you. Should you find yourself returning to your dark room, hold onto it. Remember that you are no longer there."

The pendant sent a small vibration through the æther when I took it, as if it recalled my touch. It was the last object I had held before the waterboard, a connection to *before* and to *now*. I sat up a little to clasp it around my neck and freed my hair from under the chain.

"Thank you," I said. "It will help." I coughed and lay back down. "We should get some rest."

"Yes."

His eyes were the only light. Perhaps it was because I was too weary to care about keeping my distance, or because I was starting to feel the cold of the abyss, but I shifted closer to his chest and fitted my head under his chin. His heartbeat kept the dead silence at bay.

I hoped Ivy would be all right. She had moved through the tunnels with ease, unafraid of everything except what might be in Versailles. As I began to drift off, trying not to cough too loudly, I thought about just how far we were from the world above. Ménard could hunt forever, and he would never find us here. As disorienting as la ville souterraine was, I knew now why it appealed to the outcasts of this citadel.

Exhaustion towed me into a deeper darkness. I had thought last-minute nerves would keep me awake, but after such a long slog, it was impossible not to fall asleep.

When I stirred awake, I reached instinctively for Arcturus, my palm finding his chest. I could sense that he was sound asleep, feel his heavy watchcoat over me. When I emerged from my warm nest, I found the air and my skin much colder than they had been when I drifted off. Everyone was still and quiet.

Everyone, that is, but Léandre.

He had dialed his headlamp down to the lowest setting and was sitting in the corner, knees pulled up to his chest, next to a plaque I had failed to notice when we arrived. Keeping the coat around me, I sat beside him. He spared me a look as I read the plaque.

"I carved this here," he said, low-voiced. "When we found this place."

To disappear between shadow and stone. I traced the letters. *To walk the buried places of the world and still draw breath. To be everywhere and nowhere, seeing all, known and unknown. To rise from the depths, never seeking the sun. To live as one already dead, and with the dead beside.*

"It describes the desire in the heart of an unnatural." Léandre shifted. "Or maybe just in mine."

"No," I said. "I think I get it."

"Okay." He tightened his jaw. "I apologize for being short with you earlier. I did not know you had been tortured."

"I understand. Your sister and lover are in danger."

He shot me a fleeting look of surprise, which was swiftly papered over. "Renelde told you." A tiny huff escaped him. "She wants to get there just as much. To reach my sister. Camille."

"La Tarasque," I said. He grunted. "Are they . . . âmes jumelles, like you and Le Vieux Orphelin?"

"In a different way. They are like sisters, toujours collées," he said. "You also have friends in Versailles."

"Yes."

"What are their names?"

"Zeke Sáenz, Nadine Arnett, and Michael Wren."

"We will find them. We will give them a safe place." He placed a hand on the plaque. "This day, Underqueen, we walk the buried places of the world and still draw breath."

"So we hope."

Léandre didn't smile.

"Yes," he said. "So we hope."

Not long after, the others began to stir awake. We ate a little. With our strength restored, the six of us set out again, through the final section of the Passage des Voleurs. I crunched the stimulant between my teeth.

We slithered down to the deepest known part of the carrières, where the air was soup and water fell like tears from the ceiling. I strode after Léandre, dull pain and trepidation climbing in my chest.

Eventually, our course took us upward once more. We scaled a series of broken metal ladders. At last, Léandre stopped. He gave me a leg up, and I grabbed the edge of a crack in the wall, lifting myself into a corbeled room. For the first time in two days, I glimpsed natural light. Léandre moved past me and unlocked two rusted wrought-iron gates.

I stepped out of a mausoleum, into Versailles.

18

Song of Swords

Dusk had almost swallowed the last smoldering of day. Over the city, the moon waxed bright and clean. It hung like a shaded lamp, offering enough light to guide our steps and enough darkness to hide in. I breathed in the still of the night and found that I was not afraid.

More than five months ago, I had escaped the first colony. Now I would take down the second.

Only spirits—and the stars—kept watch over the cemetery. Shadows drew their fingers through the snow. We gathered around a tombstone, which Ankou shunted aside to reveal a stockpile of arms. Among them was the flare gun, which Renelde tucked into her waistband. I reached into the grave and picked up a combat knife.

Ankou lifted out a shotgun as if it were his firstborn child. Only when he set it aside and removed an axe from his backpack did I realize he was an axinomancer; that weapon was his favored numen. Its handle was etched with feathers and bones and patterns that looked distinctly Celtic. He pressed a tender kiss to the blade.

I took note of the others' auras. Léandre, who armed himself with knuckle-dusters and a pistol, was a physical medium—if possessed, he could be a help or a hindrance in a fight. Renelde was a fury. As I tried to get a handle on her aura, I realized why it felt so familiar. She was like Danica.

"Renelde," I said to her, "your aura—it reminds me of someone I know. Can I ask what kind of fury you are?"

"I would love to be able to tell you." She took a pair of knives from the tomb. "No one is like me. I go into long trances, sometimes glimpse the future. Even in *Des Mérites de l'Anormalité*, I could not find myself. Is your friend in London?"

"Athens."

"I'd love to talk to them one day. It can be a lonely feeling, not knowing where you fit."

Arcturus kept watch while we armed ourselves. Though he had owned a knife in the colony, I had only ever seen him fight with spools.

When we were ready, Ankou and Léandre shoved the tombstone back into place, and Ankou laid his axe on top of it. He struck the end of the handle, and the axe began to spin, luring the nearest spirits. The æther trembled. When the axe came to a sudden halt, glazed with ice, Ankou looked satisfied and signed to me.

"As we suspected," Léandre translated. "Southwest. The nearest anormaux are in the same direction as the Château de Versailles."

"Good," I said. "Let's go."

We climbed over a wall and stepped into the city, footsteps muffled by deep snow, flakes catching in our lashes. This place had been frozen in time, like Oxford. Even though I sensed no one nearby, and there was no evidence of cameras, we kept off the main paths.

Renelde and Léandre led the way. We crossed streets, passed a burned-out church, and continued up a deserted boulevard, wind scalding our faces. That and the stimulant made my teeth clatter.

In the first colony, the city had been alive, to a degree. Gas lamps had glimmered on the streets. Duckett had run a pawnshop. The more fortunate humans had been allowed to leave their residences and wander. There had always been a risk of running into a Rephaite, but I had been able to sneak out most nights to visit Liss and Julian in the Rookery.

There was no shantytown here. No wanderers. If the first colony had been hell, this one was purgatory—a liminal, unfinished space, where the sinners of Scion would wait for judgment. The city was empty.

All of it, that is, but the Château de Versailles.

At last, the palace came into view, bathed in the ashen light of the moon. Every dreamscape I sensed was near or inside it. Most remnants of the monarch days were tragic ruins, but this building had been restored to its former magnificence, ready to house the Rephaim. I climbed with Malperdy and Arcturus to the roof of the former royal stables so we could take stock of the exterior defenses.

The approach to the palace was vast and cobblestoned. Malperdy handed me a small pair of binoculars, and I took in the lofty gates, covered in gold leaf and polished to a glow.

No fewer than thirty soldiers guarded them.

"Shit." Cold to my core, I lowered the binoculars. "Krigs."

They were stock-still, standing at precise intervals in front of the gates, their stances identical and disciplined. Ognena Maria had told me once that Vance made her soldiers stand for hours during the winter—to prove they could endure, that they felt nothing. She thought they were somehow changed during their training, to make them numb inside and out.

I had expected many things, but not the army. I had been a fool to assume they were all involved in the invasion.

"Stealth was always our intended approach." Arcturus narrowed his eyes. "We can infiltrate the palace without alerting them."

"This is a fucking joke." Malperdy looked as if he could spit in disgust. "Versailles was our place."

I tried to ignore the line of soldiers and concentrate on the palace. It was a city unto itself, more than large enough to house prisoners, guards, and keepers alike. Other than the soldiers, there were no obvious defenses. Just as I had hoped, the tunnel had taken us under them all.

"There are at least sixty humans inside. And—" I counted. "Only four Rephaim."

"That is not enough," Arcturus said.

My mind raced. "Could Rephaim tolerate *any* Emite blood without turning?"

"A drop or two."

"It must be concealing more of them." With great effort, I strained my sixth sense, to no avail. "If Jaxon has distributed it—if he's using it himself—then he suspects I'm coming."

Arcturus said nothing to comfort me on that front.

The three of us returned to street level. "Soldiers," I said to the others. "We should be able to avoid them if we're careful."

"Careful." Léandre stared at me, nostrils flaring. "We are dead if they get one glimpse of us."

"So we don't let them," I said. "If you want to turn back, you can guard the cemetery. I'm going in."

He looked away. Renelde laid a hand on his arm.

"Léandre," she said. He glanced down at her and gave a stiff nod.

We made our way north through the never-ending snow, still avoiding the wider streets. The side entrance to the palace would take us into the gardens near a fountain that had once been called the Bassin de Neptune. From there, we could assess the rear defenses.

Three dreamscapes were just ahead of us. A trio of Vigiles were stationed behind iron railings, next to a guardhouse with a mansard roof. None of them had their weapons at the ready.

We took shelter in a doorway, out of sight. "There is no way around those three." Léandre motioned to Ankou, who drew his axe. "Mal, you tempt them out."

"I've got it," I said.

Malperdy frowned. "What?"

In answer, I leapt from my body and flashed between their dreamscapes. By the time I returned, all three Vigiles had collapsed, and the taste of blood smeared the back of my throat.

We approached the boundary together. Malperdy climbed the wall beside the railings, sprang across to the guardhouse roof, and dropped back to the ground in a crouch. The rest of us followed him. And just like that, we were over the boundary, into the heart of Sheol II.

The Bassin de Neptune was full of frozen water. Sculptures that must once have served as fountains were now bone dry and dressed in moss. One of them held a dull gold trident.

The palace loomed on high, silhouetted by the moonlight. Most of its windows were dark. A snow-laden forest stood between us and its walls. I thought of one of the stories Arcturus had told me, about a princess cursed to sleep forever in a castle ringed by thorns.

Snow glistened in my hair. Renelde was in the lead, with me just behind to warn her of incoming Vigiles. There were about thirty dreamscapes in the gardens, each a trap that one wrong turn could spring.

We passed more stagnant water, where statues wallowed, before we reached the opening that led into the nearest grove, and the rusted gate that blocked our way. Renelde broke through a snow-bank, revealing a hollow beneath, and slid under, leaving clouds of breath in her wake. When I followed, the corner of the gate cut deep into my left calf. I bit down a hiss.

"Careful." Malperdy reached through the bars to touch my shoulder. "Are you okay?"

"Think so."

Hot pain swelled from the cut as I crawled after Renelde. In the distance, a storm was gathering. If our luck held out, the sound of it would mask our approach.

Thick foliage tangled over our heads, heavy with powder. The plants had long since broken their bounds and overrun the foot-path. Twigs rolled against my knees, buried under the snow, and twigs snared on my hair.

When a bank of cloud snuffed the moon, we all fell still, our breathing heavy. I couldn't see a thing until Renelde switched on her headlamp and angled it so it was visible to all of us. We followed it, up to our elbows in snow. It seeped into the cuffs of my gloves and chilled the back of my neck. I reached the end of the path with a raw nose and numb lips, covered in dead leaves.

I stopped.

A figure stood guard in the grove, at the top of the steps that would take us closer to the palace. A flicker of lightning revealed a dark-haired Rephaite. Beside me, Renelde lay flat on her stomach, her lamp extinguished. When she reached for her gun, I caught her wrist.

Somewhere behind me, a twig cracked. The Rephaite turned in a swing of cloak. Fear paralyzed me. Renelde started to crawl backward, breathing hard.

A shadow brushed past. Arcturus. I made a vain grab for his coat, swallowing a sound of protest, but he was already in the open, hailing the other Rephaite in Gloss.

What happened next was unclear. It was too dark to see anything but the glint of eyes before both Rephaim blurred out of sight. I sprang to my feet and ran after them, revolver in hand. Moonlight spilled from above again, stripping the ground white.

I found Arcturus kneeling in the snow beside the fallen Rephaite. "He will wake before long," was all he said.

"What were you *thinking*, taking him on without a weapon?" I said in a heated whisper.

"It was his weapon I wanted."

He rose with an exquisite sword in hand. Its blade was the length of my arm, and it looked for all the world like a seamless blend of glass and pearl, iridescent where the moonlight touched it.

"It has been a very long time since I last held an opaline blade." He gave it a satisfied spin, making the air rush and the æther vibrate. "This will serve."

Seeing him with a blade gave me a strange feeling. Renelde, who had now caught up with us, did a double take. "What the fuck is that?" she whispered to me. "Looks like a frozen rainbow."

When the other three reached us, we padded up the steps and down another thorny path. Now the Château de Versailles was to our left, and we were level with it. Cast-iron gas lamps illuminated its façade.

"We have to find another way," I said. The moon disappeared again. "The moment we leave the groves, we're exposed."

"There *is* no other way." Renelde leaned a fraction of an inch out of our cover. "Where are the Vigiles?"

"Over there." I nodded to the right. "They're moving, but not in this direction."

Malperdy got his binoculars out again. "I can see the window." He lowered them. "Still broken."

He handed me the binoculars. Even with the gas lamps, it was difficult to find, but I finally made it out. Above two pairs of white pillars, a third-floor window was missing most of its glass, as if someone had launched a piece of furniture through it.

With a deep breath, Malperdy duckwalked forward, the coiled rope slung over his shoulder. Ankou stopped him, grasping his wrist with a murmur.

"I'll check the coast is clear up there," Malperdy muttered, hands just visible in the light from the mansion. Ankou pressed his lips together. "As soon as I lower the rope, join me."

"Be careful, Mal." Renelde readied her pistol. "We are right behind you."

"Super." Malperdy blew out a breath. "Wish me luck."

He darted out from the grove, across a stretch of snow, and fell into a crouch behind a hedgerow. I waited, not daring to breathe. If anyone was watching the grounds from the windows, they would have had a clear shot at him, yet the night remained silent.

Malperdy must have had the same thought, because he made his next dash, straight for the palace walls. He was quick as a fox. Quick as the sudden unveiling of the moon.

Not quick enough.

The gunshot cracked the night like a stone through ice. We all dropped to the ground, so fast my chin almost hit the snow. Cold soaked into my undershirt as a soul-rending scream curdled the air.

"Fuck," Léandre breathed.

To his left, I could hear Ankou, his breathing ragged. Beside me, Renelde clenched a fist to her lips. "Paige," she whispered thickly, "can you tell if the sniper is still there?"

"There are too many people." I spoke under my breath, my heart thunderous. As Malperdy let out an agonized sob, a shudder in the æther made me climb to my feet. "Vigiles. Move."

The five of us retreated, stepping in our own footprints. I sensed the Vigiles descending on Malperdy.

"Now we are trapped," Léandre said, once we were back in the middle of the grove. "Like rats."

My gaze was on the unmoving Rephaite. In unison, Arcturus and I looked at each other.

"Warden can get us past the snipers." I hauled the sodden cloak off the Rephaite and thrust it at Arcturus. "Quickly."

He swung it over his shoulders and knelt to strip the Rephaite of his leather gloves and sword belt. The others watched as he put them on and pulled the other Rephaite into the overgrowth, out of sight.

"Des empreintes," a voice bellowed. A beam of light gleamed through the close-knit branches. "Les cambrioleurs ont de l'aide. Trouvez les—"

Our group splintered. I swerved right with Arcturus and Renelde, down the path we had taken from the Bassin de Neptune, while Ankou and Léandre charged to the left. Thorns and branches ripped at my hair. At the end, we vaulted over a gate and ran south, down a new path.

Dreamscapes were closing in. The little stimulant had almost worn off: my limbs were leaden, my chest tight. I swung off my backpack, grabbed an auto-injector from inside, and slowed for long enough to stab it into my thigh. With a jolt of pain, the adrenaline was in, and I was running after Renelde and Arcturus. Already I could feel my body waking up.

I shoved past another rusted gate, and suddenly we were out in the open, exposed, and the dreamscapes were too close. "Wait," I whisper-shouted to Arcturus and Renelde, who both stopped. "They're coming."

"Get behind me," Arcturus said.

His tone brooked no argument. I grasped Renelde by the arm and dragged her behind Arcturus with me. "Don't say a word," I breathed into her ear. She tensed.

Eight Vigiles burst from the foliage and trained their rifles on us, shouting at us to drop our weapons and get on the ground. Seeing a Rephaite, they stopped. Renelde gripped my elbow.

"Vigiles," Arcturus said.

His voice was utterly cold, as it had been on the night we met. Having lived with him for weeks, I realized just how much he had been performing in those days, how much effort it must take him to wear this mask. It unnerved me to see him dressed like the enemy again.

"My lord." One of them stepped forward. Her armor identified her as the squadron commandant. "Forgive me, but—"

"What is it, Vigile?"

The commandant held her nerve. "I don't recognize you." Her London accent took me by surprise. Weaver must have stipulated English guards here, which spoke volumes about his feelings on Ménard. "Have you made yourself known to the Grand Overseer?"

"You do not recognize me, despite the fact that I have been stationed here for a sennight," Arcturus said, in the same glacial tone. "Perhaps all Rephaim look the same to your feeble eyes."

Another Vigile was clearly on the verge of shitting himself. "My lord, we would never be so—"

"Not that it is any of your concern, Vigile, but I am Elnath Mesarthim. And this is Paige Mahoney, enemy of the blood-sovereign, who I found roaming this grove as if she were a tourist. Your so-called *vigilance* is wanting." Arcturus took hold of my collar. I struggled against his grasp. "One of her accomplices has already been apprehended, but there will be more. Comb the grounds immediately. I will escort these two to the Grand Overseer."

"But Paige Mahoney is dead," another Vigile said. His accent was French. "We were told."

"Then I can only conclude that this is her identical twin, Vigile. Either way, she will be processed."

"My lord," the commandant said. "Of course." She paused, then spoke into her transceiver: "Rooftop west, this is 502. Hold your fire. I repeat, hold your fire. Sentinel approaching your position with two unknowns. Establish relative safe zone from the Parterre du Nord."

"*Received*," came the response.

There had been nothing this slick in the first colony. Nashira was taking no chances.

"You're clear to approach, Lord Elnath," the commandant said. I wished I could see her face through the visor. "Please proceed."

"Efficient of you, 502," Arcturus said, not looking at her. "A pity you were not efficient enough to stop these intruders entering in the first place."

"Yes, my lord. Apologies."

She led her squadron back into the labyrinth of groves, leaving us in the snow. As soon as they were out of sight, Renelde released her breath.

"We have to find the others." She wet her lips. "And get Malperdy."

I searched for them in the æther. "Ankou and Léandre are heading deeper into the gardens. Malperdy is inside." My temples ached. "We have to take this chance to get in there."

Renelde looked toward the palace. A moment later, she took a deep breath and gave me a small nod. I followed her out of the grove.

Vases spilled winter-blooming flowers. I kept my head down as we walked on either side of Arcturus, in full view of the windows. My knees shook. That Vigile had told the snipers to hold their fire, but if they suspected a ruse, they might decide to ignore the order.

No gunfire came. Just the crunch of boots, the sluice of breath. When we reached a wide set of steps, I risked a glance to my left. Darkness stained the snow where Malperdy had fallen.

Arcturus reached a tall pair of doors, which two Vigiles opened for us. I stepped into the gloom beyond and found myself in a gallery of pale marble, where two braziers flamed. A bloodred carpet covered the floor. This was the Lower Gallery, which ran below the Hall of Mirrors.

"Lord Elnath. Allow us to escort you to the Grand Overseer," one of the Vigiles said.

"Unless you believe two unarmed humans to be a threat to me, Vigile, I will not require a chaperon," Arcturus said. "Get outside and search the groves. Bring any infiltrators to the north wing, alive and unharmed, or the blood-sovereign will hear of your incompetence."

The Vigile offered a smart bow. "My lord."

They both made themselves scarce, leaving the three of us alone.

The Lower Gallery was attached to the central vestibule of the palace, which had smooth red pillars, veined with white, like meat. I leaned on one of them.

"Okay. We're in." I tried to slow my breathing. "There are two clusters of dreamscapes. One in this wing, one in the other. They might be prisoners, or they might be Vigiles in a guardroom."

Renelde held a hand to her chest. "What about Malperdy?"

Finding him was harder. "North wing. This floor."

"He is alive, then."

"For now," I said. She suddenly pinched her nose. "What is it?"

"Le Vieux Orphelin. He is . . . sending me an image. A door." She blinked several times. "I will search the north wing and start to move prisoners toward the reservoir, as planned. With any luck, I will intercept Léandre and Ankou."

"We've got the south wing," I said. "Good luck."

Renelde was gone without a sound. Pain throbbed deep in the flesh of my calf, and my trouser leg was damp inside. Arcturus turned to the front doors.

When he opened them, the frigid air hit me again. So did a shimmer of sleet. As we strode across the black-and-white marble at the front of the palace, I dared not look over my shoulder. The windows of the King's Apartment watched over this courtyard. In the distance, through the fog, I could make out the vanguard of soldiers, their silhouettes sketched out by gas lamps.

Don't turn around.

Arcturus silently opened another set of doors, and we were back inside, out of sight of the soldiers. A wide staircase took us up to the former apartments of the queens of France. With my fatigue tided back again, I took them two at a time.

"Jaxon will be in the King's Apartment. I'm sure of it," I said to Arcturus, once we reached the top. "Free any prisoners in this wing and wait for that flare to go up. I'll join you as soon as I can."

"Very well." His gaze flicked across my face. "Good luck."

"And to you."

We took off in opposite directions.

Faded gold leaf shone dully on the walls, reflecting the torches that burned at regular intervals. I crossed a room that must once have been a bedchamber, so ornate and floral it was like being inside a chocolate box. Next was a square antechamber. When I tried the gilded doors inside it, neither of them budged.

I listened. There was no sound from within, but I could just perceive a dreamscape.

Jaxon had locked himself in.

Then I heard it. Music. "The Thieving Magpie"—one of his favorites—was playing beyond the doors. The volume climbed until it was booming through the corridors.

He knew.

Like wasps in a nest, dreamscapes stirred across the palace, as if the music were some hellish public alarm clock. Sensing a gust of movement on the floor below, I spun on my heel and pelted back through the apartments. The music was a grindstone on my ears and jaw.

Arcturus had forced the doors to the south wing. I shoved through them. The Rephaite keepers must carry keys. I would need his strength to take one of them down.

Jaxon could lock himself in as tight as he liked. He was the one who had taught me not to let any lock bar my way.

The music became frantic, deranged. I skidded into a hall with an arched ceiling, four hundred feet long, where chandeliers dripped wax and cast small ripples of gold on the floor. Paintings towered on the walls, each showing a victory in the history of Scion. No dreamscapes called out from the æther here, but I no longer fully trusted my sixth sense. Emite blood could be hiding them.

Two mirrored doors flanked a wall-sized depiction of the Battle of the Iron Gates, which dominated the end of the gallery. I made for them.

The music came to a sudden halt. I stopped, too, sensing a presence behind me. When the sixth sense failed, human intuition stepped in, warning me of danger, a predator. I lowered my hands from my ears and turned.

A Rephaite had appeared at the other end of the hall. Golden hair, long and unbound. Hooded eyes, hot as the ninth circle of hell, the yellow of molten steel.

"XX-59-40." His voice, and that number, froze my blood. "What an unexpected delight."

Thuban Sargas. I snapped my arm up, aiming my revolver at him.

He stepped closer, cloak grazing the floor. Even in the half-light, I could see that his gloved hands were slick, and that he was holding something. Something like a dead animal.

"Your friend had a pitiful tolerance for pain." Darkness dripped from his trophy. "I put him out of his misery once he told me who he had brought with him. Such is my mercy."

That thing in his hand was no animal. It was cinnamon hair, still attached to a bloody lappet of skin.

Malperdy.

Thuban had scalped him.

"I wasn't sure you had any more marbles to lose, Thuban." As I spoke, I was searching the æther for Malperdy. Nothing. "I thought you liked to play for a while before you killed."

I had to keep Thuban occupied. If he was talking, he wasn't chopping pieces off me.

"I no longer have a great deal of patience for the *sound* of human beings," Thuban confessed. "Once I relished your screams, your pleas, your weeping. Now I find I prefer your absolute silence. Even the cadence of your breathing is a vexation."

Something had come unhinged in him. Even the façade of his restraint had evaporated.

"I will make an exception for you, fleshmonger." He started to close the space between us. I backed away. "Your screams will ring in every corner of this palace before I present what remains to the blood-sovereign. Perhaps I will give her that lovely hair . . . separately." He cocked his head. "If you are here, then the concubine is close. Unwise of him to leave you alone. I wonder how many fingers I will have to remove before he hears your cries."

I kept moving, trying to maintain a safe distance. "You couldn't beat Arcturus at a game of cards, let alone a duel."

"We shall test that theory when he comes." A mockery of a smile. "Tell me, now. Is 24 with you?"

At this, I stopped.

"Ivy," I said, my voice full of loathing, "is alive and fighting. She survived you, Thuban."

"Did you expect to disappoint me with that news?" he asked. "No. It pleases me. What a pity it would have been if she had succumbed after our games. We have so many more to play, she and I." He let the scalp drop to the floor with a wet *slap*. "What passed between us in the colony was nothing. When I have her back in my possession, you will wish you had slit her throat."

"You will never lay a finger on her again, you twisted hellkite." I clicked back the hammer. "I'm curious, Thuban, if you'll indulge me. Why haven't they made you the blood-heir?"

Taunting him was a dangerous game. The sight of him filled me with such revulsion and anger that it made my hands shake.

"I have one idea," I went on. "Nashira finds you embarrassing. Your clairvoyance is nothing special. You torment humans—who stand no chance against you—because you have nothing else to recommend you."

I had touched a nerve. His eyes burned hotter.

"To be a Sargas," he said, "is to be power." Another step. "I do not care to be blood-heir. Pleasure would then have to bow before duty, and there are such pleasures to be tasted here. I learned where to cut a human to make it bleed, but not to let it slip away into death. I learned how many pieces I could slice. Which bones cause most agony when broken."

As he spoke, memories pounded through me. Flux warping my mind. The branding iron on my shoulder.

"I wonder why you look at me with such disgust," Thuban said, "when humans have invented so many creative ways to inflict agony on each other. I would never have thought of some of them myself. Have you heard of a brazen bull, or a breaking wheel, or keelhauling?"

"Medieval brutality," I said. "You're nothing, Thuban. Just a low grunt who does filthy work, so pathetic he has to prey on the helpless."

"You will come to regret each word that just left your rotting mouth."

He flew at me.

A ringing *bang*, and the first slug pierced his chest. The sound barked against my ears. I fired again and again, the shock of the recoil shuddering up my arms, but Thuban kept coming, impervious to the onslaught of hot lead. He was a colossus, a god, his sarx like metal. After five shots, I lashed out with my spirit.

Power crested in me like a wave. Thuban stopped in the face of it, his teeth set against the pressure of my dislocation. I retreated as fast as I could toward the doors, just about keeping him at bay. Then his features morphed, and he was Suhail Chertan, and I was strapped to the waterboard, at his mercy. A spasm of terror made me lose my grip.

Thuban was on me before I could so much as gasp. His gloved hands locked around my throat, lifted me right off my feet, and slammed me against a painting. He choked off my cry.

"I could kill you now," he said against my ear. My eyes streamed, and a tortured sound escaped the burning pinhole of my throat. "You say I prey on the helpless. You are not. Your spirit is a weapon. Yet now we are here, which of us has true power? Is it you, with your wayfaring spirit—or is it me, with enough strength in a finger to snap you in two?"

He spends his time pulling the wings off mayflies, Kornephoros had said. *I prefer prey that fights back.*

The taste of blood was in my mouth. I pushed with my spirit as hard as I could, but Thuban Sargas was a Rephaite—a god without gifts, but a god nonetheless. I could feel my face turning puce for want of air, my hands beating of their own accord at his chest, my boots scuffing the columns of his legs. His hands turned me into a trapped moth, brittle and fluttering. He could crush my windpipe on a whim.

When he finally released my throat, I coughed until I almost retched. As my head dropped, I spotted them.

Keys. An iron ring of them, attached to his belt.

"I will soon find the concubine," Thuban whispered, "and when I do, I will keep you together somewhere for a time, before I present you to the Suzerain." I turned my head in disgust. "You can watch each other writhe in agony."

Heat filled my eyes as he drew my aura toward him. Red branched through his irises.

"Exquisite," he said, soft as velvet. "But no. The blood-sovereign would be very angry if I damaged your aura."

Tenderly, like a lover, he peeled the brace off my left hand.

"This happened in the first colony." He curled his own hand around my wrist. "Can it truly still pain you?"

"Not as much as your fucking voice," I bit out.

He tightened his grip until I felt the drumbeat of blood through my arm. His thumb dug into the middle of my palm, and fingers vised the back of my wrist. Like a child discovering a toy, he began to turn my wrist clockwise, as if to find the point at which a light would come on.

Unlike a child, he knew exactly what he was doing. What he wanted to know was how I differed from the other humans he had tortured. What dialect of pain my body spoke.

My palm now faced my shoulder. My face scrunched up as he forced it farther, and a warning ache radiated into my palm, my fingers.

"Such delicate bones," Thuban breathed into my damp hair, his eyes so close they tripled in number. I could smell the blood on his gloves. My skin was smeared with it, my whole frame trembling in revulsion. "Scream, now. Scream for the flesh-traitor who dares to call himself a Rephaite."

Cheeks streaked with blood, I clenched my teeth and steeled myself, even as the fine bones ignited. I would not cry out when my wrist broke again. I would not give him the satisfaction.

"Thuban," a voice barked.

The pressure lifted. I gasped in relief. As if he was tossing a rag aside, Thuban hurled me across the hall. I crashed to the floor, rolled over, and slewed along the marble, throat on fire, until a pillar stopped my slide. Coughing, I looked up to see Arcturus, his sword bright in the gloom.

Without even knowing it, I had summoned him to my side.

"Concubine." Thuban let out a chuckle. "I knew you would come for the human. Like a hound to its master."

"I have come for *you*." Arcturus held his gaze. "Let us end this, Thuban."

"Do you not consider this rotting meat capable of fighting its own battles?" Thuban sneered, while I used the pillar to drag myself up. My wrist throbbed with each brutal cough. "Do you admit now that they are the inferior species?"

"I did not come here to answer your questions," Arcturus said. "I came for the song of swords."

Gone was the temperate musician who had fashioned me a music box. The mere sight of a Sargas—his enemy—had transfigured him into a metal soldier, a soulless giant. Even to me, in that moment, he was chilling.

One step took him over the threshold, into the hall where Scion commemorated its battles. Thuban swept back his cloak and drew his own sword with a sound like ice being cut. With all the mental clout I could muster, I called a word to Arcturus.

Keys.

His gaze flicked to me, then to Thuban. To his belt. When he looked back up, his eyes kindled, and I followed his line of sight. Four figures had emerged, like specters, from the darkness at my back.

A deathlike cold stole over my flesh as the silent Rephaim strode toward us, each holding a sword. Leading them was Situla Mesarthim, who I remembered well from the first colony. She was a ruthless mercenary, and resembled Arcturus so strongly it was unnerving. The other three were unfamiliar. I was caught between the newcomers and Thuban.

Arcturus could beat one Rephaite. Maybe two. Five against one was a death sentence.

Run!

I willed him to hear me again, but all he did was stare out his fellow Rephaim. His executioners.

"You spineless piece of shit," I wheezed at Thuban. "Can't even fight one Ranthen on your own."

"This is what is known as a trap, fleshmonger. And you just led your lapdog directly into it," Thuban sneered.

He bore down on me again and hauled me up by my hair. My boots squeaked on the marble. Arcturus started forward, eyes ablaze.

"Concubine," Thuban called to him, "perhaps you would like to choose which part of her I cut off first." He angled the blade across my abdomen. Even through my clothes, I could feel how keen that edge was, how effortlessly it would rip skin and muscle. One wrong move, and my viscera would be on the floor. "You know her parts far better than I do, after all."

Unfortunately for Thuban, he had forced me into a position that let me reach my combat knife. In one movement, I drew it and rammed it into his neck, right under his jaw.

Thuban let out an ear-piercing note of Gloss. The instant his grip loosened, I forced his elbow up and twisted myself under it. The iridescent blade caught my skin at an angle, leaving a trail of searing cold pain, like an ice burn. A cry of shock tore from my throat. I regained my footing and sped to Arcturus, who swept me behind him and lifted his sword.

"Are you hurt?" he asked roughly.

Blood seeped beneath my undershirt. I rucked it up to see a shallow cut from navel to hip.

"It's not deep," I rasped. Across the hall, Thuban pulled the knife free and spattered the floor with luminous blood. "I need his keys. Jax locked himself in."

Arcturus widened his stance. "I will see to it." The other Rephaim kept coming. "Stand back."

Before I could, Situla rushed us. Arcturus flung me out of the way of her blade before he blocked it with bone-shattering force, the movement so fast I almost missed it. He disarmed his next challenger and slashed his back clean down the middle, drawing enough ectoplasm to cast them all in queasy light. Now he wielded a sword in each hand. On cue, music struck up again —this time, the infernal gallop from *Orpheus in the Underworld*. Spirits came swarming from all over, drawn to a clash between Rephaim.

Situla sent her blade shivering toward Arcturus. It glanced off one of his swords, and his next swing came close to cutting her in half—but the others were already on top of him, attacking like a pack of wolves.

Thuban let out an appalling not-laugh. The fight took them to the middle of the hall. I watched Situla crack Arcturus in the jaw— hard enough to dislocate it on a human – before she hurled a spool at him. He swept it aside and locked one of his swords with hers, fending off more blows with the other.

Fuck this. Stiletto in hand, I ran straight for the Rephaim, charging the æther with pressure as I went, and launched myself at Situla. She tried to shake me off, but I impaled her hand with the blade. I dropped from her back, ducked her sword—its gleaming flat passed over my head, so close my scalp turned cold—and stabbed again, right through her boot and into her heel. Though I evaded her next blow, she caught me by the back of my oilskin, and before I knew it, she had latched onto my aura like a tapeworm.

Blood ran from my eyes. I kicked wildly at her. The æther was sucked away from me as Situla wrung my connection to it. Her eyes turned a terrible red. Arcturus saw and threw one of his swords at her back, forcing her to release me to avoid it. I hit the floor. When her blade seared up again, I was still too shaken to move.

She hesitated.

Her sword hung over me, an inch from splitting my skull. I stared at her, disconcerted. Her face was drawn, eyebrows knitted tight, knuckles straining against her glove.

Then Arcturus attacked his cousin, bringing the fight with him. He was sure-footed, his bladework assured and formidable, fluent in violence. Situla fended him off with one sword. With her free hand, she lifted me, and—with what felt like all her inhuman might—lobbed me toward the doors. I slammed into the floor a third time and groaned.

"Paige!"

Arcturus tossed something after me. The ring of keys. One of the other Rephaim went for them just as I did. I snatched them by my fingertips and kicked her as hard as I could in the nose.

Arcturus could hold his own here. He had been charged with protecting the god-sent family—defensive fights were in his bones. My presence would distract him. I rolled to my feet and barreled out of the gallery.

"Stop her," Thuban bellowed over the music. "Mirzam, Heze, bring the dreamwalker to me!"

Back across the checkered floor. The two Rephaim tried to come after me, but Arcturus blocked the doorway in my wake. I sprinted like I never had through the royal apartments, my heart in my throat, wrist still pounding, and almost crashed headlong into the locked white doors.

The keys were sticky with blood. One after the other, I tried them, unable to still my trembling. The knell of blades continued in the distance. While I could hear it, Arcturus was alive.

A key with a flower-shaped bow fitted the lock. I turned it and pushed both doors open.

Once you reach the city, you are to take one action, and one only. You are to assassinate the official in charge of it.

The Hall of Mirrors stretched before me. Ahead, gilded sculptures held salvers of buttery candles, offering them up to a baroque ceiling. To my right, mirror after mirror captured their glow, divided by pilasters, facing a line of arched windows. Chandeliers flickered and sparkled overhead, laden with cut-glass embellishments, not yet illuminated for the night. Ménard must have replaced the ones the perdues had looted.

The music stopped. Each footstep echoed. As I crossed the floor, my reflection walked beside me, stiletto in hand. The woman in the glass was filthy and haunted, copper hair tangled from the journey through the carrières, more urchin than an assassin.

One of the mirrors doubled as a folding door. A man sauntered through it, cigar in hand. He wore a green lounging robe over pressed trousers and polished shoes.

"Hello, Jax," I said quietly.

Jaxon looked me up and down. And there was that smile. Like that of a father beholding his child.

"Paige." My name left him in a whisper of smoke. The dragon in his lair. "There you are, wayward daughter. Welcome, O my lovely, to the realm of the forsaken. Welcome to Sheol II."

19

Hell or High Water

Jaxon Hall had been gaunt when I had last seen him in the Westminster Archon. Now the gray in his hair was black again, and his cheeks had filled out a little. Yet still there was something drained about him, as if he were a garment put through one too many washes. No glimmer in his eye. Neither mischief nor malice on his fine-cut lips. He was just a man.

Just one man.

"You were expecting me." I broke the silence first. "So soon?"

"Of course," Jaxon said. "I told you I would be in France. I extended you an invitation." His gaze flew over my face. "You look well. Better than you did at our last reunion, in any case."

"I could say the same for you." I kept the stiletto out of sight. "Sorry to disturb your beauty sleep."

"Oh, ma chère traîtresse, never mistake a lack of respectable daywear for indolence. I was up all day doing the sort of tedious paperwork that comes hand in hand with immense power." He rubbed his shadowed eyes with his free hand. "Sleep is quite the extravagance nowadays."

"Well, I didn't think it was your conscience keeping you awake."

"Did the weight of the crown wring your skull of everything I taught you?" Jaxon said, with an air of irritation. "Morals, Paige, are for the lucky ones. Conscience is for those who have the luxury of choice."

"And what are you if not a lucky one, here in your shining palace?"

"One who climbed to these heights from nothing. One who works in the dark, unacknowledged." Thunder rolled outside. "I have always fought for the preservation of our kind, thankless though it is."

It was all too easy to imagine that the two of us were the only people in the palace. In the world. There was no sound here, among the mirrors, save the storm. There were worse places to die. I thought of the silver pill in my pocket, and I wished I could offer it to him. It would be cleaner than what had to come next.

"You have red tears," Jaxon said, impassive. "Did one of those Rephaite brutes use your aura?"

I wiped my cheek. "As if you care."

"If I didn't care about you, Paige, would I have butchered nine people for you?"

"Please don't try to impress me with that again. You didn't even bother to butcher them yourself."

"Why bloody my hands when others are so willing to do it for me, darling?"

"True. We all did your dirty work for so long, I can understand how you got used to it."

I walked a short way past him. Jaxon observed me, but stayed where he was, cigar aglow.

"I thought I'd find you in the King's Apartment," I said. "We all know what happens to kings in Scion . . . but you never can resist a throne, can you?"

"Well, you did steal mine from under me. It was only proper that I reigned elsewhere." His tone was light, but his stance told a different story. He was ready to counter me with his boundlings. "Congratulations on finding me. I would ask how you did it, out of academic interest, but I now know—as Scion does—that you will never share what you would sooner keep a secret."

His words woke something deep inside me. A small and flightless something that cried out to be nurtured.

"Did you know what they were doing to me, Jax?" Sleet washed down the windows, reflected by the mirrors. "Did you have any notion of what they were doing in that basement?"

Jaxon, for once, had no answer. I made out his dimly lit profile in the nearest mirror.

"They poured foul water down my throat until I choked on my own vomit. Starved me. Beat me. Left me in my own filth in the freezing dark. For days. All while you were living in luxury."

"And would you undo it, Paige, if you could?" The question was perverse in its tenderness. "Or has it made you stronger?"

Unexpected heat prickled in my eyes.

"You did," I whispered. "You did know." Suddenly the stiletto was out, and I lunged for him, ready to skewer his shriveled heart, all thoughts of mercy gone. "Cléir cháinte. You were like a father to me—"

Before I knew it, he had dropped his cigar to catch my wrist, and I froze as if I were still a young girl, terrified of his wrath.

"Make no mistake, Paige," he said, "that if anyone is your father, I am. A father protects his progeny. A father sees potential and nurtures it. A father seeks justice for the sorrow of his child. The pointless amaurotic that sired you did none of those things. Who did?" His hand was cold. "All you have suffered, all you have survived—all of it has armored you. Who can break you now, Black Moth, now there is nothing left to break?"

At this, my other hand—my weaker hand—came up. He went very still as my revolver touched the underside of his chin.

"There is one thing left to break," I said. "Whatever irrational affection I still have for you."

Jaxon raised his eyebrows.

"I was sent here to kill you, Jax," I said.

The storm loomed right over the palace. All I could hear, beneath the thunder, was the roar of my own blood.

"To kill me." Jaxon smiled. "Come, Paige. We both know this is posturing. You had a golden opportunity to end my life during the scrimmage, but mercy stayed your hand."

"Perhaps I've changed."

"Oh, yes, Underqueen. Anyone could see it. You transform yourself to weather the seasons, just as I do." Lightning stripped his face to the pallor of bone. "I almost hoped, when I saw you here, that you might have accepted the offer I extended in London. To save yourself."

"Surely you know me better than that."

"Of course," Jaxon said, soft as a lullaby. "I know you better than anyone, my Pale Dreamer."

"I have one regret," I said. "That I still don't understand you. I've never bought the idea that you were just another mindless follower of the Rephaim. Authority always chafed on you, Jax."

"I thought the same of you. Yet you say you were *sent* to kill me." Jaxon seemed unruffled by the gun. "Who commands you?"

As he spoke, I checked the æther. The others were all in the north wing. Still no sign of the flare.

"It doesn't matter," I said. "All of us are puppets in the Republic of Scion." I held his gaze. "I'm onto your right-hand man, too. The Rag and Bone Man. Or should I call him Mister Rackham?"

"So you are now a contract killer." Jaxon looked intrigued by the prospect. "How the plot thickens. Will you really not indulge me, darling, and tell me who it is that wants me off the board?"

"I've indulged you more than enough in this lifetime."

The camera was a tiny weight beside my collarbone. All I had to do was put a bullet in him.

Just one bullet.

In just one man.

"If you want to claim a nice bounty for Rackham, it's no skin off my nose," Jaxon said. The cigar smoked on the floor between us. "He had his uses, but he has been more of a liability than an asset for some time now—and the only thing I despise more than incompetence is incompetent audacity. He tried to have you murdered. You ought to claim your vengeance for it."

"I've you to deal with first." I pressed the revolver a little harder into his chin. "Haven't I?"

"Honeybee, I taught you better than this. I taught you respect for the finer things in life, and what it takes to win them."

My grip on the gun tightened. I had once told him that my father called me seileán—honeybee—and he had stolen it.

"If you must be so gauche as to shed blood in such a charming location," Jaxon continued, "at least have the decency to do it with your spirit." His smile was strained. "How dull it would be for a man of my reputation to die by something as insufferably *amaurotic* as a gun."

"I can't do that." I raised a bleak smile of my own. "I would, Jax, if I could."

"My murder is intended to send a message, then." His gaze sliced to the doors. "No need to explain yourself any further. I believe I know who is pulling your strings."

I turned.

Arcturus had arrived, still holding his swords. Rephaite blood streaked his face like war paint.

"Arcturus Mesarthim." Jaxon let out a soft laugh, drawing me back. "My, my. It *is* you."

I used the distraction to break his grip and step away from him. Jaxon seemed too diverted by the reunion to notice.

It was jarring to see them both in the same place, these people who had left such deep and disparate impressions on my life. After more than twenty years, Arcturus was face-to-face with the traitor who had crushed his faith in humans, whose selfishness had caused him untold suffering.

"Jaxon Hall." His tone was curt. "You looked different when I saw you last. I did not know your name then."

"You look just the same. How delightful to meet in person," Jaxon said congenially, as if we were all sharing a drink in a coffeehouse. "I did glimpse you in the colony, but always from a distance." He had the impudence to smile. "Still in chronic agony from the scars, I trust."

"As it pleases the blood-sovereign."

"You have some fucking nerve, Jaxon." The words raked up my throat. "To stand there with a smirk on your face after the endless betrayals, the gray market, the *laundering* of voyants—"

"I have shed my skin many times. Underneath, I remain a serpent. My nature, darling. Inescapable." Jaxon gave me the look I had once craved from him, that look of approval and pride. "So you uncovered the laundering. Clever of you. She *is* clever, beneath all that exhausting valor," he added conspiratorially to Arcturus, "but then, I did teach her. It seems *you* have failed to learn any lessons, Arcturus, when it comes to placing your trust in human beings."

I raised the revolver again. "You—"

"Peace, Paige," Arcturus said. "He can do no more harm than he has already inflicted on me."

"Austere as ever, I see." Jaxon let out a dark chuckle. "And ever in need of human faces for your revolutions. You are a peddler of masks. A ventriloquist. A bodyguard without a cause, purpose-less—*pointless*, really—since the fall of the Mothallath."

Arcturus was very still, an iron cast to his features. Eyes bright as fire, yet devoid of warmth.

"Oh, yes," Jaxon said, clearly savoring this. "I know all about your family. Loyal to the very end. Blindly devoted to old ways and indifferent gods, and all but extinguished because of it. Still, you seem to have won the eternal loyalty of my mollisher, the new recipient of your so-called protection." Another crooked smile. "Do you know what he can become, Paige?"

"Yeah, I got that memo, thanks." My hand was clammy. "How long have you known?"

"Since my first day in Sheol I. Clear as starlight."

"Of course. Clever you."

"You would have guessed, too, prodigal daughter, had your wits not been dulled by misplaced affection." He stared back at Arcturus, his gaze cold. "Would that I could go back and butcher Hector Grinslathe with my own hands this time. Not just because he stole Paige, but because he delivered her to Sheol I, to *you*. And look at what she has become under your . . . tutelage. So righteous. So much more liable to die in some pointlessly heroic manner."

"I see what Paige has become," Arcturus said, "and it has nothing to do with either of us, Jaxon."

"Does it not trouble you that she was my puppet long before she was yours?" Jaxon asked him, silken. "Do you never catch a glimpse of me in her? Do you never feel even a stirring of disgust toward her for not being able to hate me—to kill me—for what I did to you?"

"We'll see about that," I said.

Jaxon looked back at me, right into my eyes. "What could possibly make you think you have it in you, Underqueen?" he sneered. "You, who are so wedded to your newfound ideals?"

"Because Arcturus is wrong," I said, very softly. "Because you made me, Jaxon Hall. Because I am your monster."

His pupils were bullet holes.

"I should be wounded by your threats," he reflected, "but no. No, not wounded. I am *proud* of you, my Pale Dreamer." And he was. Pride glittered in his eyes and hooked the corners of his mouth. "Come. Ignore the order to murder me. Elect not to waste any more time on a lifelong failure like Arcturus Mesarthim." He held out a hand. "Let me show you my true intentions at last, O my lovely. The plans I have been formulating."

"You know how I'll respond to that offer, Jax. You've made it once before."

Jaxon grabbed hold of my arm. Arcturus moved forward. I thrust out a hand to stop him.

"There is more to this," Jaxon said under his breath. "This conflict is about to change, Paige. Every numen sings of it—the dream of the end, the war of the veils." My skin broke out in gooseflesh. "Face it by my side. What is a mollisher, after all, without a mime-lord?"

Behind him, a red light burned to life above the gardens, turning the rain on the windows to blood.

"Free," I said, "to rule herself."

I stepped back, breaking his grip with one wrench, and pointed the revolver straight at his heart.

Jaxon made no further attempts to dissuade me. For once, his face was blank. He was the White Binder, and he was above fear. I held the revolver with both hands and pulled the hammer back.

"I know things, Paige. About you. About your family," Jaxon said. "Shoot me, and the secret goes to the æther."

"Don't you dare," I forced out, "mention family. You don't understand the concept."

"Did I not make you a new one?"

My hands trembled. The world narrowed down the end of the gun and the blur of the face before me. There was no strength in my arms, my hands. Jaxon was still alive, and his smile was returning, and time was running out.

He had left all the humans of the first colony to die, and the Ranthen to suffer for twenty years. He had divided and preyed on the syndicate for coin. Time and time again, he had proven what he was.

And yet suddenly I knew I couldn't shoot him in cold blood. If this was another scrimmage, or if we had met on a battlefield, I might have been able to justify taking his life. Not like this.

Defeat crashed over me in waves. Disgusted by my own weakness, I held out the gun to Arcturus.

"I can't," I said stiffly. "He's yours. If you want your revenge, take it now."

After a silence, Arcturus took the revolver from my hand and studied Jaxon, who lifted his chin.

"You wouldn't do it. Not to her," Jaxon purred. "Perhaps if it was just the two of us. No doubt your hatred of me has deepened over twenty years, each twinge in your scars refining it, honing it."

Arcturus turned the revolver over, so it caught the light. He did not aim it. Neither did he let go of it.

"Your rage is a dark thing, Rephaite," Jaxon said, toneless now. His face was devoid of emotion. "It has matured like wine in a deep cellar, locked away for decades. Perhaps you would tear me to pieces, like the mindless beast you can become." He stepped toward Arcturus, palms turned out, and nodded to me. "But will you indulge your grudge in front of Paige? Will you reveal your inhumanity by murdering the only father she has left?"

"Don't listen," I said to Arcturus. "He's trying to get into your head. If you want to kill him, do it."

The silence seemed to go on for eons. Jaxon was still now. I waited, taut as wire, for the gunshot. For the burnt and bitter smell of death.

When Arcturus folded the gun back into my numb hand, my knees almost gave way.

"I told you," he said quietly. "There are always other ways to fight." He took a step back. "I will not kill an unarmed human. Not even this one. I am no Sargas. If that makes me a fool, so be it."

Jaxon attempted to look unmoved, but his chest sank as he released a long-held breath.

"A lovely sentiment. I can see why you two are so fond of each other," he remarked, his voice tinged with a darkness I remembered. "But once again, Arcturus . . . *ghastly* decision-making."

He pressed two fingers to the crease of his arm. As the warmth drained from the air, frost clouded every mirror and crystallized the condensation on the windows. He had summoned a boundling.

"Stop," I barked. "Jaxon, you *snake*—"

Too late. It had already come.

I knew it by the shape in the æther. The same poltergeist I had encountered at the scrimmage. The essence of a man who had torn five women apart and congealed into an all-consuming black hole.

"Fuck," I breathed.

"Defend me, my friend," Jaxon called to it, "and drive out the intruders." His fingertips were still pressed to his forearm. "I brought you an old playfellow, but if you could remove the lady from my presence first . . ."

I had no time to react before the Ripper obeyed. It seared across the gallery, lifted me right off my feet—like a noose—and smashed me with unearthly force into one of the mirrors.

Glass shattered around me. My head struck metal. An instant later, the pendant awoke. The shock had barely registered when I fell back to the floor and crumpled, leaving a spiderweb of cracks on the mirror. The æther shrieked around the fractured numen. Before I could gather my wits, let alone rise, the Ripper flew up, loosened one of the chandeliers, and brought it crashing down between me and Arcturus, snowing the floor with glass.

I shielded my eyes. My ears were full of a muffled roar, my skin clammy. Somewhere, Jaxon was shouting. I half crawled toward the doors, smearing blood in my wake. The poltergeist bore down on me, and I could feel an incorporeal hand on my throat, cold as winter, the *fingernails* of Jack the Ripper . . .

A huge, intricate spool hurtled over me, driving the poltergeist right out of the gallery. Then Arcturus was there, and I was up, and we were careering away from the Hall of Mirrors.

"Find me again, darling," Jaxon called. "Choose voyants, not Ranthen. I'll be waiting for you, somewhere in this world. Do *try* to take care of my dollymop, now, Arcturus!"

His laughter chased us out of the gallery. With a livid spike of strength, I lashed out my spirit and dealt him a blow hard enough to silence his crowing and bowl him to the ground.

Arcturus just about managed to hold onto me and one of the swords. The other glinted in our wake. I had thought that cutting down Jaxon might stop the Ripper, but it was still following his last command. My back was wet, my head ringing. I had failed, and Ducos would soon know.

That meant I had nothing left to lose.

Drops of sweat froze to diamonds in my hair. Somehow, by dint of propping each other up, we reached the broken doors to the south wing. Instinct made me pull them shut behind us. Halfway to the staircase, Arcturus collapsed, and I went right down with him.

"No, no." My breath gusted, thick and white. "Arcturus, get up. We have to keep moving—"

"Free the prisoners. Leave me, Paige."

Behind us, the doors flew off their hinges. As the poltergeist screamed toward us again, I gave in to the rush of anger and fear. Throwing away the last of my self-preservation, I ran to meet the spirit, my left hand outstretched so the three letters carved into my palm were on display.

KIN

"Go," I commanded, as I had when I faced the spirit in Senshield. "Be gone into the outer darkness—"

Pressure detonated from the scars. It was like the force that thrummed from me when I dislocated, but far stronger. The poltergeist slowed. Though I was just about holding it back, the waves of defense only served to incense it. I harnessed the power that seemed to come from nowhere.

"Fine," I shouted at it. The pressure intensified. The Ripper forged onward, a shrieking mouth in the æther. "Come on, then, Jack. Come and get your dreamwalker at last."

327

I thought it would do just that, that it would smash me between the walls until I was nothing but gore and shards of bone. Instead, the poltergeist was suddenly reeled away, as if caught on a line. The pressure ceased at once, and I buckled against the wall, light-headed.

Outside, the flare had guttered out. With gritted teeth, I took a flaming torch from the wall and thrust it into the nearest curtain. Fire raced up the fabric, to the wood-paneled ceiling. I set every curtain in the corridor alight, then the portraits: Georges Benoît Ménard, Frank Weaver, Abel Mayfield, Irène Tourneur, the whole ghastly theatre of marionettes who had made all of this possible. As their faces melted, I took the flashlight and hurled it into a tapestry.

Burn that place to the fucking ground.

Flame painted the corridor with fitful light and shadow. I ran back to Arcturus and towed his arm around my neck, but his frame was so large, and mine was so fragile. With a sound of frustration, I folded back to my knees beside him.

"Arcturus." I grasped him by the shoulders. His body was rigid. "Come on, I can't lift you—"

"I know." Tendons strained against his glove. "Run, Paige. Save yourself."

"No."

And then—even though the ceiling was on fire, even though I knew I was a moonstruck fool for doing it—I framed his face between my hands and forced him to look at me.

"Do you still want me?"

The light in his eyes had almost gone, but now it returned.

"Tell me you do." I kept hold of him, breathed the words against his lips. "Tell me you'll fight."

Fire burned at my back. Nowhere had ever been less safe. Yet in that single moment, there was only us, together in the cradle of another revolution, just as we had been when all this had begun. Arcturus cupped my cheek and pressed his brow against mine, his body softening, a wordless surrender. He didn't tell me, but I knew. Because I knew him.

"Get up," I whispered, "and come with me to Paris."

This time, when I rose, he rose with me.

He led me down the stairs, away from the blaze. It was so hot. Smoke hung in the air. "Stay here and keep a lookout." I coughed into my sleeve. "I'll get the prisoners."

Leaving him by the stairs, I dug the keys from my pocket and ran down the corridor, past room after deserted room, weaving around four unconscious Vigiles. When I reached the gathering of dreamscapes, I slewed to a stop and opened the nearest door. A paraffin lamp guttered on a guéridon beyond.

"Who is that?"

I switched on my headlamp, illuminating a wall of bars. A thin brown arm reached through, belonging to a man in a white tunic. It took a moment to recognize him with a beard—to find the scar on his forehead, the amber eyes, the freckle under the left one.

"Paige," he breathed.

"Zeke." With a sigh of relief, I grabbed the bars. "You're alive."

"You came for us." He clamped his fingers over mine with a weak grin. "Nadine said you would."

"Of course I did." I held up the keys. "Do you know which is the right one?" When he nodded, I passed the whole set through the bars to him. The cell beyond reeked of sweat and piss. "Where is Nadine?"

"Thuban took her a few hours ago." Zeke was starting to stammer. "I have to find her."

"We will."

He found the right key, and I unlocked the cell. Twelve hollow-eyed voyants in white tunics began to shove past. "Michael," I croaked, searching their grimy faces. "Zeke, was Michael in here?"

Zeke was ushering the voyants out, helping those who were too weak to rise alone. "Who?"

"Michael Wren. He's unreadable, about your age, doesn't talk much—"

"He was here," an augur said, "but they took him away yesterday." His hair was lank, and he leaned hard on Zeke. "I don't know where."

We had missed Michael by a matter of hours. I beckoned the voyants into the corridor. "Stay close to me, all of you. We're leaving."

"They'll shoot us," a voice said.

"Well, the roof's on fire, so we've no choice." The acrid smell of smoke was stronger. "We're not going past the snipers. There's another way out, through the tunnels under the palace."

"Like you said, Paul," Zeke murmured.

The augur nodded, looking satisfied. "The old hydraulics."

Arcturus waited for us at the end of the corridor. Now he was away from the poltergeist, he was visibly stronger.

"Warden." Zeke stared at him. "You came, too?"

Arcturus nodded. "It's all right," I said to a medium, who had shrunk away from him with a whimper. "He's a friend, I promise."

We moved as fast as we could, given the state of them all. I shepherded them under a flight of stairs to avoid two squadrons of Vigiles. At last, we reached the Lower Gallery, where we had entered the palace. It was already hot and dry as an oven.

A constellation of dreamscapes shone ahead. Ankou and Léandre were at the other end of the Lower Gallery, guarding the doors to the north wing, the latter newly armed with a Scion-made assault rifle. The carpet was swampy under my boots, and it reeked of something familiar, so strong my eyes watered. Léandre saw me at once.

"Paige." He beckoned my group. "Through here, all of you, now." As they hurried into the north wing, he said, "Renelde has gone ahead. She has Le Vieux Orphelin and your friend Nadine."

"Nadine?" Zeke said, catching her name. "What did he say about Nadine?"

"She's okay. She's out," I said in English, and pushed him through the doors. "Come on."

I turned with my revolver drawn when I sensed more dream-scapes. Thuban burst through another doorway, shadowed by Situla and eight more Rephaim.

Ankou pumped his shotgun and pointed it straight at Thuban. We were so close to freedom, so close I could taste it, thick as the smoke that was leaching through the ceiling and beneath the doors.

"Just let us walk, Thuban," I called to him. Each word stabbed me in the chest. "Don't disappoint the blood-sovereign again by letting this place burn."

"If you imagine that you and the concubine are going to leave here with your heads," Thuban said, as he passed a brazier, "you are sorely mistaken."

I stared as he came into the firelight. His right eye was a pit, and ectoplasm had dried on his cheek.

"An eye for an eye, Arcturus," Thuban hissed. "I will pluck hers from her skull and watch her swallow them."

All at once, I recognized the oily smell beneath the smoke. Paraffin. My gaze went from the soaked carpet to the chandelier above, laden with candles. Léandre aimed his pistol at it.

Thuban began to run. As I bundled Zeke through the doors, Léandre emptied his pistol into the chandelier. One of the bullets shattered its fixture, and as we all piled into the north wing, it plummeted. I had barely pulled Léandre through before the chandelier crashed straight into the sea of paraffin.

The conflagration was blinding. The candles ignited half the gallery, forming a wall of flame between us and the Rephaim. Thuban disappeared behind them. Léandre and Ankou slammed the doors shut.

The rest of the escape was a series of flashes, with darkness between. The sprint across another parquet floor, seeing only by glints of moonlight. The first soldier that fired through the window. Using my last bullet—the one meant for Jaxon—to splinter a scarlet visor. Watching Ankou hurl his axe across the room and Léandre finish the soldier off with a knife across his throat. When Ankou stopped to wrench the axe free, its blade glinted with blood.

Then a small room, full of silhouettes. Léandre shoved me ahead of the prisoners, through a half-open door that could have been part of the wall, onto a stone set of steps.

"Go," he called after me. His hands were covered in blood. "I will guide this group."

I went. At the bottom of the steps, I lurched right into a shallow pool. I shone my headlamp to the left—to the west—and illuminated a subterranean chamber. Water lurked around a line of pillars, which disappeared beyond my light. This was the abandoned reservoir that ran beneath the long parterre behind the palace. The smell made me grope for the pendant between my collarbones.

I turned right, as Renelde had instructed, into an arched tunnel. Hearing Zeke behind me, I sidled between two moss-covered pipes, ducked beneath another, and made for the end of the passage ahead. My calf now ached so deeply that I was afraid to put too much weight on it.

Frigid air chilled my skin. Renelde must have found a way to street level. When I saw a shaft of moonlight, I switched off my headlamp and came to a dead end. With a surge of adrenaline, I planted my boot on a loose brick, grasped the edge of the opening above, and hauled myself up, into the snow on Rue des Réservoirs. Blood drenched my trouser leg.

We were out of the palace. Now to escape the city.

Zeke climbed out of the tunnel behind me. Arcturus came next. High above us, black columns of smoke were pouring through a swallet in the palace roof. Flames raged across the upper floor, where I had left Jaxon helpless. I could no longer sense his dreamscape.

Halfway back to the cemetery, I came to a clumsy stop, holding a stitch in my side. There was one more thing I had to do. I opened the top of my oilskin, angled the camera toward the inferno, and pressed the tiny button on its side until it made a distinct *click*.

Ducos would have something to send to her superiors. As I limped after Arcturus and Zeke, I sensed every soldier from the front of the palace leave their post and storm inside.

In my wake, Sheol II burned.

****

Volcanic orange illuminated the sky. The air was thick with the stench of burning hair and smoke. Maria would be proud of me, reducing a magnificent seventeenth-century palace to cinders.

Back through the city, dripping blood. Arcturus gave me a boost over the cemetery wall. Waiting near the mausoleum was Ivy, armed with her crowbar.

"Paige," she called. "Are you hurt?"

"Not badly." I went to her. "You came."

"I had to." Her eyes were dark mirrors for the sky. "Renelde has already taken Le Vieux Orphelin through. She said the tunnel would collapse if we all went at once." Her gaze dipped to my throat, where bruises must have already formed. "Thuban *was* in there, wasn't he?"

"Yes."

"Tell me you got a decent shot at him."

"Rammed a knife right in his neck. And Warden took his eye out."

A look of surprise, then grim satisfaction. "Well." Her smile was thin. "For now, that will help me sleep."

"Mahoney?"

I turned. A whisperer was slumped against a nearby grave, breathing hard.

"Nadine?" I crouched beside her. "Is that you?"

"Somewhere under the bruises." A weak smile cracked her lips. "Took you long enough to find us."

Zeke had cleared the wall. He came straight to Nadine, and she wrapped an arm around him as he spoke to her in gentle tones. Skin had been flayed from the backs of her fingers, leaving them raw and bloody.

"Go, now," I called to Ivy. "I'll wait for Léandre and Ankou. They have the prisoners from the south wing."

Zeke half lifted Nadine to her feet. When she saw the darkness in the mausoleum, she almost bent double. Her shoulders heaved as Zeke led her inside. Ivy saluted me with the crowbar and went after them.

"Go with them," I said to Arcturus. "I won't be far behind."

After a moment, he said, "Be safe, little dreamer." Then he followed the others into the mausoleum, leaving me alone among the dead.

I willed the others to appear. When Léandre arrived, a half-conscious woman in his arms, I rushed to meet him. Ankou fired his shotgun from the top of the wall, while Léandre pushed me toward the mausoleum.

"Vite. Into the passage." He all but threw the woman at me. "Take my sister."

Ankou pumped his shotgun and let rip again. A ghastly sound answered, loud as a horn. A legion of voices in one cry.

Emim.

"Léandre," I barked at him. "The prisoners—"

"Leave them to me," he snapped back. "Just get my sister out!"

The mausoleum closed around me, black and airless. I tried to support the woman—La Tarasque—with what little strength I had left in my arms. She was raw-boned, long white hair streaming around her shoulders, and from the look of her, she had just been possessed. I guided her into the hidden entrance, then slid in after her and pulled my headlamp back on.

By the time we reached the ladders, La Tarasque had woken up a little. "Climb down," I urged her. "Hurry."

She placed her bare feet on the rungs, looking as if she had no idea where she was. I hoped she had the self-awareness to hold on.

We descended, one ladder after the next, back into the Passage des Voleurs. At last, we reached the bottom. La Tarasque draped her arm around my neck, too spirit-drunk to walk in a straight line. We were almost halfway back to the sleeping chamber by the time I hauled my focus to the æther.

There were still only four dreamscapes behind us.

Logic kicked in first. The prisoners must have been dosed with Emite blood, too. Yet my heart pounded, and my instinct warned me to go back. I helped La Tarasque sit and wrapped my oilskin around her.

"I'll be back," I told her. "You're all right."

She managed a dazed nod.

I started to run back to the ladders. Léandre was already off them and marching. Hot on his heels were Ankou, a silver-haired man with a cloaked aura, and a polyglot. No one else.

"Where are the others?" My voice cracked. "Léandre?"

"We could not bring all of them down here." He brushed right past me. "They will have to take their chances in the woods."

All feeling deserted my limbs. Jaw trembling, I caught up with him and grabbed his arm with a ferocity that took us both by surprise. He snapped around to face me, his features knitted with impatience. Ankou marched on.

"You left them." My voice was a string, wound tight enough to snap. "You abandoned all those people?"

"I sent them toward the Forêt de Meudon. They have a chance, at least," he said. My backbone turned to ice. "I only ever agreed to take *our* people through this tunnel, Underqueen. You thought we were going to be able to take more than thirty prisoners back with us?"

"And these two?" I said hotly. The strangers tensed. "Did they pay for the privilege of a way out?"

"They kept up."

His lips were set in a determined line. "This was always your plan," I breathed. The realization clotted inside me, choked me. "You always meant to leave them." I shook my head. "They'll never make it through the forest. You don't know what's out there, what will happen—"

I turned and broke into a run.

Anyone who tried to leave through the forest would die. The Emim would hunt them. The traps would get them. I sprinted back to the first ladder and grabbed a rung. Before I could get a foothold, Léandre hauled me away from the ladder and tackled me into the wall.

"Vous allez rester avec nous," he snarled, trying to pin my arms. "They will kill you, and Le Vieux Orphelin needs you!"

"Putain d'imbécile. Espèce d'enfoiré—" I thrashed against him. "They needed *us*. You thought we were here to rescue our friends and no one else? What kind of cold-hearted bastard are you, Léandre?"

"I made the call. I told you. Here," he said through his teeth, spit flecking my face, "I am king."

White-hot fury burned through my mind, erasing all caution, all restraint. I belted my spirit right across his dreamscape, sending him reeling away from me with a roar of surprised anger.

My vision crackled. He lashed out and clipped my cheek with his knuckledusters—by accident or on purpose, I had no idea, but I shoved him in return and lunged for the ladder again. When he ripped me back down, we both hit the ground in a turmoil of fists and teeth and boots. I rolled over and bashed a knee between his legs, but he kept hold of me, trying to drag me away from the ladder, the voyants, the promise I had made them.

He slammed me back into the wall. Hands around my wrists. My back arched and my chest bucked, and then I was a trapped animal, a savage bear, and I couldn't breathe, couldn't think, had to tear myself free. My skull thudded into his, hard enough to rattle my teeth and make him bellow in pain. Blood poured down his chin. As we grappled wildly for the upper hand, I heard it. Felt it.

Movement. In the air, in the ground. Somewhere in the dark, a breaking-away. A change. A crumbling. A wrongness. Léandre stiffened, his nostrils flaring.

First came the roar. In the distance, then not in the distance. And then came the water.

A *wave* of water.

All at once, it was everywhere. Erupting through cracks in the right wall of the tunnel. Pouring from above us. The sound and taste of it moved my legs before my mind had fully grasped the danger. As fear electrified my bones, my nerves, it also shut my throat.

Flood.

Adrenaline booted me in the gut. In unison with Léandre, I ran.

Water soaked my hair and clothes as we pelted down the Passage des Voleurs. It was behind us, around us, blinding me. Through the fog of sheer terror that blurred my thoughts, I remembered what Renelde had said. That the water in these tunnels must come from an underground spring or lake. (A lake. It had to be. An *entire lake* was coming in.) Reaching the top of Apollyon was our only chance. I screamed a warning down the golden cord: *Flood. The tunnel is flooding. Run!*

In return, a chilling tremor.

Ahead of us, Ankou had thrown La Tarasque over his shoulder and reached the top of the steep incline that led back to Apollyon. I thought of the plaque Léandre had carved, the words that would soon be underwater, along with the entire Passage des Voleurs.

Léandre reached the slope and scrambled up it, his hands and boots slithering. We were going to drown here. All of us. Bloated and dead. The knowledge paralyzed me.

Léandre looked back, face dripping. He was almost at the top. I was at the bottom, frozen stiff. "Paige," he shouted, and started to slide back down. I could only stare up at him. "Marcherêve, give me your hand—"

Too late. A devastating wave smashed me off my feet, sweeping me into the abyss.

****

When I was a child, my grandparents took me once a year to Lough Béal Sead, a jewel in a necklace of blue lakes in the Galtees. We would hike to it from the little village of Ros an Droichid. The first time, I was four years old, and my grandfather carried me most of the way.

We had gone late in the autumn, before the frost could really set in. The gorge was often cloaked in cloud, the lake so cold it burned, but for Mamó, swimming in it it was a ritual. Each time she emerged ruddy-cheeked and weak, and she had to huddle in front of the fire for days before her bones warmed up again, but it fortified her in a way I knew I might never understand.

That first year, I had watched with unease as she struck out into the fog. My grandfather was left to keep an eye on me, but there had been a difficult calving the day before, and he dozed off. Curious and worried, I had walked to the edge of the mist-covered lake and waited for Mamó to return. And when there was no sign of her, I decided to find her myself.

I jumped.

All I had was a proto-aura then. No power yet to let my spirit wander. But the water awakened an instinct that had slumbered within me, waiting for the right time to emerge. I remember being fascinated by the pale twists of my hair, the way they fanned out in front of me. How I became weightless. How, even as I sank, I was unanchored from the earth.

And how that feeling was addictive.

How it freed me.

I had been smiling when Daideó pulled me out, white as ice and shivering. I hadn't realized at all—not once—that in the water, I was dying.

****

337

I was alone. And blind.

A trickling nearby. The waterboard. My eyes flew open. I needed to get away from it—that *sound*, the smell, it soaked me in goose-flesh—but I was afraid to move, afraid to know how badly I was hurt.

My mouth was dry as ashes. I tried moving my fingers and toes. They worked.

Not the basement. The bottom of the pit.

Through a solid ache in my skull, I tried to think. Clearly I was deeper than the Passage des Voleurs.

Head rolling, I groped for my headlamp and switched it on. It was cracked, and the battery ran low, but a wavering light revealed yet more dripping tunnels.

These ones seemed natural. Caves, not quarries. Behind me, water cascaded down a curtain of flowstone, stinking of sulphur. I struggled away from it, heels sliding on the damp floor.

"You have got to be joking." I pulled at my collar, gasping for breath. "Wasn't the f-fucking reservoir enough?"

A blurred memory returned to me. Grabbing onto something —slippery rock—and hoisting myself up, out of the torrent of foul-tasting water, onto what I had thought was an escape to higher ground. I had scrambled on my stomach through a rabbit hole of a passageway, driven on by the will to survive. Then the plummet. My head must have struck a rock.

Somehow, in my last bid to live, I had found a way between the Passage des Voleurs and this cave system, buying me some breathing time.

I needed to utilize what I had left. To stay calm and think.

The Passage des Voleurs must slope downward. Right now, water would be pooling at its end—rapidly, if the lake was large. If my theory was right, it would not be long until it rose enough to fill these caves, as well as the human-made tunnels that must not be far above me. I could only have been unconscious for a few minutes, or it would already be here.

Palms sweating, I turned my lamp upward. More water torrented from the opening I had fallen through. It was moving faster than before.

My labored breathing punctured the silence.

I was below the bottom of the earth. I would run like a frightened rat through these caves until the lake caught up with me. That was how it was going to end, after everything.

My hand clammed into a shaking fist. Screwing my jaw shut, I staunched my bloody head on my sleeve and got to my feet.

Water was starting to cover my boots. If it was rising, there was no *down* in these tunnels. Nowhere for it to drain. There was only *up*. I forged on, half running, boots splashing. I was almost in the next cave when I sensed another presence in the æther and slowed down.

A perfect circle of ice lit the cave. In the dark, it had an eldritch glow, as if hit by moonlight.

Close to it lay an Emite. Too weak to do anything but exist, it was a ruin of papery gray sarx, swarmed by its corrupted aura. Lidless white eyes stared into mine. It had entered this realm right below the beacon of the colony, but found no flesh to sustain itself.

This had been a Rephaite once. A god. I wondered which family it had been from, whether it would have been an ally or an enemy. Unable to grab me, it let out a sound like a wounded animal and crumpled. All I could do was retreat from the chamber and leave it to starve.

Murky water swilled around my knees. It was so cold. My thighs ached with the effort of wading. I retched more than once, but dread forced me onward, into the infinite black. My calf was ablaze where I had caught it on the rusty gate. Numbness set in everywhere else.

A tunnel took me upward again, a short way out of the flood. Before long, I came to a pool. A lower tunnel, already full of stagnant water. The moment I saw it, I stopped.

It could be a way out.

Darkness or drowning. Hell or high water. I let out a strangled shout of frustration and knotted my fingers in my hair, panting. I tried to hold my thoughts together in the cracked glass of my skull.

There was one other way. My shaking hand went to my pocket, where the silver pill waited, offering an escape from the nightmare. Better than the excruciating pain of water piercing my lungs. That could not be the last thing I felt. It couldn't. My eyes pressed shut.

My shoulders heaved. I started to undo my pocket, fingers slick and clumsy on the fastening.

No.

Somewhere in the black roar of the water, a clear thought. My hand wrapped into a fist again. The pill was certain death. If I could just swim, I had a *chance*, slim though it was. If not—if I died now—then Suhail Chertan had killed me. By stealing my ability to swim, to control my panic, he had murdered me from a country away. No one would ever find my body.

Cold sweat drenched me. I took the vial from my pocket and threw it into the tunnel behind me. This time, I would fight for my life until my last breath. With trembling hands, I stripped off my sweater and removed my heavy boots, then buckled my backpack on again.

Damn Suhail all the way back to the Netherworld. I had come this far. I had crossed the Couloir des Noyés and destroyed Senshield and seized the crown of London and I was still alive. I meant to stay that way.

Shaking uncontrollably, I crouched beside the pool. Behind me, lake water was bubbling up the way I had come in, like vomit from a boiling stomach. My body rattled like a bag of dice.

My headlamp failed. The abyss was here. All I could hear was the rush of the approaching flood. All I could see was the same crushing blackness I had only just survived before. I heaved in a breath and plunged headfirst into the pool. My fingers scrabbled at rough stone. Without any light, all I could see was Suhail. *Perhaps the Underqueen would care for a drink.*

My chest tightened to the point of agony. Already out of breath. I thrashed my way back and broke the surface with a gasp. My lamp sparked on for an instant, long enough for me to see that the cavern was now half submerged, the lake crushing my air pocket. It was too late. More water sprayed from the ceiling, blinding me. I screamed into the void. Not for help. None was coming. Hair plastered to my face, fingers jammed into my ears, I waited for the end.

I wanted you. I wanted us. I whispered my confession, willing him to hear. *I'm sorry. I was a coward, too.*

My scream cracked into nothing. But then something drew my hand to the pendant. The æther quaked. In a strange, detached state—acceptance, perhaps—I exhaled through my nose. When the water had almost filled the tunnel, I took the deepest breath I could. Then I kicked off the ceiling and propelled myself back into the passage, hard and fast.

This was it. No way back. With no light, I used my hands to navigate, keeping one above my head to protect it from crags. Suhail materialized in front of me, here to watch the death I had denied him once before. Bubbles erupted from my lips. Fatal panic crested again. I tried to swim through him and shatter his image. My headlamp flared, banishing his face for an instant, but in my head, he was still laughing.

To disappear between shadow and stone.

My legs thrashed. My fingers groped for purchase. Just as water burned my nose and I thought my chest would rupture, I shattered the surface. Coughing and weeping, I crawled out of the second pool, and with a violent retch, I brought up the last meal I had eaten.

I gasped for breath. My headlamp flickered on again. I raked my soaking hair out of my eyes and looked back to see the pool already surging in my wake. The lake was coming. With a panic-stricken sob, I shoved myself up and ran. I clambered up walls and lurched through more tunnels, ascending now, always on the rise. Chips of limestone cut my soles, but I couldn't stop. The lake was still after me. When a tapered crack in the wall appeared, I twisted sideways and writhed my way through it, scraping half the skin off my hip.

A ladder. My hands clapped onto it. Somehow, I had found my way to the carrières. Arms shaking, clothes stuck fast to my skin, I scaled the mine shaft. The muscles in my thighs and calves scorched, but I kept going, rung after rung, until I could crane myself over the top.

To rise from the depths, never seeking the sun.

I had gotten up the ladder, but the effort had squeezed out my last drop of strength. I lay unmoving. Weakness would finish me off. I was going to pass out. Eventually, the water would take me.

The headlamp went out for good. The blackness of my tomb closed over me. I listened to the distant swash of the water, closer by the moment.

When I heard the voice, I thought I was hallucinating. Then a lamp half blinded me. Cool and bony hands found my arms. I looked up to see the silver-haired voyant who had entered the mausoleum with Léandre and Ankou.

His face was distinctive, the skin almost stretched. Something about his dreamscape was familiar, even to my fear-addled senses.

"Wait," I slurred. Everything was spinning, his face sliding in and out of focus. "I know— I know you."

He offered a gentle smile. I looked down to see an empty syringe in his hand. A milky drop hung from the tip of the needle.

"No, darling," he said. "You never did."

My bones were disappearing. When my hand dropped to my side, I could have sworn his face came with it.

I have shed my skin many times, he had told me. *Underneath, I remain a serpent.* I heard my own hysterical laughter. Darkness came to claim me yet again, but this time, I embraced it.

20

A Promising Start

Candlelight. Softness under my back. My eyelashes were sticky, but I could feel enough to tell that I was lying on a rug. Someone had peeled off my wet clothes and covered me with sheets. I was warmer.

Too warm. Scorching with fever, worse than before. A listless throb filled my leg, and my hair smelled of bonfire smoke.

Shh, Paige, it's okay, lie still. Deep, gut-wrenching coughs. *Dangerous . . . sepsis . . . she needs a hospital . . .*

Still underground. Not lost anymore. I tried to recall how I had gotten here, to wherever this was, but all I could remember was the roar of water and the sound of my own screaming.

Paige. A voice I trusted, a hand cradling the back of my head. *Paige, you must take this.*

Lip of a glass. Bitter pill. Trickle of water over my tongue. All around me, waking nightmares: a golden blade, the soldiers, the anchor. My final glimpse of my grandmother, her face riven by fear, as if she had seen everything that would happen if I slipped between her fingers.

My breath caught fire. To quench it, I swallowed. I wanted it to stop. All of it. I was deep under a sea of my own making.

So I fled to my dreamscape—to my flowers, wilted, swamped by water. As the fever flashlighted my limbs, I relived the moment I had asked if he still wanted me. The heat in his eyes that set me alight. I dreamed his hands to my tender skin, to places no one had ever touched.

I must have made a sound. A figure came into my mausoleum, and there was relief on my smarting back, some kind of liniment. The fire melted it down to water, and the water seeped inside me again, beaded on my face, drowned me from within. I was molten. Trickling back to the bottom of the earth, too loose and shapeless for the floor to hold me. Then a hand took mine—breaking my fall—and I pressed my brow to its scarred knuckles.

Paige. His voice. *Stay with me, little dreamer.*

I wanted to stay. So I clung onto that hand, to that voice, to him. I fought with everything I had left.

Darkness banked the flames at last. I cooled back into a solid form. When my eyes cracked open again, the inferno in my flesh was gone, supplanted by fatigue.

A low ceiling domed over me. I was in the carrières, and from the number of dreamscapes, I was directly under the citadel once more, far away from the hellfire in Versailles.

I smelled fibrin gel. When I could muster the strength, I slid my bare leg out from under the sheets and saw a livid stripe on my calf, lined with stitches. Bandages wrapped my wrist and waist.

I was alive.

And Sheol II was gone.

Weakness bound me to the rug. I thought of the voyants we had left in the colony, what horrors they might be facing now. As I floated in a doze, I was aware of someone trimming the candles. A hand on my forehead. Blankets wrapping the cold log of my body.

And finally, a voice.

"Paige."

Slowly, I turned my head. Nadine peered into the cave. She wore a knitted gray dress over tights, and her hair fell in damp waves to her jaw.

"Are you awake?" she whispered.

"Just." My throat was dry as sawdust. "Never thought I'd ask this again, but is there any water?"

She disappeared. With effort, I lifted my right hand to see a small dressing where a cannula had been. I was wearing a camisole and shorts with a button-down shirt over the top. From the size of the shirt, it belonged to Léandre.

Nadine returned with a goblet, which she helped me hold and drink. "Where are we?" I asked.

"Paris," she said. "Le Vieux Orphelin has his own little system of carrières under Passy—his appartements privés." Her accent was crisp. "Only his gang know about it. And now us." She sat on the patterned rug beside me. "I cannot believe you chose this moment to wake up."

"Sorry. I'll go back to the brink of death."

"I'm serious. Warden has barely left your side, and the minute he agrees to go back to the surface, you open your eyes." She shook her head at me. "Poor timing, Mahoney."

Shadowed memories of his presence crossed my mind. "Why has he gone to the surface?"

"Because we're down to the last crumbs of food. He took pity on all our sad faces and said he'd get some." Seeing my expression, she said, "I'm sure he'll be back soon."

The Rag and Bone Man was still out there. He had caught Arcturus before.

"Yes," I said.

I tried to sit up. Nadine put down her mug of tea to help me.

"You've been out of action for a week," she told me, and gave me another sip of water. (A week. Ducos would have returned from her assignment.) "We think something down there got into the cut on your leg, and Warden said you were already sick. Even when he got your medicine from the surface, I didn't think you'd make it. God knows how you did."

I managed to shift onto my side, leaning on my elbow. "The æther must not want me yet."

"You're lucky that puncture in your back didn't get infected, too," Nadine said. "What *is* that?"

"Had to have my lung tapped." I scraped back my greasy hair. "They waterboarded me. In December."

"Jesus. Sorry, Paige."

"Thanks." Now that I was used to the candlelight, I took a proper look at Nadine. She was a little thinner than she had been when I last saw her, her hair a little longer. "How are you?"

Slowly, Nadine picked her tea up again. "Better than I was in the tunnels. Warden had to carry me up the mine shaft," she said. "Still, I can't say it was a great hardship, clinging to such a fine pair of shoulders." I returned her smile. "Now I'm just . . . tired. So damn tired."

She sipped her tea. Her lips gave the faintest quiver.

"The new Bone Season hadn't officially started," she said, more to herself than to me, "so we didn't have to fight the Emim. And Zeke and I were only there for a few weeks."

"Doesn't matter how long you were there. A day or a year, you learned how it feels to be among indifferent gods."

While her face gave nothing away, her collarbones lifted, and her fingers blanched on the mug.

Her fingers. The tools she used to work her numen. Someone had dressed them, but even after a week, she must be in excruciating pain. Only one Rephaite could have done something like that.

Nadine caught me looking. "Thuban," she said. "Le Basilic, we called him. He tried to take Zeke, so . . ."

"So," I said.

With a nod, she took a jar of pills from her pocket and necked one with the last of her tea.

"That was some rescue, by the way. Sneaking in through ancient quarries and burning down the Château de Versailles. Hardcore." She glanced at me. "I don't know why you came for us, Mahoney, but I'm not too proud to thank you. I would have died in there otherwise."

"I came because we're still the Seven Seals."

"And look at where it got us. A power-crazed ghoul of a boss and a scrapbook of traumatic memories."

"What did you think you were signing up for, Arnett?"

"Yeah. I guess we both should have known what we were getting into." Her smile was weary. "We were kids, I suppose. Or maybe just suckers. Kids know a bogeyman when they see one."

The talk of Jaxon knotted my insides. He might be a smoking corpse by now.

"Mind bringing me up to speed on what happened in the tunnels?" I asked. "It's all a little hazy."

Nadine obliged.

Realizing the passage would soon be underwater, Léandre had run at full speed to warn the others. Against all counsel—and no doubt sensing my terror—Arcturus had tried to go back for me, but the sheer volume of lake water had caused the tunnel to collapse. Up to their waists, rocks crashing down around them, the group had been forced to abandon me to my fate.

"I was in an air pocket." Under the pall of fatigue, a memory squirmed. "Did . . . someone find me?"

"Yeah," Nadine said. "Once we were out of the ossuary, Le Vieux Orphelin ordered a search of the carrières in case you'd escaped another way. One of the people from the colony found you passed out—the Scottish guy with silver hair. The water was almost on top of you. He carried you out of there just in time."

I pressed my temple. There was a reason that silver-haired man was important, but it eluded me.

"Where is he now?" I asked. "The man who found me."

"Renelde dropped him off at Gare du Nord." She took a rolled-up blanket and wrapped it around herself. "Jax sent us to Paris not long after the scrimmage, if you were wondering. Tricked us into a Scion vehicle. He said we were going to a safe place. That should have been our warning."

"Can I join you?" a voice interrupted.

Someone else had popped their head into the chamber. "Ah, mon frère." Nadine patted the rug. "Please."

A clean-shaven Zeke stepped inside. "Stop showing off with the French."

"Right, like you never show off with the Spanish."

"It's not very useful in Scion. Although maybe it will be soon." He sighed. "Hey, Paige. I'm glad to see you awake."

"Glad to see you alive," I said.

"Thank you." He set a wooden board down. "Here. It's not much, but it's all we have until Warden comes back."

It was enough. Dry-cured sausage and ham, a dish of thick cookies, and slices of orange cheese with a crust, along with a steaming kettle.

"You're a lifesaver." I scraped the grit from my eyes. "Are you doing all right, Zeke?"

"Yes, I'm okay. Just some bumps and bruises." He sat down beside his sister and poured clove tea for all three of us. "I am not hurt. But I am very angry that Léandre left the other prisoners behind."

"That makes two of us."

"Three," Nadine muttered.

"I guess he had his reasons," Zeke said. "And some of them might have found a way through the forest." His brow darkened. "But I can't sleep, thinking of what they might have faced there while we were safe."

"Not that safe," Nadine pointed out. "Paige could have died."

We all fell silent. "How long has Warden been gone?" I asked, breaking the leaden pause.

Zeke checked his new watch. "Half an hour. It's almost six."

"Morning or evening?"

"Evening." He gave Nadine a gentle prod. "You know Warden had to carry Dee like she was an eighteenth-century damsel?"

"Oh, shut up, Ezekiel." Her answering prod in his ribs made him wince. "Give me an abandoned mine shaft when my brain chemicals are in harmony, and I'll beat you to the top with my hands tied." She sandwiched a slice of cheese between two cookies. "Warden does seem like he might *not* be a vicious sadist," she added. "Which is comforting."

"I can confirm that he's never shown any interest in torturing either animals or people." I took a delicate sip of the tea. "Did any of the Rephaim try to protect you in the colony?"

"Nope. A solid wall of disdain." She motioned to the platter. "Come on, Zeke. Get involved."

There was a lull between us while we demolished the meal. I needed to get my strength back.

"I promise this isn't me holding a grudge," I said, once there were only crumbs on the platter, "but I've been curious about why you chose Jaxon at the scrimmage." I offered a wry smile. "Was I so bad in comparison to a megalomaniac?"

I was only half serious, but neither of them smiled in return.

"You must have thought I hated you, Paige," Nadine said, after a long silence. "When we were in the gang."

"Not at the beginning."

"No. It was different then," she said. "But then our plans changed. As mollisher, you had a better salary than any of us. I needed that money. So I decided to do my best to get your job."

I had always wondered why our friendship had turned sour. "Why did you need money?"

"I'd found a way for us to get back across the Atlantic. Scion engages in limited trade with certain free-world countries, including the States," she said. "International cargo ships go intermittently from Le Havre. Costs a fortune to stow away on one, but it's possible."

I raised my eyebrows. "You want to go back?"

"I haven't been able to send one word to my family in four years, Paige." Her stance was defensive, her eyes hard. "Yes, we want to go back."

"I would have helped you, Nadine."

"You wanted to start a revolution against Scion. You needed every penny for that. I had no guarantee that you'd hand over enough from your war chest for us to pay our way out of here."

She traced the tattoo etched into her wrist. A musical note with an *x* instead of an oval at its head.

"There was a reason we left in the first place," she said. "We weren't safe in Canada. Or Mexico. But I don't think it will be a problem now, after so long."

I looked at Zeke, who was toying with his shoelaces. "And Nick?" I asked him quietly.

"It's over between us," he murmured. "I chose Dee. He chose you." His shoulders dropped. "Where is he now?"

"Sweden."

Swallowing, he rubbed the ruler-straight scar on his brow. "I hope he finds his parents there. He often said how much he missed them," he said. "If you see him again, please—" He breathed out.

"Tell him I'm sorry, Paige. I loved him before I knew we were leaving."

"Well, it's probably wise to get the hell out of Scion," I said. "All-out war is very close."

Zeke leaned forward. "No. Paige, you don't understand. We don't want to run from Scion. We want to join the revolution." His face was intent. "You need people to speak out in the free world. To reveal the atrocities, the truth. We wanted to bear witness."

"Except this conversation is pointless now," Nadine said bitterly. "I took any dirty job I could get my hands on so I could scrape enough coin together for the two of us. And Jaxon took it all."

The long hours she had spent away from the den, busking her fingertips purple. I had been too wrapped up in my own plots to see Nadine hatching her own.

"I understand why you'd want to go. Especially now," I said. "And I'm sorry you lost the money."

"Yeah. Me, too." Nadine sighed. "Guess we can always save up more, unless we make some rich friends here."

That reminded me of my own plans to get money to the Mime Order. I needed to get out of here and back to the safe house, try to explain things to Ducos. The black smoke that had poured from the palace must have been visible from twenty miles away. Everyone in Paris must have seen and smelled it.

I threaded my arms into a cardigan, and Zeke helped me rise. "I'd better introduce myself to Le Vieux Orphelin," I said, pressing his wrist in gratitude. "Could you let me know if Arct— Warden comes back?"

"Sure," Nadine said.

"Thanks. Is there somewhere I can wash?"

"A hot spring," Zeke confirmed, with a pleased look. "At the end of the tunnel."

"A hot spring in Paris?"

"I know." He chuckled. "I guess you get to live in luxury when you spend time with the Underqueen."

****

The sanctuary was something like the other carrières, but it had a cozy feel, and the limestone walls were reinforced with brickwork. A warren of caverns branched off a central arched tunnel, which was lit by skulls with candles in their mouths. Each skull was identified by a name on a plaque: ETTEILLA, LA TRIANON, LA VOISIN. I touched three fingers to my brow.

Breathing still ached. My legs wobbled. I kept one hand on the wall as I peered into some of the grottoes. One was hung with paintings that had somehow escaped the Supreme Purge, when the French had burned any object—be it painting or sculpture, numen or relic—that failed to conform to the values of Scion. Some paintings showed angels in the religious sense, the creatures after which voyants had named a class of spirit. Others didn't strike me as illegal, but they were raw and twisted in a way most Scion denizens would find unsettling. One portrayed a screaming man, an eagle clawing at his liver.

The next room housed illuminated manuscripts, prayer books, scrolls, and grimoires, most of them displayed on stands. A third held a collection of exquisite numa. This place was a museum not only to all that Scion had taken away, but to our history. The lost history of clairvoyants.

Among the tomes was a leather-bound book of prophecy, written in several languages. One tercet had been underlined in red. I studied the crabbed and smeared writing.

The scion will awaken thrice in blood—
once for life, once for a crown,
once to bring the tower down.

There were dreamscapes nearby. I glanced once more at the book before I left.

In the opposite chamber, I found Renelde playing a silent game of tarocchi with La Tarasque. Both of them looked tired. Nearby, Ivy was zipped into a sleeping bag, dead to the world. Save for a graze on her brow, she looked unhurt. Peaceful.

"Oh. Underqueen," Renelde said. Her eyes were raw. "Good to see you awake. How are you feeling?"

"Could be worse." I gathered the cardigan around myself. "You?"

"As well as can be expected." She put down the cards. "Malperdy . . . was a little brother to all of us."

"I'm sorry. He seemed kind."

"He was." With a sigh, she nodded to the woman opposite her. "This is Cam, otherwise known as La Tarasque."

"Underqueen," Cam said in a low-pitched voice. Her flaxen hair trailed in a messy plait to her waist. Though they resembled one another, she had a broader nose and a smaller chin than Léandre. "I want to thank you for helping me in the tunnels. I had just been possessed."

"Don't mention it. Is Ivy all right?"

"Yes." Cam turned toward her. "She is welcome to stay with us for as long as she wants."

"Léandre wanted to talk to you as soon as you woke," Renelde told me. "Will you see him?"

"No." I would thrash it out with Léandre, but not now. His proud scowl would remind me of all the people we had left behind. "Did you know about his plan to leave most of the prisoners, Renelde?"

"None of us did. I suspected he was keeping something from us, but believe me, I had no idea," she said. "When he sent me ahead with Nadine and Le Vieux Orphelin, I was under the impression that everyone else would follow."

Cam toyed with her plait, eyes downcast. "All right," I said.

"If you want to use the spring, you are welcome," Renelde said. "There is a small bathroom next to it."

"Thank you."

Trying not to think of how Malperdy had died, I left them alone. Thuban Sargas would have survived the fire—of course he would—but I hoped Nashira would punish him for the loss of the second colony.

For a cramped alcove that several gangsters pissed in every day, the bathroom was a civilized affair, with buckets of water for washing and a hole carved into the floor, which led to another bottomless drop. I crouched over it. When I passed the water-spotted fragment of glass that served as a mirror, I decided not to look.

A cleft in the wall led to the spring. Steam ruffled from its surface. Except for the candles at its edge, the cavern was dark. My heart thumped, but I was too burned-out to give way to fear.

I stripped down to the camisole and shorts and dipped a cautious foot into the pool. Candlelight rippled across its surface. A shelf of smooth rock at its edge would let me sit in it up to my shoulders. I got in gingerly, trying to ignore the sting in my wounds and the gooseflesh that rushed over my arms and stomach, and found that it was wonderfully hot.

And I could savor it. It felt good.

Perhaps my fear had reached its peak. Perhaps fighting it to the death in those caves had finally allowed me to defeat it. I hardly cared if this lasted—for now, I would relish being unafraid. I would let the heat unknot my muscles and steam the chill out of my bones.

I had forgotten what a pleasure it was to be wrapped in warm water. Droplets glittered across the ceiling. I breathed in the steam and drifted in a trance-like state, light and relaxed for the first time in months.

Something caught my eye as I basked there. A bust of a woman in an alcove, sculpted from dark stone, a wreath over her waving hair. I sat up to take a closer look.

"Her name is Marianne."

A start went through both me and the water. A figure had arrived at the mouth of the cavern.

"Underqueen." The voice had a muted quality to it. "We often share the spring, but I understand if you would prefer to bathe in private."

The solitude had been restful, but I thought I knew who this was. And he might bring something better than peace and quiet.

"No," I said. "By all means."

"Thank you."

The newcomer strode to the other side of the spring. I caught a glimpse of him through the thick billows of steam. He was about my height, perhaps a little taller, with midnight skin and sinewy muscles. Dark, tightly curled hair was trimmed close to his scalp. His hands were long and fine-boned, and his aura was that of an oracle.

As he entered the pool, I saw that his face was wholly hidden by an elegant gold mask. Floral embellishments surrounded the eyeholes. In this gloom, those openings looked empty.

"Marianne." He motioned to the bust. "She is the embodiment of Revolutionary France. A popular representation of liberty and reason. I keep her image in all of my hideouts. Sometimes I talk to her, as I spoke to the statue of the Maid of Orléans beside my throne."

A man who conversed with inanimate objects. "Do you chat to your collection of skulls, too?"

"Hélas, pauvre Yorick," he recited. I must have looked blank. "You are not familiar with Shakespeare."

"Oh, him," I said. "His plays sometimes washed up at the black market. I skimmed *The Tempest*."

"That one is popular among anormaux here. And yes, I do occasionally consult the skulls of the great voyants who came before us," he confessed, "but Jeanne and Marianne—opposites, in some ways—are my true councillors. Jeanne reminds me to embrace the visions of the æther. To speak out, no matter the cost. And Marianne reminds me why France strayed to Scion. We are republican to the bone here, suspicious of monarchy and religion. These are pillars the anchor also despises."

His voice was smooth, molten. It lacked the velvet quality I had noticed in other soft-spoken people, like Arcturus—that subtle edge of roughness, like a match being struck.

"Yes, Marianne carries the anchor well. And yet, we are also revolutionaries here in France. We do not brook tyrants for long. I hear the old cry like a drum in my head—*liberté, égalité, fraternité*. We have none of these now. No vote or voice. Only the impression of safety."

A brief silence pealed.

"Le Vieux Orphelin," I said. "Ignace Fall."

The mask tilted. "May I ask where you heard that name?"

"I read it. In a ledger belonging to the Man in the Iron Mask."

"Ah."

He rested his elbows on the edge of the spring. His fingers were long, one adorned with an unusual silver ring.

"Le Vieux Orphelin. The Old Orphan," I said. "Tu ne me parais pas particulièrement vieux."

A short, rich laugh. "Ankou told me you spoke French. A welcome surprise," he said. "Nevertheless, I would prefer to hold this conversation in English, the language of our mutual enemy. I would enjoy plotting their downfall in the tongue they compel us both to speak."

"If you like." My nape was slick with sweat. "I didn't know there were any hot springs in Paris."

"Only this one, buried deep under the district of Passy. I discovered this small quarry with Renelde. There was never much trust between myself and my fellow grands ducs, so I thought it wise to have a hideout. I was right."

We fell into silence for a time. Carefully, I tipped my head back into the water to soften my hair.

"Elegant."

I looked back at him. "What?"

"Your neck. Tell me," he said, "when you set out to defy the anchor, did you ever imagine what a neck would look like without a head upon it?"

"I didn't need to imagine," I said. "I'd seen it on the screens before."

"You saw it recently, I know," he said, "when your own father was murdered with the Wrath of the Inquisitor. A sword with a gilded blade, to show there is glory in the death of a traitor. Scion does like its symbols. In that, the republic is not so different from a monarchy."

I watched the mask.

"The rulers of old wore crowns and jewels to proclaim their divine authority. They believed these trinkets would protect them, and for a long time, they were right. Until their trinkets became their downfall, and their subjects saw them for what they were beneath. Mummers. Frauds. Mortals dressed as gods." His voice rang in the gloom. "I understand that under Haymarket Hector, the mime-lords and mime-queens of London fell prey to the same weakness for . . . trappings."

"Theatrics went too far under my predecessors," I agreed, "but I'm not above using greasepaint myself. It can be a weapon. A disguise."

"Oh, yes. But props must be wed to decisive, committed action. When I was told about the speech you made when you became Underqueen, I thought we might share that sentiment."

I decided not to reply. Best not to seem too eager.

"This first meeting of ours is unusual, but promising," he remarked. "Here in this spring, Underqueen, we have no crowns, no jewels, no costumes. No means to disguise ourselves."

"Says the man in a mask."

"I hope you will indulge that small hypocrisy." He lifted his fingers to the edges and gave a pull. "It cannot be helped."

It must be surgically attached to him. The thought was like a hand around my throat.

"Le Basilic threatened to remove it in the colony. He went into some detail about the ways he would attempt it," he said. "Fortunately, Underqueen, you came before he could."

I waited for him to continue, strangely fascinated.

"A mask allows a person to transcend the limits of one body, one face," he said. "I have built a reputation in Paris. It is inevitably disappointing to find that the subject of any legend is no more than a man. So while Le Latronpuche and La Reine des Thunes showed their faces to our subjects, I became my mask, my costume, and it became me. I made them whisper. I made them wonder. And when you make people do that, they start to tell their own stories." His skin gleamed in the warmth. "I trust your wounds are healing now."

"Yes," I replied. "Thank you for your hospitality."

"It is the least I can do to thank you. Hard though it is that we lost poor Malperdy, he will be remembered." The mask was still. "I want you to know that I have spoken to Léandre about his decision to direct most of the prisoners to the Forêt de Meudon. Much as it pains me to admit it, he acted reasonably. Had any more of them joined us, it would not have been you alone who was swept into the flood."

I looked away.

"I was in a similar colony," I said. "We left people behind then, too. It was difficult for me to accept."

"I understand. As does Léandre." He reached up to an alcove and removed a bottle. "An eighteenth-century vintage. Saved from the ruins of the last wine estate razed in the Médoc. Would you care to taste it with me?"

"That's very kind of you," I said, "but I don't care for wine." I needed a clear head for this.

"Very well."

He retrieved a goblet. As he stretched, I noticed a wound had been sutured under his left pectoral.

"The candles in my appartements privés are kept alight through pyromancy. Noonday—one of my perdues—recently mastered a new talent. Once, she could only glimpse the future in the flames. Now she can command spirits to carry them." He lowered himself back into the pool. "I have witnessed the rise of this phenomenon in Paris. Voyants unlocking their abilities. Our power grows with every sunrise."

"I saw the same in London."

Le Vieux Orphelin poured some of his priceless wine.

"Underqueen," he said, "my only experience of the Rephaim is as their prisoner. I wonder if you will tell me your story, share what you know of them. I should like to know their aims."

"Where shall I begin?"

"The beginning," Le Vieux Orphelin said, "though of course, that is never where one thinks it is."

For the next half an hour, I told him most of what had happened to me over the past year. My imprisonment. The rebellion. Senshield. The Ranthen. I also told him the truth about the Emim. By the time I was finished, my fingertips had creased. I had omitted my work for Domino—I still meant to protect the network—but most of my life was laid bare.

Le Vieux Orphelin ruminated for a long while.

"So," he concluded, "the curtain is drawn back at last. Scion is no republic, but a puppet empire for a monster." He topped up his goblet. "Here in Paris, we honor cartomancy as a high art. One card has appeared in most readings. L'Impératrice. Always inverted."

The Empress. A woman in a crown of stars. Upright, it was a hopeful card, of abundance and growth. Inverted, it spoke of a suffocating presence. Something that moved against nature.

"We are ruled by gods," Le Vieux Orphelin mused. "Now, it seems, we must go to war with them."

"We are already at war," I said. "Portugal has fallen. Spain will follow. Nashira Sargas wants our world, and I mean to stop her claiming it."

"I believe you. I sent eyes to your citadel when I heard a scrimmage would be held," he said. "When they told me about you—a former mollisher who wanted to turn a rabble of thieves into an army—I sensed the winds of change had blown on London." He cradled his goblet in one hand. "I share your vision of a world without Scion. We have both borne witness to the Rephaim."

"And you understand the need to work with the Ranthen," I said. "I know it might be hard to stomach, after the colony."

"Au contraire. My experience there convinced me that help from their side is necessary. Such is Rephaite power, and our fragility."

"Would you consider a temporary alliance with anyone from Scion?" I asked. "If they shared our desire to stop Nashira."

"Of whom do you speak?"

"Benoît Ménard."

His mask tilted up. "Ménard," he said softly.

"Yes. I happen to know that he despises the Rephaim," I said. "He thinks of them as just as unnatural as us. He planned to eventually use Sheol II to imprison them, as well as anormales." He was silent. "You two have a history. You met about twelve years ago, in Lyon, during a period where his public record is suspiciously vague. I presume you wouldn't be amenable to the idea of cozying up to him, but I have to ask."

Le Vieux Orphelin fell into a deep silence. So deep I thought he must have washed his tongue down with the wine.

"Ménard is a vicious and fanatical individual," he said at last. "His hatred of our kind runs very deep. I think he would burn us at the stake if he did not want the smell of melting flesh on his streets."

"And yet," I said, "he is willing to work with anormales, under certain circumstances."

"How do you know this, Underqueen?" he asked quietly. "When did you cross paths with the Butcher of Strasbourg?"

"I infiltrated his mansion to find Sheol II. When he caught me red-handed, I thought he would kill me," I said. "Instead, he offered me an alliance, of sorts, until the Rephaim have fallen."

"You are fortunate to have survived that experience. What was your opinion of his offer?"

"I still haven't formed one. I'd like to hear yours," I said. "I don't know whether a truce with him is a wise idea. Everything in me recoils from the thought. All I know is that he despises the Rephaim. For him, we are a means to an end—and we could use him the same way."

"It does not surprise me that he hates them," Le Vieux Orphelin said. "Knowing what Ménard is, I confess, I would find it exceedingly difficult to tolerate him in any capacity. I also doubt he would be willing to work with me." He swilled his wine. "Let us . . . give this matter some thought, and return to it later. For now, will you permit me to explain my proposal?"

"Of course."

"There is one step we must take before all others, and that is to eliminate the Man in the Iron Mask. I think it best for a small group of four or five of us to catch him unawares. Once he is in custody, my perdues can emerge from hiding without fear of his followers."

I nodded.

"I will then gather the syndicate on the Île des Cygnes—an old refuge—where I will have summoned the other grands ducs. I can think of some convincing pretext. Once they arrive, I will accuse them of treachery. It will be easiest if they confess. If not, we may have a fight on our hands."

"And that's where you need me."

"Yes. I need you at my side. That will carry weight among the anormaux, which I will need to defeat Le Latronpuche, since he has many of them in his pocket. Unless we can prove there is a trail between him and Scion, I have no proof of his dealings."

"I have proof," I said. "Proof that Le Latronpuche was involved in the gray market. The same ledger I mentioned earlier."

"Intriguing. May I see it?"

"Certainly. It's on the surface."

"Thank you. It will help me to build a case against Le Latron-puche." He drank. "Underqueen, I know about Operation Albion. I know your friends and supporters are in considerable danger. If the Mime Order is to survive, it must double in strength. I offer you a way for it to do that. If you agree, I can announce our alliance to the syndicate on the Île des Cygnes."

The voyants of London and Paris, bridged at last, after over a century of estrangement. This might be the most important alliance I ever made, and I had no intention of running into it in haste.

"I promise you soldiers for your army," Le Vieux Orphelin said, "and coin for your cause."

"And in return, I give you my backing, and you usurp Le Latron-puche and La Reine des Thunes?"

"As you usurped the White Binder, your own mime-lord," he said. "Not for selfish gain, but for the sake of all anormaux. For the sake of humankind."

The mask denied me his expression, but his tone rang with sincerity and conviction.

"The thought of an alliance between our two great syndicates is a very compelling one." I allowed myself a brief smile. "I need to return to the surface to . . . consult with my network, but I'll give you an answer as soon as I can."

He nodded.

"We should take another day to recover before we attempt to find the Man in the Iron Mask," I said, rising from the hot spring and enveloping myself in a towel. "I don't know about you, but I think I need it."

"Of course. Your fever was severe," Le Vieux Orphelin said. "I was captured on Rue de Grenelle, near L'Hôtel des Invalides. Perhaps we should begin our search for the Man in the Iron Mask there."

"Actually, I think you were the exception. He usually hunts near the Court of Miracles. There's a symbol he uses," I said. "A skeletal hand."

"I will send messages to my eyes on the surface," he said. "Let us meet at the Métro station of Sentier, then—on Sunday, at half past eleven in the evening. If you need me before then, you may find me here."

"Very well."

"Before you leave, Underqueen," he said, "I hope you will permit me to present you with a gift. It comes with no conditions." He climbed from the spring and reached into another alcove. "This is simply a small token of admiration, from one revolutionary to another."

With a towel around his waist, he walked toward me. I took the wooden box he offered and tipped open its lid.

Bedded in silk was a white mask. Its lips were crimson, and an ornate black moth spread its wings over the cheeks, with holes cut out for my eyes. The white sections were latticed with very fine cracks, imitating the way paint looked after aging. It was a work of art.

"Stunning." I ran my fingertip over the nose, the lips. Someone had studied my face before creating this. "Who made it?"

"I did. It is a passion of mine. I crafted masks for all of my perdues, telling their stories," he said. "Sometimes theatre is necessary to earn an audience, Underqueen. And the revolution needs that audience. But if our roles are to be more than trappings—more than cheap distractions—then we must occupy them. Live and breathe them. I have done that for eleven years, since the day I first covered my face with this mask."

I glimpsed his eyes, dark and incisive. I wondered who he was, and what had driven him to resist.

"If you and I are to fight the gods, we must become mythic ourselves," Le Vieux Orphelin said. "With this, whenever you desire, you can conceal Paige Mahoney—all her fears, all her sorrow, all her rage—and inhabit Black Moth. You can write her story. You can sing it to the streets of Paris. And I promise you, this citadel will call eternally for more."

I had never had a costume. In the scrimmage, I had fought as the Pale Dreamer, the mirror of the White Binder, even when I had declared myself as Black Moth. Perhaps it was time.

"Thank you." I closed the box. "You can call me Paige. In private, of course."

"Paige." He inclined his head, and I returned the gesture. "I look forward to our next meeting."

He took his leave. I set the box down by the pool and began to dress, keeping the mask in view. It was the only proof that the meeting had been any more than a heat-induced hallucination.

****

The clothes I had been left were well-made and warm. By the time I returned to my sickroom, someone had lit a stove. I sat beside it until my hair dried.

My backpack sat in the corner. The camera was safe inside. I hoped the photograph had survived—but the water had reduced my dissimulator to mush.

I moved about, restless, folding the sheets into the corner, rolling the rug I had lain on for days. I was so distracted, I didn't notice him until he spoke.

"Paige."

My head snapped up. Arcturus was standing at the threshold.

Seeing him snatched the breath from me. He was here. He was fine. I wanted to go to him, but sudden trepidation stopped me.

"You're back," I said.

"Yes. And you are awake."

"At last." I couldn't take my eyes off him. "Nadine said you were with me the whole time."

"Hm."

He let the drape fall across the entrance, silencing the muffled conversations in the rest of the appartements privés. Now that we shared the same firelit space, I could hardly think for wondering if he had heard my confession as the water closed in. If the golden cord had carried it to him.

I wanted you. I wanted us.

"I was just with Le Vieux Orphelin," I said. "We laid the ground-work for an alliance between the syndicates. In the bath. Which is . . . very normal."

"I am pleased to hear it." His flaming gaze rested on mine. "It is done, then. Sheol II is no more."

"Yes."

The magnitude of it settled over us. Together, we had struck another blow against Scion.

"Domino might cut us off for what happened," I said. "Ducos told me that discharged agents have to take white aster, to erase

362

their memories of the network. Then again, blue aster could undo that, if we can find it."

He narrowed his eyes. "Blue aster."

"Yes. Scion uses it," I said. "They feed blue aster to the subject and it lets them see recent memories."

"That is a lie, doubtless planted to frighten voyants. Blue aster can make memories clearer, but only an oneiromancer can see them."

"Oh." Scion had really hoodwinked the syndicate there. "I see. Could *you* restore my memories?"

"In theory, I could reverse the effects of white aster, though I have never attempted it. Memory is complex. And fragile."

There was a brief silence. In that silence, I remembered the fire. The taste of the smoke when I had asked if he still wanted me. The smoke, and what had come before it.

"Arcturus—" I looked away. "I forgave you for lying to me about the Emim. That was nothing in comparison to what I did to you by not killing Jaxon. And I don't expect your forgiveness."

I sensed his gaze on my face, but couldn't meet it. Suddenly my stomach was tight with shame.

"If our roles were reversed," I went on, "if you had once been close to the person responsible for *my* torture, if you had still cared too much about him to be able to hurt him . . . I'm not sure I could forgive you." I folded my arms. "Jaxon was right. Some deep part of you must resent me for it."

"No. In truth," Arcturus said, "I expected it. You are not an executioner, Paige Mahoney."

"But this is war. I need to have the spine to kill. I left Jaxon alive once before, out of mercy, and I lived to regret it."

He stepped toward me. For a moment, I thought he would embrace me, but he stopped before our auras could touch.

"Mercy," he said, "is an undervalued quality. It is what sets you apart from Scion. In any case, Jaxon Hall is either dead or a condemned man. Nashira will kill him for his failure to protect the colony." His voice was low. "I deceived you because I was loyal to Terebell. You may no longer be loyal to Jaxon, but in your heart, you will always feel you owe him a debt you cannot pay. He opened a world to you. He was father and savior and friend."

"That was the past. And everything he told me was a lie."

"And I am an oneiromancer. Of all people, I understand the enduring power of memory."

Slowly, I looked back at him, finding only candor in his face.

"Forgive me," I said.

"I already have."

He closed the space between us then. Cupped his fingers beneath the tips of mine, barely touching me at all. He held me as if our hands were spun from glass, not scarred and hardened by our battles.

Strange how a feeling could blossom where once there had been nothing. Then again, I had never felt *nothing* for Arcturus Mesarthim. Never been indifferent to him. From the instant our eyes had met, we had reacted, like fire and kindling. First with fear and hatred, then a quiet respect, and then something else. Something that had never stopped burning.

"I wanted to go back for you," he said. "I tried."

"I know you did. Nadine said."

"Hm. As it turns out, you did not need me or anyone. You confronted your fear alone."

"I did," I said, my voice almost too soft to hear, "but . . . I don't want to be alone tonight."

He was very still. I moved my fingers, tracing the broad mount of his thumb, the burl of bone at the side of his wrist. Except for the size and strength of them, his hands were so human-like. I wanted to know them. I wanted to know the precise slant of his collarbone, the depth of the curve in his back, the way his mouth felt on all of my skin. I wanted to know every inch of his body, and for him to know every inch of mine.

Our gazes locked fast.

"Do you wish to return to the safe house?" he asked.

I thought of the honeyed light through the windows, the place I had started to feel I belonged.

"Yes," I said. "Let's go home."

21

Overture

It was almost nightfall by the time we surfaced on Rue des Eaux. Renelde had arranged for a buck cab to pick us up from a street near the Champ de la Tour. With the dissimulator ruined, I wore a scarf over my face.

The Eiffel Tower smoldered across the river, illumined in lambent orange, as if the wind had showered it with embers. It loomed, its spire half swallowed by fog. Impossibly beautiful.

We crossed the nearest bridge over the Seine. I wanted to look at Arcturus, to break the silence, but I did neither. Whatever we said next had to be said when we were alone. The golden cord was still and taut.

Above, the tower. Emberlight and the pendent dark. Below, the hidden world that sheltered the forsaken. And I walked liminal between them, with a god at my side and the streets like dying coals around us, waiting to be stoked. The fire was in the citadel, in his eyes, in my skin.

The cabbie drove us to the right district. From there, each step lasted far too long. Cloud steamed from my lips, and the air drank away the heat of the spring, but I no longer felt the cold. Every moment, every breath, moved me closer to my end. There was no more time to waste. I had come so close to death again. Now I meant to live with abandon.

In the hallway, I took off my coat. He did the same. I tried not to wonder what would happen if I kept undressing until there was nothing to keep me from his sight. I imagined him taking me in his arms, hunger overcoming his eternal self-possession. And I imagined him just standing there, silent and arcane, his gaze as sensual as a touch.

Without looking at him, I went up to the apartment. A minute later, he followed.

There was no one else there. In the parlor, I switched on a lamp, which gave just enough warm light for us to see by. A note was folded on the mantelpiece, dated from Thursday the nineteenth. That was yesterday. I read the neat handwriting.

I will try again on Sunday. When you return, stay indoors. I have news for you.

"Paige."

His voice stilled me. I caught sight of myself in the nearby mirror. Hair curling thickly, wet at the ends. Cheeks flushed by the cold. Eyes dark with want, their pupils bottomless.

"In Versailles, you asked if I still wanted you."

As I became aware of his silhouette in the mirror, I wondered how I had ever thought that I could stop myself from falling. Just the sight of him made me shiver like a stricken bell.

"Yes," I said. "I realized how I felt. About you. How I never stopped feeling. And because—" My courage almost failed me. "Because I hoped you might still feel the same way about me."

There was a furnace in his eyes. We had all but acknowledged it, yet it remained unspoken.

I had denied it for too long. Smothered and stifled it, buried it deep—yet still the song was rising. I had precious little knowledge of desire, but I knew it now. I knew its name.

The shutters were halfway open, letting in the glow of a newly lit streetlamp. It struck a high contrast to the heat of his eyes. We regarded one another in silence.

"Liss read my cards," I finally said. "The fourth was the Lovers. The Spaewife told me to stay close to that person, to be certain of who it was. And I am." My throat felt small. "Jaxon tried to make me doubt you. He failed. Now he wants you to doubt yourself. He's afraid of what we are together. Afraid of what we represent, and everything we could become."

My skin was too cold and too warm at once. I walked into the light from outside, toward him.

"I called you a coward once. I was a hypocrite," I said, softer. "I was wrong to break it off with you. I thought it was necessary. That I had to feed every inch of myself to this war to keep it burning."

My palm found his sturdy chest.

"I know I'm mortal. I know it can't last," I said, "but I can't stop feeling this way. I've tried. It's too strong." I looked deep into his eyes. "I need you with me. I want us to try."

"We did try." He held my gaze. "You need no one, Paige. You saw the sense in our separation before I did."

"What?"

Under my fingers, his heart was a war drum. Where mine hammered, his was slow, set on its never-ending course.

"I give no credence to the doctrine of flesh-treachery. Too many Rephaim do." His voice was hardly there. "If what has passed between us was ever proven beyond doubt, your life would forfeit."

"I'm not afraid."

"I am." His thumb brushed from my cheek to my temple. "I am afraid."

I reached up to hold his wrist. "You said your fear wasn't my cage."

"But it is mine. This time, I must keep to its bars." His eyes burned low. "I wanted you, Paige. I still do."

His affirmation of it sent a chill across my abdomen.

"But to place you in greater danger than you have already faced —to prize that desire above your life—is more than I can justify," he said. "It was selfish to take you in my arms, knowing what that touch could bring."

"No." I touched his face. "That night, in the Guildhall—I felt so afraid, and so alone. And despite everything you had been told to believe about humans, you held me. It showed me who you really were. Someone who would put everything in his world at risk to do the right thing."

"Everything. And everyone," he said. "Including you." He lowered his hand. "If I had cared enough for your life, I would never have held you again."

I closed my eyes as he walked toward his room. This was not how I thought this night would end.

"I'm not the Mothallath." My voice snapped the quiet. "You were never duty-bound to guard me." He stopped. "My life is mine to risk as I choose. I choose to risk being with you."

Still he remained on the threshold of the room.

"I can't give all of myself to this war. I'll lose my mind," I whispered. "I am ready to fight to the end, but I need one thing—just one—that the revolution doesn't touch. That is not meant to further it. Not a scheme, or a tactic." A tremor raided my voice. "I want to show one person my true face. I want . . . just one place, one safe place, where I don't have to be Black Moth. Otherwise she will consume me."

It was some time before he moved again. Only when his door closed did I grasp that he was saying no.

****

There was always sound in this district of Paris. Music from the coffeehouse on the corner. Snatches of laughter from nearby Rue des Arcs. And blue tone. The endless breath of the citadel. Tonight, it all seemed so much quieter, as if Paris had at last fallen asleep.

In the safe house, there was silence. For want of a distraction, I took a proper shower, only shivering a little, before I brushed my teeth and found a nightshirt. In my room, I changed the sheets.

A snow moon tipped its light over Paris. Wrapped in a blanket, I opened the windows and huddled on the ledge behind the balustrade.

Underneath his armor, he was losing a long battle with himself. I saw that now, as I had failed to truly see before. I nearly went into the parlor—except I had already made my confession. I had told him, in no uncertain terms, what I wanted. Now it was his choice.

When the cold set in, I knew. I had been a fool to hope it would ever work between us. I was mortal. He was as ageless and distant as his namesake. I would be his mayfly lover, dead after a day. It was over. I returned to bed and tried to fade into sleep, but my heart kept drumming me awake.

Just before midnight, I sensed movement. Arcturus was no longer in his room. Little by little, I sat up, all my attention fixed on the æther. And then he was at my open door.

Time clotted, slow as honey dripping from a comb. He came to sit on my bed, and for a long time, neither of us moved.

"It is a splendid and terrible thing," he said, gaze on the wall, "to be Rephaite, and to feel so acutely for a human. It has brought wonder to my existence to learn the deepest truths of yours. To find that, though we are different, we are also alike." His voice was a long shadow. "And yet it has also brought fear. Fear of everything that could curtail your life—even time, which never touched me. Even my own arms around you."

Slowly, I turned his face.

"Fear is a constant for us mortals," I murmured, "but so is the knowledge that no matter what happens, no matter how careful and afraid we are, life does end. So you might as well take every shot you get." I looked up at him. "You said I didn't need you. Maybe neither of us needs the other. We both know how to be alone. Is it not enough that we want each other?"

Smokeless heat rose in his eyes.

Our meeting was quiet. Guarded, as if he really was afraid I would shatter at the slightest touch. He let me guide his brow against mine, and I felt myself be kindled by his aura.

"Paige."

That was all he had left. Just my name. I touched my lips to his.

It was hardly a kiss. Just a whisper of my mouth on his, a give and take of breath. Tilting back, I idled my fingertips along his jaw, then his lower lip—full and smooth, curved like the limb of a bow. Calling my courage, I stroked the tip of my tongue across that lip before I drew it into my mouth.

Deep in his chest, resonance. The taste of him woke a dream of red drapes. I held his nape, exploring his mouth with a tender slowness that could only stem from certainty. I could touch him now. I meant to savor it.

"I can offer you nothing," he said. "Only a song in the shadows."

"Sing it to me," I whispered back.

One of his hands cradled my leg. He traced the same wound that had set me on fire.

He gathered me into his arms—gently, carefully, so I could breathe. My hands were on his sarx, his lips hot and sure on mine. Our kiss deepened as his fingers strayed into my hair.

All seven of my senses were in freefall. I broke the kiss and started to unbutton my shirt. At first, he only watched—and just that, the *watching*, it set me alight—before he abetted its fall from my shoulders, and his hands moved up the bare skin of my arms.

Before, we had been grasping at stolen moments, always in the limen. This was different. Every look, every touch, was a piece of a promise. Commitment to our crime.

His gaze seared over me. He stroked his thumb over my lips, soft and reverent. For the first time, I was aware of a new power. Not possession. Not the crown. Something else.

As he dipped his lips to my collarbone, tasted the hollow of my throat, I took him by the hand and led it to my breast. When he cupped it, a fractured sound came, unwilled, from my lips. I was lost to the discovery of pleasure, unable to do anything but let myself be touched.

For so long, I had treated my body like a burden, a weight to be cast off. Forgotten its potential for softness. My skin was still tender from the heat. Every touch was heightened, shivering. He kissed my neck and each of my ribs, and when I was taut with frustration, he drew the delicate tip of my breast into his mouth. My mind drifted to a day when I had found a smoked-glass shew stone at the black market. Claiming its polished beauty, knowing I would be executed if I was ever found with it in my possession. I had kept it because it was beautiful. Because holding it was an act of defiance.

At last, I found the clarity to return his touches. The divot at the base of his throat. His broad shoulders and the ledge of his collarbone. I smoothed my hands around his sides, to the scars on his back, and he lifted his gaze back to mine. He watched my face as I ran my fingertips over the mutilation, letting him know where I was and where I meant to go.

After a moment, his tension dissolved, and he lowered his head to me again. I was intensely aware of his mouth on my other breast, the warmth of it ribboning to my abdomen. Breathing hard, I unbuckled his belt. He raised his head, and our lips came together. I slid off my underwear—his hands joined mine—and then it was only me in his arms.

He looked at my face for a long time. Even as I tensed in expectation, I almost lost my nerve. I was so different from what he knew.

His gaze moved down my body. I held still. A human might have whispered in my ear, told me I was beautiful or perfect, but not him. For a long time, all he did was look, opaque, eyes on fire. When I was sure the silence would last forever, when the tension of waiting would snap me in two, he drew me against him, into the moonlight. It illuminated my hair, transfigured it to flame, and ousted the few shadows that had draped me.

He could see every part of me. Every inch, down to the last scar and freckle. Another chill of reserve almost made me glance away. To counter it, I placed my hands on his chest.

"What are you thinking?"

Speaking eased my nerves. His calloused palms came to rest on my waist first, then the fingers he had almost lost.

"That if wanting you is treachery," he said, "then let me always bear these scars." My arms circled his neck, and his lips grazed my jaw. "Let them be a badge of pride, not shame."

I thought it would undo me, hearing his voice that deep, that close. When we melted onto the bed, he was careful not to trap me, never holding me too hard. Before long, there was nothing human-made left on him. Just long contours of limb and muscle. I had been so lost in his embrace that the æther had almost faded from my notice, but now I reached out to it, and it magnified every touch, every breath. The golden cord seemed to surround us.

This could not be wrong. Every instinct in me spoke of rightness, of balance, of synchrony.

As his breath warmed my ribs, I tilted my head back and exhaled. Doing this—crossing this line—might snap the constant pull between us. I yearned for that pull. It steadied me.

And yet I wanted more. I had waited enough.

His kiss made the skin of my abdomen shiver. His hands cradled the backs of my knees.

"This," he said, "is an overture."

His voice was little more than a tremor in his throat. I felt it everywhere.

"Learning a duet entails time. And patience. Calls for us to move as one." He found a sensitive place at the back of my thigh, and I breathed his name. "I want you to show me where to touch you. I want to know—" he rolled a thumb over the wing of my hipbone "—how to make your body sing."

He already did. I couldn't remember how to breathe, or what it was to not be burning.

His hands returned to my knees. I trembled as he guided them apart, my head tilting back in anticipation.

"Do you want this?"

"Yes," I whispered. "Yes."

Arcturus pressed a kiss to my thigh. I breathed in as the powerful muscles of his back shifted, and then I was lost in a new and exhilarating language. A song that only we could share.

He knew what he was doing. Rephaim must not be so different from humans in some respects. Heart pounding, with his hands on my hips, I threaded my fingers into his hair. All reserve had disappeared at the first touch, transforming into want, into vastness. It seemed impossible that my body could feel this much, *be* this much, and somehow not break into pieces.

Small, instinctive sounds passed my lips as he carried me to the edge of a precipice. I cleaved to him, afraid to let go, every limb fighting the call to surrender. Surrender had no place in war.

But this was no war. Not here, in this room.

He never rushed. As my hips surged and my hand twisted into the sheets, I thought of the bird in the music box, and the golden key that wound it. He coaxed me closer and closer to the brink, and there he held me until the bird came to life and took wing.

****

We lay still and soft-limbed after that. As much as I wanted to draw him into me, it was enough, for now, to be in his arms. To look up and always find him close enough to kiss.

We both had our dark rooms. Now we had this one, too.

My back was against his chest, my head supported by his arm. A calloused hand smoothed up my waist. I felt heavy enough to sink through the bed, yet my senses were as light as air.

His voice broke a long stillness. "You would tell me if I hurt you."

I looked at him over my shoulder. "You didn't think those were sounds of discomfort, did you?"

"Humor me." He held my gaze. "Last time you were intimate with someone else, it caused you pain. You told him it did not matter. Urged him to continue."

The memory pierced me for the first time in months. The hollowness and fear of it.

"I wasn't thinking straight that night," I said, almost too softly to hear. "I don't think I . . . feel that way unless there's already a connection. Like ours." I covered the hand on my waist with one of mine. "And it was different with an amaurotic. As if he couldn't reach all of me."

"Even so." He lowered his lips back to mine for a lingering moment. "We may both have auras, but you are not a Rephaite. If I do anything to disquiet you, I would like to know."

"Mm. So long as you'll tell me if I do anything to disquiet you."

"You have my word."

A siren called outside the cracked-open window, and a slurred voice shouted in French. I couldn't tense at those sounds, as I often did. Not with him gently exploring my hair, as if he was contemplating how to untangle it.

"I have resented my gift," he said, "for it does not let me forget." He drew my hair to one side of my neck and kissed the atlas of my nape. "I could not forget the room where I was scarred." I hooked my fingertips between his knuckles. "Yet neither can I forget this room."

He stroked down my abdomen. I half closed my eyes as he circled my navel—the tiny hollow that marked me as human as surely as his eyes marked him as Rephaite. All the while, I willed him not to stop.

We fell silent for a while, immersed in the possibilities of touch. He kissed my jaw, my shoulder. I tilted my head back. As my hand strayed along his side, I felt the very tips of the scars.

"Will you let me see them?" I asked him softly. When he looked away, I held his face. "It's all right if not. I just . . . don't want you to feel as if you have to hide them, either."

After a small eternity, he turned onto his side, so I could see the broad span of his back. I sat up slowly to look.

There were more than I had wanted to imagine. His back was an iron trellis of scars. The larger ones were raised welts, as thick as my little finger, while the smaller ones were hairline threads across his shoulders, like cracks in glass, that spoke of slow, meticulous cruelty. How he had restrained himself from shooting Jaxon, or kept up his façade of loyalty to Nashira after she had inflicted this on him, I could only guess.

He was still as I traced each scar. They were smooth as wax. It took him some time to relax into my exploration, but when he did, he was as heavy as if he was sleeping. When I had touched each one, I slung my arm around his waist and embraced him from behind.

"You will not be comfortable there for long," he said.

The scars did feel strange against my bare skin, but I pressed my cheek to them. "Hush. I'm asleep."

"Hm."

****

We both drifted off for a while. When I stirred, we were bathed in moonlight, and we had somehow traded positions, my back to his chest again. The crook of his right arm cupped my elbow. I held his left hand between both of mine, fingers intertwined. His face was tucked into my neck.

If you do not come back within the sennight, I will find another way to escape this place. I breathed in hard when I remembered, tightening my chest. *I will hunt you, Paige Mahoney.*

When I coughed, Arcturus opened his eyes. His scarred fingers skimmed my arm.

"I broke my word to Kornephoros," I murmured. "It's been more than a week."

"If he comes for you, we will deal with him."

There would be consequences foreverything that had happened. What remained to be seen was just how many.

"You feared that caring for me would distract you from the revolution. It can be otherwise." His voice was almost too low to hear. "We will end the gray market. We will unite the syndicates. All will be well."

With a nod, I turned to face him, and he traced down to the base of my spine. I rested my head on his chest.

"I know," I whispered. "I believe you."

****

The sky held a gray inkling of dawn when I woke a second time. Arcturus was silent beside me, his palm over the dressing on my back, as if he had meant to protect it. He had not slept once while I lay fevered. Now he had withdrawn into a deep slumber, turning him into a statue.

I curled an arm around his neck and tucked my head under his chin. He was still here. Both of us were still here. A long beat passed before I snapped upright with a jolt, realizing what had woken me.

Two familiar dreamscapes were heading straight for the apartment. Ducos and Stéphane. With a low curse, I disentangled myself from Arcturus and dived out of bed. Ducos would likely not care if she thought I was sleeping with my associate, but I was taking no chances.

"By all means, you carry on sleeping, you big clot," I hissed. "I'll handle the pissed-off spies by myself."

Without stopping to wait for a reply, I threw on my underwear and half ran to the wardrobe, where I grabbed the first shirt and trousers I saw. The blouse was barely done up—buttons in all the wrong holes, naturally—by the time Ducos came sweeping into the parlor.

"Ducos." I cleared my throat, conscious of my unruly hair. "Didn't think you'd be here until Sunday."

"Steph has been keeping an eye on the building. They saw a light on when they drove past last night." Ducos placed both hands on my shoulders, the gesture almost maternal. "Are you injured?"

There was a sharpness in her gaze that set my nerves on edge. She seemed worried and suspicious in equal measure. It was not an expression I had seen her wear before.

"I had an infected wound. Took me a few days to recover and get back here. Otherwise I'm fine," I said. "We got to the city through the carrières, in the end. There was a flood. Dirty water."

"I had no idea the carrières extended as far as Versailles." Ducos moved past me. "How did you find your way?"

"I had some help from locals. They didn't know about the assignment."

"Locals."

"Yes. They're clairvoyants."

Ducos sank onto the couch with a long exhalation. Her cheeks held a touch of high color from the cold. Stéphane walked in, wearing a pair of tinted spectacles and a leather jacket.

"Flora," they said. "Good to see you alive."

I nodded. "Stéphane."

"Well?" Ducos asked me, gaze intent. "Is the Grand Overseer dead?"

Our eyes met. I swallowed, and for the first time, I wondered if I should be afraid of her.

"I had no time." I took the micro-camera from the mantelpiece. "But it's likely he died in the fire. In the palace."

When Ducos slowly held out a hand, I placed the camera into it. Stéphane removed their spectacles, eyebrows raised.

"I had heard there was a significant fire to the west of Paris," Ducos said. "But not that it was the Château de Versailles. A building that has stood for some four centuries, that has seen the rise and fall of sovereigns and republics." Pause. "How did that happen, Flora?"

There was a dangerous silence.

"I set it," I said.

To my right, Stéphane let out a long breath. "You are insane," they breathed. "This will enrage England."

"That's why I did it."

For several moments, Ducos was speechless.

"Explain yourself." There was a hairline crack in her veneer. "Tell me why you did not carry out the assignment I gave you. Why you chose, instead, to commit first-degree arson."

"The city was heavily guarded. Even with my gift, it was impossible for me to reach the Grand Overseer." The lie came smooth as buttermilk. "I reasoned that destroying the colony was the next best thing. That Domino could pin the blame on Ménard, creating even more friction between France and England. That place was the source of all their tension, and now—"

"—it is in ashes. Like our plans," Ducos barked. "I did not tell you to improvise, Flora. You are expected to heed your orders, not question them, nor tailor them to suit your own scruples."

"You didn't mind me tailoring the plan when I was taken into the Hôtel Garuche. You must have known I would adapt to my circumstances again," I said. "Retreating would have scuttled a priceless opportunity. Did you really want me to back out after a two-day crawl through hell?"

"Yes." Without raising her voice, Ducos managed to express the depth of her anger and disappointment. "You should have retreated, returned here, and informed me that you could not reasonably complete your assignment. That would have been the proper course of action for a sane individual. Instead, you decided to demolish our plans, plans that have taken months of blood and sweat and risk to lay." She rose. "I stressed the delicate nature of your role in Domino. I explained the unpredictability and danger of the situation in Europe."

"You did," I said. "Ducos—"

"That target was not chosen at random! He was chosen because his death would sow tension without *shattering* the relationship between England and France. By setting fire to the colony—the root of their disagreement—you may have pushed the two countries into all-out war. The Suzerain could do anything in retaliation."

"So be it," I snapped. "If Scion is at war with itself, it isn't at war with your benefactors. Command can dole out my punishment. Until then, am I still a member of Mannequin?"

Ducos looked as if she had half a mind to hit me. Stéphane puffed out their cheeks.

"I have no time for this now," Ducos finally said. "Albéric—the agent who takes care of the safe houses—has dropped off the radar. We have no idea where he is, or why he isn't responding to any attempts to contact him. As a precaution, we would like to move you and your auxiliary to a different part of the citadel. I have eight people to relocate by tonight."

"I will collect you at ten," Stéphane said to me. "Pack some clothes and food. If that's not too dull an order," they added under their breath.

I tried not to feel the loss too deeply. Wanderer that I was, I should have known better than to try to grow roots.

"Until I send my report and receive a response, you remain one of my agents, and you will be treated as such," Ducos said. "You see, to me, and to Stéphane, the rules of this sub-network are not flexible. Or optional." She turned her back on me. "Stay put until we return. If you even *think* about stepping outside this apartment—"

With a last shake of her head, she strode out in a waft of dark hair and a swing of scarf. Stéphane hung back.

"How badly have I fucked up?" I asked them quietly. They answered with a tiny shrug.

"I would not want to be you right now." They put their spectacles back on. "Enjoy your last day in Rue Gît-le-Cœur. A week from now, you might not have a roof over your head. Or any memories in it."

22

Lady of Paris

FEBRUARY 21, 2060

The horizon was as red as if the fire still burned. I watched the sunrise from the roof. Fog breathed into every nook and alcove of Paris, laced over the dark crests of the river, blanched the sky to the pink of salmon. I was sure the air was still spiced with the tang of smoke.

Beautiful though it was—this ancient, haunted citadel—there was a disquieting stillness to the morning. The sky was blood mixed into milk. The people down below were shadows, rendered faint and faceless by the mist. I trapped my breath and blew pale flags of cloud into my palms.

This was the coldest winter I could remember. Even on the farm, where all of us had been runny-nosed and the cowshed had been warmer than the house, I had sometimes found wild primroses or a sunburst of coltsfoot in February. Here, the air withheld even the rumor of a thaw.

We were leaving this apartment, where I had started to heal after the hardest trial of my life. Another lost home to add to my list.

Steam gusted from my mug of coffee. My lips were sweetly tender. I traced them, lost in thought.

I hoped Ducos was wrong. There would be repercussions for the loss of the colony—grave ones—but if Nashira was so enraged that she executed Ménard and Frère, a significant threat to her reign would disappear.

By nine, Arcturus had still not risen. Days without sleep must have drained him. I slid back through the hatch, suddenly self-conscious. By night, it had been so easy to let go of my inhibitions. In the cold light of day, it might be different. I might remember all the risks again.

Only one way to find out. I brushed my hair back, took a deep breath, and opened my bedroom door.

Golden light spilled into the room. He was still in bed, on his side, exactly as I had left him. As soon as his features came into relief, my nerves evaporated. I wanted him as strongly as before.

The feeling vanished as I sat on the bed at his side. He was stone-cold to the touch.

"Arcturus."

His eyes cracked open.

"Is it the scars?" I asked. When he managed a nod, I placed a hand lightly on his shoulder. "Tell me what to do."

"You cannot ease it." He could barely speak. "Not without amaranth."

"Did you not bring any with you?"

"Our stores were low. The others needed it."

"You needed it as well, you bull-headed idiot."

Now I was this close to him, I sensed pain. Agony barked from his rigid jaw, the tendons of hand and neck, his tortured muscles. Nashira was seizing her vengeance for the loss of another colony.

"All right." I was afraid to touch him too much. "Do you think you can move to the parlor?"

After a minute, he eased into a sitting position and draped an arm around my shoulders. Between us, we got him down the corridor, into the parlor, and onto the couch. I fitted a cushion under his head and held a glass of wine to his lips. Even swallowing took him effort.

"You're all right," I said, keeping my voice steady. "It will fade."

He moved onto his side with a nod. I got some covers from the bedroom and slipped under them with him, as if I could lend him my warmth. He rested his cheek on my chest, and I propped my chin on the top of his head, wishing I could draw some of his pain out through the cord.

For a long time, my breath was the only sound. At last, Arcturus lifted his head to look at me.

"Paige," he said, "I know this is new to you." His hand moved across my stomach, to my hip. "I meant what I said. It was an overture. What comes next, we will write together."

"I know."

We looked at one another for a while. I brushed his hair back.

"Will we just play it by ear, then?" I asked softly. "Or do you know what you want from this?"

"I want you with me." He set his forehead against mine. "That is all I know."

I had said those same words to him once. I took his face between my hands and breathed him in.

"Ducos and Stéphane came this morning, before you woke," I eventually said. "We have to leave this place tonight." I sighed. "And I don't think we have a future with Domino."

Arcturus held my waist as I told him what had happened. Every so often, his muscles tightened, and I held him close.

"If Domino severs the connection, I imagine Le Vieux Orphelin will allow us to take shelter in Passy." He returned his head to my chest. "We should see what is happening abroad."

It had been a while since I had checked the news. I reached across to the coffee table for the remote.

"*—Weaver has sanctioned the execution by firing squad of Esteban de Borbón, who will be the last King of Spain,*" Scarlett Burnish was saying, her control as ironclad as ever. I sat up. "*Esteban took his family into the Bascilia de San Francisco el Grande, telling them that God would keep them safe. Instead, he shot and killed his wife, Queen Antonia. He shot and killed their heir, seven-year-old Luciana. He shot and killed his father-in-law, barrister Torben van Buskirk, who died attempting to protect his granddaughter.*"

The blood drained from my face.

"*These crimes, reminiscent of those of the Bloody King, serve as judicious proof that monarchs, like unnaturals, have no place in the civilized world*," Burnish said, eyes glacial. "*The anchor will rise over Madrid.*"

"They killed them all," I murmured.

Not for one moment did I believe King Esteban had committed those murders. Scion had killed his family in that church. When he was executed, he would remind the world of why it should turn to the anchor, away from crowns and gods.

Arcturus interlocked our fingers. He knew there was nothing to say. From the sound of it, Spain was all but defeated. Now King Esteban was in custody and accused of murder, the Prime Minister would have little choice but to surrender.

In two and a half months, the anchor had taken the whole of the Iberian Peninsula.

It was an hour before the pain eased enough for Arcturus to slip back to sleep. I stole away to make breakfast. I ate two rounds of honey on toast before I began to pack.

My only possessions were the music box and the parcel from my father. I retrieved the latter from under the wardrobe, though I still had no stomach to open it. Both went into my backpack, along with as much spare clothing as I could fit. Finally, I slid in my weapons, my dossier from Domino, and the ledger I had stolen from Ménard.

Except for the money and some clothes, Arcturus had brought nothing with him from London. I did, however, find one of the swords from the colony under his bed.

For the rest of the day, I watched the news from the armchair, too bone-weary to do anything more. All the raconteurs could talk about were the evils of monarchy, and how Scion would soon release Spain from its bonds.

At noon, there had been a break in the cycle—an announcement that Inquisitor Ménard was investigating the possibility of terrorist involvement in the recent fire in a Type A Restricted Sector. He appeared briefly on-screen, instructing those responsible to come forward and confess.

He must have known it had been me, but he was keeping that close to his chest. I frowned. This would have been his perfect chance to pin the blame on me and the Mime Order and to somehow turn that against Weaver.

His face, as ever, gave nothing away. He was too well-trained for that. I wondered what the mood was in the mansion. Whether he feared retribution for his failure to protect the colony.

Every now and then, Arcturus flinched awake. Each time, he would look around the room with hot eyes. Like something caught in a trap. Seeing me nearby, he would quiet and return his head to the cushion.

At five, I muted the news. There was nothing left to do but wait for Stéphane. I lay down next to Arcturus and cuddled up to him, my head tucked under his chin. Still half-asleep, he pressed a kiss to my hair and lifted the covers over my shoulders.

And I let myself imagine it could always be like this. That no matter the consequences of what we had done—and what we had yet to do—he would always be there to face them with me.

I must have slept. The light outside was dim and blue by the time a sound jerked me awake. It cut into my skull like a bone saw—the doorbell, the one nobody had ever used. All of the agents had keys.

Somehow, Arcturus kept sleeping. I sat up and listened. Someone with the wrong address, perhaps. Kids playing knick-knack. There were plenty of reasons, none of them sinister, why somebody would ring a doorbell. As I stole downstairs, my attention rolled to the æther.

I knew that dreamscape. Furious, I slid the chain aside and cracked the door open to find a hooded figure on the doorstep, shoulders dredged with snow. I recognized that tight-lipped mouth.

"What the hell are you doing here?" I said in a cold undertone. "How did you know where I was?"

Léandre brazened me out. "Ivy told me."

"Kindly give her a bump on the head with that crowbar for me." I started to close the door. "Goodbye, Léandre."

"Stop." He wedged a dirty boot between the door and the frame. "You are to make an alliance with Le Vieux Orphelin. I am his heir.

Since you chose to childishly avoid me earlier, I came to resolve this . . . quarrel." A muscle twitched in his cheek. "There is somewhere we can go. Very close."

I glanced over his shoulder. An old black moto was parked against the wall.

"I have to be back before ten," I said.

"You will be."

"Fine. Wait there."

I shut the door in his face, leaving him to gather snow.

In the parlor, Arcturus was still asleep. I gave him a gentle shake and whispered his name, to no avail. His scars were still too cold.

I didn't like to leave him like this. Still, as much as it pained me to admit it, I did need to thrash out my bitterness with Léandre. As quietly as I could, I laced on a pair of heeled boots and buttoned my coat, then scribbled a note.

Léandre turned up. I'll be back before 10.
Codladh sámh.

I left it on the couch beside him. As I turned to leave, something made me look at his face once more. I traced the elegant lines of his brow and jaw, and his lips, soft in repose. At least he was peaceful. I placed a kiss on the top of his head before I left.

Léandre was in exactly the same position when I stepped outside, as if he had done nothing but stare at the door since I left. We headed east on foot, following the river along the Quai des Grands Augustins.

Snow tufted around us. We both tensed as a squadron of night Vigiles strode past on the other side of the road, but they were too far away to glimpse our auras, and they seemed preoccupied.

Léandre stopped at the end of the Pont Neuf, and we sized up the building that loomed to our right. Its bell towers presided over a public square, where vendors sold postcards and paintings.

"La Grande Salle," I said.

"Once she was called Notre-Dame. She belonged to all Paris, and Paris belonged to her. It has been almost nine hundred years since her first stone was laid." Léandre folded his arms. "This is where Ménard married Frère. In a fortnight or so, they will hold a masked ball here. The Butcher of Strasbourg is not a theatrical man by nature, but, much like Le Vieux Orphelin, he understands the power of a symbol. A guillotine. An anchor. A building like this."

It was a spectacular feat of construction. The cathedral still had its rose windows, though the kings that had once reigned above its doors had been decapitated. A compromise between two factions: the anachorètes who believed that all religious buildings should be demolished, and those who recognized its beauty and wanted to cut away pieces of it until it was fit for Scion. The wooden spire had burned away in a fire set by the anachorètes.

"I'm fairly sure we won't be invited," I said, "so I'll assume you didn't bring me here to ask for the first dance."

"No," he said. I was starting to wonder if Léandre had ever cracked a smile in his life. "I heard you liked to climb in London. I am learning. I know the world below Paris. I would like to learn the world above." His expression was mildly pained. "Your advice would be . . . helpful."

I took the measure of the building. This was one kind of olive branch I could get behind.

"You have chalk?" I asked Léandre. In answer, he passed me a pair of textured gloves. "All right. Let's see what you can do."

****

And that was how I came to be clinging to a Gothic cathedral in Paris as dusk painted the citadel in shades of blue and gray. I had expected guards—Nick and I had often had to dodge private security when we climbed buildings in London—but clearly Scion had better things to do than watch a glorified clock.

We climbed up the south-facing side. Léandre needed little guidance. His long arms and legs gave him a spider-like ease. I occasionally pointed out a handhold if he fell behind, which he acknowledged with a grunt.

The cathedral offered crockets and ledges in abundance, as if she wanted us to scale her. I had spent a long time underground of late, but this was what my limbs had always itched to do. To make every building my ladder and stairway.

Climbing made me miss Nick so much it ached. I wanted to know that he was all right. Weeks had passed since I had left him on the dock in Dover. I hoped that wherever he was in Sweden, and whoever he was with, he was reclaiming the rooftops from Birgitta Tjäder.

Nick was used to leading a double life. He would have worked out how to be a rebel and a spy.

Léandre hurdled a balustrade and began to climb again. Just ahead of him, I grabbed onto a stump that must once have been a gargoyle. When I was high enough, I hoisted Léandre up by the arm, onto the edge of the roof, which provided us with a bridge to the bell towers. Its sides were alarmingly steep, treacherous with ice. We shimmied along it.

We finally stopped in the open-air gallery at the front of the cathedral. Paris sprawled before us. Léandre sat down and huffed into his hands, legs over the edge. I stayed on my feet.

"Not bad," I said. A curt nod. "You go first, then. Since you brought me up here."

"I do not apologize for leaving the prisoners behind."

I let out a mirthless laugh. "Great start."

"You saw what happened," he said to me. "The Passage des Voleurs collapsed. I told you from the beginning that there was a risk of that." He took a leather pouch from inside his coat. "If we had gone with your plan, all of those people would have drowned."

"Instead, most of those people are dead in a forest. Or worse," I said. "You allowed me to believe that we would try to save all the prisoners."

"I never said that."

"You knew exactly what you were playing at." I stared out at the blue lights of the citadel, the dark slick of the river. "I don't want lies or half-truths anymore. I've had plenty of those from too many people."

Léandre took a narrow sheet of paper from the pouch. He held it open with one hand and used the other to sprinkle a line of shriveled aster petals across it.

"I knew you would make a fuss if I was honest," he said. "That you would be irrational."

"It isn't irrational to care about people, Léandre. I might have been too optimistic to believe we could save them all," I conceded. "Maybe it just isn't possible to break into a government-controlled facility and get everyone out alive."

"That was my opinion," Léandre stated. "Would you have listened to me if I had been frank?"

I ground my jaw.

"I fought to get those prisoners out of the palace," he continued. "Ankou and I waited until everyone was through the reservoir before we stopped defending the entrance. Even when the soldiers came inside."

"You should have told me your plan from the start. I could then have told *you* that sending them all into the Forêt de Meudon was not an option," I said. "You don't know what's in those woods."

"I didn't then. I think I do now." Léandre glanced sidelong at me. "Something chased us to the cemetery. An aura like a swarm of flies." He rolled the cigarette and skimmed the tip of his tongue along the edge of the paper. "Les Emim, no?"

"Yes." I finally sat beside him, bracing my heels on a ledge, and took off the gloves. "Most of what was in the pamphlet was real. Based on things that happened in the first colony."

"But the pamphlet depicts the Rephaim as saviors," he said. "And those guards in Versailles were not."

"Rephaim aren't good nor evil. They're as complicated as we are. Having said that," I said, "a fair number of them do want us dead, mutilated, or enslaved, so best to always approach with caution. As for the pamphlet, someone edited it without my permission."

Léandre took a vesta case from his coat and removed a match, which he used to light his roll-up, releasing the cloying scent of aster.

"If it means anything to you, I am sorry." He pocketed the case. "Not for the plan itself, but for hiding it. Now that I know you want honesty, no matter how brutal, I am happy to deliver it."

"I can't imagine everyone appreciates that attitude," I said. "Does Le Vieux Orphelin?"

"Yes. He does." He exhaled blue-tinged smoke. "When he rules this citadel, things will change, Underqueen. As soon as the Man in the Iron Mask is gone, he will summon all of the leaders of the Nouveau Régime, and there, we will confront that bastard, Le Latr—" His eyes narrowed. "What is happening down there?"

I followed his gaze to the Quai des Grands Augustins. As soon as I saw what he was looking at, I stood. Multiple squadrons of Vigiles had descended on the quay in armored vehicles, red lights glinting, no sirens to betray their approach.

With my heart north of its rightful place, I waited. They were moving out of sight of our vantage point. I identified their drivers in the æther and waited for them to keep moving up the quay.

Then I felt the convoy stop. And I felt where it stopped.

On the corner of Rue Gît-le-Cœur.

"No." The word left me as a rasp. "No. They can't—"

Léandre had risen. "Your bodyguard."

Like a shock of iced water, fear drenched me. Without a strategy, without a single thought for caution, I turned on my heel and ran for the roof. The golden cord quaked as I screamed his name through it.

ARCTURUS, RUN!

Léandre intercepted me. He pinioned my waist with both arms—stopping me, like he had stopped me in the tunnels. "Paige, wait," he snarled in my ear. "You can't help him now—"

"I can." Labored breaths sawed through me, hard as sobs. "I can. Let me go, let me go to him—"

"You are not going down there to get shot or arrested," he snapped. "You think you're going to fight off all those squadrons on your own, Underqueen? What are you, a fucking tank?"

My knees could barely hold me. With a last flare of strength, I shoved Léandre off and threw myself back to the edge of the gallery, grabbing onto a column to keep myself from falling. Without the sirens to warn him, and with little strength to run or fight, Arcturus would not escape.

ARCTURUS, GO, NOW!

A vibration rang in answer. I sensed him move—my heart soared—before the Vigiles stormed in, and his dreamscape was in a moil of them, and it was too late, he was lost.

What followed was a torture I had never thought possible. Unable to see the arrest, I lived every moment of it in the æther. The blow that brought him down. (I buckled, as if they had struck me as well.) His stillness. (I slid down the column, onto stone.) The slow drag to the vehicle.

I let out a low sound of denial, my head vised in my hands. Léandre was beside me, and I could hear him speaking, but all I could do was cling to the feel of that ironclad dreamscape, as if by holding onto it I could keep Arcturus from what was to come.

He was going back to his dark room. The one he had never truly escaped. Nashira had no more use for him now. She knew from experience that he was too strong to give way under torture, that all she could do was dispose of him.

The vehicles drove off. A few Vigiles remained behind, presumably to lie in wait for me. With a last flicker, Arcturus disappeared from my perception. I pressed my brow to the column.

"Paige." Léandre broke the terrible silence. "Did they take him?"

It was a moment before I could speak. "Yes."

By unspoken agreement, we stayed in the gallery. Safer up here. Only when a dreamscape came to my attention did I stir from my detached state.

Ducos was on her way back to the safe house. I needed to intercept her before she ran straight into the Vigiles.

"I have to get down there." I sounded distant even to my own ears. "Léandre, you should go."

"Paige, wait." Léandre grasped my shoulder. "If not for you, I would have lost the two most important people in my life—my sister and Le Vieux Orphelin." His face was set. "I will help you get Warden back. To repay that debt. The other perdues will help you, too, once the Man in the Iron Mask is dead."

"I'm going after Arcturus first."

The last time Nashira had seen him, I had been in his arms. She was the only other person who knew the truth about us, because she had seen it with her own eyes. Her cruelty might be my only hope. She would want to punish him for that betrayal before she took his head.

I had time to save his life.

"If you're serious about helping me," I said to Léandre, "get yourself safely back to Passy. I'll find you there."

Lips pursing in the fuzz of his beard, Léandre squinted across the citadel, his low-set eyebrows knitted.

"I will expect you soon. Be careful, marcherêve," he said gruffly. "They will be looking for you, too."

I clambered back to the roof and started to edge along it. Arcturus had taken bullets to shield me, dived into an ice-cold river to drag me from its grip. Now it was my turn.

Climbing down was unbearable. Even as every instinct screamed at me to hurry, I had to place my boots and hands with care—not just so I wouldn't fall, but to make sure no sharp-eyed Vigiles caught a glimpse of me. Twice I slithered on the ice and almost plunged to my death. In my wake, the bells rang out.

When I was low enough, I let go of my handhold and flumped into a snowdrift, then beat the flakes from my coat, hitched my scarf up to hide my face, and started walking. Ducos was approaching from somewhere near the University of Scion Paris.

I sped up. As soon as I glimpsed her on Rue Serpente, I crossed the street to stop her.

"Isaure," I called.

Ducos looked up from under a snow-flecked umbrella, lips parting with her intake of breath. "Flora." She pulled me left, into a doorway. "Cordier got you out in time, then?"

"Cordier?"

"Yes, Cordier. She called me to tell me that your safe house was under attack. We were cut off, so I came—" Ducos stopped, her hand tight as a cuff around my arm. "You didn't see her?"

"No. I was across the street when it happened. Somehow they didn't spot me." My voice shook. "Ducos, Warden was still inside. They took him."

The cords of her throat shifted. "Stay calm." She brought me under her umbrella. "Is your dossier still in the safe house?"

"Everything." My breath came in white gusts. "Everything is."

The ledger that exposed the corruption in the Parisian syndicate. The music box and the parcel from my father. If Scion had found my backpack, they had everything I possessed in the world. Everything but the mask I had left in the appartements privés.

Ducos checked the street, then started to walk again, taking me with her. She linked our arms as if we were the closest of friends, dipping her head close to mine as she spoke.

"Here is what's going to happen," she said under her breath. "Stéphane is nearby. You are going to get in their car and leave this district. You will be installed in a safe house in Rue Vernet, and you will stay there until I tell you otherwise. Meanwhile, when the coast is clear, I will see if there is anything left at Rue Gît-le-Cœur."

"I can't stay indoors." My heartbeat was a fist on velvet, thick and heavy in my ears. "I have to get to Warden."

"No rescue attempts. I told you."

She took me through a number of streets before she stopped near a telephone box. After a short wait, Stéphane pulled up, and Ducos bundled me into the heated interior of their car.

"Her auxiliary was detained. I will keep looking for Eléonore," she said in French. "Take her."

She slammed the door and walked back into the snow. I shivered uncontrollably, dread and nausea puncturing the icy shell around me.

"Where is Rue Vernet?"

I sounded nothing like myself. Stéphane glanced at me. "Very close to the Arc de Triomphe and the Grand Cours. Expensive area," they said. "You will not be there for long."

It was among the most famous districts in Paris. It was also north of the river, much closer to Passy.

"You never found Albéric, then," I said.

Their long hands tightened on the wheel.

"No," they said, in clipped tones. "If Cordier has also been detained, I can only think that one of the other two agents has betrayed us. Mannequin is compromised." Silence. Then: "Do you know how long the average lifespan is for a spy in the Domino Program?"

"Do I want to?" I asked dully.

"No." Stéphane let out a mild chuckle at that. "But know one thing, Flora. All of us are on borrowed time."

I was quiet for the rest of the journey.

Stéphane dropped me in Rue Vernet with a key, a small amount of money, and a new dissimulator. I waited until the car was out of sight before I smoothed the dissimulator onto my face and strode back into the snow. The golden cord was soundless and unmoving, but I poured a promise into it.

I will find you, I told him. *Hold on. Just hold on.*

23

Evenfall

The Eiffel Tower gleamed before the late-afternoon sun. There were dreamscapes at its summit—as well as a tourist attraction, it was a transmission station for use in national emergencies—but I had evaded all notice as I climbed into its northern leg, where I had spent most of the day. Concealed in the snow-lined latticework, I watched the Scion Citadel of Paris.

A night and almost a full day had passed since the arrest. My gaze darted across the frozen citadel, to the stone-built tower that was the Bastille. Bleak and windowless, the prison cast a long shadow over the nearest district.

Though my eyes were dry, grief vised my throat. I was tired to the point of numbness, but not in my bones, not in my limbs. It was the same desolation I had felt after I had watched my father die. The detached sense that nothing really mattered. Loss was not a sharp pain, but a formless gray that rounded off the edges of the world.

I pinched myself to stop it from taking me. Arcturus was not lost yet. He was imprisoned—badly hurt, no doubt—but I could save him. Unless I saw his head on a spike, I would not give up on him.

Le Vieux Orphelin had advised me against this vigil, but I needed to see as much of the citadel as possible. Arcturus was usually a guiding star in the æther, even at a distance. Now darkness had stolen between us. My internal compass was broken, the needle spinning. He might be anywhere.

Scion knew my abilities. They must have force-fed him a drop of Emite blood to conceal his location.

Sooner or later, it would start to wear off. In the small window of time between one dose and another, I had to be able to determine his precise location in the citadel. This viewpoint would help me do that.

Hold on. I willed him to hear me. *I'm here. I'm with you.*

A heavily disguised Léandre waited a long way below me, electing not to venture any higher than his perch. His moto waited in the Champ de la Tour. The moment I felt a shiver from the golden cord, he would drive me in the right direction. Le Vieux Orphelin had reluctantly given him permission to help me, but regretted that he could not send any more of the perdues to my aid, with the Man in the Iron Mask still at large. It was already a great risk to send Léandre. Nadine and Zeke had offered to help, as had Ivy. I had a burner phone to contact them.

A shift in the æther made me stiffen. My gaze snapped eastward, straight toward the Île de la Citadelle.

This was it. The compass had trembled, pointing me to him. Breath clouding, I started to climb down.

I'm coming. I repeated the words like a prayer. *Hold on.*

Mindful of the ice, I returned to Léandre, who was crouched at a juncture between iron girders, breathing into his hands. Seeing me, he raised his eyebrows and pulled his climbing gloves back on. My dissimulator had unsettled him at first, but he seemed to have got used to it.

The stairs took us most of the way down. Close to the bottom, we ducked into the latticework again to avoid two maintenance workers, who were speaking in voices thickened by colds. We dropped unseen to the ground, and then we were back into the dirty snow, running south.

Léandre unlocked his moto and tossed me a helmet. I climbed onto the back and wrapped my arms around his waist, and we were off.

With more Vigiles than usual on the south bank, Léandre crossed a bridge over the Seine and drove on the other side. The cord flickered. I followed it—my seventh sense—as I had once in London, when the Rag and Bone Man had buried Arcturus, thinking nobody would find him. The golden cord was a living tie between our spirits, and it was making itself known to me. A light glinting in murky water.

I stopped Léandre with a gesture. He pulled over, and we found ourselves staring once more at the Île de la Citadelle, this time at the splendid complex that occupied its western side. Cone-shaped roofs topped the crenellated towers.

"There?" Léandre said.

"Yes," I said. "Somewhere in there."

He tightened his grip on the throttle. "La Forteresse de Justice. That would make sense."

There would be no justice done in that place. "We need to see its defenses."

With a nod, he drove on. As I slung my arms around him again, I tried not to look at the towers.

The sun was leaving bloodstains on the sky. Léandre went as far as the Pont au Change, where we had to dismount and walk the moto between us. It was hard to tell it was a bridge, so tall were the houses and shops that towered on either side of it. Jewelers and pawnbrokers and goldsmiths plied their trade here, peddling the riches of Scion. People shouldered around us, breath feathering, hunting for bargains or trying to forge a way home through the concourse of wrapped-up bodies. People who had no idea that a fugitive now walked among them.

At the end of the bridge, we both climbed back onto the moto. Careful not to slow down, Léandre took us along the main boulevard of the Île de la Citadelle, past the elaborate gates of the Forteresse de Justice, home of the Inquisitorial Courts. A dozen soldiers, armed and armored, were posted both in front and beyond them, on the steps, as well as two Punishers, the elite Vigiles.

Nashira. Only she would have brought those bodyguards. I sensed her now. Even though the cord was somehow blocked again, I could sense Arcturus, too. His dreamscape was so close.

Hold on.

Léandre left his moto locked beside a tree. We strode down the nearest steps to the river path and walked until we were in the darkness under a bridge, where we both took off our helmets.

"You can't go in there." He made it fact. "Le Vieux Orphelin would say the same if he were here."

"There's an entrance to the left of the gates. A passageway. I saw it as we passed," I said under my breath. "That place is not the Bastille or the Archon. There are windows, multiple exits—"

"If it's so easy, why hasn't the Rephaite already found a way out?"

"Because they'll have him restrained." I tried not to picture him bound like Kornephoros, flowers twined around iron chains. "I didn't say it would be easy, but it's not impossible. I'll need a diversion, a disturbance—something like a brawl on the Pont au Change. It will draw the soldiers away from the fortress."

"People could get hurt. You know what krigs are like."

"A small fight will do. Just enough to get them away from the entrance, not to open fire. You could make that happen."

Léandre drew a long breath in through his nose and folded his arms.

"We might have to use your free-world friend. The Québécoise," he said. "You will have one shot at this, marcherêve."

"I only need one."

Léandre didn't point out my low chances of success. We both knew how insane it was for me to break into another Scion-controlled building and expect to come out alive, but I had done it more than once. He took a burner phone from his coat and made a call.

Arcturus, I'm coming.

****

Dusk approached the Scion Citadel of Paris. Stars tinseled a dimming sky. Far below, all seemed peaceful as sunset drew to a soft close. Portugal had fallen. Spain was almost won. All was well.

On the Pont au Change, a woman elbowed through the crowds. Clad in a velvet coat and tinted lenses, she could have been a raconteur or a fashionable denizen of the Rive Droite. Gloves hid her peeled fingers. She marched to a stall that glittered with jewelery—a stall that had appeared not long before—and slammed her handbag onto it, unspooling scarves and banknotes from inside.

"You. Cheating swine, you lied to my face," she snapped in French. The vendor straightened, tensing in expectation of a fight. "Everyone, gather round and mark the face of a charlatan!"

Her own face was so fury-stricken, nobody paid much attention to her accent, which was not quite French. A crowd gathered, drawn to the prospect of a spectacle. The pickpockets of the bridge ought to have been circling this affluent denizen, but none of them went near her.

"You are mistaken," said the vendor, with pockets full of bribe money. "My gems are among the finest in Paris."

"I have the evidence," the woman proclaimed, fist clenched. Nadine was enjoying herself. "He claims to sell the best emeralds of the Rila"—she emptied a succession of lucent green jewels onto the table, drawing gasps of wonder at their size, the brightness of the gold that connected them—"but I ask you, do these look like emeralds to you?"

At this, she dropped the lovely necklace to the ground and slammed down the heel of her boot. The ersatz jewels shattered beneath it, brittle as boiled sweets.

Outrage erupted at the sight. People craned to look. Already, those close enough to overhear were beginning to suspect that they might also have been hoodwinked. Teeth bared, the vendor overturned the table. Every one of his jewels soared, yet none of them broke as they scattered the cobblestones. Quick-fingered gutterlings darted for the treasures.

"See," the vendor bellowed over the clamor of angry voices. "This woman accuses me of forgery, but she is the only one holding false jewels. It was not me who sold her that necklace!" He pointed at her. "She is a liar. She probably made the damned thing herself."

"Only an unnatural would accuse an honest person of lying," the woman retorted. The word froze the crowd. "Perhaps you work for the grands ducs, who terrorize us from the shadows. Perhaps you fund their criminal activities with the sale of forgeries!"

Now the scent of a fight was in the air. With my mask in place and a hood over my hair, I watched as more and more people were drawn into the disagreement. As words became shouts, then shoves, then blows. And then I watched the soldiers clock what was happening.

One of them nodded to the others. Moving in regimented unison, they stepped from their posts.

Léandre and Nadine had bought me time, but it was sand in an hourglass. I could not waste one grain. I sprinted for the Forteresse de Justice.

I ran through the side passage and into the courtyard beyond, where I stared up at the nearest building. Arcturus was much closer than I had realized. I took in the high walls of the church-like edifice, topped with a dark wooden spire.

Dreamscapes were closing in. Guards, no doubt, called to cover the front gates while the soldiers were away. With little choice, I slipped into the building and closed the doors behind me.

The crypt-like space beyond was barely lit. There was still a rosy glow in the sky, but the windows in this place were small. Gilded struts streamed like sunrays from the ceiling, swooping down to kiss the tops of crimson pillars. It did not strike me as a likely entrance to a prison.

I found a winding stairway in a corner. Nerving myself, I began to climb. At the top, I stopped, wonderstruck.

This was definitely not a prison.

I was standing in the corner of a jewel box. Stained-glass windows soared to a starry vault high above me, which was crisscrossed by ribs of gold. The moribund light of dusk spilled in, scattering the marble floor with splinters of a rainbow. For several moments, I could do nothing but absorb it, the shimmering iridescence of the hall.

Though its name eluded me, I knew of this place. A former chapel, it was famed for these spectacular windows, which had once portrayed hundreds of scenes from a religious text. Wanting to preserve its beauty, if not its purpose, Irène Tourneur had ordered the medieval glass to be rearranged. Now the windows narrated the story of Scion. Not all of it, of course. Just the parts we were allowed to know.

Chandeliers were suspended on chains, so delicate the candles seemed to float in midair. By their light, I could make out a figure at the other end of the chapel. Unbound. With a low sound of relief, I crossed the hall and all but threw myself onto him. My arms went straight around his waist.

"Arcturus." I pressed my cheek to his chest. "I'm sorry. I'm sorry I took so long."

Relief had clouded my vision. That was why I missed the change in him. I had looked without truly seeing.

His stance was stiff, his arms at his sides. When I drew back and saw his face, his eyes gave me an unanticipated chill. Their light was that of a long-extinct sun, a dead and distant echo.

I took half a step away and found that he was dressed from head to toe in black. That was usual. The uniform, however, was not. Boots covered him to the knee, a silk-lined cloak swept to the floor, and leather gloves were pulled halfway up his forearms.

This was how he had dressed as blood-consort.

"Arcturus," I said, unnerved.

He said nothing.

His appearance, and his silence, almost stole the words from my tongue. I recovered enough to say, "We need to go. Before the soldiers—"

"Neither of us is leaving, 40."

The number stopped my blood. Dark memories woke in the back of my mind.

"What did you call me?" I whispered.

Red-hot brand. Nameless, numbered.

The Emite blood. It had to be. They had given him too much, and it had affected his mind. That hardly explained why he was dressed like this. Why he was standing free as a bird.

The night before last, his hands had discovered my body, and his eyes had seldom left my face. They were fixed on my face again now, but too intensely. As if he wanted to melt skin from bone.

"Arcturus," I said, "what—"

"Do not presume to use that name."

Through the encroaching fog, I racked my mind for an explanation. He was acting. This was some kind of tableau, like the one

Hildred Vance had created for me in Edinburgh, designed to devastate my sanity. I glanced up at the ceiling and toward the rose window, searching for cameras, for snipers, anything to help me understand.

"There is no one watching us," came his cold voice. "Were you so convinced I cared for you that you are unable to face the alternative?"

He sounded so unlike himself that I almost laughed, but the mask of his features locked my voice box.

"Jaxon Hall once gave you a warning. He told you that Terebell Sheratan ordered me to seduce you," Arcturus said. "He was not so far from the truth. I was not ordered. I chose. And I did not do it for Terebell."

A numbing agent was rushing through me, anaesthetising every limb. As if in preparation.

"No," I said, after an excruciating silence. "You can't have been acting. Not all this time. You would have—"

"Perhaps I should help you understand," Arcturus said softly. "The blood-sovereign needed information about the clairvoyant syndicate. She wanted Jaxon Hall, who had eluded her for years. When I discovered that you were his heir, I saw an opportunity to retrieve all that she desired. Without her knowledge, I set out to do this."

Every hair on my arms stood on end as I stared up at him.

"Through past actions, I was already a traitor. It was not such a fall, to become a flesh-traitor. To gain your trust," he said. "In London, I found out all I could about Jaxon Hall. I stayed at your side while you investigated the gray market. After the scrimmage, once I knew exactly where he was and all that he had done to mock Rephaite rule, I paid Jaxon a visit. I forced him to return to the anchor. I also delivered three of the fugitives who escaped from the first colony."

Their corpses on a scaffold, on a screen. Jaxon, gaunt and tired in his borrowed finery.

"No," I said again, faintly.

"I decided to remain by your side. To learn every secret of every clairvoyant organization," Arcturus said, "so that one day, we Rephaim could eradicate them all. You were thorough: London,

Manchester, Edinburgh, Paris. You never questioned whether you should tell me all you knew."

Through me, he knew our leaders, their organization, their hideouts. I had let him into every part of my life without a second thought.

He knew about Domino, too. About Ménard.

He knew *everything*.

The enormity of my error stared me in the face. With this, he could not just damage the revolution. He could destroy it. Every person I loved would swing from the gallows, and they would be there because of me.

I had shown him how to win. How to make sure that Scion would never face a flicker of resistance.

"I see you are recognizing the scale of your complicity," Arcturus said. "You were generous to furnish me with so much information. Of course, I could not have foreseen how far you would go to reach Senshield, else I would have stopped you then."

My knees were about to give way. This had to be a last ripple of fever, a terrible hallucination.

"I could have gone on. There seemed to be no end to your gullibility. But the time has come for me to return to the blood-sovereign, and to share all I have learned," Arcturus said. "We will crush every pocket of revolution. Together, we will claim this world." The corner of his mouth crooked in a taunting smile. "The Rephaim are in your debt, Underqueen."

I had sometimes wondered whether I could tempt him to smile. Not like this. That smile was a dissimulator on him, twisting him into a stranger. I drew my first breath in what felt like an eternity.

"Nashira is . . . taking you back," I said. "As her blood-consort."

"Such is her mercy. She knows that all I did, I did for her. Would you not say I have earned my reward, Paige?"

Hearing my name on his tongue had never felt like mockery before.

"Tell me." I raised my chin. "How exactly were you serving her when you came to my door the other night?"

No answer. Just that awful, ill-fitting smile.

"You are Arcturus Mesarthim, a leader of the Ranthen. You were loyal to the Mothallath. You despise the Sargas," I said, forcing myself

401

to sound calm and reasonable, "and you have done everything in your power, for centuries, to bring them down. Do you deny it?"

"I was a traitor then. But the Mothallath are gone," he said, "and it is because of humans."

"Arcturus—"

"After Jaxon betrayed me in the first rebellion, I realized that the blood-sovereign was right about you. Humankind must be bridled. Portugal is defeated, and the King of Spain is dead. You will lose."

"Enough." I stepped closer, fear boiling into panic and anger. "Arcturus, please, stop this. However she's threatened you, whatever hold she has over you, we'll find a way out. We can—"

"There is no *we*, fleshworm," he cut in. "Your reign is ended. You are nothing but corrupt flesh, rotting on the bone."

Against my will, I flinched in the face of his contempt. The night in my room gleamed across my mind, and for an unbearable moment, I saw it through a lens of Rephaite hatred. I rendered myself lewd and disgusting.

Our gazes locked. I searched for any trace of him from that long, dreamlike night, when everything had made sense. Any remnant of his warmth, his tenderness. All I could see before me was a statue. An automaton. A mimic. Something that wore a human shape, but was not, and had never been, human.

Through the ringing in my ears, I became aware of the dreams-capes beyond the walls. I was out of time—but I had to try, once more, to wake him up. To pull him from the brink. Not just for myself, or for him, but for the revolution.

"Arcturus. Warden." I stood as close as I could without touching him. "Listen to me. The world Nashira wants is not the answer. Don't go back to her. Don't stay here to be displayed like a trophy for the rest of your days. Do not be complicit in our extinction."

I might as well not have spoken for all the response I got. Abandoning all caution, I reached up and took his face between my hands, as I had not long ago, forcing him to look me in the eyes. A void looked back at me.

"I *know* this isn't you. Even if—even if it started out as a pretense, I don't believe you were pretending. Not that night," I said. "Remember the person you were before. The person who fought for the Mothallath. For clairvoyants. For humans." I grasped his gloved hand. "The person who held back a blade with his bare hands to *stop* Nashira Sargas."

He looked down at my fingers, wrapped around his leather-clad ones.

"I want to spend my life with you," I told him. "I want to bring Scion to its knees with you. I want a future with you." My throat ached. "It's not too late to do the right thing. You don't have to tell Nashira about the syndicates. Don't condemn thousands of people to death. And don't choose the side I'm not standing on, because I don't think I can bear to be your enemy."

Nothing. I tried to use the cord, to make him understand, but it was frozen solid. I was screaming into an abyss.

"Walk out of here," I whispered. "You will never be a war trophy to me."

His gaze seared into mine once more.

"You are not escaping," he said. "Not this time."

He shoved me off, hard enough to jar my bad wrist, and then— suddenly, terribly—his hand swung up to strike me.

One of the first things Nick had taught me was how to duck a punch. Plenty of fists came at you in the syndicate, no matter who you were. Avoiding this one should have been second nature.

But in that moment, I just stood there, too stunned to move. Time seemed to slow. I came to the far-off realization that one solid blow from that fist would crumple my skull. He actually meant to kill me.

He had revered my body with those hands. Now they would break it.

Death never came. Just before Arcturus could land the blow, his eyes gave a livid flare, and he pulled his arm back, so hard it was as if it had been wrenched by a string, or a shield had flown up in front of me. Such was my shock, all I could do was stare at him in silence.

"No," he said, after a long beat. He was still all over again, eyes flat. "Even with gloves, I will not dirty my hand."

My knees shook. I was rooted to the spot. Arcturus Mesarthim, as I had known him, would never have raised a hand to a human. Not to me.

Not for anything.

New footsteps sounded on the marble. In a stupor, I turned to see the architect of all my suffering. Nashira Sargas, the Suzerain, her golden hair combed to a high shine.

She was flanked by Situla Mesarthim, who looked no worse for wear after the fire, and Graffias Sheratan, who I remembered from the first colony. The sight of Nashira filled me with dread in a way it never had before my torture. I was alone and virtually unarmed with three—four—enemy Rephaim.

My nerves hardened to steel. I was twofold. Paige Mahoney was in too much pain to breathe, but Black Moth had to stand and do her duty. She had to warn the syndicates of the betrayal.

It was my fault. Now I had to fix it.

Nashira joined Arcturus and laid a hand on his arm. The sight of it tore my guts out.

"He's a flesh-traitor, Nashira." Bitter hatred almost strangled me. "Why would you take him back?"

"Be assured, 40," Nashira said to me, "that I will cleanse Arcturus of your influence. His flesh-treachery was for a cause, but he accepts that he will need to be punished for it. I will deliver."

Hers was the voice that so often disturbed my sleep. I remembered the way she had looked at me in the Westminster Archon just before I escaped her. Hellfire in her eyes.

There was a draft in the room. The rear doors to the chapel stood ajar. I had to keep her talking.

"Can he not speak for himself?" I asked.

"Arcturus is *not* himself after months of your words in his ear."

His dreamscape gave a strange vibration. I scrutinized his face, but his expression stayed the same.

"You escaped me in London," Nashira stated. "I would have let you die there. It would have been excruciating—humiliating—but it would also have been over in one night. Now I think I will keep you alive for a little longer before I claim your spirit. Arcturus will need to wean himself from the flesh. And to feed. Perhaps you can continue to tend to his needs for a time."

Disgust shivered through me. "I take back everything I ever said," I told him. "You *are* a coward. And a fucking hypocrite. You're a monster."

Still the same callous gaze.

"It is you who is monstrous, fleshworm," he said. "You are an affront to the natural order."

The Devil. I thought of the card Liss had shown me. *They'll make you think you're tied to them forever.*

We are bound together by a golden cord . . .

"Arcturus is no coward to commit flesh-treachery for the cause," Nashira said. "He will tell me everything about the Mime Order and Le Nouveau Régime. And when they are driven into the open, your thieves will soon be trapped by their own citadel. Because now that I have you back . . . I also have Senshield."

The implication sank in. All she needed to reactivate the scanners was the spirit of a dreamwalker.

"Fear not. I will ensure your people understand precisely how it happened," Nashira continued, softer. "That their Underqueen invited a wolf into her flock. Into her bed." She motioned to the other two Rephaim. "Take her to the Bonbec Tower, and tell the others to feed on her whenever they desire. Together, if they choose."

Before I could run, they had seized an arm each, and they were hauling me away from the blood-sovereign and her betrothed.

"Don't think you've won this," I shouted at Nashira. "We are everywhere now. Not just in London. Not just in Paris. We are under the ground and over your heads, on every street and rooftop. We will multiply, like the rats you claim we are, and bring the plague that will consume you—"

"No," Nashira said, and turned to put her gloved hands on Arcturus again. "You will consume yourselves. As you always have."

That was when I surrendered to it. The hopelessness, the terror and confusion and rage. I pulled it all in.

And let it all *out*.

It came exploding from my dreamscape. An unearthly flare of pressure, violent as the surface of the sun, that seemed to come both from within and without. I called, and in the distance, something *answered*.

All four Rephaim stiffened. A windstorm raged in the æther—a storm charged by my wrath. Situla and Graffias dropped me as if

I had burst into flame. Without so much as touching them, I had brought gods to their knees.

Hatred burned white-hot in my veins. I could barely keep hold of it. With what little control I had left, I concentrated it all on Nashira. Shockwaves slammed into her, one after the other, and for the first time since the colony, when I had briefly taken hold of her dreamscape, her composure slipped. Her eyes blazed as I forced her, at last, to take a step back.

Wetness ran from my nose and soaked into the collar of my shirt. I fitted my mask over my face.

"Tell Gomeisa the moths are coming," I told Nashira, "and there are more of us than you can count."

As I turned, Arcturus snared my gaze across the hall. And for a heart-stopping moment, I could have sworn his eyes became lambent and alive once more, and I could have sworn that—for a fraction of a heartbeat, a whisper of time—he looked like himself, and not a shell.

Then it was gone, and I ran for my life.

Out through the doors to a roofed balcony. On my right, scaffolding. I flung myself onto it and climbed, muscles screaming. The two Rephaite guards came after me, but I was already clambering over the top, onto a flat and icy roof. My arms shook with the effort.

Straight ahead loomed a sheer wall, no handholds whatsoever. Sensing the Rephaim follow, I drew the pistol Léandre had given me, pointed it to my right, and fired into the nearest window. Without so much as a breath, I hurdled through it.

Straight across a deserted room. I aimed my shoulder and smashed through another window, back into the frigid air, landing hard on my side in the snow. I shoved myself straight up, cleared a gap, swerved left, and pounded down a stretch of snow-covered roof. Behind me, a searchlight glared on at the highest point of the Forteresse de Justice and performed a slow rotation. It illuminated my footprints and caught up with me just as I climbed to a new section of the roof. The siren doubled in volume.

The Forteresse de Justice must be packed with soldiers. I ran as I never had in my life—not even on the night I was arrested, the night that started all of this. They had caught me that time. This time, thousands of lives depended on every inch I put between myself and the enemy.

He could always find me. Just like I could always find him. For the rest of my life, I would be chained to a traitor.

Sparks near my boots. The first hail of bullets. I was running out of roof, melted snow carrying me too far, too fast. I managed to twist at the last moment and grab hold of a window frame, the force almost pulling my arms out of joint. Desperate for breath, I scrambled down using sills and ledges and landed in a crouch on a tiled slope, only for ice to throw off my footing and send me over another edge. The snow on a lower rooftop broke my fall.

One spring took me down to a parked car. I hopscotched across two more, hit the ground running, and slammed out of the Forteresse de Justice. The wrought iron gate clanged shut in my wake.

My boots splashed into slush. I stumbled, bruised and dazed. People stared at me, and I realized how it must look for a masked figure to have just burst out of the home of the Inquisitorial Courts.

Somewhere behind me, a pair of doors crashed open. Voices roared at me to stop. I sprinted away from the gun-mounted lights, past frightened people, toward the dreamscape ahead. Soon I could see him as well as sense him, standing by his moto near the Pont au Change.

"Léandre," I shouted.

His face flicked toward me. Seeing my pursuers, he snapped down his visor and flung me a helmet. The moto was moving before I had even fully climbed into the saddle.

"Where is he?" he called to me as I threw an arm around his waist. "Where is Warden?"

"Just go!"

He twisted the handlebar and gunned the moto over the bridge. Bullets ripped into the pavement behind us, and then we were speeding away from the Île de la Citadelle, back into the shadows of Paris.

****

407

Léandre abandoned the moto under an archway. We ran north, taking narrow streets and shortcuts wherever we could. All the while, I choked out tearless sounds, as if I was being ripped apart from within. He grabbed an umbrella from a hotel, pulled me close, and opened it against the snow.

Sirens echoed all across the citadel, and a helicopter shone its light onto a nearby street. Léandre knew his way. He walked me down to the river, into the shadow of another bridge. There was a set of steps beneath it that led straight into the swift-running waters of the Seine. He pulled me down to sit on them, so we could speak without anyone seeing our faces.

"Is Nadine safe?" I asked.

"She's fine. We have to keep moving," he muttered, "but tell me what happened. So I know where to take you."

I shook uncontrollably. Léandre draped his coat around my shoulders, but nothing could keep out the chill in my bones. The chill of shock.

"Paige." He grasped my shoulder. "Is he dead?"

All I could do was stare at the black river. I moved my lips, tried to explain.

"I wish he was," was all I could say. "I wish—"

The tears were silent at first. Then came sharp breaths, then huge, brutal sobs that wrenched my ribs and stemmed from deep in my stomach. Léandre edged an arm around me, and I wept into his coat, so hard I was almost choking. Hideous sounds that racked my whole frame.

The first meeting of our lips. The long nights. The lilt of my own laughter when he danced with me in a derelict hall. He had crafted that music box by hand, each part chosen to reflect me.

"Sorry." I mopped my cheeks, chest heaving. "Sorry, Léandre."

He gave me a last, uncomfortable pat on the head before he backed off, looking relieved.

"Has he changed sides?" he asked me.

I nodded, then shook my head. Hot tears drenched my cheeks. "No. Maybe. I don't think he was ever on my side." I scrunched my hair into my hands. "Fuck. I don't understand."

Léandre delved into his backpack and unscrewed a flask. I accepted it and took a few gulps of brandywine.

"Tell me what happened," he said again. "Be quick."

With effort, I wadded down my panic enough to make room for my breath. "He said he was working for the enemy all along. Spying on us. He's one of my high commanders—" My mind darted ahead. "I have to send someone to London. To warn them. Nadine and Zeke, they could go."

"Do they have papers?"

"No."

Léandre considered.

"The merchants," he said, more to himself than to me. "They'll have a way." He scooped an arm under both of mine and hauled me to my feet. "Come. I will arrange it with them."

"Call Nadine first. Now," I said, "before she gets rid of her burner or goes underground. Tell her to get Ivy and Zeke and meet us somewhere near Gare du Nord." Raw-eyed, I looked across the river. "We have to warn London. Before this destroys everything."

24

Steel Queen

The train left Gare du Nord at ten past nine. Since I had my dissimulator, we risked the Métro, keeping a sharp eye out for night Vigiles. By half past eight, we were in a cookshop opposite the station, waiting for the others. The dissimulator was giving me a headache, and my knee ached where I had bruised it on the roof. It was the only physical reminder of what had happened.

Léandre took a sip of his coffee and observed the other customers, fingers drumming on the table. Now and again, he shot me a disconcerted look and pressed his lips together.

If the blood-consort had already told Nashira everything he knew, soldiers could be descending on the Mime Order at this very moment. I could only hope they were no longer all in one place. That they had returned to the cell-based structure as soon as Senshield had failed. Glym would have done that—he was rigid in his efficiency—but Ivy had told me they were still using the underground shelter.

My hand shook as I lifted my cup of saloop. It took all my restraint to just sit and wait. Stillness was a threat. It let me think. If I faced what had just happened, I would snap, and I had to be as cold as rock for just a little longer. For the syndicate. For the revolution.

At ten to nine, Nadine and Zeke arrived, both ruddy-cheeked with cold, the latter with a backpack on one shoulder. They both squeezed into our booth. Nadine wore a peaked hat at an angle.

"Ivy can't risk coming in here." She moved her fringe out of her eyes. "What happened?"

I wet my lips.

"Léandre," I said, "give us a moment, will you?"

It was the first time I had spoken since the bridge. With a curt nod, Léandre slid out of the booth. "You have five minutes before we need to leave."

He moved to stand by the door. Zeke lowered his scarf.

"I need you to go back to London," I said. "To take a message to the Mime Order. Warden has betrayed the revolution. He knows of three major clairvoyant organizations in Britain. All of them need to be aware of the danger." They exchanged a baffled look. "Léandre has secured a place for you on a train to Inquisitors Cross."

"We don't have papers anymore," Zeke pointed out. "What if there's a spot check?"

"It's a cargo train. Someone will see you onto it. Someone else will meet you on the other side." As I spoke, I glanced at the transmission screen above the serving counter. "This leak is my fault—I should be the one risking the journey—but I need to stay here, to consolidate our alliance with Le Vieux Orphelin. We'll need him in the weeks to come. I trust only the two of you and Ivy to do this for me. To make sure London gets this message."

"How can you be sure Warden betrayed us?" Nadine asked under her breath. "What did he say?"

"Enough."

"No way. You didn't see how he was in Passy. He did not leave your side *once* while you were sick—"

"And you didn't see him today. He was playing a long game, Nadine," I said quietly. "I have to safeguard the syndicate. That is my duty as Underqueen."

Nadine gave her brother a frustrated look. Zeke bit the inside of his cheek.

"Your syndicate thinks we're traitors," he said. "They watched us walk away from your side."

"Eliza will hear you out. Ivy knows the way to her," I said. "Once you find Eliza and Glym, tell them to warn the communities of Edinburgh and Manchester that their hideouts may be compromised. And tell them to move the London voyants to the shadow houses."

Nadine frowned. "What?"

"Glym knows about them," I said. "A few safe havens I kept from the Ranthen. Our voyants will be pressed for space, but they'll be safe."

"You had a contingency plan," Zeke murmured. "In case the Ranthen ever betrayed you."

"Yes."

I reached into my coat and removed a thick brown envelope— the one I had inadvertently carried from the safe house, full of Ranthen money. The blood-consort must have left it in my coat, trying to convince me he was on my side. Buying my trust however he could.

"I know what a risk this is. And I don't expect you to do it for nothing." I slid the envelope across the table. "For your ship home. I presume the smugglers you know are in London."

Nadine took the envelope, feeling its thickness. "You need this," she said. "For the revolution."

"Not that money. I don't want it anymore."

"Come with us," Nadine pressed, voice low. I shook my head. "Dreamer, I lived with you for two years. I can tell you're not in a good place. Come home to London, just for a few weeks."

"Nick would not want us to leave you behind," Zeke agreed. "You shouldn't be here alone."

"I can't go off course at such a crucial moment. Not when I'm so close. And I have the perdues now." I looked back up at them. "There's one more thing. Eliza and Glym need to make it their priority to destroy the Senshield scanners. If Scion ever captures me again, or finds another dreamwalker, they could be reactivated very quickly. Work out a way to get those things off our streets."

"Should we tell the Ranthen?" Zeke looked nauseous at the prospect. "About Warden, I mean."

Terebell. It felt like so long since I had last seen her, even though it had only been a couple of months. I hadn't thought of how she would react when she heard the news.

"Yes," I said.

Léandre returned and leaned into the booth. "Time to go," he said, ignoring the bitter look he got from Zeke. No reconciliation there. "A friend is waiting in the station."

I got up. Léandre reached for his cup, downed the last of his coffee, and shuffled a few notes onto the table.

We crossed the street and walked toward the well-lit building. Gare du Nord was the largest station in Paris, its primary link to the Scion Citadel of London. Ivy waited by an entrance, so bundled up against the snow that she was little more than a dark pair of eyes, recognizable only by her dreamscape. I peeled off my dissimulator and pressed it into her hand.

"Open it and hold it onto your face until it sticks," I said under my breath. "Hurry."

"No," she husked. "Paige, you need it—"

"I can get another one. Take it."

She did as I said. When it was done, she fingered her cheeks and brow with a grimace, her features strained into those of a stranger. It was the only protection I could offer her.

"I know you might not want to go back to the Mime Order," I said, "after everything."

"No," she said. "I want to stay here. Maybe join Le Vieux Orphelin, if he'll let me be a perdue."

"Then as soon as you've seen Eliza and Glym, come straight back. But I need you to bring someone with you."

She raised an eyebrow when I gave her the name, but nodded.

"Okay. If he'll come." She hesitated. "Paige, I'm sorry. That Warden tricked you."

I wanted to tell her it was all right—that I would be fine—but I couldn't. Before I could think of a reply, she embraced me. I wished she could stay, and reminded myself that she would be back soon.

When we parted, Ivy took a deep breath and reached into her back pocket.

"Take this." She handed me a small tool, like a key. "It opens standard Scion manholes. If the Rag and Bone Man hasn't scarpered, he'll be underground and near a voyant district."

"You don't mind us going after him without you?" I asked.

"He's just a puppet. Just a man." Her face was a washed slate. "It's Thuban I want. If it takes me the rest of my life, I swear on the æther, my face will be the last thing he sees in this world."

She spoke with soft conviction. Looking into her eyes, I believed her.

"All right," I said. "Come back soon."

Zeke was next to hug me. Even his coat was cold. "Goodbye, Paige. Thank you," he said. His stubble tickled my cheek. "I really hope we see each other again."

"I don't. For your sake." I patted his back. "Good luck with the journey."

"We'll need it," Nadine said dryly. "Crossing an ocean will be the easiest part of this." She drew me close to her with one arm and spoke against my ear: "Thank you for the money. And Paige, it will get better. It never stops hurting, but it gets easier to carry. I promise."

This time, I could barely even nod in answer.

"We are going to take the fight to the free world. This is our official sign-up to the Mime Order," she continued. "If you ever make it out of this nightmare republic, make sure you find us. My parents live on Anticosti Island. It's beautiful."

"I hope you make it there." I drew back and tried to smile. "Safe travels, Silent Bell."

"À notre prochaine rencontre, Pale Dreamer."

At that moment, a woman stepped out of the station, clad in the winter uniform of a train conductor. She conferred with Léandre and Nadine in swift French before she marched back in.

My friends followed her. Nadine gave me a last, troubled look over her shoulder before she disappeared through the doors, into the glowing warmth of the station.

"You're certain they'll be safe?" I said to Léandre.

"I am certain of nothing. But that contact has never betrayed us," he said, face half-lit, "and since Ivy is disguised, there will be no temptation to turn her in for a bounty. They are as safe as they can be." He opened his stolen umbrella again and pulled me under it. "There are cabs near here. We have to get back to Passy before someone sees your face."

"Warden knows about Passy." My jaw was rattling. "He could already have told Scion."

"For now, we have nowhere else to go." His hold on my shoulder firmed. "Le Vieux Orphelin sent eyes to Rue Montmartre. You were right. The Man in the Iron Mask does hunt there. And now we know where he is hiding."

The thought of a hunt in the dark was almost enough to unhinge me. My boots hit the ground too hard, the impact jolting my knees. The ground felt too close. Everything did.

Paige Mahoney needed sleep. Needed to be alone somewhere. But until the gray market was gone, I had to be Black Moth. I slid a hand into my pocket and traced the cold and molded features of the mask.

When we had played chess, the blood-consort had taught me an unusual tactic called the king walk, or steel king. Generally, a player protected the king at all costs and kept it out of the way, safe from capture. It waited quietly and let other pieces fall in its defense.

But the king had the capacity to fight. It could sit and tremble in the wings, or it could march up the board, straight for the enemy side, and attack. It might even win the game.

I would heed that lesson. I had hidden for too long. Queens could be steel, too.

I walked on.

****

On Rue Montmartre, blue streetlamps glowed through gently falling snow. Four of us had gathered for the hunt. Le Vieux Orphelin walked at my side, Ankou on the other, Léandre just ahead.

I still didn't have the ledger. If it was gone, so, for now, was our proof.

There were manholes here and there, each a potential door. When Ankou touched my elbow and pointed, I followed his line of sight. The façade of the nearest building was more elaborate than those around it, decorated with personifications of Scion values. One of them—Diligence—stretched out a stone arm. From its wrist hung a swatch of threadbare red cloth.

A hand surrounded by crimson silk. A soothsayer had seen a vision of this in London, when I had asked her a question about the Rag and Bone Man. The silk fluttered now, like a flag, a welcome. The hand on that pale arm pointed straight to our right.

We entered the street next to the building. Boarded-up windows and a stained mattress. No one to be seen. You could disappear without a trace into a street like this. When we reached the manhole, I crouched beside it and took out the tool Ivy had given me. Ankou helped me hoist it up.

When the way was open, the four of us stood around it. I clipped the wings that flapped in my stomach. After the carrières—after the flood—this should be nothing.

A ladder took us under Rue Montmartre and onto a bridge. Water rushed beneath it, flushed through by the storm drains, and my breathing deepened.

Blue light leaked in through a vent above us. It only took a moment to spot the ribbon: red silk again, tied around the handle of an otherwise inconspicuous hatch. Léandre crouched and lifted it, revealing a spine of rungs, brittle with rust, that led down into absolute darkness.

Nick had told me once that grief came in waves. The hot denial had come and gone. This next one must be a cold wave, come to numb me. My limbs felt wrapped in layers of lead.

I climbed in first. Into the bones of the old sewer, long since buried by the new. One of the rungs snapped under my boot near the bottom, and I plunged knee-deep into reeking water.

My throat clenched. I took off my mask so I could breathe. With a small cough, I groped in my oilskin for my flashlight and illuminated a large chamber, partly flooded. Seeing a ledge, I waded out of the sump and hoisted myself onto it.

Next, my light revealed a smaller tunnel. There had to be a dry area, somewhere the Rag and Bone Man could keep his captives until they could be transported.

A stench congealed in my throat. Something visceral, rotten. I pressed my sleeve to my nose.

"I can feel a dreamscape." My voice belonged to someone else, someone hollow. "Very faint."

And familiar. I just couldn't think where I had felt it before. Ankou showed me his scanner, which confirmed that there was a single, unmoving person nearby.

We stole into the second tunnel. The Rag and Bone Man seemed to like the spaces between the ribs of citadels—the forsaken corners where dust gathered, almost lost to the world above. He must relish the fact that he alone still used them. Here and there, smeared over the crust of filth on the walls, I glimpsed a reddish spray that could only be blood.

My fear calcified into a sense of purpose. For months, I had craved this confrontation, and now, at last, I was close. I walked out of the tunnel and switched on my flashlight.

And there he was. On the floor, a dark lake was congealing around him.

There was his travel-stained greatcoat. There was the sinister helmet that magnified his labored breaths. Gauntlets covered his hands, which were holding in slick pink snakes of intestine.

Le Vieux Orphelin waded to a stop beside me. "We are too late to deliver justice," he said.

"No," I said. "He's alive."

I knelt beside the Rag and Bone Man, the specter who had haunted me since my escape from the colony. He reeked of shit and gore. With gloved hands, I unfastened the bolts that closed the helmet and lifted it from his head. And I shone my flashlight on his face—a face I knew.

Thin gray hair, slimy with sweat. A crooked mouth, meant for smiles, peeled back over bloodstained teeth. Purses of puffy skin under his eyes, which were glazed in the agony of a slow death.

Le Vieux Orphelin crouched on the other side of him. "Do you know this man, Underqueen?"

"His name is Alfred." I set down the helmet. "An old friend of the Grand Overseer."

Alfred from the Spiritus Club, who had helped me publish a pamphlet to warn voyants about the threat of the Rephaim. Jolly, apple-cheeked Alfred, who used books to touch the æther, who kept a tin of cookies in his office and thought reading was a miracle.

He was among the last people in the world I had expected to see behind that mask.

Alfred finally noticed me. The gaze I had once thought kind was now cold and greedy.

"Hello, dear heart," he rasped. I had to lean close to hear him, close enough to smell his foul breath. "I would bow if I could."

I was already hollowed out from one betrayal. There was no more heat in me for anger.

"You never did tell me your surname when we met. I think I know now," I said. "Rackham. Alfred Rackham."

Alfred ground out a chuckle. "So," he said, "s-someone let my name slip. I was not as careful as I should have been when we first began our trade." Red bubbled at the seam of his lips. "Alfred Hayhurst Rackham, founding member of the gray market."

Alfred.

The hawk-eyed scout who had plucked an impoverished Jaxon Hall from a garret and shown his words to the citadel. Who had profited from the bloodshed *On the Merits of Unnaturalness* had left in its wake. Who had stitched a monster into being. He had seemed harmless, with his passion for good literature and his quaint little office.

He and Jaxon had known each other since before the latter had been taken to Sheol I. Since before he was even called Jaxon Hall. It was because of the pamphlet they had published together that Jaxon had been arrested in the first place. On his return, he must have gone straight to his old friend—his redeemer—to tell him the secret behind Scion.

And so the two of them had decided to branch into a new line of business. To take advantage of the knowledge Jaxon had attained.

How blind I had been.

"It was you who edited *The Rephaite Revelation*," I finally said. "You made it glorify the Sargas."

"Too easy. All of it was too easy. N-no one would suspect a fusty old fellow with a penchant for poetry and cake." A damp wheeze of laughter escaped him. "Be grateful I only hindered you, Paige. I did try to have you removed from the game altogether, if you recall."

The bag over my head. A saw-toothed blade.

"Jaxon had Hector and his entire gang slaughtered for selling me to Scion," I said. "You were very brave to try killing me after that."

"Oh, he was most upset when he found out. Threatened to spatchcock me if I touched a hair on your head again." His eyes were unfocused. "He always . . . keeps his promises. In the end."

That was when I looked down, at the wreath of flowers on his chest, like the ones sold at the black market, intended to be read counter-clockwise. I picked it up. One by one, I decoded the flowers.

White puffs of bittercress: *paternal error*. Monkshood, purple and poisonous: *treachery*. Fragrant bay leaves with golden blooms: *I change but in death*. Barberry, like drops of blood: *sourness of temper*.

And last, white clover: *think of me*. A sign-off as mocking as it was tender.

"The Grand Overseer is alive."

The tunnel echoed my words. I thought of the man Nadine had mentioned, the silver-haired binder who had carried me away from the flood. When I tried to remember the period between that desperate swim and waking up in Passy, there was only white.

And I wondered. I wondered whether Jaxon, who had worked in the same building as Scarlett Burnish—a spy for Domino—could have somehow got his hands on a dissimulator. Whether he could have worn it to escape the burning Château de Versailles, tacked himself to our group as we left, and dented my memory with white aster when I put two and two together.

Even as I thought it, I sensed truth. I had told him I was onto the Rag and Bone Man. He had been confident enough in my talent to be sure that I would find this place, this wreath.

Paternal error. He had made a mistake by trusting Alfred. Jaxon Hall had lost his temper at last, and this was the consequence. It was also his apology. He had ended Alfred—just as he had ended Hector, except this time he had done it himself. He had carved his old friend like a leg of lamb.

If I didn't care about you, Paige, would I have butchered nine people for you?

Please don't try to impress me with that again. I closed my eyes. *You didn't even bother to butcher them yourself.*

"How could he have survived?" Le Vieux Orphelin wondered aloud. "He did not escape with us."

"I think he did. With a new face."

"The man who saved you."

"I think he gave me white aster." I touched my temple. "But he made sure to tie up the final loose end of the gray market." With the wreath still in my hand, I looked back at Alfred. "It's over."

I should let him bleed out. Deny him the threnody. Leave him to scream in the æther forever. A peddler of flesh deserved no better than this agonising death, this grave.

Except Jaxon had killed him for me, as a gift. And I did not want anyone to die like this in my name. Not even him.

I prepared to do it with my spirit. It would be clean and digni-fied. Then a broad hand came down on my shoulder, and I raised my head to see Ankou, who held out his sickle.

"An Ànkou, in Breton myth, is the reaper of souls," Le Vieux Orphelin said. "This soul should be yours, Underqueen. Let him begin his own Empire of Death."

The blade was a dark grin of steel. Ankou gave me a grim nod, his mouth a line. Slowly, I took the sickle.

Alfred no longer seemed able to speak. Blood seeped between his knuckles where he held his guts in. His gaze darted to the sickle, then my face.

He had harvested us for the season of bones. Even he knew this was justice.

If I'd had the silver pill, I might have given it to him—but I would not use my gift to take his life. That was one mercy I was not prepared to offer this time. Paige Mahoney had shown mercy too often for her own good. Black Moth was someone else. Someone to fear.

420

I placed her mask back over my face.

"Alfred Hayhurst Rackham," I said softly, "be gone into the æther. All is settled. All debts are paid." I rested the blade of the sickle on his throat. "You need not dwell among the living now."

****

The smell of blood clung to my clothes as I climbed the ladder back to the surface. Once everyone was through, Le Vieux Orphelin closed the manhole behind us, leaving the Rag and Bone Man to rot in his reeking tomb.

In a hundred years, someone might find his skeleton and the rusted sickle and wonder what had befallen him, this nameless corpse at the bottom of the citadel, this man with an iron mask beside him. Until then, he would be forgotten.

I could think of no more fitting end.

25

The Winged Victory

I lay on an unfamiliar bed, iron-cold and silent. Outside, the sun had dipped below the rooftops. I slept in the day now, and rose at night, as I had in the colony. Darkness made everything softer.

Rue Vernet was quiet this evening. I stared at the wall, my arm half-numb under my head.

Tomorrow night, I would join the perdues on the Île des Cygnes—one of the natural islands of the Seine—to await the arrival of Le Latronpuche and La Reine des Thunes. Léandre had forged them a summons from the Rag and Bone Man, sealed with a wax stamp we had taken from the corpse, which showed the skeletal hand. Mélusine had ensured it was delivered.

Unbeknownst to them, Le Vieux Orphelin would be waiting, with the patrones gathered as witnesses, to accuse them of all their crimes. If the syndicate accepted the evidence and ousted Le Latronpuche and La Reine des Thunes, I would step from the shadows and announce the alliance between the syndicates of London and Paris. I would show the world I was alive.

Except that I didn't feel alive. Not fully. Part of me had been swallowed into that hall of stained-glass windows, entombed there like a queen of old.

The part of me that could never have drawn a blade across a human throat. The part of me that would have flinched.

Now I felt nothing. Just as I had felt nothing when I washed the blood off my hands and face and neck. It had been a mercy kill, yet there had been no mercy in my hand. Only resolve.

Distantly, I knew I needed to get up. Wash, eat, pull myself together. The most I had moved since noon was to turn from my side to my back to my other side.

When I slept, it was in jolts. Often I stirred, thinking there was an arm around my waist, somebody there. Then I would remember, and the sharpness of it would pierce me again. For the first time in weeks, I craved the drug they had forced into me in the Archon, the one I had sweated out in the safe house. Anything to eclipse the harsh light of reality.

It was almost dark by the time I got up and faltered down the corridor, to the kitchen. I needed to turn on the heat. I could do that. Once I had found the right switch, I took a jug of lemon barley from the fridge, poured a little into a glass, and drank until I coughed.

Just before the fridge thumped shut, I glimpsed a coffee press on the counter. And suddenly I was on the other side of the Seine, and there was Arcturus, in the amber sunlight, handing me a steaming mug. Though my lips clamped together, they trembled. I wanted to shatter the coffee press. I wanted to buckle. That memory was a lie. All of it had been part of his act.

I had wondered what the æther had been trying to tell me when Liss read my cards. If Arcturus Mesarthim was meant to be my lover or my downfall. Now I knew. He was the Devil.

My breath shook. Heat suddenly leaked down my cheeks; I brushed them roughly with my sleeve. Every time I thought I had turned myself to ice, something opened the cracks again.

Since I had run from him, the golden cord had been so still that I could no longer feel it. A small mercy. If I couldn't feel him, perhaps he could no longer feel me. Or find me. I would still have to abandon this place soon, just in case. I could never stay in one hideout for long. I would have to be rootless for the rest of my life.

I looked hard at the ceiling. When I could draw a steady breath, I returned to the room and the rumpled bed. I had to sleep, had to think clearly for tomorrow. As I turned onto my back, I remembered another bed. The warmth of him beside me, around me.

It was the only thing I didn't understand. Why he had allowed himself to fall so far into flesh-treachery. He must have reasoned that the more I opened my heart to him, the deeper he could drive the knife.

He had been right. Even now I knew the truth, the memory of that night made me ache for his touch again. He was a poltergeist, haunting me from wherever he was now, and his phantom hands still held me close, held me prisoner. I slid into a drowse, my cheek pressed into a cushion.

It was a long time before I heard the door. A figure entered my den and switched on a lamp.

"Flora."

My eyelids scraped apart. Ducos was sitting on the bed, one eyebrow arched.

"You had better not be drunk again." She gave me a sharp tap on the cheek. "What is the matter with you?"

"Fine," I rasped.

"Yes, you look it." Before I could object, she hoisted me into a sitting position. Knotted curls fell over my brow. "You need a shower. And a comb. And a clean shirt. When was the last time you ate?"

"Not sure." The skin under my eyes was raw. "What day is it?"

"Tuesday. The twenty-fourth." She felt my cheeks, my forehead. "Out with it, then."

She needed to know. "My auxiliary," I said. "He went to Scion. You and Stéphane should find new aliases."

"Are you saying he has double-crossed you?"

I managed a small nod. "I don't know how much he might have told them."

Ducos kept her cool, but I could almost hear the gearwheels of her mind at work.

"I did not expect this." She took something from the floor. "I found this behind the safe house in Rue Gît-le-Cœur. I assumed your auxiliary or Cordier had thrown it outside to keep it from Scion."

My backpack. With leaden arms, I reached for it, then carefully undid the zip. Inside was everything I owned, including the ledger.

"He can't have," I said, too softly for her to hear.

Ducos moved to sit in a nearby chair. A belt rode high on her waist, and her trousers were turned up to show off heeled leather boots. I had never felt like more of a mess.

"You had feelings for him," she said. I was silent. "It happens. In this line of work, we walk on the edge of a knife. If he softened that edge for you, you should not blame yourself. We have all trusted the wrong people at one point or another. Cordier, in particular, always looked for someone to dull the blade." She breathed out. "She is gone. There was blood near the safe house, so we must presume her dead or captured. As for Stéphane, I have sent them to sub-network Figurine. This may be the end of Mannequin."

Out came her silver case. She picked one of her trim cigarettes from it.

"I wondered who betrayed us," she said. "Perhaps it was your auxiliary, after all. Or someone else." She lit the cigarette with a snap. "For now, I will hold the fort alone. My work is important, and I have not spent thirteen years in Scion to give up now. We can rebuild."

"Alone." I managed a tired smile. "I'm out, then."

"Yes," she said flatly. "You burned down a seventeenth-century palace. You are out."

"Oh, that. I almost forgot."

"Command agreed with my conclusion that you are not well-suited to the role of intelligence officer. You are too personally invested in the fight against Scion. Consequently, your access to our safe houses, identification documents, dissimulators, and other provisions have all been revoked, effective tomorrow. I trust you have somewhere else to go."

"Yes."

The numbness absorbed her words. I might have cared, if things had been different. Now it was just another loss.

"Command also agreed with me," Ducos said, softer, "that the Mime Order has great potential. As do you." She blew smoke through pursed lips. "You cannot do my job, Paige. It is not your calling. But you can be a valued associate of an intelligence network. We have contacts who are not intelligence officers, people who could provide Domino with vital assistance in the years to come. I convinced my superiors that you could be one of them."

I watched her, not quite daring to believe it.

"You will not be dosed with white aster," she went on, "and if you can provide me with proof that your organization is ready to fight, you will receive financial support. You will still be attached to the Domino Program. We can work together." She looked me in the eye. "This is the best outcome."

We had another source of coin outside the syndicate. We could be more than just a rabble of thieves.

We could still beat Scion.

"I know a way to prove our organization is more than ready," I said. "Meet us on the Île des Cygnes tomorrow, just before midnight."

"Given your track record, I will come armed." Ducos rested her cigarette on the nightstand and dug back into her coat. "I am going to break the rules and give you something. Because I like you, Paige, in spite of the headaches you have given me."

She held out a sealed tube. I took the dissimulator.

"Do not lose it," she said, "because that is the last one you will ever get."

"Ducos," I said, "thank you. Foreverything."

"Don't thank me. Just . . . shower."

She took the dossier from my backpack, then retrieved her cigarette and left without a backward glance. I sat where I was for a long time, holding my stippled arms.

Somehow, I did as she asked. I rose and stepped into the bathroom, where I confronted my own face in the mirror. Ashen and blotchy, eyes bloodshot, hair clumped in knots, the dye faded. My mask leaned against the mirror. Slowly, I drew a thumb across its features, hard and inert, cold to the touch. I turned away from its empty stare and pulled off my nightshirt.

I shivered under the shower for a while. When I emerged, I dried off and returned to the bedroom, my hair dripping. I tucked it into a woolen hat before slinging on a coat and boots, picking up the backpack, and unlocking the doors to the balcony. I got one heel onto the balustrade and used it to reach a ledge above, and from there, I clambered onto the roof.

The illuminated Arc de Triomphe sent a fire-like glow into the sky. Traffic beeped and roared. I sat down and opened the backpack, taking out the only objects I had left to my name. The leather-bound ledger, my inheritance from my father, and the songbird box, exquisite and delicate. It was a miracle it had survived being thrown from a window.

My fingers curled around it. Before I could second-guess myself, I held it over the edge of the roof.

All I had to do was loosen my grip. The music box would shatter on the pavement below, the song inside forever silenced. There would be nothing left—nothing concrete—of his connection to me.

"Slán," I whispered.

My ribs seemed to constrict. Instead of loosening, my fingers tightened. My weakness struck again. Even if this box was part of the lie he had spun for me, it was the most beautiful thing I had ever owned. With an unsteady intake of breath, I pressed it to my heart.

It was him. All I had left of the person I thought he had been, the person I had believed would be at my side for years to come. It was a castle in the sky. Breathing in stabs of white fog, I shoved it all the way to the bottom of my backpack and crammed the ledger on top of it. Smashing it would be a waste. I could at least find an antiques dealer to take it off my hands.

All that remained was the gift from my father. I took the penknife from the front pocket of my backpack and dug its blade under the lid. When it broke, I allowed myself to wait for a moment—only one—before I cracked it open and tilted the lid up. Its hinges were stiff.

Inside, cushioned by dark velvet, lay a folded leaf of paper. With care, I opened it. The handwriting was familiar.

It just wasn't my father's.

I was curious to see if dear, dull Daddy left you anything in his will. And, lo and behold, he did. Sitting pretty in the Bank of England.

I'll be waiting for you, darling. Come and see, Pale Dreamer. Come and see.

Wind stripped flurries of snow from the rooftop. I sat there, staring at the words, until the paper came apart between my hands and the two pieces fluttered into the night.

When I returned indoors, I went straight back to the bathroom. I took the ceramic face and held it up to my own. And I watched Paige Mahoney—all her fears, all her sorrow, all her rage, and all her weakness—disappear behind dark wings. Instead, someone else stared back.

Black Moth.

****

The Île des Cygnes lay right in the shadow of the Eiffel Tower. Separated from the quay by a thin collar of water, the tiny island was home to nothing but storehouses awaiting demolition. A bridge had once tethered it to the riverbank, then a foot tunnel, which had been closed to the public for years. Fortunately, Le Vieux Orphelin had a key to the entrance.

The Eiffel Tower glowed like something newly forged. As I walked, I didn't let myself recall how I had felt when I had last seen it. Someone else had felt that anticipation and newness and resolve—the woman underneath the mask.

The perdues were waiting at the rusted gate to the tunnel. We pulled it shut behind us and strode between graffiti-coated walls, Ankou lighting our way with a signal lantern. Léandre met us on the other side.

"Le Vieux Orphelin is already here. So are the patrones," he said. We followed him up a slight incline. "Underqueen, for the time being, stay out of sight. You are our trump card."

"Did you meet my contact?" I asked him.

"Yes. I made sure no one cut her throat."

He led us through a thicket, into a stone-paved area surrounded by dilapidated buildings, where a figure waited. While the face was new, the dreamscape belonged to Ducos.

She tensed at our approach, one hand in her pocket. "It's me," I said to her, stepping forward while the others walked on. "Glad you made it."

"The feeling is mutual. I was beginning to wonder if you had decided to stay in bed." Ducos relaxed a little. "I am no longer your supervisor, so I know you are not obliged to answer this question, but why on earth have you chosen to wear a mask representing a notorious fugitive?"

"Just a touch of theatre." I nodded to the nearest derelict. "There are a lot of anormales in there. Don't draw attention to yourself."

"Must I remind you that not drawing attention to myself is the essence of my occupation?"

"No amount of training is going to make you look clairvoyant to people who really are."

"And what happens if they notice?" she asked, impassive. "A mob hangs me from a lamppost?" She considered the nearest derelict. "Or something bloodier, perhaps. That building used to be an abattoir."

A bleeding grin around a neck. A flood of metallic darkness over my fingers, soaking my clothes.

"Just keep your head down," I said.

Léandre waited for us to catch up. He led us through the doors of the largest building, where Le Vieux Orphelin waited in the gloom, hands clasped behind his back. He was dressed in a crimson-and-gold doublet, cinched with a silver belt, and dark trousers tucked into boots.

"This must be your amaurotic companion." Le Vieux Orphelin inclined his head. "Madelle."

Ducos eyed him, taking in the mask, the clothes. "Yes," was her only reply.

Le Vieux Orphelin walked on, beckoning me alone to his side. I smelled dust and abandonment.

"Were you able to recover the ledger?" he asked. I handed it over. "Thank you, Paige. This is a priceless gift."

"Only if he revealed his real name to anyone," I reminded him. "But I might be able to help with that, if it comes to it."

He slowed his pace to turn the pages. When he saw his own name—his real name—his hold on the ledger tightened. "Let us hope the patrones listen." He shut it. "I will call you forward at a timely moment."

"We need to be quick." I closed my eyes before I spoke. "Arct—Warden can trace me in the æther. He hasn't come after me so far, but I think it's only a matter of time. I can risk staying for about half an hour, ideally less, before I need to get moving again. To throw him off the scent."

"Trace you?" The gold mask turned in my direction. "How is such a connection possible?"

"I wish I knew."

Le Vieux Orphelin withdrew into a short-lived silence. "I will be concise," he said. "As soon as the alliance is ratified, Léandre will take you back to Passy, if you would be willing to spend a night with us. I would like to return to the subject of Georges Benoît Ménard."

"Of course." I swallowed my pride. "In truth, I'd be grateful for a bed. I just lost the place I was staying in."

"You are always welcome with us."

Voices resounded nearby. Ahead, two rusted doors were drawn apart for us, and we stepped into a dark and sonorous hall, which years of neglect had distorted into a bizarre dreamscape. Thick pipes swam in and out of the walls. A concrete staircase ended in midair. Rubble had formed a cairn beneath a vast hole in the roof. Past the haze of ochre light from the tower, the night was clear. The ceiling was a yawning mouth that rattled with a thousand stars.

At least a hundred voyants had gathered, their puffs of breath drifting up to the rafters. These must be the patrones and other influential members of the syndicate, along with well-chosen witnesses.

Le Latronpuche and La Reine des Thunes had not yet arrived.

"Ignace," I said quietly, and sensed him turn. "When did you decide to put the mask on for good?"

After a pause, he answered. "When there was too much inside me that I could no longer hide."

I was grateful, then, for the frozen lips of my own mask. They covered the tremor in mine.

Ducos came to my side. I melted into the back of the crowd with her, while Le Vieux Orphelin ascended a creaking set of stairs and stepped onto a platform, where everyone could see him. Léandre stood behind him.

"Friends," Le Vieux Orphelin called, "good evening. It has been some time since I last set foot on this island."

Absolute silence descended on the hall.

"How good it is to see you again," he said. "How long it has been since we gathered like this. We grands ducs spend much of our time among the bones, concealed from Scion. Not all of you can afford to hide with us in the dark. You have mouths to feed. You have coin to earn, often in the face of extraordinary danger. Or perhaps you wish to live in the sun. Not the shadows."

Every face was raised, every gaze intent.

"We, your leaders, may seem complacent and distant to you. You may even have asked yourselves if we notice the hardships of life in the Republic of Scion France. My friends, I have noticed. I have seen. I have walked among you as often as I can, and I have witnessed the need for justice. Since I was a child, I have fought back against our enemy. And I have waited for the opportune moment to turn that fight into a war." He paced his stage. "I have summoned you here to what I believe will be the cradle of that war."

Mutters.

"First, however, it falls to me to turn the knife inward. Though it hurts me, I must reveal the enemy within. Only then can we turn to those who threaten us without," Le Vieux Orphelin said. "Four years ago, you elected me one of your grands ducs, and I vowed that I would never leave Paris; that I would never abandon the anormaux of this citadel. I vowed that I would always work for their good, for their betterment—and to do that, I had to live alongside them." His forefinger snapped up. "This year, I was forced to break that vow."

"What is he talking about?" someone whispered near me.

"He has gone mad."

From her expression, Ducos agreed. Nonetheless, she was listening.

"I have seen many wrongs in my time in Paris. But never had I thought that it was possible for this family—*our* family—to turn against itself," Le Vieux Orphelin went on. "For several long weeks, I was a prisoner of Scion." The whispers turned to mutters. "Because I was betrayed. Betrayed by the very people who swore to protect you from the anchor. Instead, they sacrificed you to it."

He had their attention. Fortunate, because a cluster of dreamscapes was approaching, two of them familiar.

"Tonight, I would like you to help me bring them to justice," Le Vieux Orphelin said, "by bearing witness to a trial." He looked toward the doors and raised a gloved hand. "Bring them in."

Two voyants heaved the doors open again. Beside me, Ducos drew in a long breath.

"Is this likely to end in bloodshed?" she said to me in an undertone.

I watched the doors. "Not if they accept the charges."

Footsteps broke the tense silence. Several flashlightes flicked toward the doors just as Le Latronpuche stepped through them.

His wig was tied back with ribbon and covered by a buckled hat, and a fur-lined cape swept from his shoulders. Beside him, La Reine des Thunes had abandoned her musty gown in favor of a frock coat. Eight armed voyants flanked them.

At the sight of the vast gathering, both of them stopped dead. Some of their voyants reached for their weapons, only for La Reine des Thunes to still them with a small motion.

"Beloved siblings-in-chaos," Le Vieux Orphelin greeted, his tone pleasant. "Welcome."

"How did—" Le Latronpuche stared up at him, open-mouthed, a startled trout. A moment later, he slapped a smile over his disbelief. "My dear brother! What a great relief to see you alive."

"Indeed," La Reine des Thunes agreed, clearly just as stricken. "An immense relief." Even in this gloom, her diamonds glistened. "We . . . feared we would never see you again."

"Doubtless," Le Vieux Orphelin agreed. The doors squeaked closed, and a voyant secured them. "I am so glad you could both accept my invitation to this little gathering." Pause. "Or were you under the impression that you were meeting someone else tonight?"

La Reine des Thunes said nothing more. One of her hands strayed toward the pocket of her coat.

"You have heard of the Man in the Iron Mask, the spectre of the slums," Le Vieux Orphelin said to his audience. "Some of you may have lost friends and family to him. I tell you now that Le Latronpuche struck a bargain with this monster. I was a victim of that bargain, as were eight others. Paul Caron, whose songs brought joy to our darkest streets, who leaves behind a spouse and child. His crime was to sing a ballad that mocked Le Latronpuche.

"Sylvie Lambriquet, the most gifted pickpocket in Grenelle, who dared to sell her prizes without paying tax to the grands ducs. Simon Cleutin, who insulted Le Latronpuche by asking him for a little coin to save his family from starvation." The muttering again, like a kicked hive. "How gravely he suffered for that mistake. He was a burden, you see. They were betrayed, sold, and left to the mercy of Scion, while Le Latronpuche pocketed a handsome fee."

"This is absurd. The ravings of a power-hungry fool," Le Latronpuche snapped. "What is this—a court of piepowders, to try us on the spur of the moment?" He raised his voice. "Treachery and avarice. I have maintained for years that he wants Le Nouveau Régime for himself, and here is the proof!"

The crowd rippled. Le Latronpuche took a bold step forward.

"Have you any evidence of this so-called bargain, Ignace," he demanded, "or is that another secret you hide behind that mask?"

"I thank you for asking that question, mon frère," Le Vieux Orphelin said. "Rest assured, I have evidence to prove your corruption. A ledger that belonged to the Man in the Iron Mask."

He held up the object in question. Every gaze was pinned to him as he opened it and skimmed a finger down the page.

"There is my name," he said softly. "And the names of our lost friends, all anormaux who have not been seen since the listed dates. Their sponsor—the person who betrayed them—is listed as one P. Waite." He showed it to them all. "This is your true name. Is it not?"

"I deny it." Le Latronpuche mustered a grin. "You would make a poor lawyer, Ignace, to bring nothing but ink to a trial—ink from a pen that could have been yours. In fact, if that ledger does belong to the Man in the Iron Mask, one might wonder how you obtained it.

Are *you* in league with him?" He whirled to face the witnesses. "Are there no others who can verify your story, give credence to your forged document? Anyone *not* from your own pack of sycophants?"

"I can."

Every head turned. It took me a moment to realize that the voice that had broken the silence was mine.

"Hello again, Latronpuche." I moved toward him, parting the crowd. "I know I promised I wouldn't interfere. As it turns out, we can both lie between our teeth."

When I was close enough for him to see me in the dimness, I removed the mask. At once, the mutters turned to high-strung chatter. I walked past Le Latronpuche and joined Le Vieux Orphelin on the platform.

"Anormales of Paris," I said to them, "I am Paige Mahoney, Black Moth, Underqueen of the Scion Citadel of London. With his brave perdues at my side, I retrieved Le Vieux Orphelin from the clutches of Scion, and from its masters, the Rephaim. And I hereby accuse Le Latronpuche of treason, of collusion with the anchor, and of human trafficking."

Le Latronpuche appeared to have frozen in place. His gaze darted from one face to another, drinking in the reactions to my appearance. He conjured another of his smiles and stepped toward me.

"Underqueen," he said in a honeyed tone, "this is a terrible misunderstanding. Of course, as I said when we last met, you are most welcome in Paris—"

"The Underqueen was alive, and you knew?" an augur shouted. "For how long?"

"Did you plan to sell her, too?"

"—but," Le Latronpuche shouted over the din, "whatever you believe you saw, whatever lies Le Vieux Orphelin has told you, it had nothing to do with me." His voice hardened. "There is no evidence that I have ever conspired with Scion."

Our gazes locked. The slippery bastard was right.

That was when the æther rang. For the first time in days, a smile pulled at the corners of my mouth.

"Actually," I said, "I have a witness. A witness who would be deemed credible in any court of law, be it voyant or amaurotic. Someone who knows you better than anyone." While Le Latronpuche looked baffled, I motioned to the voyants at the back of the hall. "Open the doors."

They obeyed. Not half a minute later, a lone figure in a tailcoat marched inside, his wig aquiver.

Last I had seen him, he had been pounding a street with his fists as his auction house burned to the ground. Jaxon had always dismissed him as an incompetent fool. He might be a terrible binder and an even worse poet, but I had never been more pleased to clap eyes on anyone.

"Oh, for the love of Nostredame and the fear of Hades," Le Latronpuche said wearily. "Please. Not like this."

"Mister Waite, welcome to Paris," I called across the hall. "Thank you for answering my urgent summons."

"You are very welcome, Underqueen." Didion was ruddy-cheeked, panting as if he had run all the way from London. "Any question I can answer, any service I can provide, it would be my pleasure and my privilege." He spoke at great speed in French. "Ask, and I shall deliver."

Ivy slipped into the hall behind him. She gave me the smallest nod.

"Thank you," I said, with a smile at Didion. "First, would you be so kind as to introduce yourself?"

"Friends, I am Didion Waite," he declared, in his element at last. "Binder, auctioneer, curator of rare spirits, and renowned author of illicit literature, including *Bring Forth the Smelling Sa—*"

"Thank you, Mister Waite," I cut in, before he could list all one hundred and forty-seven of his published works. "I only have two questions, if you'd be so kind." I pointed at Le Latronpuche. "Who is this man?"

"His name," Didion said, almost slavering in triumph, "is Pantaléon Waite." He took his time over each syllable. Le Latronpuche looked as if he had just aged twenty years. "It was given to him by our late mother. You see, Underqueen, this man is my elder brother."

"Half brother ," Le Latronpuche said under his breath.

"Thank you again, Mister Waite," I said. "And may I confirm that this"—I took the ledger from Le Vieux Orphelin—'is his signature, to the best of your knowledge?"

Didion came up the steps to accept it. In the silence that followed, not a single breath was drawn.

"Oh, yes." He snapped it closed. "Pantaléon published several works of his own in London," he added, with a sly look at Le Latronpuche. "I took the liberty of bringing some of his many *rejected* manuscripts with me, written in his own hand. Perhaps you would like to compare them."

"You truly have thought of everything," I said. "Thank you kindly, Mister Waite."

He bowed to me with a flourish and stepped back. Le Latronpuche gritted his gray teeth.

"Have you anything to say?" I asked him.

"I do not, Underqueen. I am going," he said, lip curled, "but I will not brook this miscarriage of justice. You shall hear from me again in due course. Mark my words, there will be—"

"Yes. You are going, Latronpuche," I said, toneless. I fitted the mask back over my features. "Into a cell. A very small one. For quite some time."

I gave no order. And yet thirty-odd voyants moved, half of them blocking the door and the others coming up behind him. Le Latronpuche shouted in incoherent rage while his own voyants towed and shoved him toward another room, there to await a stronger prison. La Reine des Thunes hovered in nervous silence.

"Douceline," Le Vieux Orphelin said. She flinched. "I know you were a part of this, but since I have no evidence against you, I cannot banish you. Join us, and you may find a path to forgiveness."

La Reine des Thunes barely hesitated before she removed the diamonds from her ears and the pearls from her neck.

"You gave these to me, mon frère." She pressed them on him with trembling hands. "Sell them. For the revolution. Everything I have, I offer to the revolution."

Le Vieux Orphelin beheld the diamonds. They were priceless contraband, representing more provisions and weapons than I could imagine.

"As do we," he said. "The Underqueen and myself."

All eyes turned to me again. I remembered standing in front of another syndicate, soaked in blood, with a crown twisted from numa on my head.

"I was no one," I said. "Just a child in Ireland when Scion came. When I almost lost my life to their violence. When I saw hundreds die." I spoke louder: "I was nineteen when they came again. When they took my name. When they tried to warp me into their weapon. That day, I resolved that I would not rest until no one in this world lives in the shadow of the anchor. Until clairvoyants can live wherever they choose, without fear and without shame."

Watched by them all, I walked to Le Vieux Orphelin. At the back of the room, I glimpsed Ducos.

"I have found a like-minded leader here in Paris. Together, we pose a far greater threat to Scion, and to their benefactors, the Rephaim. It is time to choose a side," I stated, "because war is coming. And there can be no middle ground against enemies like these."

"From this day forth, if you stand with us, Le Nouveau Régime and the Mime Order will be one army," Le Vieux Orphelin called. "By your grace, my friends, we will unite our two syndicates. Let us bridge the sea. At the dawn of this new decade, let us teach the anchor what it is to be afraid."

For a long time, there was silence. I took in their faces, waiting, my nerves tuned to every subtle change in their expressions.

Then someone took a step forward. Katell, the woman who had opened this syndicate for me, her baby in a sling. She crossed her thumbs, pressed her fingers together, and fanned them outward, so they looked for all the world like wings.

Then came a muster of raised voices, and hands lifted, and then there were fifty of them, a hundred, more. An eclipse of moths—a storm, an army, soaring from the depths of night.

****

437

In the end, after everything, the coup had been bloodless. A far quieter victory than the scrimmage in London. I had never expected Didion Waite to be the key—but if there was one thing I had learned in the last year, it was that in a puppet empire, everyone had their role to play.

Le Latronpuche might swing from the old gibbet at Île Louviers, or be handed over to the Vigiles, or granted a second chance. I would have no part in that decision. I had not come here to rule. Le Vieux Orphelin would see to his people, and I would see to mine. But we would lead them with a common goal.

The gray market was gone. So was Sheol II. Domino would collaborate with the Mime Order. It was more than I could ever have asked from my time in this citadel, where my father had promised we would go one day.

Never had victory felt so cold.

The patrones disappeared back into the citadel. Soon, only a few of us remained on the island. Still wearing her dissimulator, Ducos stood at the riverbank, where I joined her, and together we drank in the immensity of the tower that speared high above us, into a hood of cloud.

"There is a transmission station at the top of it," she said. "For emergency broadcasts." Fog unfurled from her lips. "There have been rumblings from my contacts in the network."

"What kind of rumblings?"

"Something to do with the fall of Spain." Her gaze was distant. "They never tell us very much. Not even supervisors. But the execution of a royal family, thinly concealed though it was . . . it has caused ripples. Scion may have gone too far this time."

"They went *too far* when they marched on Dublin," I said. "Our Taoiseach called for aid. No one ever came."

We stood side-by-side for a long while. Ducos reached into her coat and handed me a phone.

"Keep this close. I'll call you," she said. "Until then, Paige, don't get yourself killed." A breeze teased her short hair across her face as she turned to face me and placed a hand on my shoulder. "Mannequin thanks you for your service. As does the Domino Program."

She walked until the darkness of the tunnel swallowed her. I gazed at the Eiffel Tower for a long time after she was gone, until footsteps broke my trance and Le Vieux Orphelin took her place.

"To Passy, then, Underqueen?"

It was a moment before I answered.

"Yes." My voice sounded distant. "Throughout all of this—every step we have taken to get here—we've just been sowing the seeds. Now our pieces stand ready. So does the enemy. It's time we tear open this war." I looked at him. "And I think I know where we need to start."

26

All the Devils

MARCH 7, 2060

The Grande Salle de Paris had never looked finer than it did tonight. A spectacular light show played across its façade. Guests from all over the Republic of Scion France were arriving in white limousines in front of the cathedral, all dressed in their best and wearing elaborate masks.

In the distance, red fireworks erupted. Across the citadel, revellers were out in force, drunk on the glory of the double conquest of Spain and Portugal.

Effigies swung from wrought-iron streetlamps. On a corner, a crowd launched another one onto a bonfire. It had straw for hair and wore a crown, and a sign was tied around its neck.

ÇA IRA, ÇA IRA, ÇA IRA
LES MONARQUES À LA LANTERNE

The execution of the King of Spain had ended all formal resistance. For trying to help a monarch escape, Pilar Brugués Olivencia had been stripped of her power and imprisoned. In Portugal, the

Scion Citadel of Lisbon had been formally named. Madrid would be next.

The Republic of Scion held eleven countries. For all intents and purposes, and with the exception of any last-ditch rebellions, it had won total control of the Iberian Peninsula. From the tip of Scotland to the south of Spain, the anchor now presented an unbroken front to its enemies.

On the other side of the empire were its territories on the Balkan Peninsula, as well as Cyprus. Sweden loomed to the north. Slowly but surely, Scion was enclosing the remaining free countries of Europe.

Eleven would not be enough for its masters. The entire world now lay in the shadow of the anchor.

A blast of wind brought me back to the present. I was with Le Vieux Orphelin on the dimly lit Quai des Orfèvres, and his arm was linked through mine, sure and sturdy. He wore a cream doublet, its sleeves woven with gold thread, the cuffs long enough to cover his knuckles. Léandre walked a short way behind. His half mask was silver, cast in the likeness of a lion.

I had not been back to the Île de la Citadelle since the night the blood-consort betrayed me. Knowing he might be close sent a bolt into my stomach.

"There is every chance, of course, that Ménard will have you arrested on the spot," Le Vieux Orphelin murmured. "I would not be surprised if he has erected a guillotine in there."

"I'll be fine." I looked at him. "I never asked if he knows your mask."

"Fortunately, no. I did not wear this mask in Lyon."

"I suppose you don't want to tell me what happened between the two of you there."

The mask tilted up a little.

"I called myself Le Vieux Orphelin," he said, "because I am a son of the æther, and because my family is this underworld. But *orphelin* has another meaning. Among the criminals and unfortunates of Paris in centuries past, the word could also refer to a goldsmith, or a jeweler. This strange life of mine began in a bookshop—and as you know well, Underqueen, stories hold more facets than jewels, and more worth than gold."

Another carnival of fireworks lit the nearest rooftops.

"There is always a price to be paid for their telling," Le Vieux Orphelin said. "The story of myself and Georges Benoît Ménard . . . I am not yet ready to pay that price. Forgive me."

I nodded. After all, he had never insisted I tell him what had happened between me and the blood-consort that night, in the place I now knew was called Sainte-Chapelle.

A limousine glided past us. I had thought it might be conspicuous to arrive on foot, but as we drew closer to the cathedral, more and more people joined us. Ordinary people who had won the ticket lottery.

Lamps and black-and-white ribbons festooned the arch over the main doors, which stood open. Candlelight glowed from between them like heat from a stove. We crossed the salted cobblestones in front of it, where the snow had been shoveled away, and joined the wending line of guests. After what felt like years, a day Vigile held out a hand for my invitation.

"Madelle Besson. Welcome." She slotted the gilded card into a strongbox. "Monsieur?"

Le Vieux Orphelin presented his invitation. The Vigile gave it a cursory look and stood aside.

The real Marguerite Besson—a French consular assistant from the Embassy of Scion England—was unconscious with the perdues. I had dyed my hair chestnut brown to match hers. Two other invitees were sharing her cell. All of them would be released, unharmed, as soon as we had carried out our task.

Ivy was in charge of watching over them. Le Vieux Orphelin had invited her to join the perdues—an invitation she had accepted. She had yet to choose a new syndicate name, but at last, after so many trials, she could start to build a new life.

An attendant took our coats. As soon as we were inside, a pall of warmth draped over me, and I gazed upward, the breath leaving me.

Thousands of white candles lit the echoing interior of the Grande Salle. Some flickered on cast-iron chandeliers, which hung from the pointed arches that divided the aisles from the main chamber. Somehow the cathedral seemed even larger from the inside, cavernous as well as tall. Far overhead loomed a rib-vaulted ceiling, almost too distant for the candlelight to touch, so high I had to crane my neck to take it in. I had never beheld a place like this, which looked as if gods had raised it—and yet it was humans that had dreamed it into being, and built it from the ground up.

For days, I had felt as if I was sleepwalking, but the lambent splendor of the place finally woke me from my stupor. Arcturus would appreciate this. With a smile, I turned my head to see his reaction to its beauty.

I was looking at empty air. At darkness. The realization snatched the warmth from me again.

He had never cared for humankind. Not the music, not the art, not me. All of it had been a lie.

Ahead, a checkered floor stretched out like a never-ending chessboard. Couples waltzed across it, conducted by a violin consort. In the shadowed aisles, behind looming columns, knots of people laughed and talked, their voices merging into resonance. It was going to take a while to find one person in this labyrinth, even if he was the man of the hour.

"Madelle?"

A masked attendant offered me a platter. I took a steaming goblet of mulled blood mecks.

"Might as well enjoy ourselves," I said to Léandre, who had materialized on my right. "Remember, keep your distance."

"I must also keep watch. You'll be hard enough to see in this gloom without a twenty-foot gap between us."

"I will be able to sense you for a time." Le Vieux Orphelin, who had caught up to us, refused a glass of mecks with a gesture. "Fear not. We will not lose sight of you." He extended a long hand to Léandre. "Come, mon amour. It has been too long since we last danced."

For the first time since I had met him, I swore Léandre almost smiled. Almost. A band seemed to constrict around my throat. I stepped into the shadowy aisle to the left.

It hurt to remember. Almost as much as it hurt to forget.

I shook myself and focused on my search. Even without the masks, it would have been hard to make out individual faces. I fine-tuned my sixth sense until the æther glittered around me. There were so many guests, creating such a crush of dreamscapes, that trying to isolate just one was like trying to pick a single crystal of sugar from a salt cellar. I stopped beside a column and took a sip from my goblet, giving me an excuse to observe my surroundings.

The place was thick with people. I was one among thousands of guests. But as I stood there, a group to my right noticed my mask. When I looked toward them, one man laughed in delight.

"Très audacieux, Madelle," he called to me. The whole group lifted their goblets. "Bon débarras aux racailles terroristes."

I raised my own goblet in acknowledgment. If they only knew who they were toasting.

Le Vieux Orphelin had paid a trustworthy amaurotic tailor to craft an outfit for me. Cut-off trousers, heeled boots, and a black dress that resembled a blazer, with long, ruched sleeves and gold buttons down the front. The overall look was elegant, yet low-key. Inconspicuous.

It was the mask that drew attention. The mask with red lips that displayed a black moth. The faint cracks in the porcelain were meant to disguise what was beneath, not reflect it. The guests assumed it was my intent to mock a dead radical, an enemy of the anchor. A little near to the bone, perhaps, but commendably daring.

That was when I finally spotted the Grand Inquisitor of France. He was ensconced in the opposite aisle, surrounded by guests and laughter. I strode back the way I had come, murmuring apologies and accepting compliments on my mask as I went. I almost stopped when I spied Aloys Mynatt, the retired Grand Raconteur of France, who I had last seen in the first colony. He was hunched by himself in an alcove, gaunt and whey-faced.

Columns rushed past as I quickened my stride. From the look of him, Ménard was about to take his leave of this circle of guests. I would have to cut through the dancers, or risk losing him again.

I stepped out from the arches. Before I knew it, I had been spun into the arms of a familiar oracle.

"You shouldn't be here." A whisper at my ear. "I'll ask you again. Do you have a death wish, dreamwalker?"

"Cade." Instinctively, I grasped his shoulder. "Not the time. I need to reach Ménard."

"In such a scandalous mask?" His right hand came to my waist. "Whose invitation did you steal to get in here?"

"Marguerite Besson."

"I am astonished they bought that. From what I hear, she's timid as a mouse."

I glanced toward the aisle. Ménard had vanished again. As we glided seamlessly into the Waltz of the Anchor, I drew back a little to look Cade in the face. His mask was wooden, beautifully carved to resemble a bear. It left only his eyes and a little of his chin on show.

"A bear," I said. "Because you're less timid, I assume."

"Well, that," he conceded, amused, "but it's a little nod to my inheritance, too." He twined his fingers with mine. Though it was warm in the cathedral, he wore leather gloves. "Fitzours. It means *son of the bear*. Did you know that the name Mahoney is linked to bears, too?"

"Yes. Vaguely," I said, after a pause. "Did you look that up?"

"Just something I know."

We whirled deeper into the tumult of dancers. In Ireland, I had loved to dance with my cousin, but somehow, I had always gotten it wrong at my school in London. I had worked hard to convince my teacher of my grace, to no avail. Still, the steps came effortlessly now.

"It's dangerous for you to be here, Paige," Cade said. "Why risk coming back?"

"To do exactly what you wanted. Cut a deal with Ménard."

"What kind of deal?"

"One he'll like."

"Well, he does need some good news. I assume it was you who burned down Sheol II." When I was silent, he chuckled. "If you wanted to stir the pot, you succeeded. Weaver called Ménard the next day. I don't know what they said to one another, but Ménard has been in a foul mood ever since, even with Luce. From the look of him, he hasn't slept in a while."

"Nashira is in the citadel. That might be why."

The apple of his throat shifted. "I had no idea," he muttered. "Now I'm worried. She might be planning to punish Ménard for Sheol II. She wouldn't think twice about hurting Luce."

I glanced toward the aisle, where Ménard was nowhere to be seen. "Speaking of Luce," I said to Cade, "I haven't seen her so far."

"She isn't here. Stomach bug," he said. "Onésime stayed behind with her."

That seemed unlike Frère. This was the greatest night of the year, the culmination of a long-awaited victory.

"I'm sure she'll be fine," I said, seeing the tension in his jaw. "She has the best medical care in France."

"Yeah, I know."

The dance was drawing to a close. As soon as the music ceased and the applause broke out, Cade walked toward the aisle with me. "Ménard is due to make a speech in about half an hour," he said. "If you insist on talking to him, I'd do it now, or you could be waiting all night."

"Did you see where he went?"

"Yes."

I followed him down another dark aisle. For a moment—just a moment—it became a tunnel, flooding with water.

Onésime might be keeping his mother company, but Mylène was the soul of the party, leading several well-dressed children in a game. A minder hushed a tearstained Jean-Michel, who clutched his blanket to his cheek. All of this was unfair to them.

Mylène was the same age as the murdered Spanish princess. She had died in a place like this.

Keeping hold of my hand, Cade led me from the aisle into the heart of the cathedral—between two of its rose windows, where a platform housed an illuminated lectern—and worked his way through a thicker swathe of the crowd. Long tables were laden with food from every nation in the empire, including a range of local specialities from the regions of France. All of this to celebrate the annexation of two countries that might now face a brutal reckoning.

When Cade touched my shoulder, I looked over it to see Ménard, much closer, deep in conversation with two of his ministers. His mask was gold, unadorned except for a small anchor etched into the brow. Leaving me by a column, Cade caught his attention and subtly nodded toward me.

Ménard raised his chin. He took his leave of the ministers and spoke to a suited woman behind him—one of his bodyguards, I assumed—before he walked back toward the front doors, Cade in his wake. I shadowed them.

It took some time for Ménard to make it out of the chamber, since everyone wanted to shake his hand and offer their good wishes. Eventually, however, he vanished through a door with Cade. I glanced over my shoulder to see Léandre, who gave me a nod from a dark corner.

Beyond the door was a flight of steps. Halfway up, another door stood ajar. Cade waited outside.

"Go in," he said. "He wants me to stay here. To subdue you if you try to attack him."

"And will you?"

"You're not going to find out, because you're not going to attack him. Are you?"

"No comment."

I brushed past him. With an amused sigh, he closed the heavy door behind me.

Georges Benoît Ménard waited in the room beyond. A table and a single lamp stood between us.

"My guards expect me to return within ten minutes," he said. "In my hand is a personal alarm." His thumb was on it. "Should I activate it, you will not escape this room."

"I've no intention of assassinating you, Inquisitor Ménard. And be aware that I have voyants outside, awaiting *my* return." I made no move to take off my own mask. "Apologies for interrupting your party, but I didn't think your personal secretary would be able to squeeze me in." I moved farther into the room. "You must have known it was me who set the fire, yet you never seized the opportunity to blame the Mime Order."

Ménard blew out a slight huff through his nose. "After I saw that you had broken into my office, I knew you must be responsible for it, even though I left no information as to the whereabouts of Sheol II," he said. "I can only assume you were able to access my safe."

"Correct," I said. "Has the Suzerain been in touch?"

He clasped his hands on the table.

"She has," he said. "France must make significant financial reparations to England for the loss, and Minister Auclair awaits execution for her failure to defend the colony. I hope you sleep well when you think of her six-year-old child, who will have no mother by next week."

"I was six when Scion marched on Dublin. I doubt that keeps you up at night." I took another step toward him. "You are now on very thin ice with the Suzerain, Inquisitor Ménard. If she decides to replace you with someone more unwaveringly loyal, you'll never live out your fantasy of a Scion without its masters. You'll either be dead, imprisoned, or stripped of your power and sent away to rot somewhere. You need leverage. A way to cling to your title."

"And you can provide this?" Ménard spoke in a soft voice. "Have you reconsidered my offer?"

"I have one of my own," I said. "The anormales of London and Paris have agreed to stand shoulder-to-shoulder against Scion. Le Vieux Orphelin is my partner in this endeavor."

His face changed in a way that chilled me.

"You have struck an alliance with Ignace Fall," he said, toneless. "He survived the fire, then."

"He did. I ensured his safe return from Sheol II."

"Good." A faint smile. "I would hate to imagine that he had burned without my knowledge."

"I confess, I was always surprised you *don't* burn people. They used to do that to us, you know," I said. "The witches and the warlocks. The people society blamed for their ills."

"What happy days," Ménard said.

I walked past his table, skirted my fingers along it. His dark gaze was nailed to my mask.

"Le Vieux Orphelin is alive and well. Together, he and I command a significant army of clairvoyants. Enough to fan our small flames

448

of revolt into an open war against Scion," I said. "Now, we could turn our attention to you first. Make public threats. Eliminate your supporters. Destroy any sense of internal safety in France. The French syndicate will certainly want that." I stopped. "Or . . . you and I could come to an understanding, as you suggested when I was your guest. A temporary, mutually beneficial arrangement."

Ménard did not break my gaze. It was like staring into a void.

"I am listening," he said. "What is it that you propose?"

"A truce."

The two words hung in the air between us.

"In the months and years to come, Le Vieux Orphelin and I want to dismantle Scion. If you like," I said, "we can start at the nucleus—England. We can ensure that, for a time, our syndicates and allies are focused on overthrowing Frank Weaver. For the time being, we will not attack you, nor those Scion leaders who wish to stand against the Rephaim."

Ménard was like a statue. For someone who despised the Rephaim, he could look just as emotionless.

"France will seem like a bastion of stability in comparison, and you—Benoît Ménard—like the only worthy replacement for a fool and a marionette," I said. "You could take England. We wouldn't be averse to that, so long as you keep working against Nashira Sargas."

"And in return?"

"You will suspend all capital punishment of clairvoyants." I placed both hands on his table. "I know you can't release all the prisoners in the Bastille without compromising your public support. That support keeps you in power. But you *can* keep the prisoners alive. You can retire the guillotines."

"And how am I to justify this sudden absence of executions in France?" Ménard asked, unperturbed. "The people expect blood. Since the dawn of human civilization, they have thirsted for it."

"You're a clever man. Perhaps you can pretend you understand the concept of mercy." I leaned closer to him. "I've been busy in the year since I was arrested. As you said yourself, I have made a great many connections that I could, at any moment, exploit. If you break this ceasefire—if you kill one clairvoyant, even in secret—I will know. Do not test us."

"That is all you want, then." He laid a hand on his mask. "An end to the bloodshed."

"For now. Prove that you can keep to this arrangement and resist your deep-rooted urge to murder innocents, and perhaps, in a few months, we can discuss the ways we might work together to bring down the Suzerain. To save humankind." I straightened. "But make no mistake, Inquisitor Ménard—this is a marriage of convenience, nothing more. We might both be human beings, but we have very different ideas of what humanity means."

Ménard dredged up a grim smile at that.

"I will announce a suspension of public executions in a week. I will say that we must show greater restraint than monarchs like Esteban de Borbón," he said. "Two years, Madelle Mahoney. That is what I will give you. Two years of clemency. If I hear a single whisper from the Mime Order against me before this truce comes to an end . . . I will burn all of you."

"I would expect nothing less." I turned away. "Enjoy your evening, Inquisitor Ménard. You'll be hearing from us very soon."

I left.

Outside, Cade was leaning against the wall, arms folded. When I blazed past, he followed me down the steps. "That was quick," he said. "Did you get what you wanted?"

"That remains to be seen." At the bottom of the steps, I turned to him. "Have you had enough yet?"

"What do you mean?"

"I'm asking you if you're ready to stop working for him. If you'd like to work for me instead."

Cade glanced up the stairs. The door had just closed above us.

"Meet me on the Pont Neuf. I need some air," he said. "Getting a little stuffy in this place."

****

We returned to the checkered floor. Cade left first, to avoid drawing attention, while I lingered in a corner. I shook my head when Le Vieux Orphelin moved to approach me. If someone saw me with him and reported it to Ménard, he would know exactly what Le

Vieux Orphelin looked like, and I could not give him that power. He had to fear the specter of the streets.

Léandre came to my side instead. "Well?" he said. "Did he agree?"

"Yes."

"Well done." He breathed in through his nose. "Although . . . all of this seems too easy."

"That's why I'd like another lick of varnish on the deal. We need someone on the inside. Someone to watch him." I glanced up at him. "Wait for me. I won't be long."

"Where are you going?" Léandre asked, but I was already heading for the cloakroom to retrieve my coat.

The cold hit me like a solid wall of ice. I pulled on the coat as I walked past the Vigiles outside, away from the light show at the front of the cathedral, past the line of last-minute arrivals and the limousines. Cade was nearby. If I could get him on side, it would make my deal with Ménard watertight. Let it be my next move in the game against Nashira Sargas.

And the blood-consort. Let him see that I was not defeated. Steel queen. Iron heart.

I crossed the cobblestones, my head bowed against the snow-flecked wind, and followed the street left toward the Petit Pont. Cade was waiting for me under a lamppost.

He had removed his mask. When he looked at me, I stopped dead. Fatigue was stone-rubbed under his eyes, which were dull and bloodshot, and his brow shone with sweat. He wiped it with his sleeve. Despite it, he was clearly feeling the cold, burrowed deep into his coat.

"So," he said, with a dour smile, "what kind of employment are you offering, Paige?"

"I need someone to make sure Ménard doesn't execute any more voyants."

"You got him to agree to that?" He chuckled. "Killing voyants is his favorite pastime. I wouldn't like to see what happens when Ménard gets bored."

"I won't go into specifics," I said, "but I could use a spy. You're close to him, Cade. You can report on what he's doing."

"To you?"

"Or one of my associates. All you'd have to do is give us a report on where Ménard has been and who he's been meeting so we can investigate. You'll be compensated for the risk, of course."

We started to walk again. Side by side, we stepped onto the Quai des Grands Augustins, which was closed to traffic for the night. Cade looked straight ahead and breathed out.

"Compensated how?" he finally said.

"Financially, of course," I said. "But there are other ways. If the baby does turn out to be yours, and if that fact is very obvious, we can get you out of there. Give you somewhere to hide."

Cade contemplated my face. Slowly, a smile turned the corners of his mouth.

"What?" I said.

"You've just . . . done so much. For voyants. And in such a short amount of time." He rubbed his hands together and blew into them. "You know it's been a year to the day since you were arrested for murdering two Underguards."

"I didn't, no. That's—" I slowed. "How do you know when I was arrested?"

"Oh, you know. Records, conversations. You're a person of interest to everyone, Paige."

The stalls were all closed tonight. Seeing them, I suddenly realized where we were. I saw the crimson sign—the sign reading RUE GÎT-LE-CŒUR, a name that spoke of a heart at peace. The safe house. I stopped.

Memories were breaking through my armor. For the first time since that night, I saw the house where I had lived with the blood-consort for months, sat with him under the stars, slept at his side.

And I saw that the door had been smashed down. That was no surprise: Nashira hadn't known he had been working for her. His mission had been known only to him.

The shattered window on the second floor was harder to explain. There had been a struggle in that building.

Why would he have struggled?

A chill seeped between my shoulders. Seeing me waver, Cade grasped my arm to steady me.

"Paige. You all right?"

"Yes." I looked at him for what felt like the first time. "You don't look well, though, Cade. Not sleeping?"

Our gazes met. "I'm fine, Paige."

The æther quivered. It was trying, desperately, to tell me something. To *warn* me. And I listened, because I was clairvoyant, and the æther was my guide.

So I looked at Cade again. I looked harder. This close, I could see the blue tinge to his mouth. The sight of that darkness made something coil like an adder inside me. He had kept a pair of gloves on as we danced, so I couldn't tell whether he had the same discoloration in his fingers. My own lips were painted by the æther, a permanent mark of my gift.

Cade was an oracle. I knew that.

Cade Fitzours, whose name was linked to mine.

I thought of Arcturus that night. His cold stare. His cruelty. How flat the light in his eyes had been for most of our confrontation—exactly the way they had looked in the mirror when I had possessed him—and how, when he had raised a hand to me, his arm had seemed to resist a command it had been given. A command to strike a blow that could have killed me.

The scar on my hand was suddenly cold. I clenched my fingers over the three-letter word there.

It would take a dreamwalker incredible strength to turn an unwilling Rephaite into a marionette. It was impossible. And yet, I had done it myself. Not for long—not for anywhere near as long as Arcturus had taunted me—but for a few moments, I had known control over a god . . .

And how could I have sensed a dreamwalker, when all my life I had believed I was alone?

My hand slid into my coat and closed around the grip of my revolver. At the same time, Cade stepped closer.

"Recognize this place, Paige?"

Warm breath on the back of my neck. I managed one stunned look into his eyes, and then—

A blow, as from a battering ram, but not into my body. Into my *dreamscape*. It smashed through my defenses, into the haven in my mind, the place no one had ever seen. I stumbled backward and fell hard on the ice, and as blood leaked from my nose, Cade bled, too.

My poppies closed in self-defense. Too late. He was already at my centre. Darkness came, swift as a falling sword, as surely as if every light in Paris had gone out.

****

I woke to the far-off sound of a siren. Not the commonplace kind that echoed across every citadel. Not an ambulance or a fire engine, or a black van looking for unnaturals. This was a measured, over-lapping drone that rose and fell in waves, far louder than the sirens in the first colony.

A deep ache filled the joints of my arms. When I shifted, the rattle of chain links followed. So did pain.

Agony crested at the front of my skull, a pressure that made my eyes prickle. Afraid to move, I drew in a delicate breath. This was deeper pain than I had ever felt in my life, as if someone had struck me head-on with a spike maul, but worse. A feeling of wrongness and violation leaked through me. Nausea roiled in my stomach, and before I could stop myself, I had coughed bile down my front. The sound of my retching was all I could hear.

Trepidation bubbled in my chest as I tried to latch onto some light. I found none. I could feel myself sliding back into my dark room, and I had nothing to keep me grounded.

No. I had to think. Whatever had happened, however I had gotten here, I needed to stay calm.

I remembered leaving the masquerade. Cade waiting for me under the lamppost. Walking together off the bridge and down the Quai des Grands Augustins—

Then nothing. Just darkness.

There was no point in screaming. No one was close. Beneath the sirens, all I could hear was my own uneven breath. Dreamwalking out of this one was impossible; the migraine was too distracting. And while Eliza had taught me to pick a lock, I had no idea how to slip a chain.

It was pitch-black. From what I could feel, I was manacled by my wrists to the wall, loosely enough that I had some range of motion in my arms. I could also feel something pressing against my side.

The phone. The phone Ducos had given me, tucked into a hidden pocket in my jacket.

I was not going to die in another dark room. Teeth gritted, I got one knee onto the floor and turned over, so I faced the wall.

Using the chains for purchase, I rose, bent my head, and unzipped the pocket with my teeth. Next, I angled my elbow so it was underneath the phone. It slid around like a bar of soap. Finally, I managed to winch it up a couple of inches, so it jutted out enough for me to bite it.

Then I realized. I was underground. No signal.

With a huff of frustration, I let the phone drop back into my pocket. That was when a door opened behind me, and Kornephoros Sheratan appeared.

"Your mistakes have caught up with you, dreamwalker." He stood in the dim light from beyond. "I trust you are feeling well."

"Kornephoros. What—" The muted light in his eyes broke the darkness. "Is this the Hôtel Garuche?"

"Indeed. You seem to be the newest test subject. Which you deserve," came the voice, "given that you did not honor your word to free me. I expected nothing less of a human."

Ménard must have come after me. His agreement to my plan had been a trap. Cade might already be dead. "I did try." My tongue felt bee-stung. "I see you got free anyway."

"I am no bird to be caged, dreamwalker."

My head was aching too much to fully take in his words. "What the hell is that noise?" I rasped. "Those sirens—"

"Civil defense sirens," Kornephoros said, with a conversational air. "They are activated by Inquisitorial authority in the event of a national or interimperial emergency. But fear not. You are quite safe here, fleshworm."

His aura loomed, and suddenly, he was there, in front of me. All I could see were disembodied red eyes.

"I said I would hunt you. In the end," he said, "someone else did. And now here you are."

Under the pain, I was waking up to a chilling reality. I was trapped in the dark with a monster, and something terrible was happening above, and I had no idea how or why.

"Who brought me here?" I croaked. It took great effort to hold my head up. "Who hunted me?"

"I am sure he will explain your situation in due course. For now, he has business with the Suzerain. I imagine he caught you by surprise," Kornephoros remarked. "Even I had no idea of what he was, or his allegiance. But it certainly opens a world of possibilities." He walked toward me. I tensed. "This is for your lies, oathbreaker."

Kornephoros brushed my cheek with one finger. White-hot pain roared from his touch. It was as if his hand was a magnet, and my jaw was iron, bent to his will. He moved to my throat, choking my cry and immobilizing me as the same excruciating pain drilled into the bones of my neck.

Then he reached upward, to where my chains were bolted to the wall. They gave way and jangled to the floor, and my arms fell heavily to my sides, numb and cold. I stared at him, lost.

"I do this not as a favor to you," Kornephoros said, "but to honor an oath of my own." He turned his back on me. "No doubt I will see you again soon, dreamwalker. Farewell."

Before I could try to question him, he was gone. And the door was open. Still nauseous, I limped toward it and lurched up the stairs beyond, holding the banisters with both hands, in so much pain I could barely see. I was trembling all over, but not just because of the cold. I felt hollow-boned, like a bird. Vulnerable, as if someone had stripped me.

The Hôtel Garuche was dark and deserted. Somewhere, a clock struck eleven. All I could perceive were two dreamscapes, which made no sense. I walked drunkenly through its corridors until I reached a familiar staircase, and from there, I entered the private apartments.

The first thing I saw was Alexandra Kotzia. She lay on her side, her hand a few inches from a pocket pistol. Red hair covered her face. Beside her lay a pallid Onésime. I went to him first and felt for breath, exhaling when I felt air whisper against my fingers. Kotzia was still alive, too, but cold to the touch, her pulse faint. Blood had dried under both their noses.

Luce Ménard Frère was nowhere to be seen.

I remembered then. Dark lips against blue-tinged skin. The shadows under his eyes. The gloves. And when those pieces came together—when I realized not only what had happened, and how I had gotten here, but the clues that I had missed—the blood drained from my face.

"Onésime?"

As the realization froze my blood, I looked up. Ménard was in the doorway, flanked by bodyguards. He was staring at his nine-year-old son, who must appear dead, and me, on the floor beside him, close enough to the gun that it could have fallen from my hand. Before I could move, before I could explain, Ménard had grabbed me with both hands by the throat and slammed me onto my back.

"So this is your attempt to ensure I keep to my end of the bargain, anormale," he hissed. I shoved at his chest, but he only squeezed harder. "You attack my family a second time?"

His hands were stronger than they looked. In any other fight, I would have beaten him, but anger had charged his muscles and steeled his grip. His eyes yawned wide and hollow, and a vein swelled in the middle of his brow. Darkness gathered at the edges of my vision.

"Where," he whispered, "is Luce?" I could feel his breath. "Does Le Vieux Orphelin have her?"

"Papa, stop!" Suddenly Mylène was there, face tearstained, voice rusty with fear. "Please—"

His gaze darted toward her. In the half second his grip slackened, I lashed out at him with my spirit, broke his chokehold, and kicked him off. Mylène grabbed his shoulders, as if she could stop him lunging after me. I coughed violently, my cheeks hot and damp, while Ménard, on his knees, wiped his bloody nose. He was breathing almost as hard as I was.

"I just woke up in your fucking cellar," I rasped. "Clearly, whoever took Luce is the same person who brought me here. The same person who released the Rephaite in your basement." I held my throat. "Most of your personal guard was at the masquerade. Someone had a two-hour window to take advantage of that."

Ménard was silent. Without looking at Mylène, he wrapped an arm around her and drew her close to him, and she buried her face in his shoulder. One of the bodyguards spoke into her radio, calling for urgent medical assistance, while the other aimed his rifle at the stairs.

"Where is Fitzours?" Ménard said to me, very softly.

I met his gaze. "I don't know."

Mylène clung to her father, lip trembling. "Papa," she said, "I want to go to the safe room now, with Onésime and Jean-Mi. Please, c-can we go?"

Though his gaze remained blank, Ménard clenched his jaw, as if in defeat. His hand came to the back of her head.

"What the hell is happening out there?" I asked him. "The sirens—"

"Get out," he said, so quietly I almost missed it. When I didn't move, he looked up at me. "Do not make me tell you a second time, anormale."

A Vigile knelt beside Onésime and gathered him up, while another started trying to wake Kotzia.

"Remember our deal," I said to Ménard, then slipped between his guards and took the stairs back to the ground floor. From there, I faltered down the front steps, into the snow, out through the wrought-iron gates to Rue du Faubourg.

Kornephoros was nowhere to be seen. I was alone in the middle of the night, with no overcoat or gloves to fend off the freezing wind. As the realization of what had just happened sank in, my shivering grew worse. Someone had hauled me off the street and chained me up for some unknown purpose, either before or after abducting Luce Ménard Frère.

I thought I knew who. I had no idea why.

The sirens joined their voices. The noise was deeply unsettling, loud enough to vibrate in my bones. Some denizens leaned out of windows above me, as if waiting for a sign.

"Hey, is this a joke?" one of them shouted across the street.

Several people ran straight past me, even though I wore no mask. It was too dark for them to see Paige Mahoney. Where they were going, I had no idea.

Ducos would know what was happening. I groped for the phone and selected the only number in the contact list. When I held it to my ear, all I could hear was a long tone. I tried to search the æther for anyone I knew, but the pain was too much, and I gave up. Out of options, I started to walk, not sure where I was going—only that I had to move, because I had someone to find. Either Cade knew how I had ended up in chains, or he had been the one to chain me.

Even though it was the middle of the night, the streets were thronged with people. Voices shouted in anger and confusion, but their voices sounded far away, too far to hear. Snow tumbled into my hair and caught on my lashes.

I was almost at the river when the streetlamps flickered and went out. Every single one.

More shouts went up. Some screams, too, high and thin. In the near distance, I could see the bright glow from the screens on the wide Pont de L'Inquisition. By the time I reached the nearer of the two, I was so cold I could no longer feel most of my face, or any of my fingers.

SCIONEYE EMERGENCY TRANSMISSION

REGULAR ANNOUNCEMENTS HAVE BEEN SUSPENDED
STAND BY FOR FURTHER INSTRUCTION

LES ANNONCES RÉGULIÈRES ONT ÉTÉ SUSPENDUES
TENEZ-VOUS PRÊTS POUR DES DIRECTIVES SUPPLÉMENTAIRES

I stared at it until my vision blurred again, trying to read between the lines. There were no platitudes from Scarlett Burnish, no gentle voice telling us to remain calm, and no indication whatsoever of why the sirens had activated. Just words on a screen, and the noise, never-ceasing.

A hand seized my bad wrist, making me gasp. A speaking medium stood before me, eyes milky, in the grip of a possession.

"The Devil," he croaked. "The Devil has deceived you."

"What?" I tried to twist my wrist free, but he only held tighter. "What are you talking about?"

"The third card. Two horns, two wings, two cloven hooves," he called over the sirens. Tears leaked from his eyes. "Why did you not heed the cards, Paige? Why did you not listen?"

Before I could speak, the medium crumpled and fell into the snow, like a puppet without strings.

The sirens soared to a key that sent a fearful thrill along my spine. Now people were starting to run in every direction. Cars skidded to a stop and decanted passengers onto the street. I turned left and kept forging through the snow, my ears aching in protest. Some unseen force was pulling me on. With every step, a piece fell into place, each one sending a hot jolt into my bones.

And then I remembered something. Something I had known for months, but had never put together.

You told me once that there was something that proved that you were always on my side. I could almost hear my own voice. *Something that would betray you . . . if anyone but me could see.*

I understood now. Far too late, I had solved the riddle Arcturus had given me. His dreamscape. The red drapes in his mind that only a dreamwalker could see . . .

He felt safest in the place he had first held me in his arms.

A moment so powerful it had transfigured his dreamscape. A moment that forever shaped him. Because somehow, for some absurd reason, I was the very centre of his world. The realization hit me so hard I almost bent double.

Arcturus Mesarthim had not betrayed me. By not trusting him, not believing in him, I had betrayed him. I had condemned *him*. I had left him all alone in his dark room.

And it was possible—suddenly, terribly possible—that I was not the only voyant who could see into his mind.

I ran.

It was a long way. Perhaps they had already moved him somewhere else, to a safer place than here. But sheer, desperate, blinding resolve propelled me through the streets of Paris. Cade was a dreamwalker. I was not the last of my kind. And for whatever reason, he was working for the enemy.

I chased the river east, toward the Île de la Citadelle. The next time I passed a screen, it switched to a different message.

SCIONEYE EMERGENCY TRANSMISSION

MILITARY THREAT DETECTED

AERIAL ATTACK IMMINENT

SEEK IMMEDIATE SHELTER

MENACE MILITAIRE DÉTECTÉE

UNE ATTAQUE AÉRIENNE EST IMMINENTE

METTEZ-VOUS IMMÉDIATEMENT À L'ABRI

No. It wasn't possible.

It had never happened . . .

It was as if night held its breath. Then an automated voice intoned the words, and the sirens increased in volume, and the streets shattered into a state of chaos. Scattered Vigiles were trying in vain to maintain order, but no one could hear them. No one stopped. I buffeted through panic-stricken people and kept running, scoured of air, my only thought to reach Arcturus. The cold was punishing, but I kept going, hands on fire, feet numb in my boots.

This had to be their vengeance. Spain or Portugal. Maybe both. One of them must have allies somewhere, and they were coming to destroy us, in retribution for the murder of a king.

The night was suddenly too still. I slewed to a stop on a bridge, one hand clutched to my chest, and looked toward the clear sky. Stars shone in their multitudes, bleak and cold, like so many scattered bullets. Every sinew and nerve and vein in my body felt drawn to them. I waited.

Then it came.

First, a sound like being underwater. My own breath. Then a bone-deep rumble that filled my ribs and resonated along my jaw, which sharpened into a whine that drowned out the sirens. My last clear thought was that it sounded like the whistle that came before a firework.

I should have run then. Instead, I watched, transfixed, as a shadow shot overhead, barely visible. And something fell.

It struck the bridge opposite mine. The obliteration that followed must have unfolded in an instant—but I saw and felt each stage as if the whole citadel were suspended in oil.

The deep pulsation of the impact. An eruption of rubble and water. The earthquake that resounded along the whole riverbed. Red-hot sparks, flung toward the stars. The terrible flare of fire, a searing yellow that ripped the dark apart and blinded me for an instant. Noise roared all around me, thunderous, in the air and across the citadel. My eardrums screamed. All my senses were lost to this fulmination of light and noise, which tore the night in two.

Somehow I was on the ground. I shielded my face against the heat. My ears rang and my eyes streamed. Gasping, I looked up to see a black thundercloud of smoke, heaping and twisting itself into a column hundreds of feet high. A tower. For a long moment, all I could hear was my own heartbeat—but no, it was too slow, and with each pulse, the ground shunted.

The streetlamps flickered back on. Across the water, the devastated bridge shed bodies and debris. There were people in the river. I tried to catch a glimpse of what had dropped the missile, but it was too late, and the night was too dark, my eyes smeared by the frigid air.

Coughs racked my chest. I hooked my fingers into the balustrade and used it to drag myself up. To my right, another explosion illuminated the surface of the river. Above, the sky was crisscrossed with tiny comets. Comets that were rapidly descending.

Instinct jolted me to life. I stumbled off the bridge and onto the south bank, joined by a mass of screaming Parisians. I was no longer a mollisher or a rebel or a terrorist or a queen. Just one person running for her life.

They would not see unnaturals or amaurotics. All of us looked the same from the air.

The bridge had been the herald. Now the bombardment commenced. Missiles rained down on Paris, hitting buildings and cars and crowds of terror-stricken people. As I broke into a sprint along the south bank, I looked up as often as I could, eyes and ears strained for any sort of warning, but it was so dark, and there was already too much smoke. In the turmoil, I shut out the æther. My mind rejected death. Every other sense engulfed the sixth. They sheared me down to nerve and blood, and desperate, primal, animal instinct.

Cold and disorientation slowed me. I collided with a man—he could have been amaurotic or voyant—and we both crashed headlong into the snow. People stampeded past me, stepping on my fingers and the toes of my boots. I curled into a ball. Somewhere close by, a child was crying.

Another missile clipped a rooftop and showered the pavement with broken tiles. Someone went down beneath them. The next explosion took out a line of vehicles. Alarms went off on both sides of the river. Everywhere, people were abandoning their cars to flee on foot.

In the distance, thunder. A far deeper explosion, felt in the very roots of Paris. A moment later, every light plunged out. Every building went dark. Every streetlamp was extinguished. Another surge of screams spiked the air as the citadel was plunged into near-total darkness.

The fires. The fires could light my way. I rolled onto my knees and got back up, choked by smoke and snow and dust. Ash between my fingers, in my mouth. I tasted blood. Not mine.

I was nineteen, trapped in a screaming crowd in Edinburgh. I was six and underneath a statue, watching as soldiers washed Dublin in blood.

Except Scion had never bombarded Dublin from the air. Not then. Nashira had paved the way to war.

And here it came.

Everywhere I turned was pandemonium. Screaming. Terror. Insanity of fear. I fought to orient myself, using the ruined bridge as the centre of my compass. The earth trembled as another bomber whined overhead. I had to stay calm. I had to find Arcturus.

To my right, a car burst into flame. The blast hurled me off my feet and into a gutter full of slush. It was in my hair, on my bare palms, soaking into my jacket. I was so cold. So heavy.

For six months, I had courted war, taunted it. This was not what I wanted. Not this bloodshed, this wild terror. I covered my head as another plane dived toward the quay, lit by its own path of destruction.

This is not what I wanted this is not what I wanted this is not what I wanted this is not what I wanted this is not what I wanted—

Blood soaked the snow nearby. I looked up to see corpses strewn across the street. Jaw blown off. Chunks of flesh. Like the carrières, but with warm, soft bodies. My mind locked it all out. Yet everywhere I turned, there were more horrors to rip open each stitch I used to seal it all away. I was six. I was stumbling over bodies and through lakes of blood. I was twenty and in hell and there was no escape. My past and present selves were side by side.

One hand in the snow. Trembling in my elbow, pressure in my wrist. *Get up.* I planted my boot on the ground. *Get up.*

Somehow, I kept going. I ran and ran until I retched on the scorched air. I skirted craters, stepped on bodies, veered away from cracked and teetering buildings. I imagined the deep wounds in the citadel, missiles shattering the delicate walls of the carrières. Paris could swallow itself whole.

I stumbled past Rue Gît-le-Cœur. And then I was almost there. I was closing in on that hall of stained-glass windows, where I had left part of myself. Left him to his fate. Yes, I could see its spire, not yet fallen. The golden cord trembled. I felt it. A gasping laugh escaped me. He *was* there. We would find each other. We could get out of here together.

I want you with me. That is all I know.

Faster. Over the bridge, onto the Île de la Citadelle. The Grande Salle was on fire. A woman was on her knees in front of it, fists buried in the snow. Her scream went on and on. I kept running, half blinded by dust.

Paige?

Arcturus—

From the east, where the sun would rise, a windstorm. A whistle. The telltale vibration in my bones. I looked up, past the flaming buildings and the smoke, to the spire. I heard him—either in my head or through the cord—call my name. I heard it like he was beside me. And with the last of my sense, one clear thought: *stop, you have to stop.* I was too close.

And then the purest, brightest, most beautiful gold, as if the sun had opened its eye and looked straight into me. And I knew it was the last light, and the æther had come to take me back into its arms.

****

I woke to snow on the backs of my fingers. My cheek was numb against wet stone.

Not just snow. Ash. Gray, flaking ash.

When I coughed, crushing pain followed. A sludge of memories, too thick to parse. I was lying on my side, half buried under shards of wood and glass, and the sky above was scarred with black. The sirens had waned, replaced by a dead silence I had thought impossible in a citadel. No blue tone. No unbroken breath of traffic.

Silence.

A heavy bar of iron lay across my leg. With a tiny groan, I pulled free, shifted onto my front, and sucked in a burning lungful of smoke. I crawled along pitifully on my stomach. My clothes and hair were thick with ash, bleached pale as bone. I tried to push myself onto my elbows, but my arms trembled too much. I kept going until I almost collapsed onto soft warmth.

A woman. Eyes dull beneath heavy lids, blood drying in her hair, a shroud of ashes. Slowly, with a leaden head, I looked up to see more corpses, as gray as me, littered all the way down the street. One man was missing most of his right arm; he lay in red snow near the ruins of the Forteresse de Justice. I looked at it. At the first place a missile had hit.

At the smoking remains of the chapel with stained-glass windows, the last place I had seen Arcturus. That glass now glinted from the snow and ash, fractured into millions of pieces. Splinters of a rainbow in the gray.

"No." I reached for the golden cord, but it seemed to slip between my fingers. "No—"

In the ruins, nothing stirred. Surely even Rephaite bone would have yielded to that weight.

My sob of denial set off a coughing fit. Smoke cooked the back of my throat. I stared with hot eyes at the place that had been his prison, the dark hall that had shone with colors. Elsewhere in the citadel, I realized, the sirens were still calling. I mustered all the breath I had left and screamed along with them, until I folded on myself and my voice burned to nothing.

I have resented my gift, for it does not let me forget. I could not forget the room where I was scarred. Our fingers twined. *Yet neither can I forget this room.*

"Paige!"

My hands curled into fists. Someone was beside me, someone I knew. A pair of buckled shoes, black against the slush. Hair less gray than mine.

"You're alive." Cordier blew out fog. "The only one here, by the looks of it. A stroke of luck for both of us." Small hands took me by the shoulders. "Paige, get up. Stand up. We have to go."

But my chest was heaving. I was awake in the ruins of everything, and suddenly I was racked by sobs, so hard and wrenching that I made no sound at all. Heat bathed my cheeks. Every memory was a knife in my core. Keeping one hand pressed to my back, Cordier swore under her breath and reached into her coat. In the bloody light of sunrise, her shadow fell across me.

"I'm sorry, Paige. I have to do this," she said, her voice almost tender. And no longer French. "It's for your own good. I promise. Everything that happens next is for good."

Before I could stop her, she clamped a cloth over my nose and mouth. It smelled of white flowers. It smelled of oblivion. I tried to resist, to push her away, to stop myself inhaling—I tried, I did—but I was back on the waterboard, icy cold and wet and smothered, all my fight was gone.

War was coming. The Devil was twofold. It was standing over me, holding my chains, and I could not remember why I had ever thought I could escape it. I closed my eyes.

And I breathed in.

A Note on Language

Since the seventeenth century, a mixed group has always been masculine in French. Even if there is one man among fifty women, the rule is the same: le masculin l'emporte sur le féminin.

Since the Republic of Scion is not a patriarchy, and since I disagree with Nicolas Beauzée's assertion that the masculine should prevail over the feminine (in any context, linguistic or otherwise), I decided that feminine and masculine group nouns would be interchangeable in Scion French, leaning toward a rule of majority—for example, "les perdues" is feminine throughout the book because more than half of Le Vieux Orphelin's loyalists are women, while "les grands ducs" is masculine because the group is made up of two men and one woman. A person's own gender identity may influence their choice of noun, especially when the makeup of a group is unknown or fluid—for example, Paige defaults to "les anormales" (feminine), while Le Latronpuche uses "les anormaux" (masculine).

There is one exception to this rule in the book: "les patrones," which combines the feminine "patronnes" and masculine "patrons." In this case, I took what seemed a golden opportunity to blend two words into a gender-neutral noun.

Although there are no examples in *The Mask Falling*, Scion French also uses the rule of proximity. Where an adjective applies to multiple nouns, its gender matches that of the closest noun, rather than defaulting to masculine.

Given their deep-rooted associations with a woman's age and marital status in the real world, I decided against including "Mademoiselle" or "Madame" in the Republic of Scion France, either for official or colloquial use. Instead, I use a portmanteau, "Madelle" (plural "Mesdelles"), an honorific that appears to have first been proposed for use in Québec. Perhaps due to its lack of etymological logic, or simply the power of tradition, "Madelle" has never seen widespread use in any French-speaking territory. However, it does have historical precedent, appearing in the correspondence of Nicolas-Claude Fabri de Peiresc as early as the seventeenth century.

My attempts to address what I see as the problematic aspects of French may be imperfect. While I studied a Romance language for eight years and understand some of their gender-based constraints, I don't speak French. More far-reaching ideas have been proposed within the French-speaking world. Some are pushing for the official adoption of "l'écriture inclusive" (inclusive writing), which uses the "point médian," allowing the feminine and masculine forms of a word to be expressed simultaneously and thereby rendering it neuter, e.g. "les écrivain·e·s." The debate continues.

Scion Sign Language (SSL) is a fictional sign language originating in the Republic of Scion England. Just as English is compulsory across all territories of Scion, so is SSL, but other sign languages remain in use throughout the empire. SSL has been shaped by the specific cultural context of Scion; signs described in the book are therefore not intended to reflect those of any real-world sign language.

People of Interest

†—For humans, the dagger indicates that the character is dead by the beginning of *The Mask Falling*. For Rephaim, it indicates that they have been sequestered.

CLAIRVOYANTS

Humans with the ability to commune with the æther. They are identifiable by an aura, the color of which is related to their specific means of connecting with the spirit world.

THE SCION REPUBLIC OF ENGLAND

PAIGE MAHONEY

Order: Jumper
Type: Dreamwalker
Also known as: The Pale Dreamer, Black Moth, XX-59-40

Born in early 2040, Paige lived a quiet life on Feirm na mBeach Meala— her grandparents' dairy farm in County Tipperary, Ireland. Her mother, Cora Spencer, died of placental abruption not long after her birth.

At the age of six, Paige narrowly survived the Dublin Incursion, during which her cousin, Finn Mac Cárthaigh, was arrested, and his fiancée, Kayleigh Ní Dhornáin, was killed. Two years later, as guerrilla war raged between Scion and Ireland, Paige was forced to move to the Scion Citadel of London when Scion conscripted her father, Cóilín. Her first significant encounter with the spirit world was in a poppy field near the Cornish village of Arthyen, where a poltergeist made physical contact with her, leaving a scar on her left palm. It was here that she met Nick Nygård, who treated her wounds.

At sixteen, Paige reunited with Nick in London, and he invited her to join the clairvoyant underworld as a member of the Seven Seals, a gang founded by Jaxon Hall. Prizing her rare form of clairvoyance—dream-walking—Jaxon made Paige his mollisher.

In 2059, Paige was detained and transported to the penal colony of Sheol I, where she learned of the existence of the Rephaim. Arcturus Mesarthim was assigned as her keeper. The two eventually put aside their differences and, with help from some of the other humans and Rephaim in the colony, organized a rebellion against Sargas rule. Paige returned to London and resolved to become Underqueen in order to expose the Rephaite threat. During this period, she came into conflict with the Rag and Bone Man and uncovered his trafficking network, the so-called gray market. She betrayed and defeated Jaxon, who was not inclined toward rebellion against Scion, to win the crown.

As Underqueen, her legacy was the neutralization of RDT Senshield. After a rigorous search across Manchester and Edinburgh for a way to destroy it, Paige surrendered herself to Scion to reach its power source in the Westminster Archon. After enduring twenty-three days of imprisonment and torture, she banished the spirit inside Senshield's core by unknown means, deactivating all the scanners. Alsafi Sualocin and Scarlett Burnish organized her escape from Inquisitorial custody. Burnish sent her to Paris to work for the Domino Program.

DANICA "DANI" PANIĆ

Order: Fury
Type: Unknown
Also known as: The Chained Fury

A former member of the Seven Seals who also worked for Scion as an engineer. She created a custom-made ventilator for Paige to use so she could sense the æther at a distance. Danica helped rescue Paige from Sheol I and ostensibly sided with her after the fourth scrimmage, but secretly applied for a transfer to the Scion Citadel of Athens two days later, disinclined to participate in the revolution.

While waiting for her transfer request to be approved, Danica inadvertently passed Paige false information, planted by Hildred Vance, which resulted in a botched raid on a warehouse and two voyant deaths. Racked with guilt, Danica unearthed a more accurate piece of information for Paige before her departure from London, which proved vital in the hunt for Senshield's core. Her status is unknown.

DIDION WAITE

Order: Guardian
Type: Binder

A poet and pamphleteer of the clairvoyant underworld and the long-term rival of Jaxon Hall. Widely considered a poor wordsmith, Didion finally rose to prominence in London when he established the Juditheon, an auction house where spirits could be sold to the highest bidder—a move that made him unpopular in some circles, since the binders in his employ would often poach valuable spirits from outside their own sections of the citadel. Didion is the younger half brother of Pantaléon Waite, a grand duc of the Parisian syndicate.

DIVYA "IVY" JACOB

Order: Augur
Type: Chiromancer
Also known as: The Jacobite, XX-59-24

Ivy grew up in the sealed-off community of Jacob's Island, where the vile augurs of London were imprisoned after the publication of *On the Merits of Unnaturalness*, which portrayed them as dangerous and unclean. She was raised by Wynn and Vern Jacob. After escaping with her girlfriend, Chelsea Neves, Ivy moved to Camden, where she worked for a kidsman for three years. Chelsea, meanwhile, became mollisher supreme to the Underlord, Hector Grinslathe.

When she was twenty, Ivy became mollisher to the Rag and Bone Man, mime-lord of II-2. During their time together, she would help him select voyants for "employment"—a euphemism, unbeknownst to Ivy, for their sale on the gray market. When she noticed that the voyants she chose were disappearing, Ivy reported her mime-lord to Chelsea, who was now known as Cutmouth. For this betrayal—which ultimately brought the corrupt Hector into the trafficking ring—the Rag and Bone Man sold Ivy to the very market she had helped to run.

In Sheol I, Thuban Sargas was Ivy's Rephaite keeper and subjected her to months of physical and mental abuse. Ivy escaped the colony during the rebellion and took shelter with three other fugitives in Camden, finally confessing her role in the gray market at the end of the fourth scrimmage. Her confession forced the Rag and Bone Man to flee from London and exposed one of his accomplices, the Abbess.

For her involvement in the trafficking ring, Ivy faced trial by the high commanders of the Mime Order in late 2059. With the deciding vote, Paige—now Underqueen—initially gave Ivy no punishment, but this angered many of her subjects. When ScionIDE and Senshield threatened the syndicate, Ivy sacrificed herself to a life in the Beneath to buy sanctuary for her fellow clairvoyants there. Her childhood friend Róisín Jacob joined her. At Paige's behest, Scarlett Burnish had them both extracted.

ELIZA RENTON

Order: Medium
Type: Automatiste
Also known as: The Martyred Muse

Raised by aster dealers in Cheapside, Eliza was next to join the Seven Seals after Jaxon Hall founded the gang with Nick Nygård. She became the breadwinner of the gang by practicing ethereal forgery, painting copies of famous pieces of art while possessed by the spirits of their creators. She remained behind when the rest of the Seven Seals rescued Paige from Sheol I and was initially skeptical of Paige's stories about the Rephaim.

For years Eliza was unwaveringly loyal to Jaxon, but chose Paige's side after the fourth scrimmage. Paige made her mollisher supreme of the newly formed Mime Order alongside Nick. She traveled with Paige to Manchester and Edinburgh during the search for Senshield's core. After Paige was arrested, she returned to London and became interim co-ruler of the Mime Order alongside the Glym Lord.

EMMA ORSON †

Order: Jumper
Type: Dreamwalker
Also known as: Fair Emma, Marie Jeanette Kelly (?)

A nineteenth-century dreamwalker, the first of her kind to be imprisoned in Sheol I. After the Ranthen released her and she escaped to London, Nashira Sargas sent the clairvoyant who would become known as Jack the Ripper to retrieve her. He was unsuccessful—either because he murdered Emma, or because she escaped.

EZEKIEL "ZEKE" SÁENZ

Order: Fury
Type: Unreadable
Also known as: The Black Diamond

When Zeke's clairvoyance first revealed itself, he was a whisperer, able to hear the voices of the dead—until a traumatic incident rendered him unreadable. Seeking help from Scion-based clairvoyants, he came to London as part of an American tour group with his younger sister, Nadine Arnett, in 2057. They joined the Seven Seals the same year. By 2058, Zeke was in a relationship with Nick Nygård.

Zeke participated in rescuing Paige from Sheol I. After the fourth scrimmage, he sided with Jaxon Hall. Paige has not seen him since.

THE FERRYMAN

Order: Augur
Type: Hydromancer

A member of the London syndicate. He blamed Paige for the expansion of Senshield and rejected her authority as Underqueen.

THE GLYM LORD

Order: Medium
Type: Physical medium
Also known as: Laurence Adomako, Glym

Known to the clairvoyant syndicate as Glym, Laurence is currently interim Underlord of the Mime Order in Paige Mahoney's absence. He was originally one of her six high commanders and has always been a firm supporter of her rule. His closest friend, Tom the Rhymer, was killed during the search for Senshield.

HECTOR GRINSLATHE †

Order: Soothsayer
Type: Macharomancer
Also known as: Haymarket Hector

The former Underlord of the Scion Citadel of London, Hector was notorious for his greed, cruelty, and sloth. Among his many vices, he was a member of the gray market. Not satisfied with the cut he was receiving from Jaxon Hall for selling his own subjects, he targeted Jaxon's mollisher, Paige Mahoney, and sent her to Scion without Jaxon's knowledge. This resulted in her six-month incarceration in the penal colony of Sheol I.

In retribution, Jaxon arranged for Hector and his gang to be assassinated by the Abbess, another member of the gray market, who was possessed by the spirit of Jack the Ripper. Along with almost all of his gang, the

Underbodies, Hector was disemboweled in his own parlor. Only his mollisher, Cutmouth, escaped—but was later killed in the same manner.

JACK THE RIPPER †

Order: Fury
Type: Berserker
Also known as: The Whitechapel Murderer

A clairvoyant serial killer who operated in the London district of Whitechapel in 1888, before the foundation of the Republic of England. Prior to the murders, he was a red-jacket in Sheol I. Nashira Sargas entrusted him to retrieve the dreamwalker Emma Orson after the Ranthen secretly facilitated her escape.

"Jack" pursued Emma to London, where he murdered several other women. He was unsuccessful in returning her to the colony. Nashira used his killing spree to bring about the fall of the monarchy and presumably executed him for his failure. His spirit—a violent poltergeist—is now among her fallen angels. After the failed rebellion of 2039, Nashira used the Ripper to mutilate several members of the Ranthen, who feel intense pain when Jack is close—or when Nashira wills it. The Abbess allowed Jack to possess her so that she had enough strength to dismember Haymarket Hector and his gang, the Underbodies.

JAXON HALL

Order: Guardian
Type: Binder
Also known as: The White Binder, the Grand Overseer, An Obscure Writer, XVII-39-7

Orphaned at the age of four, Jaxon Hall was an impoverished gutterling until 2031, when he shot to underworld fame as the author of *On the Merits of Unnaturalness*, a pamphlet that divided clairvoyants into seven "orders" and caused an outbreak of gang warfare in London. His writing attracted Scion's interest, and he was subsequently arrested and transported to the penal colony of Sheol I for Bone Season VIII. Upon discovering a nascent rebellion against the Sargas family, he betrayed it in exchange for his own freedom. This resulted in the massacre of almost every human in the colony and the disfigurement of the Rephaite conspirators, including Arcturus Mesarthim.

Although it was initially agreed that Jaxon would remain under Scion surveillance for the rest of his life, he slipped the net, returned to the underworld, and built a new life as mime-lord of I-4, founding a gang named the Seven Seals and calling himself the White Binder. Meanwhile, unbeknownst to his gang (including his mollisher, Paige Mahoney), he maintained contact with Nashira Sargas—never meeting her in person— and began selling her rare clairvoyants for the Bone Seasons, accruing significant wealth in the process. Several other syndicate members joined this enterprise, including the Rag and Bone Man, the Abbess, and even the Underlord, forming a trafficking ring known as the gray market.

Jaxon attempted to become Underlord in 2059 and came close to it, but Paige betrayed him and used her gift to force him to yield. With the gray market exposed and the crown no longer in his grasp, Jaxon revealed himself to Nashira, defected to Scion, and was granted the title of Grand Overseer. His motives for his actions remain unclear.

JED BICKFORD †

A former Underlord of the Scion Citadel of London. He was found dead in the Thames with a knife in his back. Hector Grinslathe, who won the ensuing scrimmage, is suspected of having murdered both Bickford and his mollisher.

JULIAN AMESBURY

Order: Soothsayer (?)
Type: Unknown
Also known as: XX-59-26

One of Paige Mahoney's closest friends during her time in Sheol I. Julian worked with Paige to plan and execute the rebellion, and was responsible for setting fires on the evening of the Bicentenary, which prevented the Rephaim from sending an assistance call to London. He never reached the escape train. Paige initially assumed he had died in the colony, but Scion is still looking for him, suggesting that no body has been found.

LISS RYMORE †

Order: Soothsayer
Type: Cartomancer
Also known as: XIX-49-1

A talented cartomancer, Liss was another of Paige's closest friends in Sheol I, where she was imprisoned for a decade, having been captured during Bone Season XIX. Gomeisa Sargas was once her keeper, but he expelled her to the Rookery, where she became a performer, specializing in aerial silks.

Frightened by stories of the failed rebellion of Bone Season VIII, Liss was initially reluctant to resist the Sargas—but after Arcturus Mesarthim saved her from spirit shock, she joined Paige and Julian in planning the rebellion. Before she could leave with Paige on the train, Gomeisa murdered her by causing her to fall from the silks.

MICHAEL WREN

Order: Fury
Type: Unreadable

As a teenager, Michael terrified his parents with outbursts of the spirit language, Glossolalia—the gift of a polyglot. Loyal to Scion's ideals, they attempted to "exorcise" him. The experience left Michael so traumatized that he became unable to speak. He fled to live on the streets of Southwark, and two years later, he was arrested and transported to Sheol I, where he was treated as an amaurotic.

Nashira Sargas gave Michael to Arcturus Mesarthim, who taught him Scion Sign Language. Michael grew to trust Arcturus and later assisted him in planning the rebellion of 2059 with Paige Mahoney. After leaving

Sheol I on a hijacked train, he and Paige were separated while fleeing the Tower of London. Michael has not been seen since.

NADINE ARNETT

Order: Sensor
Type: Whisperer
Also known as: The Silent Bell

Nadine joined the Seven Seals in 2057 after coming to Scion on a college tour. The secret aim of the trip was to get clairvoyant help for her elder brother, Zeke—a former whisperer, now unreadable. The two evaded their tour guides and disappeared into the citadel. A whisperer with a talent for the violin, Nadine's main work for Jaxon was earning money through busking in Covent Garden. She chose to side with Jaxon after the fourth scrimmage.

NICKLAS "NICK" NYGÅRD

Order: Jumper
Type: Oracle
Also known as: The Red Vision

Born in the Scion Republic of Sweden, Nick—a child prodigy—was training as a doctor when his younger sister, Karolina, was murdered by soldiers under the command of Birgitta Tjäder. This incident led Nick to the path of rebellion, and he resolved to move to England, the heart of Scion, to fight the anchor from within. He first met Paige Mahoney in the small Welsh town of Arthyen.

During a visit to London, Nick met Jaxon Hall and became the first member of his gang, the Seven Seals. After meeting Paige again, Nick brought her into the gang. He has been her closest friend and confidant ever since, and served alongside Eliza Renton as mollisher supreme. Siding with Paige after the scrimmage forced him to part from his boyfriend, Zeke Sáenz, who chose to support Jaxon.

Nick was drafted into the Domino Program at the same time as Paige and sent back to Sweden to stir up anti-Scion sentiment there.

OGNENA MARIA

Order: Augur
Type: Pyromancer
Also known as: Yoana Hazurova

Born in the Bulgarian mining town of Buhovo in 2025, Yoana Hazurova was among those who rebelled against Scion's incursion into the Balkan Peninsula. At the age of fifteen, she joined a youth army under the command of Russian insurgent Rozaliya Yudina, who was killed in a psychological trap by Hildred Vance.

Following a failed resistance in Sofia, Yoana was imprisoned for several years and sentenced to hard labor in the new Republic of Scion Bulgaria. She escaped across the Black Sea and traveled on foot across Europe, seeking a large community of fellow clairvoyants. Eventually, she found sanctuary in London, where she became mime-queen of I-5 and took the alias Ognena Maria, the name by which she is now most commonly known. She is a trusted friend of the Glym Lord.

When Paige Mahoney won the scrimmage, Maria became one of her six high commanders and traveled with her throughout the search for Senshield's core. After its deactivation, the Domino Program sent Maria back to Bulgaria to rekindle the resistance there.

THE RAG AND BONE MAN

Order: Unknown
Type: Unknown
Also known as: L'Homme au Masque de Fer (The Man in the Iron Mask)

The former mime-lord of II-4, leader of the Rag Dolls, and a key member of the gray market. One of his three mollishers was Ivy Jacob, who discovered his involvement in clairvoyant trafficking and reported it to Haymarket Hector's mollisher, Chelsea Neves, in late 2058. In retaliation, the Rag and Bone Man sent Ivy to Sheol I.

After the rebellion in Sheol I, Paige came into conflict with the Rag and Bone Man in London when she found Arcturus Mesarthim imprisoned in his lair. As Paige grew closer to discovering the gray market, the Rag and Bone Man organized an unsuccessful attempt on her life. He also arranged the murder of Neves to ensure she was unable to stake her claim to the crown. Finally, after the end of the fourth scrimmage, Ivy told the truth about the market, and the Rag and Bone Man fled London with a bounty on his head. Since relocating his "business" to Paris, he has taken a new alias, L'Homme au Masque de Fer.

THE SCUTTLING QUEEN

Order: Augur
Type: Capnomancer
Also known as: Roberta Attard

Leader of the organized clairvoyants of Manchester, the Scuttlers. Roberta feared Paige's arrival would bring Hildred Vance's wrath down on the city, and so offered minimal assistance in the search for Senshield's core. Paige subsequently released her imprisoned younger sister, Catrin "Cat" Attard, from death row at Spinningfields Prison.

Catrin used her Vigile contacts to facilitate a successful raid on SciPLO Establishment B, where Senshield scanner-guns were being manufactured. However, Catrin also used the raid to serve her own ends and assassinate the Minister for Industry, Emlyn Price. Rumor has it that she went onto kill Roberta and become the new Scuttling Queen.

THE SPAEWIFE

Order: Soothsayer
Type: Cartomancer
Also known as: Elspeth Lin

Leader of the organized clairvoyants of the Scion Citadel of Edinburgh and maternal aunt of Liss Rymore, the Spaewife holds court in the South Bridge Vaults. She assisted Paige when she came to Edinburgh in search of Senshield's core.

ANKOU

Order: Soothsayer
Type: Axinomancer

The last member to join the perdues, Ankou is a wanted fugitive for unknown reasons. He is an expert in weaponry, with a particular fondness for axes and hatchets, which he uses to connect to the æther. His name refers to a Breton personification of death.

LE BATELEUR

Order: Augur
Type: Capnomancer

One of the patrones of the Nouveau Régime. He is also a member of the perdues.

CADOC "CADE" FITZOURS

Order: Jumper
Type: Oracle
Also known as: David Fitton, XX-59-12

As a spy for Georges Benoît Ménard and Luce Ménard Frère, Cade engineered his own arrest and transportation to Sheol I under the name David Fitton in early 2059. He quickly rose through the ranks of the colony to become a red-jacket. His immediate fate after the rebellion was unknown to Paige.

KATELL

Order: Soothsayer
Type: Crystallist

A low-ranking clairvoyant who lives in the largest Court of Miracles, in Rue des Forges. Her spouse, Paul Caron, has recently gone missing.

LE LATRONPUCHE

Order: Guardian
Type: Binder
Also known as: Pantaléon Waite

One of the three grands ducs of Paris. He was born in France and lived in London for sixteen years, as did his younger half brother , Didion Waite, who stayed behind when Pantaléon returned to Paris. His syndicate name comes from Louchébem, Parisian and Lyonnaise butchers' slang.

LÉANDRE RATH

Order: Medium
Type: Physical medium
Also known as: Le Prince Creux

Compagnon d'armes and lover to Le Vieux Orphelin. Brother of La Tarasque. They were the first to join the perdues when Renelde and Le Vieux Orphelin came to the Scion Citadel of Paris.

LOUISE GILBERT †

Order: Soothsayer
Type: Cartomancer

One of the purported founders of the clairvoyant syndicate that developed into the Nouveau Régime. She was invited to read for Marie Antoinette, and frightened the Queen so greatly that she was forced to leave court. In Paris, she connected with a younger cartomancer, Marie-Anne Lenormand, and they formed the early syndicate.

MALPERDY

Order: Sensor
Type: Sniffer

Also known as: Mal

A member of the perdues with a gift for climbing and rappelling. His uncle abandoned him when he was a child, forcing him to become a pickpocket. After Malperdy tried to rob her, Renelde du Linceul took pity on him and invited him to join the group.

MARIE-ANNE LENORMAND †

Order: Soothsayer
Type: Cartomancer

Arguably the most famous and successful clairvoyant of the French Revolution, Marie-Anne Adélaïde Lenormand (or Le Normand) was born in Alençon in 1772. At the age of fourteen, she moved to Paris, where she opened an establishment on Rue de Tournon and began to tell fortunes.

Aged twenty, Lenormand befriended fellow tireuse de cartes Louise Gilbert, and together, they resolved to make themselves indispensable to both sides of the French Revolution. Lenormand was more daring than Gilbert, and purportedly read for such figures as Empress Joséphine de Beauharnais and Maximilien de Robespierre in her lifetime. Despite being imprisoned at least twice, she survived the long period of upheaval and died in 1843.

MÉLUSINE

Order: Augur
Type: Hydromancer
Also known as: Naila Clary

A member of the perdues who has concealed the extent of her allegiance to Le Vieux Orphelin, allowing her to report to him on the activities of his fellow leaders, Le Latronpuche and La Reine des Thunes. She also heads a small gang of hydromancers based in the district of Montparnasse.

LA REINE DES THUNES

Order: Augur
Type: Cryomancer
Also known as: Douceline Marchand

One of the three grands ducs of the Parisian syndicate. She wears jewels that once belonged to Marie Antoinette.

RENELDE DU LINCEUL

Order: Fury
Type: Unknown
Also known as: Renée Gilson

Renée Gilson spent her early years in the Scion Citadel of Lyon. She became involved in clairvoyant society there when she was still a child and attracted the interest of a gang boss, Burchard Louvel. She escaped his influence a short time after befriending Ignace Fall, a bookseller in Vieux-Lyon. They were living together by the time Georges Benoît Ménard arrived in the citadel in 2046.

After coming into conflict with Ménard in 2048, Renée and Ignace—now known as Renelde du Linceul and Le Vieux Orphelin respectively—relocated to Paris and formed a gang, which would eventually become the perdues. It was Renelde who discovered Apollyon, the lost tunnel leading to Versailles.

LA TARASQUE

Order: Medium
Type: Physical medium
Also known as: Camille "Cam" Rath

A member of the perdues, sister of Léandre Rath. La Tarasque refers to a fabled Provençal creature, made of parts of several animals. Her real name is Camille Rath.

LE TROUVÈRE

Order: Sensor
Type: Polyglot

A clairvoyant in the service of Le Latronpuche.

LE VIEUX ORPHELIN

Order: Jumper
Type: Oracle
Also known as: Ignace Fall

Ignace Fall grew up in the Scion Citadel of Lyon, where he owned a bookshop in the ancient district of Vieux-Lyon. At age seventeen, he met Renée Gilson, whom he befriended. The two set up home together and became lovers. When Georges Benoît Ménard was posted to the citadel, the three of them came into unspecified conflict, and Ignace took the alias Le Vieux Orphelin.

Le Vieux Orphelin and Renelde finally escaped to Paris in 2049, where they gathered a gang of loyalists, the perdues. By this point, Le Vieux Orphelin had permanently masked himself. Popular, compassionate, and intriguing, he was made a grand duc within a few years, ruling alongside Le Latronpuche and La Reine des Thunes. When Paige first hears of him, he has been missing for several weeks.

AMAUROTICS

Humans who are not clairvoyant, sometimes known as rotties. They have no connection to the spirit world and are unable to sense it.

ABEL MAYFIELD †

The Grand Inquisitor of England before Frank Weaver. He oversaw the conquest of Ireland, for which he is most commonly remembered. He died of a stroke in 2050, at the age of sixty-two.

ALBÉRIC

A field agent working for the Domino Program, responsible for the safe houses of sub-networks Mannequin and Figurine in the Scion Citadel of Paris. His name is an alias.

ALEXANDRA "ALEKA" KOTZIA

Personal assistant to Luce Ménard Frère, born in Greece in 2036, three years before the Balkan Incursion. Kotzia moved to Paris at twenty to work for the Inquisitorial family and is now among their most trusted employees. She is married to Charlotte-Marie Deschamps, a popular journalist for the *Daily Descendant*.

ALOYS MYNATT

The former Grand Raconteur of the Scion Republic of France. He attended the Bicentenary in Ménard's stead and ensured that Cadoc Fitzours could deliver his intelligence to the Hôtel Garuche. Having witnessed the power of the Rephaim, Mynatt retired and moved to Arles. A suitable replacement has not yet been found.

APRIL WHELAN

Grand Inquisitor of the Scion Republic of Ireland. She is the first Grand Inquisitor of the country, succeeding the Taoiseach, Eóghan Ó Cairealláin.

BIRGITTA TJÄDER

Also known as: The Magpie

The Chief of Vigilance in Stockholm and commander of the Second Inquisitorial Division of ScionIDE. Rumor holds that she controls the weak-willed Ingrid Lindberg, the Grand Inquisitor of Sweden. Known as the Magpie by her enemies, Tjäder is a merciless Scion fanatic with a zero-tolerance approach to all degrees of lawbreaking. Soldiers under her command executed Karolina Nygård and her friends for the crime of drinking alcohol—the slaughter that Nick Nygård joined Scion to avenge.

CÓILÍN Ó MATHÚNA †

Also known as: Colin Mahoney

Paige's father, son of Gráinne Uí Mhathúna and Éamonn Ó Mathúna, and elder brother of Alastríona Ní Mhathúna. He spent most of his career working in Dublin as a forensic pathologist, leaving Paige in the care of her grandparents in Tipperary. Scion conscripted him in 2048, and he and Paige relocated to the Scion Citadel of London, where he legally anglicized his own name and Paige's Irish middle name, Aoife. Their relationship grew strained over the next few years.

Colin was arrested on the same night as Paige in 2059. After being released for a time under supervision, he was rearrested and tortured for information about her. Hildred Vance had him publicly beheaded as part of an elaborate attempt to force Paige out of hiding.

DANIELA GONÇALVES

President of Portugal, a key target of Operation Madrigal.

ÉAMONN Ó MATHÚNA

Paige's grandfather, father of Cóilín and Alastríona, and spouse to Gráinne, with whom he ran Feirm na mBeach Meala, a dairy farm close to Bearys Cross, County Tipperary. His fate is unknown.

ELÉONORE CORDIER

A field agent working for the Domino Program. She is the medical officer for sub-network Mannequin. Her name is an alias.

EÓGHAN Ó CAIREALLÁIN

The last Taoiseach of Ireland, who led the country during the Dublin Incursion and the ensuing Molly Riots. He was executed by hanging after Ireland surrendered to the Republic of Scion.

ESTEBAN DE BORBÓN

King of Spain and a member of the House of Bourbon. His consort is Queen Antonia, and they have one daughter—the heir apparent, Princess Luciana. His father-in-law is Dutch barrister Torben van Buskirk.

FRANK WEAVER

Grand Inquisitor of the Republic of Scion England. He succeeded Abel Mayfield, who ruled Scion when it conquered Ireland. Prior to Operation Madrigal, Weaver had no military victories to his name.

GABRIELLE AUCLAIR

Minister of the Interior for the Republic of Scion France. She has one daughter, Nora Auclair.

GEORGES BENOÎT MÉNARD

Also known as: The Butcher of Strasbourg

The Grand Inquisitor of the Republic of Scion France, usually known as Benoît Ménard. Originally from Strasbourg, Ménard studied law at the University of Scion Paris. After his graduation, he worked for the Inquisitorial Courts as a judicial clerk and continued rising through the ranks for several years before being posted to the Scion Citadel of Lyon, where he served as "expert counsel" to the Ministry of the Interior from 2046 to 2049. During this period, he came into conflict with Renelde du Linceul and Le Vieux Orphelin.

After leaving Lyon, Ménard served for close to four years as Minister for Justice before succeeding Jacquemine Lang as Grand Inquisitor after a unanimous vote by the Inquisitorial Courts in 2053. He is spouse to Luce Ménard Frère, with whom he has three children: Onésime, Mylène, and Jean-Michel. His mother, Sophie Ménard Chaillou, lives in the Scion Republic of Greece.

GRAHAM HARLING

Grand Admiral of the Republic of Scion England, the highest-ranking member of the Inquisitorial Navy. He has overall command of all sea forces across Scion.

GRÁINNE UÍ MHATHÚNA

Paige's grandmother, mother of Cóilín and Alastríona, and spouse to Éamonn. Gráinne was born on the island of Cléire, a Gaeltacht. Having spoken primarily Gaeilge during her own childhood, Gráinne made sure it was Paige's first language. She ran Feirm na mBeach Meala alongside Éamonn in the years before the conquest of Ireland, during which she was forcibly separated from Paige. Her fate is unknown.

HILDRED VANCE

Grand Commander of the Republic of Scion England and authority maximum of ScionIDE. She has been hospitalized since Paige destroyed the core of Senshield while they were both inside Victoria Tower. Patricia Okonma, the deputy Grand Commander, is currently acting in Vance's stead.

IRÈNE TOURNEUR †

The first Grand Inquisitor of France. She was a popular and resolute leader who presided over the de-religionization of the country, declared the Supreme Purge, and otherwise administered the transition to the Sixth Republic.

ISAURE DUCOS

A field agent working for the Domino Program. She is the supervisor of sub-network Mannequin and receives orders for its agents from Command. Her name is an alias.

LUCE MÉNARD FRÈRE

Also known as: Madelle Guillotine

Spouse and official representative of Georges Benoît Ménard, the Grand Inquisitor of France. Frère was born in the Scion Citadel of Toulouse and studied at the University of Scion Marseille, earning a first-class degree in Scion History. She met Georges Benoît Ménard in 2047, at a dinner party in Grenoble, and married him two years later. The couple has three children: Onésime, Mylène, and Jean-Michel. Frère is currently in the second trimester of her fourth pregnancy. Her mother was Caroline Frère, the former Minister of the Exchequer.

Paige first saw Frère in person during her imprisonment in the Westminster Archon in November 2059, where Frère was representing Ménard.

PILAR BRUGUÉS OLIVENCIA

The Prime Minister of Spain. She is one of the targets of Operation Madrigal.

SCARLETT BURNISH

The Grand Raconteur of the Scion Republic of England, Burnish is the host of Scion's only news station, ScionEye, and the voice of public service announcements in English throughout the empire. She has held this position since 2052.

On New Year's Day, Burnish unexpectedly helped Paige escape death in the Westminster Archon and revealed that she is a deep-cover agent in the employ of the Domino Program. She took Paige, Ognena Maria,

Nick Nygård, and Arcturus Mesarthim to Dover and sent them to Paris (Paige and Arcturus), Sweden (Nick) and Bulgaria (Maria). Despite the risk, she returned to work the next day. She was allied with Alsafi Sualocin.

STÉPHANE "STEPH" PAQUET

A field agent working for the Domino Program. They are the courier for sub-network Mannequin. Their name is an alias.

STYX

Elected king of the toshers and mudlarks of the Scion Citadel of London and guardian of the Beneath. His community coexisted with the clairvoyant syndicate of London until a group of syndies tortured and killed a mudlark in 1977.

Upon the declaration of martial law in November 2059, Styx struck a deal with Paige Mahoney and Wynn Jacob, agreeing to let the syndicate hide in an abandoned deep-level crisis shelter in the Beneath—on the condition that they would send a clairvoyant to his community to replace the mudlark who was killed. Ivy Jacob chose to go. Róisín Jacob accompanied her.

REPHAIM

Immortal humanoids of the Netherworld, a decayed and uninhabitable dimension that once served as an intermediary realm between the æther and the corporeal world. Rephaim exhibit similar abilities to clairvoyant humans.

THE RANTHEN

ARCTURUS MESARTHIM

Type: Oneiromancer
Also known as: Warden of the Mesarthim, the concubine, the blood-consort

The former Warden of the Mesarthim—the guardian and ruler of his family—Arcturus was among the most devoted to the Mothallath family, whom the Mesarthim were sworn to protect. Despite repeated accusations that the Mothallath were responsible for the Netherworld's deterioration, he remained loyal and fought on their side during the Waning of the Veils. When the war was all but lost, Nashira Sargas blackmailed Arcturus into a betrothal to signal the surrender of the Mesarthim family, forcing him to part from his existing mate, Terebellum Sheratan. Arcturus was given the title of blood-consort.

On Earth, Arcturus spent most of his time confined to the penal colony of Sheol I, where he and several other members of the Ranthen hatched an ill-fated rebellion against the Sargas in November 2039. After a young Jaxon Hall betrayed the plot, Nashira slaughtered almost the entire human population of the colony and punished the Rephaite participants by using a violent poltergeist to mutilate their backs.

Following the betrayal, Arcturus developed an intense distrust of humans, though he tried to protect them by fighting the Emim in secret, limiting injury to the red-jackets. In March 2059, he reluctantly took Paige Mahoney—a dreamwalker—as his "tenant" in the Residence of Magdalen. With the approval of the Ranthen (and the vocal disapproval of Paige), he helped her to hone her skills, hoping she would be able to defeat Nashira at the Bicentenary. Nashira, meanwhile, wanted Paige trained so she could absorb the gift of dreamwalking at its fullest. After six months, Arcturus and Paige sparked a mass breakout with help from some of the other humans and Rephaim in the colony.

After being captured by the Rag and Bone Man in London, Arcturus reunited with Paige, who rescued him from the Camden Catacombs, and became one of the high commanders of the Mime Order following her coronation as Underqueen. He and Paige had a brief and illicit relationship before she ended it, afraid it would become a distraction—or that his fellow Ranthen would discover it, leading to the dissolution of the alliance. After the destruction of Senshield, Arcturus volunteered to accompany Paige to Paris.

Arcturus is an oneiromancer, able to make others "dream" their memories, and to experience them alongside the subject. In the colony, he used this gift to judge whether or not Paige could be trusted.

ALSAFI SUALOCIN †

Type: Unknown

Alsafi was a Ranthen double agent throughout the Waning of the Veils and continued in that role on Earth. Masquerading as a Sargas loyalist, he remained with Nashira after the rebellion in Sheol I and fed valuable information to his fellow Ranthen. He colluded in hiding most of the clairvoyant syndicate of London in the Beneath, having already created a network of human contacts within Scion, which allowed him to send Paige Mahoney, Ognena Maria, Tom the Rhymer, and Eliza Renton north to Manchester and Edinburgh to find the core of Senshield.

After Paige disabled the core in London, Alsafi carried her from the ruined Victoria Tower and dueled with Nashira to give Paige time to escape. Nashira beheaded him. Scarlett Burnish, his ally, subsequently got Paige out of the building.

TEREBELLUM "TEREBELL" SHERATAN

Type: Unknown
Also known as: Warden of the Sheratan, the sovereign-elect

Terebell was Warden of the Sheratan before the civil war and still uses the title. Throughout the Waning of the Veils, she was a ferocious supporter of the Mothallath and fought for them alongside her mate, Arcturus Mesarthim. When the war was lost and Nashira took Arcturus as her betrothed, Terebell fought Nashira in single combat and lost.

Like all of her fellow Rephaim, Terebell was forced to relocate to Earth in 1859. In Sheol I, she, Arcturus, and a number of their old allies resolved to stage a coup against the Sargas with the help of the humans in the colony. Terebell was named sovereign-elect of the new and clandestine Ranthen. She was among those who were scarred in punishment after the failed rebellion of 2039, and assisted with the successful rebellion of 2059, after which she escaped the colony.

Terebell is currently co-ruler of the Mime Order, with Paige Mahoney and Laurence Adomako as her human counterparts.

NASHIRA SARGAS

Type: Binder
Also known as: The Suzerain, the blood-sovereign

Blood-sovereign of the Rephaim and creator of the Republic of Scion, Nashira is the highest power in the empire, but uses the Grand Inquisitors of England as her puppets and mouthpieces. She shares her authority with Gomeisa Sargas, her fellow blood-sovereign.

Formerly a scholar, Nashira spearheaded the war against the ruling Mothallath family during the Waning of the Veils, which resulted in their complete destruction. After her victory, she blackmailed Arcturus Mesarthim into becoming her blood-consort to demonstrate the surrender of the Mesarthim family. She then led all of the Rephaim across the veil to Earth, where she established Scion, with herself as its supreme authority. She spent the next two centuries presiding over the penal colony of Sheol I while Gomeisa largely remained in London.

After Jaxon Hall informed her about the imminent rebellion of 2039, Nashira allowed the Emim to kill almost every human in the colony and used the spirit of Jack the Ripper to torture the Rephaite instigators, including her own blood-consort. When Paige Mahoney arrived in the colony in 2059, Nashira tasked Arcturus with training her, partly as a test of his loyalty. Her plan backfired when Paige and Arcturus struck a tentative alliance and organized a second, successful rebellion. Nashira is the only person to have witnessed their first embrace at the Bicentenary.

Nashira is a "super-binder" who can not only bind spirits, but use the gifts they had in life. This necessitates her killing her victims in a specific manner. The enraged spirit of Jack the Ripper is among her entourage of so-called fallen angels, and she can use it to cause the scarred members of the Ranthen excruciating pain on a whim. She is responsible for the doctrine of flesh-treachery, which prohibits physical contact between humans and Rephaim.

GOMEISA SARGAS

Type: Unknown

The male blood-sovereign of the Rephaim. Although he had one human slave—Liss Rymore—Gomeisa was rarely in Sheol I, instead spending most of his time in the Westminster Archon to keep a close eye on his Grand Inquisitors. He was nonetheless present for the Bicentenary, where he killed Liss. He is also thought to be the mastermind behind the conquest of Ireland, which he accomplished through his most powerful puppets, Hildred Vance and Abel Mayfield.

Gomeisa can harness apport, the energy of breachers—a rare and highly dangerous gift, which essentially makes him telekinetic. Currently, this ability has no name, and no one else is known to possess it.

GRAFFIAS SHERATAN

Type: Unknown
Also known as: The Gray Keeper

A low-ranking Rephaite who previously lived in Sheol I, where he was responsible for overseeing the small amaurotic population of the colony.

KORNEPHOROS SHERATAN

Type: Osteomancer (?)

Kornephoros initially fought on the Ranthen side in the Waning of the Veils, but betrayed the star-sovereigns at the eleventh hour, resulting in the fall of the Mothallath family. Nashira rewarded him with the title of Warden of the Sheratan—a title formerly held by his cousin, Terebellum —and he now serves as her emissary. Arcturus Mesarthim is one of his former mates.

He appears to be a kind of osteomancer, able to connect with the æther using bones. His touch can cause excruciating pain. In the past, during his brief stays in Sheol I, he used his talent for the bones to read the future for Kraz Sargas.

KRAZ SARGAS †

Type: Unknown

The former male blood-heir of the Rephaim. When he caught Paige stealing supplies in Sheol I, she used the pollen of the poppy anemone and a bullet to incapacitate him. He is presumed to have been sequestered. His replacement has not yet been chosen.

SITULA MESARTHIM

Type: Unknown

A brutal mercenary in the service of the Sargas. She is one of the very few members of the Mesarthim family to be staunchly loyal to the usurpers.

SUHAIL CHERTAN

Type: Unknown

A low-ranking Rephaite. In Sheol I, he was charged with keeping the peace in the Rookery—the slum that housed the performers. He was assigned to torture Paige after her capture in November 2059, with the aim of forcing her to disclose the whereabouts of the syndicate. Despite subjecting her to physical and mental torment, he was unsuccessful.

THUBAN SARGAS

Type: Unknown
Also known as: Le Basilic

Thuban was one of the keepers in Sheol I, notorious for his cruelty. Ivy Jacob was his only human slave during Bone Season XX. He subjected her to six months of torture before her escape in September 2059. Known as Le Basilic, after the basilisk, a creature with a fatal gaze.

VINDEMIATRIX SARGAS

Type: Unknown

The female blood-heir of the Rephaim. She has spent most of her time on Earth creating and supervising a network of spies who predominantly operate in the free world.

Glossary

Æther: [noun] The spirit realm, accessible by clairvoyants. Rephaim are dependent on access to the æther.

Amaranth: [noun] A flower that grows in the Netherworld, though not as bountifully as it once did. Its essence helps to heal and soothe spiritual injuries. The Ranthen use the amaranth as their symbol.

Amaurotic: [noun *or* adjective] Non-clairvoyant. Clairvoyants sometimes call amaurotics *rotties*.

Anakim, the: [noun] In traditional Rephaite belief, the Anakim are higher beings who created the æther and abide in a realm beyond the last light. The Mothallath family claimed the Anakim had sent them to reign in the Netherworld, and compelled their fellow Rephaim to worship them. The Sargas family were particularly skeptical of this claim. See also *Mothallath family.*

Anchor: [noun] The symbol of the Republic of Scion, often used as a metonym for it, e.g. countries are described as being "in the shadow of the anchor" when they come under threat from Scion.

Aster: [noun] An ethereal drug. See also *Regal* and *White aster.*

Aura: [noun] A link to the æther, which can manifest in a number of colors. With the Netherworld fallen into decay, Rephaim must now use clairvoyants" auras as a bridge to the æther, since their own no longer function as they once did. Both clairvoyants and Rephaim often refer to this process as *feeding.*

Bicentenary, the: [noun] A key event in recent Scion history, the Bicentenary was the celebration of two hundred years of Scion rule, held in *Sheol I* in September 2059. The *Great Territorial Act* was to be signed on this night, and Nashira intended to kill Paige in front of the assembled guests.

Binder: [noun] [a] A type of human clairvoyant from the fifth order. Binders can control a spirit (a boundling) by marking its name on their body, either permanently or temporarily, or attach a spirit to a location using a small amount of their own blood. [b] A name used for a Rephaite with similar abilities, though Rephaite binders are also able to make use of the clairvoyant gift the spirit had in life. In this case, the boundling is called a *fallen angel*, of which Nashira Sargas has several.

Blood-consort: [noun] The title of a blood-sovereign's mate. Previously held by Arcturus Mesarthim when he was betrothed to Nashira Sargas.

Blood-sovereign: [noun] A ruler of the Rephaim. There are always two blood-sovereigns, one male and one female, with two blood-heirs to support them. Under the Mothallath family, the equivalent title was *star-sovereign*.

Bone Season: [noun] A harvest of clairvoyant—and some amaurotic—humans, organized by Scion to appease the Rephaim, and to compensate them for protecting humankind from the Emim. For two centuries, clairvoyants were detained over the course of each decade and sent together to the penal colony of *Sheol I*. Paige was drafted into Bone Season XX.

Boundling: [noun] A spirit that obeys a binder.

Breacher: [noun] A spirit that can affect the corporeal world and cause injury. Poltergeists—angry, vengeful spirits—are the more common of the two classes of breacher. Scars left by a breacher will often ache and feel colder than the rest of the body. It is thought that banishing the responsible breacher with the threnody may stop the pain.

Brekkabox: [noun] A fast-food chain in the Republic of Scion, specializing in all-day breakfast.

Dissimulator: [noun] A form of free-world technology, apparently unknown to Scion, that changes the wearer's face. The Domino Program issues them to many of their field agents.

Dream-form: [noun] The form a spirit takes within the confines of a dreamscape. It may or may not reflect how an individual looks physically; rather, it is a self-image. Once a spirit leaves a dreamscape and enters the æther, it no longer has a clear form.

Dreamscape: [noun] The seat of the spirit. A mental space between the flesh and the vastness of the æther, not unlike an airlock. Clairvoyants can consciously access their own dreamscapes, while amaurotics may catch occasional glimpses of theirs when they dream. Although trauma can distort its appearance, a dreamscape will generally take the form of a place the individual feels calm and safe.

Dreamwalker: [noun] A very rare type of clairvoyant with the ability to project their spirit and possess other beings. Before leaving their body, a dreamwalker must "dislocate" their spirit from the centre of their dreamscape, which causes a wave of ethereal pressure. Dreamwalkers have the ability to access dreamscapes other than their own and display unusually high sensitivity to the æther. Paige can sense ethereal activity up to a mile away.

Emim, the: [noun] [singular *Emite*] The purported enemies of the Rephaim. They are known to feed on human flesh, and their blood can be used to mask the nature of a clairvoyant's gift and to stop dreamscapes being perceived. The Emim carry an infection called the half-urge.

Flux: [noun] Fluxion, a psychotic drug causing pain, hallucinations, and disorientation in clairvoyants.

Gloss: [noun] Formally, *Glossolalia*. The language of spirits and Rephaim. Among humans, only polyglots can speak it.

Golden cord: [noun] A link between two spirits. Very little is known about it, except that it allows for a degree of communication and emotional transmission. Arcturus and Paige share a golden cord.

Gray market: [noun] A trafficking ring founded by Jaxon Hall after he broke the terms of his release from *Sheol I*. In London, the gray market specialized in procuring clairvoyants of interest and selling them to the Rephaim. While Nashira Sargas did accept clairvoyants from the market, she forced Jaxon to shut it down when he pledged himself to her service in late 2059.

Half-urge: [noun] [a] An infection carried by the Emim, which can be transmitted to Rephaim. Its effects on the human body are temporary, as human blood appears to be able to destroy or stall it. [b] Rarely, Rephaim may use the same term to describe the disfigurement caused by contact with the poppy anemone, which can make them appear as if they are in the early stages of "true" half-urge.

Kidsman: [noun] A class of syndicate voyant. They specialize in training young gutterlings in the arts of the syndicate.

Krig: [noun] A slang term for a ScionIDE soldier, from a Swedish word for war.

Last light: [noun] The end or centre of the æther, the place from which spirits can never return. It is rumored that a final afterlife is encountered beyond it. In traditional Rephaite belief, it is the abode of the Anakim.

Mecks: [noun] A nonalcoholic substitute for wine, with a syrupy consistency. It can be served hot or cold and comes in three flavours: white, rose, and red ("blood"). Alcohol is illegal under Scion law.

Mime-lord or mime-queen: [noun] A gang leader in the clairvoyant syndicate of London. Together, the mime-lords and mime-queens form the Unnatural Assembly. Under Paige Mahoney's rule, they have become commanders of small "cells" of clairvoyants. They are roughly equivalent to the *patrones* of Paris.

Mime Order, the: [noun] An alliance between London's clairvoyant syndicate and some members of the Ranthen, led by Paige Mahoney and Terebell Sheratan, founded in 2059. Its long-term aim is to overthrow the Sargas family and bring down the Republic of Scion.

Mollisher: [noun] In London, a clairvoyant associated with a mime-lord or mime-queen. Usually presumed to be [a] the mime-lord's or mime-queen's lover, and [b] the heir to their section, though the former may not always be the case. The Underlord's or Underqueen's heir is known as a mollisher supreme. Paige chose two: Nick Nygård and Eliza Renton.

Mothallath family: [noun] The former rulers of the Rephaim, who claimed to have been sent by the Anakim to reign over the Netherworld. Originally, they were the only Rephaim who could cross the veil to walk among humans. During one of their crossings, an unknown event caused the Netherworld to begin to decay. The Sargas family blamed the Mothallath and declared war on them, finally usurping them. The Mesarthim family, which was duty-bound to defend the Mothallath, supported them to the last.

Mudlarks and toshers: [nouns] Amaurotic outcasts in London. Mudlarks scavenge for valuables on the banks of the River Thames, while toshers forage in the sewers and storm drains. They claim the deep tunnels of London—collectively known as the Beneath—as their territory. The two communities, while distinct, are closely intertwined and share a leader, who almost always takes the name Styx upon election.

Netherworld: [noun] The Netherworld is the domain of the Rephaim. It is a middle ground between Earth and the æther that once served as a place for spirits to come to terms with their deaths before they moved onto the last light. It has not served its original purpose since the Waning of the Veils, during which it began to fall into decay. The Ranthen still make infrequent journeys to the Netherworld to harvest its dwindling supply of amaranth, and there are pockets of Rephaim who have attempted to continue living there, though they are in constant danger from the Emim and must return to Earth frequently for aura.

Nouveau Régime, Le: [noun] The Parisian clairvoyant syndicate. Based in the carrières (quarries) of the citadel, it is thought to have been founded by cartomancers Marie-Anne Lenormand and Louise Gilbert. Its leaders are the three grands ducs: Le Latronpuche, La Reine des Thunes, and Le Vieux Orphelin.

Novembertide: [noun] The annual celebration of the Scion Citadel of London's official foundation in November 1929.

Numen: [noun] [plural *numa*, originally *numina*] An object or material used by a soothsayer or augur to connect with the æther, e.g. fire, cards, blood.

Off the cot: [adjective] Insane; reckless.

Opaline: [noun] A Netherworld material, thought to be the only substance that can sever Rephaite bone. As its name suggests, it resembles opal.

Patrones: [noun] Local commanders of Le Nouveau Régime. They are roughly equivalent to the mime-lords and mime-queens of London.

Penny dreadful: [noun] Cheap, illegal fiction produced in Grub Street, London, the centre of the voyant literary scene. Serialized horror stories. Distributed among clairvoyants to make up for the lack of fantastical literature produced by Scion. Penny dreadfuls cover a wide range of supernatural subjects. Paige paid for the distribution of one titled *The Rephaite Revelation* to warn the London syndicate about the hidden threat of the Rephaim, but it was edited without her knowledge to glorify the Sargas.

Perdues: [noun] Members of Le Vieux Orphelin's gang. They are loyal to him above their loyalty to Le Latronpuche and La Reine des Thunes.

Poppy anemone: [noun] A red flower that severely weakens and injures Rephaim. Direct contact with the poppy anemone or its pollen will cause their sarx to become disfigured. Rephaim will occasionally call this disfigurement the *half-urge*, as it resembles the early stages of a far more serious condition of that name.

Psychopomp: [noun] Once charged with guiding spirits to the Netherworld, they now carry messages between Rephaim. They are wary of humans. In the Netherworld, they take the form of winged creatures with a haunting song.

Ranthen, the: [noun] [a] Rephaim who fought on the side of the Mothallath family during the Waning of the Veils. [b] An alliance of Rephaim who oppose the rule of the Sargas family and believe in the eventual restoration of the Netherworld. Also known as *the scarred ones*. Most of the present-day Ranthen were also Ranthen during the civil war.

Red-jacket: [noun] The highest rank for humans in *Sheol I*. Red-jackets were responsible for protecting the penal colony from the Emim. In return for their service, they were given special privileges.

Regal: [noun] A street name for purple aster, an ethereal drug, used by clairvoyants for recreational purposes.

Rephaite: [noun] [plural *Rephaim*] Also *Réphaïte* (French). See p. 491.

Rottie: [noun] See *amaurotic*.

Saloop: [noun] A hot, starchy drink made from orchid root, seasoned with rosewater or orange blossom.

Sarx: [noun] Rephaite skin. It has a slightly metallic sheen and does not age.

ScionIDE: [noun] Scion: International Defense Executive, the armed forces of the Republic of Scion. The First Inquisitorial Division is responsible for national security; the Second Inquisitorial Division is used for invasions; the Third Inquisitorial Division—the largest—is used to defend and keep control of Scion's existing territories.

Scrimmage: [noun] A battle for the position of Underlord or Underqueen, usually triggered by the death of the Underlord or Underqueen in the absence of a mollisher supreme to take over. Paige was the victor in the last scrimmage—the fourth in London's history—after the murders of her predecessor, Haymarket Hector, and his mollisher, Cutmouth.

Senshield: [noun] A form of ethereal technology used by Scion, capable of detecting certain kinds of clairvoyant, currently deactivated. Its rapid development throughout 2059 caused a crisis within the clairvoyant community of London, which was forced into hiding to avoid detection by the Senshield scanners installed across the citadel. Paige spearheaded a mission to disable them and succeeded when she banished the spirit that powered Senshield's core in the Westminster Archon.

Sequestration: [noun] The decapitation of a Rephaite with an opaline blade. The word the Sargas family has chosen for this process seems to indicate that they view it as an act of isolation or confiscation rather than outright destruction. Sequestration stops the half-urge taking hold.

Seven Orders of Clairvoyance: [noun] A system for categorizing clairvoyants, first proposed by Jaxon Hall in his pamphlet *On the Merits of Unnaturalness*. The seven orders are the soothsayers, the augurs, the mediums, the sensors, the guardians, the furies, and the jumpers. The system was controversial due to its assertion that the "higher" orders were superior to the "lower," but was nonetheless adopted as the official form of categorisation in the London underworld. It also had significant influence in Paris.

Seven Seals, the: [noun] The former dominant gang of I-4 in London, cofounded by Jaxon Hall, its mime-lord, and Nick Nygård. The other members were Paige Mahoney, Nadine Arnett, Danica Panić, Eliza Renton, and Zeke Sáenz. The gang was based in the district of Seven Dials. Paige was its mollisher.

Silver cord: [noun] A permanent link between the body and the spirit. It allows for a person to dwell for many years in one physical form. Particularly important to dreamwalkers, who use the cord to leave their bodies temporarily. The silver cord wears down over the years, and once broken cannot be repaired.

Spirit shock: [noun] A dangerous and potentially fatal condition arising from an inability to connect with the æther. Clairvoyants who go into spirit shock will usually die or succumb to amaurosis, often resulting in long-term weakness and anguish. Rephaim can also experience a similar condition if they fail to connect to the æther through clairvoyants' auras.

Spool: [noun] [a] A group of spirits. [b] [verb] To gather several spirits into a group. Spools are used in spirit combat.

Syndicate: [noun] A criminal organization of clairvoyants. There are large syndicates in the Scion Citadels of London and Paris. Members specialize in mime-crime for financial profit. They are known as *syndies* in London.

Threnody: [noun] A series of words used to banish spirits to the outer darkness, a part of the æther that lies beyond the reach of clairvoyants.

Toshers: [noun] See *Mudlarks and toshers.*

Underlord or Underqueen: [noun] Head of the Unnatural Assembly and mob boss of the clairvoyant syndicate. Paige Mahoney became Underqueen after she won the fourth scrimmage in November 2059.

Unreadable: [noun] A voyant whose dreamscape has collapsed due to trauma and grown back with impenetrable armor, losing their original gift in the process. Michael Wren and Zeke Sáenz are both unreadables.

Vigiles: [noun] The Republic of Scion's police force, split into two main divisions: the clairvoyant Night Vigilance Division (NVD) and the amaurotic Sunlight Vigilance Division (SVD). NVD officers are granted thirty years of immunity from justice before being executed for their unnaturalness.

Voyant: [noun] Common shorthand for a clairvoyant.

Waitron: [noun] Gender-neutral term for anyone in Scion's service industry.

Waning of the Veils: [noun] Used to describe both the catastrophic event that triggered the decay of the Netherworld and the ensuing Rephaite civil war, fought primarily between the Mothallath and Sargas families. After the Sargas usurped the Mothallath, the Rephaim abandoned the all but uninhabitable Netherworld and made the crossing to Earth, where they established their puppet empire, the Republic of Scion.

Westminster Archon: [noun] The highest seat of power in the Republic of Scion, in London. It is the workplace of most of the Scion Republic of England's key officials, including its Grand Inquisitor, and sometimes houses members of the Sargas family and their allies. Paige was tortured in its basement.

White aster: [noun] A powerful amnesiac; *blue aster* is said to undo its effects.

Acknowledgments

Writing *The Mask Falling* has been an extraordinary journey. It's surreal to think that I've been chipping away at this installment of the Bone Season series since 2012, when I fell head-over-heels for Paris. As *The Mime Order* was my tribute to London, so this book is my love song to the City of Lights.

Thank you for waiting so patiently for it. I know it's been an unusually long gap between installments of the Bone Season, and even if I've left you on a brutal cliff-hanger, I hope you loved this one as much as I've loved working on it for the past eight years. I really can't believe we're halfway through the series.

Just as Paige would be nowhere without her army, I would be nowhere without mine. Thank you to my ever-phenomenal agent, David Godwin, and everyone else at DGA: Heather Godwin, Kirsty McLachlan, Mary Scott, Philippa Sitters and Sebastian Godwin, and Lisette Verhagen at PFD.

To my editors, Alexa von Hirschberg and Genevieve Herr, who made *The Mask Falling* the best it could be. Alexa, thank you for eight years of wise, witty and compassionate editing—I wish you all the best in your next adventure.

To David Mann for another humdinger of a cover, and Emily Faccini for her beautiful illustrations. I'm so lucky to have both of you working on my books.

To the extraordinary global team at Bloomsbury Publishing, including Alexandra Pringle, Allegra Le Fanu, Amanda Shipp, Amy Wong, Ben Turner, Callum Kenny, Carrie Hsieh, Cindy Loh, Emily Fisher, Genevieve Nelsson, Hermione Davis, Imogen Denny, Jack Birch, Janet Aspey, Jasmine Horsey, Josh Moorby, Kathleen Farrar,

Laura Keefe, Laura Phillips, Lauren Molyneux, Marie Coolman, Meenakshi Singh, Nancy Miller, Rachel Wilkie, Rosie Mahorter, Sara Helen Binney, Sarah Knight, Sara Mercurio, Phil Beresford, Nicole Jarvis, Philippa Cotton, and Trâm-Anh Doan.

To Lin Vasey for copyediting, Ciarán Collins for the Irish translations, and Chloe Sizer and Will Tennant for their early feedback on *The Mask Falling*. It was a privilege to work with all of you.

To the brilliant Bone Season advocates—thank you for continuing to show so much support and passion for this series.

To everyone at my French publishing house, De Saxus, especially Sam Souibgui and Volodymyr Feshchuk—thank you for sending me on a wonderful, inspiring French tour that ended up shaping this book in ways I never expected, and for giving the Bone Season series a new life in France.

The Bone Season translators all over the world, including Benjamin Kuntzer, Lenka Kapsová and Regina Kołek. Thank you for bringing this story to readers I wouldn't otherwise have been able to reach.

To everyone in the book community: authors, bloggers, booksellers, librarians, reviewers—I am so proud to be here.

To all the people who have inspired, cheered, helped and supported me in various ways throughout this journey, including Alwyn Hamilton, Claire Donnelly, Evie Tsang, Harriet Hammond, Holly Bourne, Ilana Fernandes-Lassman, Jay Kristoff, John Moore, Katherine Webber, Kevin Tsang, Kiran Millwood Hargrave, Krystal Sutherland, Laura Lam, Laure Eve, Leiana Leatutufu, Lisa Lueddecke, London Shah, Melinda Salisbury, Nina Douglas, Peta Freestone, Richard Smith, Vickie Morrish and Victoria Aveyard. And of course, to my incredible family, who are always there when I need them.

To all NHS employees, because they deserved to be thanked at every available opportunity.

This book is dedicated to my grandmother, Ann Preedy, who passed away in November 2019. She loved me unconditionally, and that love extended to anything and everything I wrote—above all, the Bone Season series. Throughout the months and years I worked on *The Mask Falling*, Grandma was forever asking me when she could read it, and whether or not Paige was going to have a happy ending for once. The fact that I couldn't finish the series before her death will always be tremendously painful, but I will strive to stitch some of her generosity and kindness into every book I write.

I miss you, Grandma. Thank you for everything. I know that if the æther was real, you'd have already come back as my guardian angel.

A Note on the Author

Samantha Shannon was born in west London in 1991. In 2013 she published *The Bone Season*, the first in a seven book series. *The Mime Order* followed in 2015 and *The Song Rising* in 2017. The series is internationally bestselling and her books have been translated into twenty-six languages. Film and TV rights have been optioned by Lunar Park. Her fourth novel, *The Priory of the Orange Tree*, was published in 2019.

samanthashannon.co.uk
@say_shannon